I0663878

Haven
Book 2 of the Orbit Series
J.S. Collyer

Dagda Publishing
Nottingham, UK

Dagda Publishing
62 Godfrey Street, Netherfield, Nottingham, NG4 2JG
www.dagdapublishing.co.uk

For Andy & Anna.
Thanks for helping me keep it unreal.

Contents

'Feeding us with violence, we face the fall of man.
Believe me and catch me if you can.'
- Apoptygma Berzerk

I

Habit made Hugo stand to attention as the officers filed out of Colonel Hudson's office. None of them looked at him as they passed.

Hudson's aide had to call him twice from the office doorway before he registered he was being summoned. Hugo unclenched his fists and made his body move. The colonel's office was very ordered. A distant part of his mind remembered that he'd always approved of that. It used to comfort him, but now it only seemed to emphasise the chaos in his head.

Hugo attempted to focus as Hudson started speaking. She was young for a colonel. Younger than him. Better at her job, too. He remembered her as Colonel Luscombe's aide, sorting the older man's life in more ways than he even realised before he retired, and knew she was even more of a force to be reckoned with now she was making her own decisions. Good decisions, most of the time.

"Commodore," she said again after a pause he hadn't noticed. "Are you listening?"

Hugo didn't answer. His heart was pounding and his fingernails were digging into his palms.

"Hugo," Hudson said, standing from behind her desk. "This is serious."

"What was the outcome?" Hugo's voice sounded low and distant in his own ears.

Heat flared in Hudson's face as she visibly controlled her temper. "Suspension. Effective immediately."

"That's not acceptable."

"I don't care if you think its acceptable. You were this close to a formal court martial. I don't even want to admit to myself the favours I've had to call in to stop formal charges being filed."

"I don't care about formal charges. I need access to my team and equipment."

"They're not your team any more."

Hugo felt something ripple over his skin, something that was almost feeling. "Ma'am, the culprits are at large."

"And they will be apprehended by the appropriate teams."

"They captured and tortured my officer. I can't - "

"No, Hugo," Hudson's brow clouded. "This is not a negotiation. You are suspended from the Eclipse unit and hereby removed as overseeing officer from all its missions. You are to turn in your pips and weapon and return home to await further instruction."

"Ma'am…" he managed to keep his voice from shaking, but only just. "I can't…I can't leave this."

"You're going to have to."

"Eclipse - "

"Eclipse should never have taken on that insane mission. You don't have the resources or the influence to pull off investigating Haven smugglers. It's no wonder it ended in disaster. It will be passed on to the Analysts."

"Ma'am," Hugo said again. "The Analysts can't follow the trail. They have no jurisdiction on Haven."

"I am aware of this. But you were reckless, Hugo. You risked too much, too soon. You know Command is looking for any chance to shut Eclipse down. And you gave them a reason."

Hugo clenched his jaw. "That team have earned their right to revenge."

"This is exactly what I'm talking about," Hudson said, voice rising. "We cannot have officers using Eclipse for personal vendettas. You got too close to this. You got cocky, soldier, and Marilyn Harvey paid for it. You've lost us this mission. You were lucky you didn't lose us the unit."

Hudson's clouded face swam as he watched everything crumble away. "We'd named him," he said, not knowing why. He couldn't see the office any more, just a dark, swirling hole he was ready to fall into and drown in. "She'd chosen a name for our son."

"I'm sorry," Hudson said after a pause. She sounded it, too. But Hugo could barely hear anything over the rushing in his ears. "But there's nothing can be done. Go home, Hugo. Go home and rest."

Δ

He knew he could do neither. He found himself in an express lift in the Medic Centre after a blurred flyer ride from Headquarters. On some level, he knew it felt peculiar to not have the familiar weight of his gun at his hip but he couldn't summon the energy to care.

Early spring sunshine was streaming through the hospital room window when he walked in, making it seem almost peaceful. The soundproof plexiglass looked out on the crowded skyways and towering buildings of central Sydney but kept the tumultuous noise at bay. The only sound in the room was the soft hush of Harvey's sleeping breaths and the single monitor she was still hooked to that purred in the corner.

He sat in a plastic chair next to the bed, keeping his hands clasped together in his lap because he was afraid his touch would wake her. His jaw was clenched so tightly that it hurt. He tried to keep his eyes on her face, on the light eyelashes resting on her cheeks, the curl of her yellow hair on the pillow and the calmness that relaxed the new lines in her forehead and around her mouth. But his gaze always slid to the laser burns under her eyebrows where they'd managed to remove some of the scarring, or the bandaging that still swathed her neck and arms, and he'd have to shut his eyes and breathe through another internal assault.

"Kale?"

He hadn't heard the door. He let out his breath and opened his eyes. His brother Giles stood in the doorway, slight frown of concern creasing his lined forehead. Hugo got up and gestured him back out of the room, clicking the door shut behind them.

"Are they still keeping her under?"

"No," Hugo said. "She's just sleeping."

"That's good," Giles prompted, searching Hugo's face.

"What do you want?"

Giles sighed, glanced through the window at the sleeping figure, then took his elbow to steer him away from the door.

"I heard about the decision today," Giles began. Hugo kept in step, not replying. "Look, Kale…I just…you're not going to do anything stupid, are you?"

"No."

Giles sighed and stepped in front of his younger brother to halt their progress. A medic shuffled by with a panel. Giles waited until she was out of sight again before continuing. "I'm serious about this. Eclipse is on the verge of breaking into the inner ring of the West Desert Movement. We need that intel, Kale. They're pressing in on the Eurasian boarders and we don't have enough landed manpower to push back a full-scale assault."

"How do you know about Eclipse's missions?"

Giles sighed. "Hudson drafted me in to review the caseload when you were…taken off duty."

"You?"

Giles frowned. "Yes. Me. I've been commanding dirt-side insurgent resistance for the last four years. The colonel wanted my take on things."

"You have no underground ops training - "

"My training is not the point here," Giles interrupted. "Eclipse is doing good work. I don't want to see it compromised. And you shouldn't either."

"I don't know what you think I'm planning to do, but you're wrong."

"Dana contacted me."

"Dana? What about?"

"She said you'd been talking to Anita Rami."

Hugo bristled. "How does Dana even know about any of this?"

"Rami called her at the academy. They're Marilyn's friends too, you know."

"This is none of Dana's business. Or Captain Rami's either."

"They are worried about you. We all are."

"Well don't be."

"I know you," Giles said, voice lowering as another medic passed by with two Service officers that glanced at the brothers as they passed. "I know what you're like when it's…personal."

"Personal?" Hugo heard the word leave his mouth and it sounded someone else's voice. "Marilyn was tortured. Our baby died. That's more than personal."

Giles rubbed his mouth, glancing back toward Harvey's hospital room. "You can't use the Eclipse team for revenge," he said, drawing himself up. "I'm sorry. We're all sorry. But tracking down the blade that worked on her and bringing him in has to be left to the Analysts. You can't get onto Haven without a Sponsor and no right-minded Havenite is going to Sponsor any Service officer after one of their own. You try and sneak onboard and get caught, there would be outcry. All our manufacturing contracts with their shipyards would be cancelled and we'd be set back years on the Mars project." Despite everything else careening round his brain, Hugo was struck by how much Giles looked like their mother when he was commanding. Special Commander Erica Hugo had exactly the same set to her brow and hardness to her eyes when she would tolerate no argument. "Not to mention it would be the last nail in Eclipse's coffin lid. We can't afford that. The Service, despite what some of Command think, can't afford it either. This New Age of Service Command has fostered more hatred then you and I even know about. We need Eclipse. We need those recruits from the underground, possibly even more than we need our increased unit numbers or the new flagship."

Hugo felt himself start to shake. He stared into his brother's face without blinking. "If you think I would compromise that team after everything that's happened, you don't know me at all."

He shouldered past Giles and strode away down the corridor,

ignoring his brother calling him back.

Δ

He sat in his armchair in the living room of his apartment. He was hunched forward with his head in his hands, staring at the streaks of sunlight that warmed the carpet Harvey hadn't liked. He tried to fight it but just like always, the memory came through so clearly it was like she was in the room with him.

Harvey was handing him a glass of blask and laughing at him as she tended to do when he told her no.

"It makes sense, you know it does," she had said, her green eyes glinting with determination. "I finally have some names. We have a chance to take them down."

"Bloodgrease trafficking is a political minefield," he'd said, sipping the blask and leaning back in the chair. He remembered how his back and head ached from the long day bent over command consoles with his lieutenants, planning the next West Desert reconnaissance mission. "Our team's not got the background or training to take on any Haven-based organisations."

"I do," she smiled wider. "Seriously, Kaleb…" she'd perched on the arm of his chair, not letting herself touch him which she did when she wanted him to pay attention. "Bloodgrease traders are parasites. Even by Haven standards. We find out enough to cut off their buyers in the Orbit, the trade will wither. Haven needs its legitimate contracts and credit flow. These slimy bottom-feeders should be labouring in the shipyards or trading official produce. But they line their own pockets with credit from illegal Orbit buyers and look to their own gain and not Haven's."

He'd sipped his drink and reached up to put his hand on her stomach, but she leaned back. He remembered with a stab of pain this distance in her eyes then as she looked at him.

"I need my own missions, Kaleb. It's bad enough our relationship means no one takes me seriously."

"They do take you seriously."

She looked away. "You're not around the research room enough to notice. I want fieldwork. And I want the smugglers stopped. Just think about it, ok?"

He shook his head, slamming back into the present. His breath went out of him in a rush and he pressed his hands over his eyes to force away the visions of Harvey a few months later after the blade had done his work.

Slowly, he calmed down. His head swirled but he wiped away the wetness on his eyes and leant back in the chair staring at the ceiling. The apartment was silent around him. His Service-issue computer panels and workstation with links to the Eclipse data-banks had been confiscated. The whole place felt very empty, like him. Empty and powerless.

He got up and booted up his personal comm station. He punched in the secure code he'd memorised. After the connect-ing screen had buzzed for a few minutes a woman's face appeared, dark hair cut into a sharp bob and dark brown eyes smiling though her face was serious.

"Commodore. I'm glad you called."

"Captain Rami," he said, voice steady for the first time in days. "I want to take you up on your offer."

Now she really did smile. "What changed your mind?"

"I can't use Eclipse. If I do they'll shut it down."

Rami nodded. "Ok then. I'll help, sir. When do you want to get started?"

He paused. "What exactly did you tell my sister?"

Rami blinked then composed herself. "Nothing. I promise."

"She knows you talked to me."

"I contacted her to tell her about Harvey. She asked how you were so I said I'd spoken to you, but nothing more."

"She asked how I was?"

"You sound surprised."

"We're not exactly close."

Rami shrugged through that. "Well I just said you were…well. Angry."

Hugo nodded. The word wasn't big enough but he could tell by the look on her face that they both knew it.

"I'll meet you tonight," he said. "I want to leave on the next shuttle. You really know where I can find him?"

Δ

The shuttle ride felt like the longest Hugo had ever known. He couldn't remember ever feeling so alone and so determined at the same time. He clutched at the cold metal of Harvey's dog tags that he'd slung round his neck under his clothes, knuckles aching with the tightness of the grip, for the whole trip.

He spent the four-hour layover in Tranquility spaceport slumped in a plastic chair with his cap pulled down low on his face staring at the floor, turning his fake ID over and over in his hands. He told himself over and over that he'd know what to say when he saw him. He didn't let himself think about what he would do if he said no.

Somehow, he fell asleep on the shuttle transfer from Tranquility to Lunar 3. He woke when the attendant shook him. She had an alarmed look on her face and the other passengers were looking his way.

"Are you alright, sir?"

He shouldered himself upright. His shoulders were tight and his throat raw. He took a shuddering breath and glared out the porthole. The attendant took the hint and left him alone. He kept himself from falling asleep again by staring out at the stars and clinging to the dog tags.

When the huge ring-shaped space station that was Lunar 3 finally came into view, something lurched inside him. For the first time since they'd rescued Harvey and he'd seen what they'd done to her, he felt a flicker of doubt.

Then he remembered that she'd wanted to call their son Thomas after the chief engineer of the *Zero* who'd lost his life in the last Lunar Uprising, and fire burned through him again, incinerating the fear and uncertainty.

He filed along behind the other passengers, out of the shuttle and into the civilian arrivals port, pack on his shoulder and head down. He handed over his ID for scanning whilst keeping his breath even. It bleeped and the customs agent waved him through. He found himself on the raised pedestrian walkway spanning the curved levels of Lunar 3's busy port.

Pulling out his panel, he checked the address Rami had given him again and turned his feet toward the lifts that would take him to the commercial levels. He drifted along the walkways and through the foot traffic in a kind of fog of numbness. It might have been one hour or it might have been four he spent floating on and off countless public shuttles and sliding walkways, before he pulled himself together to find himself staring at the door of a boarding pod. The minutes stretched on as he stared at the number on the door, aware of nothing over the slow slug of his pulse in his ears and the roll in his gut.

Finally, he pushed the buzzer.

There was muffled movement from inside, a long pause, then door slid open.

"Hugo," Webb said after staring for several moments. The clone of his one-time commander looked alarmingly unchanged from when he'd last seen him three years previously, when they'd parted ways on the roof of the Memorial Music Hall in Sydney. Hugo's own hair held more grey than then, but Webb's hair, which he'd let grow out to the length it had been when they had first met, was still an even, midnight-black. He was still lean, although now a little on the thin side, his vest and cargo trousers hanging a little loose. There were new scars on his arms and face. He'd also re-done a lot of his predecessor's tattoos, with the addition of an original one on his right bicep: stark black lines of the Roman numeral for the number two.

The younger man's face started off blank with surprise but shifted into a more guarded look as he glanced over Hugo's shoulders and kneaded the gun he had in his hand. "You're alone?"

"Yes."

"What in the name of hell are you doing here?"

"Can I come in?"

Webb narrowed his eyes slightly. "Am I under arrest?"

"No."

Webb examined him a moment longer then stepped back to allow Hugo in. The boarding pod was barely big enough for the two men, the bunk and the work bench bolted to the wall. There was a consumables dispenser with a dirty cup balanced in the slot installed behind the door, a computer panel with a locked screen on the bench and a single bag, open with a spill of clothes, computer panel casings and wires sprawling onto the bed.

"I suppose you know what time it is?"

"You're up, aren't you?"

"I guess," Webb replied. "You look like shit, by the way."

Hugo rubbed the growth on his jaw and frowned. "I've had a long trip."

"You want a coffee or something? At least, I think it's supposed to be coffee."

"No."

Silence stretched for a second or two until Webb laughed. It wasn't a nice sound and his smile had a hardness to it that Hugo had forgotten about.

"I know you were never the greatest one for small-talk, Hugo. But as you're the one that's turned up in the ass-end of nowhere in the middle of the night-cycle...the conversational ball is kind of in your court."

Hugo straightened, fumbling for where to start. "I need your help," Hugo finally managed.

Webb's eyebrows lifted slightly. "*You* need *my* help?"

Hugo nodded. "I need someone with your experience. And expertise."

"You mean *Webb's* experience and expertise."

"They're yours now."

The clone snorted.

"You kept his name…" Hugo said quietly, watching the other's face.

"It's not like he was using it."

"You said -"

"I know what I said," Webb snapped. "Do you want to get to the point?"

"I need you for something."

"The charming Colonel Hudson has tried to rope me into Service shit before," Webb said. "I told her -"

"I know what you told her. She wanted to bring you in to face threat charges."

One corner of his mouth turned up in a sneer. "She should have known better than to ask. As should you."

"This isn't for the Service, Webb. This is…personal." The word was thick in his mouth.

Webb's eyes narrowed. Hugo watched him take in his lack of uniform or insignia. Their gazes met again, then the younger man sighed and looked away. "Look, Hugo. It's really late…"

"Will you at least hear what I have to say?"

"No."

"Webb…"

"I said no. I have a deal to make. I don't have time."

"Tomorrow then."

Webb blinked at him. For the briefest moment Hugo saw all the hardness fall away from his face and he just looked surprised. Then he closed back up again with a slight frown. "It's that important to you?"

"Yes. At least hear me out. If you do and say no, I'll leave."

Webb frowned harder, then moved towards the door, shaking his head. "Fine. I'll meet you tomorrow."

"When?"

"Mid-cycle," Webb said, gesturing towards the door.

"Where?"

"Oh, Christ in heaven. Here." Webb grabbed the panel Hugo had forgotten he was holding and typed in some numbers and handed it back. "This is my wrist-comm number. Find somewhere, anywhere, bring food, and message me. I'll meet you."

"You will?"

Webb shrugged. "I'll try. Now please, get the hell out of here."

Δ

Hugo knew there was little point but he booked himself into his own boarding pod for what remained of the night-cycle. He stared at the ceiling, lit by the dull glow of a colony streetlight bleeding in around the blind. It was just the right shade of orange to make his head ache. When he did sleep, his dreams were fractured and violent. He decided he preferred the headache.

He sent Webb a message the next day as soon as he'd found somewhere to meet. With nothing else to do, he sat down on the bench he'd chosen at the edge of civilian rec area to watch Lunar 3 life roll by. There were a couple of children playing on some playground equipment with watchful guardians nearby. Their shouts were loud and happy and the play area was well-lit, but the spread of metal and concrete beyond still showed scars of the Lunar Uprising. There were fenced-off piles of rubble, hastily-patched metal workings in the hull above their heads and chunks missing from megablocks that rose against the artificial horizon. Most of the damage had been repaired or built over on the moon, but credit clearly did not flow so freely on the colonies. Nevertheless, the adults watching their charges laughed and chatted and the children played on.

As the meeting time approached he went and fetched food and returned. He watched the chrono on his wrist panel as mid-cycle came and went. He stayed put on the bench, checking his wrist panel every few seconds. He was just beginning to think that his old crew-mate wasn't coming when a hand clapped him on the back.

"What, is your commodore's salary not enough to stretch to a restaurant?"

"We're less likely to be overheard here."

"Oh yeah, sure," Webb said with a crooked grin as he dropped his bag on the floor and sat sideways on the bench. "Two spacers hanging about in a kids' play area eating Chinese food. Real discreet. You better have got kung po."

Hugo passed the carton over and a pair of chopsticks. Webb dug in without looking up. Hugo thought the other man looked far better than he had a right to after so little sleep.

"Right," Webb said around a mouthful of food. "I launch for the moon in an hour, Hugo. Whatever it is you want, make it quick."

Hugo poked at his rice with his chopsticks, forcing his mind to be ordered and his voice to be steady.

"Four months ago an Eclipse Agent was kidnapped and tortured. She has undergone weeks of therapy, physical and mental, but can't remember enough of the encounter to produce much evidence."

Webb chewed for a while. "Do you know who did it?"

"We have a good idea."

"Ok…what's this got to do with me?"

"I've come to you because the case has been reassigned to the Analysts. But I know they won't follow the trail with what little evidence there is. The agent kept her written records to a minimum and she…" Hugo paused, hoping the blood he felt rushing to his head wasn't showing in his cheeks. "She doesn't remember much of her life before the attack."

"What, she doesn't remember anything?"

Hugo took a second to answer. "Some things. Not everything."

"Did they drug her or something?"

"We're not sure. There was nothing detectable in her system, but the Analyst's catalogue of substances isn't exhaustive. Either way the…nature of what was done to her suggests a…professional."

"You think someone hired a blade?"

Hugo nodded, watching the children chase each other around the climbing frame.

"Bummer," Webb muttered.

Hugo took a breath and carried on. "If we find this blade, we'll find out who hired them. For this job...and others."

"Ok," Webb set aside his food carton and leant forward, resting elbows on knees. "As wonderfully bleak as this is, I'm almost afraid to ask again...where do I come in?"

"The Analysts can't hunt this blade down," Hugo continued. "If they've gone where we think, no one in the Service has the authority or the reach. But they need to be found. Only they will have enough evidence to bring whoever hired them to justice."

"This is why you should have a *Zero*," Webb muttered. "Then you've got a paid team you can disavow easily to do your dirty work."

"Eclipse is better funded, better resourced and better trained than the *Zero* was."

"But?"

"I've been suspended from Eclipse and removed from my rank. Eclipse has been forbidden to pursue the matter."

"Suspended, huh?" Webb said, eyeing him warily. "What for?"

Hugo clutched his hands together so they wouldn't shake. "The agent's capture happened under my command. They've held me responsible."

Webb didn't say anything for a while. When Hugo looked at him, he dared hope he saw some sympathy in the younger man's face but he turned his attention back to his food before Hugo could be sure.

"So," he said. "Whilst you're officially suspended, any rules you break, oh, I don't know...say, running off, using any means you have to find this blade and drag them to trial by the seat of his pants, can't come back and bite your pet Service team in the proverbial?"

Hugo swallowed and looked away as the adults across the play area started to gather the shouting children together. "This is something I need to do, with or without Eclipse. But I can't do it on my own."

Webb looked at him. His eyes were narrow and hard again. "And this noble and self-sacrificing partner in crime you're hoping to recruit here. What do they get out of it?"

"I believe Colonel Hudson would be suitably generous to anyone who helped bring in such a dangerous perpetrator. So long as they were brought in in a fit state to testify."

"How much are we talking?" Webb said, sounding careful and not looking at him. Hugo wondered what was going through the clone's head but his face was unreadable.

"Whatever you think your contribution is worth. And...there's one other thing in it for you."

"Oh?"

Hugo turned to face the other man. He looked at him until the other man returned his gaze. "What was done to the agent...I've seen it before."

Webb's frown deepened.

"I believe the blade we're after may be the same one who..." Hugo faltered, gathered himself. "I believe he's the man who interrogated you on the *Tide*."

Webb blinked slowly. "Ariel?"

Hugo nodded.

Webb's jaw tightened. Then he leant back on the bench, dangerously slow. "Let me get this straight, Commodore. You need someone with Service-level skills, but who doesn't have a nice pressed uniform to get bloodied up or a position to threaten. But it's ok, I should want to do it, because I'm helping track down the man that pumped me with neuro-enhancer and sliced off my skin, in order for you to buy his co-operation with protection?"

"He won't walk, Webb."

"Bullshit," Webb said, standing and shouldering his bag. "You forget I was in the Service. I know how it works."

"Webb -"

"Screw you, Hugo," he said, turning to go.

"Zeek," Hugo stood, grabbed the other man's sleeve.

Webb shook him off. "I've given you my time and I've given you my answer, which is all I agreed to. I'm leaving."

Hugo watched him stalk across the play area and vanish through the gate without looking back. He slumped back against the bench and rubbed his aching temples. A distant rumble sounded as a shuttle pulled in at a platform above his head. He watched his wrist panel and waited five minutes before getting up and following Webb towards the docks.

Δ

The anger pulsed behind Webb's eyes. Damn Hugo for bringing all that back up. He punched the commands into his ship's control panel with more force than was necessary.

"Mark and countdown, *Nod*."

"Mark, Control," Webb muttered in response to his communicator. "Ready to begin launch in ten."

"Roger."

Webb continued his checks, pressuring the hatch, running systems diagnostics and scans. A changed reading on his interior temperature scan made him blink and then scowl in anger. He drew his gun.

"Show yourself, Hugo." Hugo stepped into the small cockpit. He kept his hands behind his back and gazed impassively down the barrel of the weapon. "Get off my ship."

"No."

"You stubborn asshole. Get off my ship, or I'll shoot you, I swear."

"With this thin little hull? You're many things, Webb, but stupid is not one of them."

Webb snarled in frustration and lowered the gun. "I'm ten minutes from launch. Will you get out of my life, already?"

"I just want to talk to you."

"*Nod*? Come in *Nod*. Send your final check results, please."

Webb ground his teeth, trying to melt Hugo with his glare. When that didn't work, he holstered his weapon with a muttered curse and turned back to the comm.

"Incoming, Control. Er...I've got a last minute addition to the passenger manifest."

"Way to go. You get lucky?"

"All due respect, fuck off Control."

Webb thought he heard a snigger over the comm. "They better have their ID handy because you're five minutes to launch."

Webb glanced over his shoulder and Hugo was nodding, producing a card from his jacket pocket.

"Transmitting now," Webb said, snatching the card and swiping it over his control panel.

"Check. Cameron Bale added to the manifest. Easy trip, *Nod*."

"Starting launch procedures now. Nod, out. Oi. Uninvited guest," he said, gesturing at Hugo. "You might want to find something to strap into."

"Where are we going?" the other man asked as he shut his pack in a locker, sat in the co-pilot chair and strapped himself in.

"*I'm* going to Pole-Aitken. You'll be lucky if I don't report you as a stowaway and have you arrested when we dock."

"You've already registered me as a passenger," Hugo pointed out smoothly. Webb wanted to hit him.

They sat in silence as Webb got the engines fired. The view out of the screen lurched and then stabilised as the ship broke gravity. The glowing numbers on the large panel above the port doors ran down to zero and the doors lumbered open to reveal a star-specked stretch of space. Nod eased out and Webb gunned the thrusters to pull them a safe distance from the colony before firing up to full power. The feeling of weightlessness rippled through his innards. His shoulders bumped against the harness and his hair floated about his face. He continued punching in commands and Nod steered into her course.

"A class three skiff?"

"I downsized. So?"

"Nothing. I've just not felt zero-g for a while."

Hugo lapsed into silence as Webb concentrated on the controls and not his tangled emotions.

"It was Marilyn."

"What?"

"It was Marilyn," Hugo repeated, voice still low, pulling some dog-tags out from under his shirt and holding them up to the light. They had Harvey's name and assignment number on. "The Eclipse agent they took. She was pregnant."

Webb felt cold rise in place of the heat of anger. He looked over at Hugo, but he'd tucked the dog tags out of sight and was staring out the viewscreen. "I'm sorry."

Hugo met his look. "They couldn't save the baby. But they saved her. Physically, at least."

Webb looked away. Nod rounded the colony and soon the moon hove into view, a white crescent ahead.

"I meant it when I said I needed you," Hugo continued quietly. "You were always better at undercover work than me. And I thought you deserved the chance to get even."

"I deserve a chance to kill the bastard," Webb said. "But that's not what you're offering me."

"No, it's not. But it's the closest thing I can offer. I want to get him, Zeek. Never mind what he can give the Service. That's Hudson's agenda. I want to make him answer for what he did. To Marilyn. And to you."

Webb stared hard out towards the moon. He could see the blinking lights of the city of Tranquility in the shadow of its crater. The cold was crawling under every inch of his skin.

"I tried to get the scars removed you know," he said, not knowing why. "Twice. And damned expensive it was too. But my skin is weird...I don't know. The lasers didn't work like they should."

He looked up and Hugo was regarding him levelly. "I'm over it as much as you can be. But every time I look at the scars, I'm back there on that table. And it's not the pain I remember. It's the way he smiled."

Hugo was quiet for a moment. Something was flickering deep in his eyes but whether it was shock, anger or gratification Webb couldn't tell. "So you'll help me?"

Webb looked back out the viewscreen. "Yes. I'll help you. But I can't promise I'll let you take him alive."

"We'll work on that later," Hugo said and there was no missing the grim satisfaction in his tone.

II

The remainder of the journey to the moon passed in near silence. Not exactly a strained one, but Hugo was aware there were things to say that weren't quite ready to be said. He focused on the moon growing larger, occasionally sneaking glances at his former commander.

Webb seemed to have no trouble at all ignoring Hugo, but even with the seemingly effortless tweaks of controls and checks of readings, there was something in the set look on Webb's face that made him wonder whether he was also chasing unwanted thoughts around his head.

The moon eventually filled the small viewscreen. The grid of lights that was Pole-Aitkin spread out ahead as their course brought them into orbit. Webb contacted Harbour Control with his manifests but there was no easy joking this time. He watched the grids widen and split into districts and blocks and soon could see the individual lights from the spacescraper windows as they broke through the atmosphere shield. His stomach lurched as the city's gravity took hold of the ship and he dropped into the co-pilot chair. Webb didn't seem to notice and he wondered how long he'd been driving this beat-up class three skiff...and what for.

"Well, Hugo," Webb said, getting up from his chair after they'd docked, stretching until his joints cracked. "I have some business to complete before we can talk any further about this crazy plan. How about you find us some boarding?"

"Boarding? For how long?"

Webb moved to the back of the cabin where he started pulling holdalls from lockers. "Tonight at least. It'll take us that long to figure out where in the hell we're going to start."

"And we can't berth here?" Hugo asked, retrieving his own pack.

"What's the matter, Hugo? Afraid of trying to get through customs with your fake ID?" He straightened and looked him in the eye. "Because you should be. The moon's not the place it used it be."

"It got me through the Tranquility spaceport just fine."

Webb raised his eyebrows. "Well, that's a good sign. Still, we need to be careful. You service types have made it hard for a guy to make an honest living these days."

"Your living is honest, then?"

Webb grinned. "More or less. But anyway, *Nod*'s only got one bunk. So, unless you're planning to get real friendly, we're going to need boarding."

Hugo retrieved his own pack from the locker and followed Webb off the skiff. The processed air in the harbour made him dizzy for a moment. He took a second with his hand against the hull to let it pass.

"You still get air-spin?"

"I've been spending a lot of time on Earth."

Webb shrugged and strolled ahead without waiting. Hugo took another breath and hurried after him when there was less chance of him staggering. The harbour activity buzzed around them and the smell of the cheap air and engine fuel threatened to awaken unwanted memories. He shook them away.

Spacers zoomed past in flyers and on mopeds, but there wasn't the grind and clank of heavy machinery or industrial lifters. Looking around, Hugo saw the berthed ships were mainly small cruisers and the queue at the exit way was mostly foot passengers.

"Not much trade in Pole-Aitken these days," Webb said as Hugo kept looking around. "Industry's moved more into the colonies."

"The Service is investing heavily in the moon," Hugo said, looking around as they moved on. "Moving the industry away and establishing more leisure and rec facilities instead. They think re-establishing it as a stopping point for Apollos Outreach

Mars project will stabilise the strip."

"They should invest in the colonies," Webb muttered. "Not burden them with more industry than they have the resources to sustain. I swear they make the same mistakes over and over again. Still, can't complain. Lack of certain fundamentals in these places keeps a fella in credit."

Hugo couldn't stop the involuntary glance towards the hold-alls and cases Webb was carrying but the man's stride was easy as ever and his face neutral. Hugo stopped himself from checking his fake ID was still in his jacket, aware of the armed Servicemen guarding the exit.

Webb went through the foot-passenger customs port without even glancing back. Hugo stood with his arms folded, resisting hanging his head to better hide his face. He had managed to avoid watching any newsreels since leaving Earth, but he was sure his suspension was big news and his face was probably doing the rounds on the solarnet. Again.

He was also sure that someone would have realised he wasn't at his apartment by now. And possibly where he was going. He didn't know exactly what Hudson would do once she found out, but he itched to be further along the trail than he was for when they came looking for him.

Still…he needed Webb. And Webb didn't yet know what he'd agreed to.

The door slid open and he straightened himself and stepped into the port. A customs officer behind a screen directed him to scan his ID card across a panel in the wall as the beam of a scanner ran over him and his pack, bleeping. Hugo made himself breathe steadily as the bored-looking woman behind the plexi-glass watched something scroll on her screen and tapped a couple of keys, then a door on the other side of the port hissed open and she waved him through. Feeling his shoulders loosen, he strolled out into Pole-Aitken.

Hugo glanced around to get his bearings and followed. "East

Quarter?"

Webb nodded. "Though it doesn't look much like it did when I first came here."

Hugo deliberately side-stepped asking which version of himself the clone was talking about. "We've sunk a lot of credit into cleaning it up."

"I noticed," Webb said, voice flat. He hoisted his holdalls higher on his shoulder, then raised his hand to flag down a taxi flyer. He bundled all but one bag into the back and then gestured to Hugo. "Get in. Head to Aitken Square. Plenty of boarding there."

"What about you?"

"I don't know how long I'll be. You've got my comm number. Let me know where you end up and I'll meet you there later."

Hugo watched him stroll away into the bustling dock traffic, clenching and unclenching his fists but reminding himself that impatience was not going to work with Webb.

He climbed into the taxi and told the pilot to take him to Aitken Square. As the flyer climbed up onto a skyway, Hugo watched the neon lights of the spacescrapers whizz past. The city didn't look much different to what he remembered once they'd left the better-lit groundways behind, apart from the black-and-grey Service patrol flyers at almost every junction and the webs of scaffolding where new sections were being added to the existing buildings.

Aitken Square was a web of platforms and walkways suspended between two megablocks at the edge of the Eastern Quarter. The flyer pulled over into a busy parking pool and he climbed out into the noise and bustle. There was a static tang in the air from being so close to the atmosphere shield and when he peered out between the buildings he could make out the flat desert of white and grey that spread to the horizon.

He was just glancing around at the neon signs advertising everything from economy accommodation to 3D film reel showings when his wrist panel bleeped. He grabbed the bags, ducked out of the foot traffic and pulled up his sleeve, blinking at the code that was flashing on the display. He frowned before searching the signs again and weaving his way across the square to a boarding house on the other side.

The Homely Inne, that was reached by a rickety walkway over a vast drop to the level below Aitken Square had nothing homely about it. The landlady in the lobby took a scan of his ID and Hugo again wondered how Webb had managed to stay so off the radar for the last three years with every boarding house and public transfer point taking records like this.

"What level of connection do you have?" Hugo said, scanning the browsing rates on a display above the counter.

"We're on the moonframe," she said, fishing keycards out of a drawer. "Solarnet too. Workstation's in your room."

Hugo nodded and took the keycard, avoiding her eyes as recognition dawned on her face, and ducked out of the lobby to find the room. The corridors were narrow with bare floors. He passed more anonymous numbered rooms, some with the sounds of TV shows or arguments leaking through the cheap doors, until he found his. He locked the door behind him, dumped the bags on one of the bunks and went straight to the workstation.

The machine booted up after only a small burst of static and Hugo was relieved to see the connections were good even if the hardware was not. Glancing around out of habit to confirm there were no cameras, he fished his interface out of his pack and patched it in behind the monitor. He took a breath and typed in the comm code that was still flashing on his wrist panel.

The connecting screen flashed for a couple of seconds before Rami's face appeared.

"Rami? What's happened?"

"Calm down, Hugo," Rami said. "Nothing's happened. I just wanted to talk to you."

"It's too risky to talk right now."

Rami raised an eyebrow. "Relax, Commodore. This is exactly

what I gave you the interface for. No one's getting through those codes. How's the ID working?"

Hugo winced. "Fine, so far."

The beginnings of a smile tugged at the corner of her mouth. "Feels odd, doesn't it?"

"What does?"

"Working on the other side again."

"I appreciate your help, Captain, but you really should minimise our communication from now on, for both our sakes."

"Yes, Commodore," Rami said with a nod. "I understand. I just wanted to reiterate…whatever you need, sir, if you need backup, my unit -"

"Stop right there, Anita."

"I mean it, sir," Rami said. "I'm not linked to Eclipse so it can't come back on your team. And you're out there blind, deaf and alone."

"That's the whole point. I have to do this alone."

"I can vouch for everyone in my unit, sir. No matter what happens, if you need backup, you are to call on me. I can have the *Assurance* with you within twelve hours."

"I would have thought your workforce would be otherwise occupied."

Rami frowned. "I'm not arguing with you. I'm telling you: you need help, you hail me. Understood?"

"Understood. Thank you, Anita," he managed.

She nodded again, the frown easing before her eyes moved to focus off-screen. "You found him, then?"

"Yes."

"How is he?"

"Same as ever, more or less."

She let out a breath. "That's good, I suppose."

"He's meeting me here. Do you want to speak to him?"

"No," she said, before he'd finished speaking. "No, thank you," she said again, calmer, though she couldn't entirely mask her emotion.

Hugo nodded, letting out a heavy breath. "How's Marilyn?" he asked quietly, after a pause.

"The same, sir," Rami said, face softening. "I promise I'm keeping a close eye on her."

"Thank you."

Rami took a breath and straightened. "Catch that bastard Ariel, Commodore. But be careful. He's hurt too many of us already."

She signed off and Hugo busied himself with checking through the supplies she had provided him with. He had a new-model computer panel, hand-grips, climbing rope and scan-proof lockbox. He had to hand it to Rami, she'd managed to get some top-level tech for him, but only being able to have what he could carry on his back, it looked like pitifully little.

He checked and re-checked his weapons, all of which had fake licences loaded into his ID. He avoided thinking about the fact that despite the increased checks and Service patrols, with the right codes he was still able to bring two hand-held semis, a Newmarc Fourshot, two boot and one combat knife into Pole-Aitken.

He was just re-stowing the computer panel after checking the code guards for the fourth time, when the door opened and Webb swept in.

"If you think finding the slummiest boarding house in Pole-Aitken is going to stop you getting noticed, you're wrong," the young man said as he slung his bag down on the other bunk and glanced around the basic room. "The landlady recognised you."

"How do you know?"

"Because when I turned up, she recognised me. And that doesn't happen unless you're around."

"It doesn't matter if people recognise me. It only matters that they realise I'm acting on my own."

"Hence our friend 'Cameron Bale'?"

Hugo nodded.

Webb shook his head. "So what now?"

"Are you done with your 'business'?"

"I'm done for today," Webb said. "I guess you better fill me in on whatever little it is you have on this creep. Come on."

"Where are we going?"

"I know I'm going to need a drink for this."

Δ

Webb found a bar with dim lights and a view over Aitken Square. There were clusters of people leaning on the bar and around the tables, mostly spacers though there were some Earth-tanned people with the wide-eyed look of tourists. Webb ordered and they took a table nearest the window. There was an awkward moment when they both wanted to take the seat facing the door. Webb relented with a sardonic look and sat in the seat facing the bar.

"Old habits die hard, I guess," he said as their drinks arrived. The waitress gave them a long look but something on her order pad bleeped and she scurried away. "So," Webb continued, though his eyes had followed the waitress. "You never got Rami to fix your face up, huh?"

Hugo touched the scar that he had got from storming the *Resolution* three years ago, but then dropped his hand. "It makes sure I don't forget," he said, not letting himself look at the white lines scarred into the skin of Webb's neck as he did so.

Webb raised an eyebrow as if guessing his thoughts. "You think you were ever likely to forget? I laid bets with myself that Harvey would have made you fix it. Guess I owe myself. Come on then," he continued, taking a mouthful of his drink. "What exactly do you have on this blade of mine?"

"Not much. He has no official record or Service profile."

"Figures."

"What do you remember about him?"

Webb looked fixedly over Hugo's shoulder as he took a drink and Hugo saw that his hand was tight around the bottle. "They called him Ariel, though if that's his real name I'm Duran McCullough." Hugo glowered and Webb grinned. "Sorry, bad example."

"You shouldn't joke about that."

Webb raised his eyebrows. "Oh yeah?"

"Yes," Hugo said. "Governor McCullough's revolution didn't die with him, or with Admiral Pharos either. There are still separatists wanting independence for the Lunar Colonies. If anyone else finds out McCullough had a son they could use you to be the figurehead of another rebellion just as Pharos did"

Webb gave him a hard look. "Not to remind you of this yet again, but *I'm* not actually McCullough's son. I'm not anyone's son, in fact. Unless you count that medic Yoshida, I guess."

Hugo felt heat ride through his face. "I don't count him as anything."

Webb leant forward on his elbows, still with an edge to his expression. "He's more my father than any long-dead revolutionary, Hugo. He created me, whatever I am. Not that I'm expecting him to show up to take me to a baseball match or anything anytime soon. What happened to him, anyway?"

Hugo clenched his fists. "He disappeared after the uprising. His arrest warrant is still standing, though."

Webb sighed and took a drink. "Beginning to see more why you need my help. Seems the Service can't pull its head out of its New Age ass far enough to find any of its enemies. Still," he added, as Hugo bit his tongue. "Can't complain as it can apparently help a guy earn some credit on the side."

"Is there anything else you can tell me about Ariel?" Hugo said to get them back on topic.

Webb shook his head. "All I know is his codename and that Admiral Pharos and LIL were one of his clients."

"You don't remember anything else?"

Webb stared at his bottle. "Only what he did. How he spoke. And that he's from Haven."

Hugo took a swig of his beer to try and drown the fluttering in his belly as he watched realisation dawn on Webb's face.

"You bastard," he growled.

"Zeek -"

"You lying bastard. All that shit about *needing* me?"

"I do -"

"Yeah, to be your fucking Sponsor to get onto Haven."

"Not just that, Webb."

"Then why didn't you just ask? Why didn't you just say, 'Webb I need to get onto Haven and you're the only unfortunate fucker in my stuck-up Service world that's been through probation'?"

Hugo laid his hands flat on the table and looked Webb in the eye. "I didn't mention Haven because I knew you wouldn't listen to anything else if I did. But what I said is true. I need you because you can get me on board, yes, but more than that. I need you because you're good at this. Because you know things. And after what this guy has done, I will do anything, *anything*, to bring him in. I thought you would feel the same."

Webb shook his head. "You don't know me as well as you think you do. I'm not the real Webb."

Hugo slammed his fist on the table and Webb jumped. "You kept his name. You kept his connections. You kept his *life*, just as I said you should. You look me in the eye and tell me you didn't have a right to them."

Webb leaned over the table. "You don't have the first damn clue what it's cost me, so don't you dare sit there and tell me who I ought to be."

The clone shoved his chair back, drawing glances, and paced away. Hugo went after him and grabbed his sleeve. Webb swore but Hugo clung on, not caring if it hurt and used his greater strength to haul the slighter man back to the table. Webb stopped pulling away but didn't sit. His eyes were blazing.

Hugo let his hold drop and deliberately sat down without breaking eye contact. Eventually Webb glanced round and resumed his seat.

"You've got a nerve, Hugo. And a bastard of a temper."

"I know."

"Is this why you only got as high as Commodore? Even with Special-Commander Mom to grease the pole for you?"

"Mother is the only reason I haven't been discharged for real."

Webb folded his arms and regarded him. "At least you're honest."

"With you? Always."

Webb glared. "Except when angling for Haven Sponsorship."

"I didn't lie."

Webb took a swig of his drink then narrowed his eyes. "Double my fee. Then I'll consider it."

"Whatever it takes."

Webb leaned forward on his elbows and looked Hugo in the eye. "Do you even have the faintest idea what you're asking for, here? Wanting to get Sponsored for citizenship on Haven?"

"I have an understanding."

"Make it bleaker. And more dangerous. Then you're getting close. If Haven knows a Serviceman has snuck onto their colony after one of their own, Sponsor or no Sponsor, lynching will be the best we can expect."

"That's why we have to be careful."

Webb surveyed him for a long moment. "You think you can do this? Even double my fee is not worth Sponsoring a guy with a temper and a score to settle. I'd rather drift myself now."

"I'll be careful."

"You'll have to be. You'll also have to do everything I say."

"You'll do it then?"

Webb drank his beer for a long moment and stared at the wall. There was something ghosting in his eyes that wasn't anger. Something colder. But then he blinked, drained his drink and it was gone. "I'll do it. If you swear you'll take my lead. And my orders."

Hugo nodded.

"Think about it first," Webb said, leaning and prodding him in the chest. "Think real hard. Because I'm the furthest away from kidding I've ever been."

Hugo finished his own drink whilst staring out the window, trying to silence the nagging doubts. But then he saw Harvey in her hospital bed when he was first allowed to see her, eyes bound shut with bandages and tubes sutured into her skin. "I've made my decision."

Webb chewed his lip for a second. That look was in his eyes again and Hugo wondered again if it was fear. It was on the tip of his tongue to ask when Webb nodded and slumped back in his chair, tapping a command into the display on the table top.

"Fine. It's your money. And neck, for that matter," he said as the waitress brought over two more beers. She deliberately didn't look at either of them this time.

"It will be fine," Hugo said after she'd gone and Webb was watched her go, jaw working.

Webb shook his head. "If a Pole-Aitken waitress is recognising you, the Haven customs crews will too."

"As I said," Hugo said. "I'll be careful."

Webb sighed and rubbed his eyes. "Fine. We'll come to that later. What is it that you do have on Ariel? Please tell me it's how to find him on that poxy colony."

"A starting point. Maybe," Hugo said, watching a couple of Servicemen patrol the edges of Aitken Square out the window. People oiled by on either side like opposing magnets. His pulse quickened when they approached the Homely Inne but they changed direction before reaching the door. "Amongst her other investigations, Marilyn…Sub-Lieutenant Harvey," Hugo corrected himself, earning another wry look from Webb, "was researching two suspected rings of bloodgrease traders."

Webb choked on his beer. His eyes were watering as he wiped his mouth on his sleeve. "Bloodgrease?" he spluttered.

"Yes."

Webb blinked, coughing and put the beer down. "Jesus, Eclipse didn't start small then, huh?"

"No."

Webb shook his head. "Wow. Never thought I'd see Harvey turn her coat."

"She didn't. She's still Havenite through-and-through. And vocal about it."

"And they gave her Service pips?"

"She proved that whilst she supports Haven and its rights as an independent colony, she doesn't support those that take advantage of it to line their own pockets with Orbit credit."

"Like bloodgrease traders."

"Exactly."

"How exactly did Eclipse plan to bring down any Haven-based organisation, bloodgrease or not? Sure, it's illegal everywhere but on Haven, but there you can't touch them."

"If we get their contacts, we can bring down their buyers in the Orbit. They can't sell if there's no one left to buy."

Webb chewed his thumbnail, eyes far away. "I guess so. Especially now it's harder than ever to smuggle anything through the blockade and even harder to get anything through the ports."

"You do seem to know a lot about this already."

Webb grinned. "I know about ports. What spacer doesn't?"

"What exactly are you doing these days?" Hugo asked carefully.

"What, you mean I don't have a special Eclipse file of my own?"

"You have a file," Hugo said, sipping his beer again. "But I suspect it only contains what you want us to know."

Webb smiled. "If you say so. By the way...how did you find me? On Lunar 3?"

Hugo shifted in his seat. "Captain Rami found you. Don't ask me how."

Webb's face blanked for a second at her name, but he nodded and said smoothly, "So, do you have the names of these trading rings?"

"There are two she had solid evidence on: one's a gang called Catiline. The other she doesn't have a name for…just some leads."

"Catiline I know. Small-time traders. Petty but not dangerous. Bloodgrease on the side I can believe, but that's all. I don't see them feeling the need to hire a blade to interrogate a Service officer. But weirder and nastier things have happened. What about this other one? The one with no name?"

"We know very little about the other one. Harvey kept most of the details to herself but even her locked files had barely anything. I think it was little more than a hunch."

"Well, I was on Haven not so long ago - "

"You were?"

Webb shifted. "Yes. And Catiline are still very much alive and kicking. They've got a couple of yards under their control and connections with the refineries, which makes sense. But their operation is low-key. They avoid enemies rather than cultivate them by doing things like going after the Service."

"I trust Harvey's hunches."

"Ok then, so, what? You think Catiline hired Ariel to find out how much Harvey had dug up on them?"

"With both Ariel and bloodgrease coming from Haven…it's a coincidence too big to be ignored."

"It's still a coincidence if Harvey was investigating more than just bloodgrease. Anyone she was looking into could have hired him."

Hugo tapped his bottle on the scarred table top. "It's the only solid lead we have to go on. And besides, I don't care who hired him. I just want *him*."

Webb swallowed the last of his second beer. He slumped deeper in the chair and rubbed his forehead. "Haven," he said with a sigh. "Shit. I can't believe I'm agreeing to this."

"He nearly killed her, Zeek," Hugo said, not looking up from his bottle. "And the state she's in…even now…I wonder if it would have been better if he had." When Hugo looked up, Webb was pale. Hugo felt his cheeks flush with anger and shame. "I'm doing this, with or without you. But I'd sooner do it with you because we stand a greater chance of bringing the son of a bitch in if we do it together."

Webb sighed again and tapped in a command for another beer. "Well then. Here we go again."

III

Webb blinked into the shadows gathered on the ceiling of their boarding room for what felt like hours before cursing silently, shoving back the thin blanket and sitting up. He clutched at his head, willing the feeling that it was about to burst apart to dissipate.

You can do this, he told himself. *Pull yourself together.*

When his breathing slowed, he peered across to the dark shape on the other bunk. Hugo's breathing was steady but he twitched and mumbled in his sleep. Webb stood and padded into the tiny bathroom and locked the door. He switched on the harsh light and stared into the mirror for a long moment before pulling off his t-shirt. His skin was spacer-pale, his tattoos sharp and black, still new-looking. But, as always, these weren't the first things he noticed.

He ran his fingers over the ruler-straight scars that went up his ribs like a tally chart. They were thicker and longer across his chest, where the scalpel had sunk deeper. Long lines in the same precise, measured hand traced from behind his ears and down his neck to his collar bone. They were still a little red from the last attempt to laser them away but the nerves were dead and he couldn't feel his own touch along them.

He breathed deep against a heat rising in his throat. His hands started to shake. He blinked away at the blurriness gathering in at the edge of his vision and clenched his fists, fingernails digging into his palms. He splashed cold water on his face, willing his blood to cool but the shaking wouldn't still. He pulled his t-shirt back on, crept out, dressed in the dark and left. Pole-Aitken's air wasn't exactly fresh but it was cooler than in the Homely Inne. He paced down walkways aimlessly, weaving amongst the night-cycle foot traffic and waiting for his thoughts to align themselves into some sort of manageable order.

The walkway turned a corner and he could see the blur of the atmosphere shield curving up above him. He stopped and craned his neck, trying to pick out the glint that was the drifting colony of Haven, out beyond the space stations of the Lunar Strip colonies. The air had calmed his shakes but still there was a swallowing feeling in his stomach. He fingered a scar on his neck, letting the memories come. Ariel's face rose before him, pale apart from impossibly dark eyes that were empty and blank, even as he smiled. The scalpel peeled into his flesh and the neuro-enhancer made it feel like his very being was pouring out with his blood.

And all because of what he knew by accident. All because of what he remembered…even though the memories didn't belong to him.

Fire flared through his veins and obliterated the chill. He turned and paced towards the nearest shuttle port. A ride later and he was back aboard *Nod*, the heat of determination burning in his belly. Even with with its heat, his hands still hovered over *Nod's* comm for several minutes before he managed to start typing. He glanced at the display chrono, trying to figure out what shift Haven would be on as the connecting screen blinked. It flashed on for several moments and he spun the command chair back and forth, chewing on his thumbnail and wondering whether or not he was hoping for an answer.

It wasn't long before the display bleeped and the screen filled with the image of the dark-skinned face of an older man with thick hair, shot through with streaks of grey and pits of scarring all up one leathery cheek. He was just pulling off a dust scarf and his hair was lank with dirt and sweat. His face was screwed up in confusion, pulling the scars deeper.

"Hey, August," Webb said, dredging a grin from somewhere. "Good shift?"

The man's face flattened out. "Fuck me. Ezekiel Webb? Is that you?"

"Long time no see."

"I heard you were dead."

Webb winced. "Who told you that?"

August shrugged. "No one in particular."

"Gee, glad everyone was so broken up."

"What can I say? You vanished that quickly, I guess some folk just assumed."

"Dead men can't fly their ships through the blockade."

"Guess not," the man said, his cracked grin showing missing teeth. "Still, that's a few folk gonna be red in the face. So, what do you want?"

"I'm coming back."

"Are you now?"

"Is that a problem?"

"Not for me, lad," August said, running thick-fingered hands through his dirty hair. "You can do as you like as far as I say. Though I know a few guys who might not be, shall we say, thrilled?" Webb felt himself flush but August continued, "So, what do you want from me?"

"I just wanted to give you a heads-up."

August frowned. "You've got your brand, lad. You don't need to ask an Elder's permission any more."

"There's more."

"I knew it. What?"

"I want to Sponsor someone."

August raised his eyebrows. "You do?"

Webb nodded, keeping his face as neutral as possible. "An old war buddy's hit a dead end. Needs a new start."

"That must be some dead end."

"I can vouch for him, August," Webb said. "He's a good man fallen on hard times."

"Takes more than that to earn a bunk here, Webb."

"Can you just meet him?"

August sighed and rubbed his temples. "You timed this deliberately, didn't you?"

"I just know how soft and gooey you can be when you're tired."

August's frown deepened. "Fine, I'll meet him, Ezekiel, but I ain't promising anything."

"Thanks, August. I owe you."

"Yes. You do. Bring all the cargo you can lay your hands on and we'll see what we can do. Hope he knows what he's getting himself into."

Δ

Webb leaving had jerked Hugo from an unpleasant dream. The sweat cooled on his skin and he didn't want to think about sliding back into it. He got up, showered and went to lean in the reception doorway and watch the activity in Aitken Square as the day-cycle kicked in and the atmosphere shield lightened. He stopped himself from trying to connect to Webb's comm. He had said all he could. He'd give Webb until mid-cycle. One way or another he was leaving for Haven today.

The thought did not rally him as much as he hoped it would.

Webb didn't come back until the day-cycle had been running for a good couple of hours and though he looked tired, he was smiling.

"We're on."

Δ

"Now, Hugo," Webb said as he battened down in the lockers in *Nod's* cockpit. It was close to night-cycle again. Webb had taken most of the afternoon to complete his 'business'. Hugo made himself sit still and not fidget with impatience as Webb did his cockpit checks. "I meant it when I said you would have to do everything, *everything*, I say to pull this off, right? *Exactly* as I say it."

"I know."

"Do you? You're not my CO anymore and it's my ass on the line too. I will not hesitate to kick yours."

"I'll follow your lead, Webb," Hugo ground out. "Tell me what I need to know."

Webb sighed as he strapped himself into the command chair. "Ok then," he said. "Jesus…I don't even know where to start. We should have taken longer to prepare."

"Ariel's trail is only getting colder the longer we wait."

"Ok, ok," Webb said. "Tell me what you *do* know about Haven."

"It's the Orbit's only independent colony. And the oldest drifting one, the original space station built by pirates before Lunar 1 was established by Horatio Webb -"

"Right, hold on, stop right there, Commodore," Webb said. "Let's get that notion out of your head right now. Haven was not built by pirates."

"They were a rebel army wanted by Earth and moon-bound Enforcers for smuggling, violence, and rebellion."

Webb gave him a sardonic look as the skiff's engines hummed to life. "That 'rebel army' started off as a community of ordinary people who one day decided they would fight back against abuse and oppression rather than just bearing it. This was before the Service, you know. This was in the aftermath of the Whole World War. Living on Earth was no picnic."

Hugo gripped his armrests and reigned in his tongue.

"When fighting didn't work," Webb continued, tapping more commands into the control panel as systems started to hum and readings ran across the cockpit screens, "they found a way to escape. *Haven* is just that: somewhere beyond the reach of authority, sure, but somewhere safe. Somewhere free."

"That's a very romantic way of looking at it."

"That's the way they look at it. Then and now. You walk onto their colony with your nose turned up and a rod up your ass, you won't get one pace past the docks. Try to open you mind."

"It's hard to be open minded about a colony where a man like Ariel can find sanctuary."

Webb exhaled sharply through his nose. "I didn't say it was perfect. I just mean however dangerous it is, it's still not what you think it is."

Hugo took a moment to process this whilst Webb cleared their launch with Control and fired up the thrusters. Pole-Aitken's ragged skyline dropped out of view. The orange atmosphere faded to black and the stars blinked into view.

"What else?" Webb said as he began to type course commands into the console.

Hugo pulled out his panel as the gravity weakened and he bumped against his harness. "There's no credit system on Haven," he said, scrolling through his notes. "Everything is bought and bartered for with labour and trade."

"Correct. Well, almost. There is still credit coming and going."

"There is?"

"They can't mine everything they need from the asteroids, Hugo. There's trade off-colony. And how do you think the Service pay for their Haven-built ships? Hugs?"

"I thought -"

"Individuals don't have credit, no. Or very little if they do. They have no use for it. But the shipyards, manufacturing plants and anyone else who trades off-colony usually does it for credit. They're supposed to turn it over to the colony's brokers, who deal it out and trade it on to bring in things the whole colony needs: medical supplies and training, specialist parts, fresh food, that sort of thing."

"Supposed to?"

Webb shifted in his seat, adjusting their speed as they fell into a long-distance space lane and the moon dropped out of view. "Well, yes. I'm willing to bet there are some points that bring credit in who find ways to keep it to themselves, those that are off-colony enough to take advantage of it. But they're lucky if they get away with it."

"If a ring of bloodgrease traders is hoarding too much credit, it might be in their interest to make sure the colony doesn't find out."

"I'd say so. You may be out of the Service's reach on Haven, but better a Service detention centre than have the Elders turned against you. Anything else? Anything that Harvey's told you and that you've not just read in the Analysts' files?"

"She was always guarded about Haven."

"Sounds about right. Havenites believe in keeping your business in your own pocket."

"You lived there. What do you know about the place?"

Webb blinked in silence for a few moments. "I just know it as somewhere to get lost when you don't want to be found. For some that can be the new beginning they would never get any other way. For others…it's a more final sort of destination."

"Which was it for you?"

Webb stiffened and adjusted a dial on the command panel. "Perhaps it's time for you to start practicing the whole minding-your-own business thing they go in for there."

"What aren't you telling me?"

Webb threw him a glare. "Never mind what I'm not telling you. Just listen to what I *am* telling you."

"I'm listening, Webb. But this is all very vague."

"I'll tell you one thing that's pretty clear: they won't like you. They don't much care for Orbit politics or developments, but they will know who you are. And who you're related to. I want you to prepare yourself now for the possibility they won't even let you in."

"Even with a Sponsor?"

"A Sponsor only vouches for you. It's still the colony's decision whether you're worth the hassle."

"Webb, we have to get on that colony."

"I'll try, Hugo," Webb said. "I just want to make sure you understand that even if we get on, don't get deported and survive long enough to track down Ariel…I don't see how you expect to just march him off his own colony with no back up, right under the population's noses."

"We get him out alive or we don't get him out at all," Hugo said, watching Webb's face closely. Webb's only reaction was a slight tightening around the jaw. "How long until we hit the Service blockade?"

Webb glanced at his instruments. "Seven hours. But we need to make a little stop somewhere first."

"Where?"

"Just trust me."

Hugo muttered then silence resumed. *Nod's* life support and engines thrummed around them and Hugo found himself lulled despite everything. He thought he would chafe at being buckled in the co-pilot seat without any co-piloting to do, but even that was oddly soothing. Webb's presence was somehow putting him more at ease than he had been in months. He had a plan, a starting point and someone who, even with his talk, he knew would do his best to get the job done.

Δ

It was a pain in Hugo's neck that woke him. He drifted back slowly, revelling in the feeling of waking from a deep and, for once, dreamless sleep. He rubbed the ache and blinked until *Nod's* cockpit came into focus.

The pilot seat was empty and the command panel was dark. The silver curve of a colony took up half the viewscreen and the words sit tight scrolled across the main display in red letters.

"Webb?" he called as he scrabbled to undo his restraints. He grabbed onto the chair before crashing into the command panel, calling out Webb's name again. When there was still no answer, he pushed off the bulkhead and floated across to the access corridor.

He could see through the window in the exit hatch that the ship was docked at the end of a colony walkway, but the hatch was locked. He was just bringing up his wrist panel to buzz Webb when there was a clanking and heaving somewhere below him. He turned and pushed himself towards the ship's hold. That door was locked as well but the sounds of banging metal and the rushing of air were getting louder.

When the hatch slid open Webb was floating on the other side, frowning at a computer panel.

"Shit, Hugo," he swore when he looked up. "You scared the life outta me."

"Where are we?"

"Lunar 5," Webb said pushing past him and down the corridor with a kick off the bulkhead. Hugo just had time to see stacks of crates battened down against the deck before the hatch closed.

"What are we doing here?" Hugo asked as he followed Webb down the corridor.

"Cameron Bale was overtaken by an unbeatable urge to sample the famous local Murgh Makhanwala."

"What?"

Webb let out a noisy sigh as he drifted back into the cockpit. "It's a curry."

"I know it's a curry," Hugo said. "What are we doing taking three hours detour out of our journey for it?"

Webb sighed. "We're not. We're making it look like you are."

"Why?"

"Fake ID or not, you're not getting through the blockade if we're boarded."

"You think we'll be boarded?" Hugo felt the blood drain from his face.

"I know we will. The Service doesn't trust me for some reason."

"I assumed they'd just hail you. Webb, I can't be seen. If the Service find me trying to sneak onto Haven it won't just be me done. Eclipse will be done."

"Relax. I've taken care of it."

"What did you do?"

Webb grinned as he fastened himself back in the pilot seat. "Our friend Bale's ID was swiped at the walkway entrance to Lunar 5 but he hasn't swiped back out again. You, under whatever guise, are now officially no longer on my manifest."

"You took my ID?"

"Well you just looked so peaceful," Webb said, pulling the card out of his jacket and flicking it across the cockpit. Hugo scrambled and managed to grab it and tucked it in his own jacket.

"Nice bit of work that, too. Rami's handiwork?"

"Yes," Hugo said, watching Webb's face as he manoeuvred himself back to the co-pilot chair.

"How's she doing?" Webb's actions were smooth as ever as he started the engines but Hugo thought the words sounded a little raw.

"She's the captain of the cybernetics unit developing the systems for Apollos Outreach."

A corner of his mouth twitched up. "Bet she likes that."

"She is a very competent officer," Hugo said as he buckled himself in.

Webb sighed. "I can see why Harvey fell for you. That sensitive side of yours is almost overwhelming."

"Are we going now?"

"Yes. Strap in. Next stop, Haven. God help us."

IV

"I should report this," Hugo muttered as he dragged himself into the scan-proof holding locker under the deck in *Nod*'s tiny cabin.

"Let's get the rest of our illegal activity done first shall we, Commodore Hugo, before your honest streak kicks back in? Comfy?"

Hugo muttered as he hunched against the cold metal with his knees up to his chin, pushing against the hinge to stop himself floating out. Webb passed him his pack. He squashed it in by his feet and Webb closed the hatch, sealing him in complete darkness. His breathing sounded harsh in the close confines.

He watched the minutes tick by on his wrist panel and told himself to stay calm when there was the clank of the exit hatch opening, followed by muffled voices. They grew louder, faded, then louder again until they were almost directly above him, but the baranium-lined metal was too thick to make out any words. He heard Webb's laugh and prayed he wasn't antagonising the blockade Servicemen.

There was a series of bleeps and then the voices faded away. Again Hugo sat in the dark and prayed. The silence stretched on.

He jumped and rubbed his eyes with a curse when the hatch was opened again.

"Well done, Hugo," Webb said, holding out his hand to pull Hugo out of the smuggling hole. "You've officially broken your first law. Come on. You can see Haven from the cockpit."

"Did they check your cargo?"

"Of course they did," Webb replied as he drifted back to the cockpit. "The Service might not have any legal right to prevent anyone coming or going from Haven, but they like to make it as difficult as possible. Look." Hugo followed Webb's finger out of the view screen. The scattered edges of the farmed asteroids drifted ahead but beyond the floating chucks of rock was one star much brighter than the rest. "Last chance to turn back."

Hugo pulled himself into his chair and harnessed himself in. "Let's do it."

Webb's crooked grin showed itself again but then he sunk himself into steering the little skiff through the asteroid farm. Hugo watched in silence as Webb piloted them between the uneven chunks of rock, the concentration chasing his smile from his face. The bright point in the distance grew. More than once Hugo noticed the flash of ship engines and heavy machinery amongst the asteroids and once they passed close enough to one of the satellites that they were able to see the suited miners working on the surface.

"I never understood why they clustered them so closely together like this," Hugo muttered.

"Huh?"

"The Haven miners. The long-range haulers bring the asteroids all the way back here just to bunch them so closely together to be mined?"

"The asteroids can't be mined any closer to the moon or Earth because the gravity throws off their stability. Humanity needs the minerals, but I don't think it would be all that pleased if chunks of rock the size of cities started raining down at random."

"Then why don't they rig up them up with thrusters like the other mining companies to keep them controlled?"

"They don't have the resources to spare."

Hugo shook his head. "It's dangerous. And illegal."

Webb shrugged as *Nod* peeled around another mountain of rock. "I'm sure they'd all be working for licensed mining companies with safety contracts if they had the choice."

The traffic increased as they left the rocks behind. Skiffs, cargo haulers and a myriad of unidentifiable craft sped to and from the satellites and the colony. Hugo dug his fingers into the arms of his chair as they swung round a lumbering freighter that was apparently going too slow for Webb, only to be faced with a runner ship coming around the other way.

Webb didn't flinch and both him and the pilot of the runner peeled away and smoothed over one another.

Webb spared him a sidelong glance through his floating hair. "How do you think Webb learned to pilot so well?" he asked, the edge of that harsh smile creeping back on his face. Hugo didn't reply.

The clone's face flattened out again when the hail light started blinking on the control panel. Hugo kept his tongue still as Webb took a moment just watching the light blink. Then he reached out and pressed a button.

"Is it just me or did it take you a while to get through the blockade, Webb?" A voice growled.

"No longer than usual, August," Webb replied quickly and Hugo peered at him, trying to figure out if he was lying. "Good to hear you. Where do you want us?"

"About 500,000 kilometres back the way you came."

Webb frowned and Hugo kept his mouth shut with an effort.

"What's wrong?" Webb asked. Silence filled the cockpit like a vacuum. "August?"

"Just get yourself in dry dock, Webb. Sector 4, bay 4534. I'll be there in an hour."

Co-ordinates blinked across the display and the audio connection was gone.

"What's the problem?" Hugo asked.

"Search me," Webb said, adjusting his course again, movements just a little more tense than before.

Webb slipped them out of the busy space lane heading to the main bulk of Haven. The colony hung like a great bloated insect against the star-specked blackness. Hugo frowned at it, leaning forward as they curved around the patchwork hull. All the pictures and vidfeeds hadn't captured how ramshackle the colony was. Hugo felt his first flush of real apprehension as he took in the bristling forests of communication antennas, a technology he'd only seen in history feeds, and the different textures and colours of the miles and miles of mixed metalwork. When it was first built it may well have been the classic wheel shape that the later Sunside colonies adopted, but there had been so many extensions and branched links cobbled on over the years it was hard to decipher the shape underneath it all.

The section that faced away from the sun blinked with a hundred different colour guidance and port lights, sprinkled like stars across the sky rather than the uniform grids of signal lights that even Lunar 1 used to guide its traffic and maintenance crews. The flat surfaces facing the sunlight were dark with clusters of thousands of solar panels in different shapes and sizes, like black eyes amongst the bruised and battered metal skin.

When they were close enough that the pitted and scoured hull filled the viewscreen, Hugo was soon dizzy from trying to understand how Webb was navigating so well. Dozens of vessels zoomed back and forth across their path without any discernible order. Relief warred with his rapidly rising dread when Webb finally turned them into a wide entry way and through a vacuum shield. His stomach dropped as they came under the sway of artificial gravity. He leaned forward to take in the sight of the small dry dock through the viewscreen. There was the usual level of activity of any port or dock, spacers and cargo handlers with equipment and lifters milling out between the berths, but he'd never seen such a peculiar assortment of vessels. They were all small, all old and all much-repaired.

"Do they remind you of anything?" Webb said as he lowered *Nod* into their numbered berth.

"The *Zero*," Hugo murmured.

A fond smile softened Webb's face for a moment. "I've wondered before if this is where they got the inspiration for the thing. May have even been built here, for all I know. I wouldn't put a few off-the-books contracts past Admiral Pharos."

"Haven-made ships are the best in the Orbit," Hugo said, rising from his chair to get a better look. "Why do their own craft look like this?"

"They don't need flagships," Webb said, unbuckling his harness and going over to look over Hugo's shoulder. "They only need something that does the job. And I don't think I've ever known a Havenite to scrap anything that even still thinks about functioning."

Hugo took in the workers nearby that had paused to watch their arrival. They were leaning on their lifters, still talking, eyes not leaving *Nod*. Hugo stepped back out of sight.

"August Sinclair will be here soon," Webb said, moving to the cockpit lockers. "He's an Elder and can decide if we get on or not in two seconds. I hope you've figured out what you're going to say to convince him you belong here..." Webb paused as Hugo's pack clinked as he hefted it out of the locker. "Hugo, did you bring guns?"

Hugo frowned. "Of course."

"You'll have to leave them here," Webb said, unzipping the pack and taking out Hugo's shoulder holster and semis.

"What?" Hugo strode across the cockpit to pull his pack from Webb. "You think I'm walking onto this place unarmed?"

"You won't walk on at all if you try to take a gun with you," Webb said.

"What are you talking about?"

"You don't know?"

"Know what?"

"*No guns*, Hugo. They're illegal here. Don't tell me that's not in any of the Analysts' files?"

"I told you, there's virtually nothing in the Analysts' files."

Webb shook his head. "Even if you managed to get one through the gate, if anyone found you with a gun you'd be lynched."

Hugo frowned harder. "Haven has the highest violent crime rate in the Orbit."

"None of it gun crime," Webb said, pulling the pack back off

Hugo and rooting through it.

"Explain, will you?"

"You feel there's something worth killing someone over on Haven, you've got to do it up-close and personal." Webb shrugged. "It's always been the way. Keeps the justice system in line."

"There's a justice system?"

Webb's mouth turned up at the corner as he handed him his much-lighter pack. "Of a kind."

"Brilliant," Hugo muttered. He waited until Webb had turned back before reaching in his pack to check the Newmarc Fourshot was still in its tiny scan-proof case in the inner pocket.

"You've got knives though, right?" Webb asked, closing up the locker.

"What, so they're ok are they?"

"I said no guns, not no weapons. We're honourable, not suicidal."

"Yes, I've got knives."

"Good," he said, holding out Hugo's baseball cap that had been his pack. "Glad to see you came at least partially prepared."

"A habit I got from you," Hugo said, pulling on the cap. He didn't look up when he knew they must have both realised that the clone hadn't been the one to make Hugo start wearing baseball caps.

"Keep it on," the younger man said smoothly. "And keep up with the whole not-shaving thing again. It might give us a chance. Let's get the cargo ready to unload."

Webb pulled on his own cap, pulling his tail of hair out the back then Hugo followed him into the hold. They started unstrapping crates in silence.

"Now remember," Webb said when the crates were stacked ready and he was lowering the cargo bay ramp. "You've got to make August believe you're a no-one down on his luck who has no other future except what's here. There's a small chance he might not know who you are, but either way, neither of us are getting into the colony, let alone anywhere near Ariel if they don't believe....oh shit."

Hugo looked up. The ramp was clanking onto the deck and Webb was rigid, staring out across the hangar. Hugo craned his neck and saw a woman with the coveralls and shaved hair of a welder storming towards them.

"Who's that?"

"Get out of sight," Webb said. "Now."

"Who is she?"

"Just...oh fuck. Too late."

The woman marched up the ramp, her thick-soled boots clanging on the metal. She stood in the entrance, big hands balled into fists at her sides and stared at Hugo with fury flushing her already ruddy face. She was small but every inch of her was stocky and bristling. "I knew it."

"Simone," Webb started, but she cut him off with a finger pointed in his face.

"What in the hell are you playing at, Webb?"

"*Simone*," a gruff voice snapped before a broad-shouldered man, not much taller than the woman, came up the ramp behind her. His face, dark-skinned and worn, was scarred all up one side and there was a finger missing on his left hand. "Not here."

"It's him, August," Simone hissed, stabbing her finger at Hugo this time. "I told you it would be."

August frowned hard at him. "Are you sure? Don't look much like him to me."

"It's him, I'm telling you," Simone growled. "Webb's 'Old war buddy'. Kaleb Poxy Hugo. I *knew* it."

"Webb, shut the hold," August said and Webb complied. The ramp coughed and groaned and all four of them stood staring at each other, Hugo channeling every effort into keeping his face neutral and his mouth shut.

As soon as the hold was closed, Simone turned on Webb again. "What in the name of seven hells do you think you're playing at, sneaking a Serviceman onto Haven?"

"And not just any Serviceman," August said calmly, arms folded and keeping his eyes on Hugo.

"We have just landed the biggest manufacturing contract Haven's had in a generation, August," Simone said, putting her hands on her hips and glaring. "The Service wouldn't send just anyone to do their snooping, would they?"

"Look, just listen a moment," Webb said and Hugo watched his face closely for any sign that he was flustered. "I don't know *what* you're thinking, but it's *not* what you thinking."

"It had better not be," August said. "Come on then, Ezekiel. Explain what's going on here."

"He's wrapped around this one's finger, that's what it is," Simone growled, gesturing again at Hugo. "What's this prig got on you anyway, Webb? Why is this the only Serviceman you've ever taken orders from?"

"Can we all just take a step back a second?" Webb said, this time looking close to actual anger. "Don't you watch the newsfeeds out here?"

"Go on," August said, though Simone looked like she was about to explode.

"Hugo's been suspended."

"Oh?"

"It's true." Hugo ventured, pleased he kept his voice steady. Three pairs of eyes swung back his way, August's evaluating, Simone's suspicious and Webb's widening slightly with warning. "The Service is done with me. And I'm done with it."

"Suspension?" August said. "That's not like getting discharged."

"No," Hugo said. "They hope I'll come round to wanting to work their way again. But I won't."

"He's lying," Simone said.

"Let's listen to what he has to say," August said. "Everyone gets a chance."

"Even Erica Hugo's son?"

"Yes," August said, looking at Simone. "The Service has broken and cast aside as many souls as anywhere else, love. You know this."

Simone took a step closer to August. "I trust Javi and Calle," she said in a calmer voice. "They've never been wrong. And they said this man is Service to the bone."

"Javi and Calle are very rich fences because they are excellent judges of character," Hugo interjected. "But I was a different person when I knew them."

"So what's changed?" August said.

There was silence for a moment. Webb stood behind August's shoulder, watching him. His face was pale. Simone had her arms crossed and her chin jutting out but she, too, waited. Hugo met August's heavy, dark gaze.

"Nothing. That's the trouble," he said. "I've been promised over and over again that things would change. I have bled and fought and lost almost everything in the name of change, only to see none happen."

August frowned. "You defeated Pharos's Lunar Uprising," he said, swinging a look over his shoulder at Webb. "And you, too. Except you left the Service behind the minute you could. You, however," August looked back at Hugo. "Did not. You won them their war, you helped them strengthen their hold on the Lunar Strip. And now you stand there and tell me you did all that for something you didn't believe in?"

"No," Hugo murmured. "I used to believe. But not anymore."

Simone was silent, though her eyes still flashed. A slight frown creased Webb's brow but August's swarthy face was still difficult to read.

"Something went wrong, huh?" the older man said.

Hugo's eyes flicked towards Webb before he could stop them. Webb shook his head almost imperceptibly and Hugo looked back to August. "I lost a lot, now and then. And all for nothing."

August let out a sigh and shook his head. "I can almost admire the fact that you had hope, Hugo. Almost. But I need to tell you: you won't find any redemption here. Haven is not somewhere to sulk. And it's not somewhere to make a point. It's somewhere you come to survive. Those that do are grateful because it's the only alternative they have. You, however," August narrowed his eyes. "Let's just say I can't believe that this is your only way out."

"I'll vouch for him, August," Webb said. "He wants out of the Service. Out of the Orbit. And he'll work for it."

"And what are you getting in return Webb?" Simone said. "What's in this for you?"

Webb lifted a shoulder in a half-shrug. "I owe him."

Both the welders weighed them up for a long minute. Then August looked to Simone and she gave a tiny nod.

August sighed. "Very well, Ezekiel. You want to take this on, I wish you the best. But I'm warning both of you now, disaffected or not, he's going to have a lot to prove. His probation may never be over."

Hugo let out a shuddering breath whilst they looked the other way, a rushing in his ears slowly fading as August and Webb shook hands. Webb lowered the ramp again as August came over and shook his own hand and clapped his arm.

"Good luck, Hugo. I mean it."

"Thank you."

"Simone? Take him through the scanner and sort his brand. I'll see what Webb's brought us to make this worthwhile."

"Your favourite, August," Webb said, patting the nearest crate. "Nutripaks."

"Brand?" Hugo asked.

"They don't hurt much," Webb said. "Now go and be good for Simone. I'll meet you on the other side."

Simone wasn't smiling. She jerked her head in the direction of the cargo ramp and Hugo shouldered his pack and followed her. They wove across the noisy dry dock, a few spacers pausing in their work to glance at him. He pulled the cap down lower on his brow, kept his head down and trotted to keep up with Simone.

"This way," she said as she ducked through some sliding doors. He followed her down a blinding white passageway with no windows and another set of doors ahead of them. "You go through."

Hugo resisted throwing her a questioning glance and went up to the black doors. A light flashed above his head and they slid open. He stepped into a small room and the door hissed shut again. There was a beeping somewhere overhead. He frowned and stepped up to the other doors but they didn't open. The beeping continued and the air began to warm.

He looked around at the blank walls and then at the dozens of small black domes bolted to the ceiling, red lights flashing in their innards in time with the beeping. He resisted the urge to fidget until finally the beeping stopped and the opposite doors slid open to admit a waft of cold and oily air. He shivered and stepped through and the doors snapped shut again behind him.

The metal bulkhead of the colony arched into darkness above. There was a set of tracking lights far, far above his head. They were a dull, underwater green instead of the white he remembered from the Lunar colonies' night-cycles and nowhere near bright enough to lift the gloom around him. The lights stretched away into the distance where he could roughly make out the jagged outlines of buildings against the dim soupy-green backdrop. There was no crowded neon of the cities on the moon and no uniform street-level flood lighting like on the colonies of the Lunar and Sunside strips. Beyond the walls of the docking area where he stood, the only light he could see was the scatterings of the few lit windows in the nearest buildings, along with a grey wash lower down which seemed to be made by sporadically placed and ill-maintained street lamps on some of the broader avenues.

The air was heavy and smelt of oil. It was also cold enough to make him shiver.

Further down on his left were large gates through which the main bulk of the dry dock traffic seemed to be coming and going. A couple of guards, not tall but bulging frames barely contained by their dark coveralls, were looking over everyone, giving the occasional spacer a sweep with a hand-held scanner. One of the guards was watching him out the corner of his eye whilst his partner did a thorough sweep of a woman with a moped, including checking her neck for something.

Hugo stayed where he was, stock-still until the doors he had come through opened again and Simone stepped out eyeing him up and down.

"Well that's the second expectation you've defied."

"Huh?"

Simone jerked her thumb back at the door. "Industrial scanner. If you'd been trying to sneak anything in, you'd be back on *Nod* already. This way." She turned and paced towards a thin-walled building that was little more than a shed shouldered against the colony bulkhead. Hugo felt his heart speed up, grip tightening on the handles of his pack and sent up silent thanks to Rami and her scan-proof box. His knees were a little shaky as he hurried after Simone.

"What's the contract?"

"Huh?"

"The biggest manufacturing contract in a generation?"

Simone narrowed her eyes. "Are you that dumb or just playing dumb?" Hugo clenched his jaw over his response. She watched his reaction and frowned. "Apollos Outreach?"

"The terraforming project?"

Simone nodded. "They've commissioned virtually everything from us."

Hugo blinked at her. "You're building everything they're using to colonise Mars?"

"There are no other yards in the Orbit which could meet the specs. Or deadline, for that matter. You really didn't know?"

"They didn't exactly publicise it."

"No," Simone grated. "They wouldn't."

"Is it night-cycle?" Hugo said, changing the subject as her brow grew stormy.

"No cycles here, Service-boy. Only shifts."

Hugo looked out over the dark gathered above him and felt something sink inside him. The door to the shed was open. They passed a couple of rooms crowded with workstations and people in headsets with charts on their displays, directing space traffic. The workstations were all mis-matched and wiring snaked between them and over the walls. Simone took them into a room smaller than the others, cluttered with dented locker banks and another workstation with a cracked display in the corner.

"Sit," Simone directed as she keyed in a code to open one of the lockers. Hugo looked round and, seeing no other chair, sat at the workstation. Simone pulled out an instrument, examining its sharp end with a frown. She pressed a control and it started to hum, the narrow point glowing red.

"What's that?"

"Lean forward," she said and Hugo blinked at her solemn face and the needle a moment longer before obeying. She pulled down his shirt collar and then he felt something biting into the skin of his neck. He hissed between his teeth and heard Simone exhale sharply through her nose.

"I really hope you weren't lying, Service-boy," she said in a low voice. "That lad's got friends here as well as enemies. If you get him lynched, you'll have to answer to them. And to me."

"I don't intend to get Webb into trouble," Hugo muttered as another line of fire was carved into his neck, hoping he wasn't lying to himself.

Simone made a noncommittal noise and released him before returning the instrument to the locker. "Don't rub it," she snapped and Hugo dropped his hand. "Wait here."

Hugo was left in the tiny room with the activity of the ramshackle building humming around him, feeling a chill of uncertainty ghosting around his innards. He shook it away and glanced around. He caught sight of a mirror propped on a cupboard across the room and went across and pulled down his collar. There were two slightly curved black bars lasered into his skin just below his shirt line. The skin around was red and angry-looking.

"You get the cross-bar after your probation is up." Hugo jumped as Webb entered the room. He dumped his pack and pulled back the collar of his jacket. "See?"

Hugo saw the slightly stylised 'H' on the side of Webb's neck just before he shrugged his jacket back up. "Come on. August says there's a boarding house not far from here that might take us."

"This is how Haven knows you've been through probation?" Hugo said, shouldering his pack and resisting the urge to rub the skin at his neck. "What's to stop someone just getting it done at any old laser parlour?"

"Step out here and I'll show you."

Hugo kept his head down as he followed Webb back out into the gloom of Haven. "Here."

Webb pulled down his collar again and Hugo saw the tattoo glowed a dull red against his skin.

"How does it do that?"

"I don't know," Webb said, striking out towards a series of ramshackle sheds across the cluttered concrete of the dock yard. "It's something to do with the track lights and whatever treatment they put in the laser. It can't be faked, either way. People have tried."

Hugo followed Webb, finding himself breathing shallowly and through his mouth. The heavy metallic edge to the air caught in the back of his throat. They ducked under an arch in the wall of one of the sheds to join a line of people filtering through onto a shuttle platform on the other side. Small knots of Havenites were milling about with lifters and bags and trolleys. The ones that weren't alone kept their heads close together when they talked. They all wore tough-wearing fabrics in grey and beige, many-pocketed trousers, sturdy boots and thick jackets with high collars. Most of them had oil or rust staining their clothing. What hands and faces he could see that weren't hidden in thick gloves or dust-scarves were scarred. Hugo was half a head taller still than the tallest amongst them. Glances slid their way and Hugo moved his gaze to his friend, who stood easy, watching the numbers on a chrono on the wall counting down. Hugo could see the top of his brand glowing red over his collar.

"You had that before," Hugo murmured, feeling his brow crease.

"Huh?"

"That tattoo," Hugo said, pointing. "The brand. You…I mean the other you…the first Webb. He had that brand."

"Yeah. He went through probation when he was seventeen, so the *Zero* could build connections here. I thought you knew that?"

"I did. I didn't realise that that's what it meant though."

"So?"

"So, if it can't be faked, how do you have it too?"

Webb shrugged. "I did it again."

"You've been through probation twice?"

"Well, no, not technically," Webb said, dark humour sparkling in his eyes. "He did it once and so did I."

"Why?"

"Aren't you glad I did?" Webb said, looking away to the shuttle rail. "Or else we wouldn't be here."

The countdown ticked to zero and an ancient shuttle lumbered to a stop at the platform. Hugo watched Webb closely as they boarded with the workers. There was nowhere to sit so they stood at the handholds by a window as the shuttle rattled away.

"You're not going to tell me why?"

"Why what?"

"Why you put yourself through probation again?"

Webb looked him in the eye. Again, Hugo saw something different in this man's face than the man he'd first met aboard Service Command. The murmur of the rocking shuttle carried on around them as he held his gaze for a long moment.

"It's not important," he said finally, and looked away.

Hugo bit his tongue with an effort and looked out the window. The shuttle clattered along its rail. Buildings interspersed with storage lots hunkered right up against the tracks. Hugo squinted but could barely see anything through the gloom. As they crossed an avenue broader than the rest he saw the single headlight of a moped cutting through the dark as it crossed from one side-street to another, laden trolley trailing behind it. The avenue curved slightly up, jumbled structures, badly lit, shouldering in on either side. The distance was just a dark green haze spreading to the false horizon. Just before the view was blocked again he caught the sight of towers in the distance, tall and glowing a brighter green, with lofty spires that reached high above everything surrounding it.

Then it was gone and it was just darkness again, broken by pools of uneven lamplight.

"There's no skyways."

"Folk round here don't have much cause for wandering far. Those that do use the shuttles. Apart from people who have cobbled mopeds together."

The shuttle stopped every so often and the carriage gradually emptied of the passengers from the docks to be replaced with workers coming to and from shifts, all grimed work clothes and tired eyes.

Sometime later the shuttle stopped at a stop that, to Hugo, looked the same as all the others but Webb, still silent, signaled that they should get off. There was no platform. They stepped onto a shadowy street and the shuttle rumbled on its way. They were left alone in the dark with concrete buildings arching up either side and an eerie silence pressing in on them.

"Where are we?"

"Still in Sector 4, I think," Webb said, voice broken with a yawn. "Been a while since I've been this far hubwards. But as August has given you permission to be here we should return the favour by sticking to his sector."

"We need to find the nearest bloodgrease refinery," Hugo said as he stepped over the shuttle rail after Webb and turned onto a virtually deserted side street.

"What for?"

"To try and track down some traders."

"Hold your horses, Commodore," Webb said as he scanned up and down the street. "You're on probation remember?"

"So?"

Webb rolled his eyes. "So it's got to look like you're here to earn citizenship. If the first thing you do is start sticking your nose into bloodgrease business, people are gonna catch on."

"So, what?"

"We've got to find some work."

"We haven't got time to work, Webb. The longer I'm here the bigger the chance of word getting to Ariel."

"You agreed, Hugo," Webb said, stopping in front of a building that, to Hugo, looked the same as all the others, except the doors were open and light spilled onto the concrete street. "Follow my lead, remember?"

"Webb - "

"Hugo," Webb cut him off, voice hardening. "You don't know this place. I do. We won't last five minutes the second anyone figures out what we're really here for. We've got to play the game."

Hugo reigned in his temper and unclenched his fists with an effort. "How long for?"

"As long as it takes."

Webb climbed the steps into the building. Hugo glanced along the dark street. The light that gathered in muddy puddles from security lights wired into the concrete walls of the buildings only made the spaces between them darker. An engine whined nearby but then faded again and all was quiet apart from the steady throbbing hum of the colony's life support.

For a second Hugo felt more alone than he ever remembered feeling before, then turned and hurried after Webb.

V

Hugo blinked in the bright front hall of the building Webb had chosen. It wasn't exactly blinding, but compared to the gloom of the rest of the colony, it was like stepping from the dark side of the moon to the light. The room was wide, its floor covered in scuffed linoleum and the walls painted grey. There were lockers bolted to one wall and a number of closed doors. Webb was pushing the buzzer on the door with a panel above that read *Building Manager.*

"Where are we?"

"Boarding house," Webb said as the sound of locks and bolts rattling came through the door. "Just let me do the talking."

A man so short he barely stood to Hugo's armpit open the door a crack. A couple of ties made of wire kept the door from opening further than a handspan and the man put his pinched face to the gap and peered at them both in silence.

"Hey there. Michalski, is it?" The man didn't move or even blink. Hugo kept himself still as Webb continued smiling. "August Sinclair said you might have a room."

The man stood peering at them a moment longer. Hugo resisted the urge to shift on his feet. "What shift you on?"

"None, yet," Webb said, with one of his disarming smiles. "Just landed. We're all yours."

The man closed the door and there was the scraping of metal on wood. Webb gave Hugo a reassuring nod and then the door was opened and the little man stepped out. His hair was slate-grey and very thick. It stuck up in wild angles as if he'd run his fingers through it a thousand times that day already. His clothes were patched and washed to that Haven-standard colour that could have started off life as black or brown but was now somewhere between grey and beige. He folded his arms over a scrawny chest and eyed them with sharp eyes. Hugo noticed that his fingers were so twisted and gnarled they were like pale claws against his woollen jacket.

"Elder Sinclair sent you, huh?" he said, his English flavoured with something like the accents he'd heard in Old Europe.

Webb nodded. "I owe him some shifts."

He eyed them both a moment longer. "Either of you any good at systems?"

"I like to think so," Webb said.

The narrow eyes fell on Hugo. "And what does this one do? Can he talk?"

Webb slapped Hugo on the shoulder before he opened his mouth. "Conversation's not exactly Kaleb's strong point. But he's got a strong back and some mechanics know-how."

"A proby, huh?" he said, keen look lingering on Hugo's neck. "You his Sponsor?"

"Aye," Webb said. "I'll vouch for him."

The little man looked between them both a moment longer, weighing them up, then nodded. "Fine. If Sinclair says you're good I'll have you. You can have the attic. But first, I need someone to look at the security system. Damn thing keeps disconnecting. Wiring, I think, but I can't keep up with the all new connection protocols. And you," he looked at Hugo, the corner of his smile revealing yellowed teeth. "Storage yard needs a good clear out. Garbage disposal is on next street over and I can't manage the lifter. Deal?"

"Deal," Webb said, holding out his hand before Hugo said anything. The man just about managed to shake Webb's hand with his twisted one. "What do I call you?"

"Webb. And Kaleb."

Michalski nodded and Hugo searched his eyes for any glimmer of recognition but the man just said, "Leave your stuff here. Tag," he called over his shoulder into his apartment. "*Tag*." There was some muttering and a scrawny boy around ten with a jumper so big it swamped him appeared in the doorway. "Take their stuff up to the attic. Then let your ma know we've got a couple extra for dinner." The boy gave them both a wide-eyed glance before taking their packs and scurrying away through another door. "This way," Michalski said, closing his own door and leading them across the hall and through the door the boy had used.

He limped along the dim corridor on the other side, Webb and Hugo following. They went past the foot of a staircase and then more closed doors to one at the end that was heavily bolted. Michalski levered the bolts back with his bent fingers and led them out into a cluttered yard, lit by a dim security light cobbled onto the outside wall of the boarding house. There were overflowing trash bins, piles of plastic and metal that could have been anything from the remains of household appliances to sections of scrapped flyers and stacks of crates containing piled bottles, cans and plastic.

Michalski tapped the nearest crate. "Here you go, Kaleb my lad. Lifter's in the shed. Webb? You follow me."

The Havenite disappeared back into the building. Webb threw a not-quite apologetic look over his shoulder as he followed.

Hugo looked at the mountain of rubbish feeling his frustration war with despair. He wanted to be angry again, angry enough to strike off into the streets after Ariel alone. But as he stood there with the silence and the shadows almost physical presences around him and the air thick with the smell of metal, he felt a shiver run over him. It had been a long time since an unfamiliar place had gotten under his skin.

He shook himself, reminding himself Webb wasn't far away and that, no matter how much it chafed, he had agreed to follow his friend's lead. He heaved a deep breath and looked around for anything resembling the shed Michalski had mentioned. Spotting a lean-to cobbled together from sheets of corrugated iron propped against the yard wall, he picked his way over, stepping around the sprawling junk. It took a heave or two to get the door open and it was only with the aid of his pocket lenslight and a few select curses he found the ancient lifter under a box of tools in the corner. It wouldn't power up so he dragged it out into the meagre light to get a better look at the controls. He tried blowing the dust out of the wiring and even turned it over to check the magnet coils but the power button remained unresponsive.

He was growling and shaking the machine when a voice at his elbow made him jump.

"It's the burners." It was the boy who had taken their bags, grinning a gap-toothed smile. "I'll fix it."

Hugo stood frowning for a second but then sidestepped and the boy knelt and pulled a panel off the side. "See? The air flow system's gone. The burners are always getting clogged."

Hugo craned his neck and watched the boy scrape away some carbon scoring from the connections and replace the panel. His throat tightened when he found himself wondering whether his own son would have liked to work with machines. He blinked back the stinging that started in his eyes as Tag hit the power button. The lifter coughed then hummed and rose off the concrete, hanging just about level.

"Thank you," Hugo said, glad his voice didn't sound thick. "Tag?"

The boy nodded then looked up as a loud booming noise like that of the ocean liners in Sydney Harbour echoed off the walls around them.

"What's that?"

Tag gave him a confused look. "Shift end," he said. "What, you don't…?" The boy paused then reached and pulled down Hugo's collar before he realised what was going on. "Whoa. You're on probation, huh? That's rough."

Hugo pulled his collar over his brand, scowling but Tag didn't seem to register and just stood there, smiling at him. He dragged the lifter over to the crates and Tag followed him.

"Where'd you come from then, huh? The Lunar Strip? They say you can see the moon *and* Earth all at once from Lunar 5."

"Sometimes," Hugo muttered as he started loading crates onto the lifter. The air started to fill with the noise of voices and feet and the occasional hum of a small engine. He couldn't see anything over the walls of the yard but lights came on in some of the windows of the surrounding buildings and the sound of doors opening and closing punctuated the growing shuffle of foot traffic in the streets.

"That's so cool," Tag was saying. "This guy from Tranquility stayed here a while. He knew Grandpa. He told me about Wasteland Buggying on the moon. He said -"

Tag was cut off by the sound of shouting. There was a loud clang of metal on metal and the nearest street lamp flickered. Tag rushed to a gate in the yard wall, heaved it open and peered out. More yells rang out along with the sounds of a struggle and Tag ran out into the street.

"*Tag!*" Hugo called, dropping a crate and running after him. The street was teeming with workers. They all looked eerily similar in the dim light, both men and women wearing hair shorn close to their scalps or else worn long and tied back. Dust scarves and goggles hid their faces and they walked alone or in twos or threes with the directionless amble of prisoners being migrated around a detention centre. Someone on a moped whirred by but otherwise people walked, gazes sliding easily off Hugo if they even landed on him.

Neither did anyone so much as glance at the two men grappling at the street corner. One, thin, and tall for a Havenite with what little hair he had left tied back in a thin braid, wielded a length of pipe with fierce desperation. His eyes were red and puffy and there were sores on the skin of his hands and neck. The other man was thicker-set and shorter but moved easier, concentrating on avoiding the pipe. They shouted insults at each other as they wrestled. The unarmed one managed to throw off the other long enough to draw a knife. Tag danced up to the small group of workers who had now stopped to watch the fight with solemn looks on their faces.

The knifeman lunged but the one with the pipe dodged and brought his weapon down on the other man's back with a slam.

"What the...?" was all Hugo managed as the crowd of foot traffic continued to oil past, uninterested and the little crowd of bystanders stood by in silence. Hugo grabbed Tag by the wrist and tried to pull him away from the combatants, who were now attempting to slam each other against the nearest wall.

"Hey, let go, I know that guy," Tag said as Hugo attempted to haul him away.

"Tag!" A flustered woman in a house coat hurried up. She grabbed Tag's other arm and pulled him to her, glaring at Hugo. Hugo dropped his hold on the child's wrist.

"But Ma, it's Sol. He might need a witness."

"There's plenty of grown-ups here to act as witnesses," the woman said, ushering Tag away. "Go and help your sister. The dinner needs serving."

Tag returned to the yard gate, muttering the whole way.

"I'm sorry," Hugo found himself saying. "I just - "

"Who are you?" the woman said, hands on hips.

"Hugo," Webb called from where he'd appeared at the gate. "Get in here. Now."

Hugo threw one more glance at the men who were now standing apart, bloodied and breathing heavily but showing no signs of finishing, then went back to Webb, the woman following and giving them both an angry glance before heading back towards the house.

"Everyone's just standing by and letting them knock seven hells out of each other. What...what is it?" Hugo added, seeing Webb staring hard at the fighters.

"I know one of them. Sol. He's a member of Catiline."

"Which one?" Hugo glanced back just as the pipe man made a mad swing for the knifeman's head.

"The guy with the knife. Wait - " Webb grabbed Hugo's sleeve as he stepped back toward them. "You can't interfere."

"They're going to kill each other!"

"They have witnesses. Let it alone."

"Witnesses? What has that to do with anything?"

"Keep your voice down," Webb hissed. "They'll be settling a score, in the open, with witnesses for their kin to see nothing sneaky gets tried. It's between them."

"If he's in Catiline, we need to talk to him whilst he still can talk."

Webb's jaw tightened, as did his grip on Hugo's sleeve. "I'm telling you, don't get involved."

"Let me go. Now. I don't care about this messed-up justice system. If that guy knows anything -"

"He won't know anything about Ariel, you pig-headed idiot. He's small-time. A petty Patch dealer. They're probably arguing over a fee."

"Patch?"

"You know, Energy Patches. Some people use them to get through their shifts."

"They're emergency treatment for heart defects," Hugo managed. "They're addictive."

"Yes, I know. Now get the hell back in here before someone sees you gawking."

Hugo wrenched his sleeve out of Webb's grip to stride away. The clone's face contorted with anger as he grabbed Hugo by the arms and hauled him bodily back through the gate. Hugo was thrown off balance, staggering when the younger man shoved him away. Webb took the opportunity to lock the gate.

"Commander Webb," Hugo growled, picking himself up the floor. "When I agreed to follow your orders, I did not agree to sitting by whilst you let potential leads kill each other."

Webb visibly gathered his temper. "I'm not your commander any more, Commodore. And even if Sol does know anything, the absolutely last thing you should do is confront him on the street with witnesses."

"What *can* we do, then?"

"Just trust me, will you? Now get finished up here. We've only got the next shift to rest then we need to get to the yards and look for work."

"I'm sick of this place already," Hugo muttered, loading another crate onto his lifter.

"Then we're in real trouble."

Webb left him. He stood and fumed with fingernails digging into palms, listening to the fight carry on out of sight. He stopped himself with his hand on the gate twice before swearing under his breath and turning back to the lifter. By the time he had it loaded and was maneuvering it out into the street, the foot traffic had slowed to a trickle. The brawling men were gone with nothing but a dent in the lamppost to show anything had happened. He scouted the area anyway, not even sure what he was looking for, but they hadn't dropped anything and there was no one around.

He pushed the lifter further down the street in a daze until he spotted someone hauling a hand-barrow full of junk around a corner and followed them. He came up on the end of a queue of people with armfuls, barrows or lifters of rubbish. Craning his neck he could see an angular hunk of metal he could only guess was a garbage disposal in the shadows between the buildings ahead. The workers all waited patiently and in silence, dumping their loads one by one and disappearing into the streets. When his turn came, Hugo lifted the metal lid to be met with darkness, a whirring of machinery far below street level and a putrid smell. He emptied the crates into the void and returned to the yard. Every time he did a trip he found himself looking up and down every street he passed and eyeing every Havenite that trudged by, but the knife-wielding Catiline member was nowhere to be seen.

Webb came and found him again when he was caked in dirt and sweat and about ready to drop. He followed him wordlessly indoors and up the stairs that seemed to go on forever. Webb gave a huge yawn as he turned an old-fashioned key in the lock of a door at the top.

Webb clicked on the light. There was a narrow cot against each wall, with a locker under each, a window and a set of shelves, broken. No workstation. No bathroom. Not even a sink. Their packs were on the cots and Hugo dropped down heavily next to his own to pull off his boots. A knock sounded just as he was searching through his pack for a clean shirt. Webb pulled open the door to Tag who stood there with two steaming bowls.

"I managed to swipe you some before it all went," he said holding out the bowls.

"Thanks, buddy," Webb said, taking the bowls and some foil pouches Tag pulled from his pockets.

Tag looked to Hugo expectantly. Webb gave him a hard look, holding out the bowl.

"Thanks," Hugo said.

Tag smiled his gap-toothed grin and scampered off.

The bowl contained something grey, like everything else on Haven, with the consistency of unfiltered engine oil, but the smell was savoury and it made Hugo's stomach clench.

"What's this?" Hugo said as Webb passed him one of the pouches.

"Nutripak," Webb said around a mouthful of his food.

Hugo ate a spoonful of the gruel and discovered it was next to tasteless but was warm and satisfying. It was gone before he knew it. He eyed the Nutripak warily before tearing off the top and taking a bite of the paste inside.

"I know, tastes like shit," Webb mumbled when Hugo scowled. "But you're not going to get all the nutrients you need from the food, believe me."

He made himself swallow the rest then was overtaken by wave of weariness. He lay back on the cot without undressing, falling asleep with the steady hum of a cranky air filter in his ears and the oily smell of Haven in his nostrils.

Δ

Webb stood at the window after waking up for the fourth time, arms folded and fingers digging into his arms. Hugo was sleeping, although he twitched and mumbled enough once again to make Webb think it wasn't soundly.

Webb chewed on his lip, willing his pulse to calm. He'd given his former captain his word, but what he'd agreed to hadn't seemed quite so real as when he'd seen Sol fending off the pipe-wielding Patch User with a bank of witnesses standing calmly to one side to make sure the fight was legal.

He stared out into the dull green dimness and took a deep breath, acknowledging that a lot more than Sol would have to be confronted before this was over.

Hugo's sharp intake of breath pulled him out of his thoughts.

"Hey, Hugo," he said, hovering by the Serviceman's cot. His dark brows were drawn together, his eyes twitched behind the eyelids and he was sweating. Webb reached out and shook his shoulder. "Hugo…ah, *fuck*. Let go, it's me."

Hugo blinked, eyes huge and the grip he had on Webb's wrist tightening. Finally, he focussed and loosed his hold. Webb rubbed his wrist, muttering, but turned away to let Hugo gather himself. The cot groaned as the other man sat up. His breathing was heavy.

"Bad dream?"

"What's happening?"

Webb flicked the light on. "We've got four hours before the next shift starts. If we leave now we can stop off somewhere on the way to the yards and I can try and ask a few questions."

"Questions?"

Webb drummed his fingers together, not looking at Hugo. "The guy we saw fighting earlier…"

"The gang member?"

Webb nodded. "Sol. He's from Sector 2. I don't like that he's turned up at our back yard."

Hugo was rubbing his temples but then went very still. "You

think he knows what we're up to?"

"What can he know?" Webb grumbled. "We don't even know what we're doing ourselves yet. But people tend to stick to their sectors. If Sol's dealing out here, well…I don't know that it means anything at all. But it's worth checking. And it's a way to start asking questions about Catiline."

"What about leaving people's business between themselves?"

"There's a difference between collaring a gang member in the street and shaking Ariel's whereabouts out of him and a few discreet enquiries about a local Patch dealer. Now, come on. You're the one that wanted to get started so bad."

Hugo rubbed his face, palm scratching against the bristle of hair along his jaw. "Anywhere to get cleaned up?"

"Shower room is on next landing down. Don't shave, though."

"I know, I know," Hugo grumbled, throwing the blankets back and stretching. He paused at the door and looked back at Webb. Webb looked up finally from his examination of the opposite wall and saw something unnerving flickering in Hugo's eyes.

"What?"

"Have I thanked you yet?"

Webb raised his eyebrows. "You haven't paid me, if that's what you mean."

"You know it's not."

Webb rubbed the back of his neck. "Don't thank me yet. Go get washed up. Time to get started."

Δ

Hugo followed Webb through the dark streets, rubbing his eyes to try and make himself focus. He felt like he hadn't slept at all but forced his mind away from why and concentrated on ghosting along in Webb's shadow. He had them moving quickly and quietly through alleys, across bridges over gaping blackness with the clanking of unseen machinery below and noxious smells rising, or between buildings shunted so tightly against one another they had to move single file between them. Again there was an eerie silence over everything and most windows were darkened. When they passed a working wall chrono, Hugo stopped long enough to adjust the time on his wrist panel to sync with Haven's thirty-hour day before Webb hurried them on.

They cut a straighter path through the sector than the shuttle rails took, the maze of alleys and roads dizzying, until the sound of voices, bustle and some music started to rise in the distance. There was light up ahead too.

So suddenly that it made Hugo blink as they stepped around a corner into a wide square that was thronging with people. There were flood lights at every level of the mismatched buildings and people came and went between their open doors, some laughing, some quarrelling, some staggering. Music spilled out of doorways and windows, as did more shouting and laughter. Webb hurried them on just as another fight started up nearby, a small gathering collecting as if on cue to stand witness.

"What is this place?" Hugo asked, looking around the busy square.

"What passes for a rec district on Haven," Webb said as he steered around a couple clinging to one another as they staggered across their path.

"What sort of recreation?" Hugo asked, eyeing a man stumbling out of a building, wiping his sleeve across his mouth before weaving his way across the yard and into another.

"Movie houses. Bars," Webb said, striking out across the square and round a group of people huddled around crates playing cards. "Not much. It's not like you get much time off to enjoy them."

"Hey!"

Webb froze in response to the shout and looked around. A man with shoulders like a bull was striding toward them, a dark look on his meaty face. "Webb? Ezekiel Webb?"

"Who is it?" Hugo hissed, seeing Webb's jaw tighten.

"Just keep your mouth shut, ok? And don't do anything. I'll handle this. Ribble," he greeted the square-jawed man as he came up to them. "Long time no see."

The man punched Webb across the face before Hugo realised what he was doing. Webb staggered back, clutching his mouth and Hugo surged forward to grab the man by his black coveralls.

"Hugo," Webb growled through his hand. "Let him go."

"You've got a nerve," the man snarled, shoving Hugo off him and looking only at Webb. "I heard you were dead. You're gonna wish you were."

"Ribble, hold on, pal," Webb said, straightening back up, wincing and wiping blood from his split lip. "I've not come to cause any trouble."

"Well, you've got trouble," Ribble growled, taking another step toward the taller man.

"Hugo," Webb snapped again as Hugo moved to intercept. Out of the corner of his eye Hugo saw Havenites beginning to form a cluster close by. He stayed where he was with an effort. Ribble gave him an angry up-and-down then turned his attention back to Webb.

"Go on. Explain yourself. What's your cowardly ass doing back here?"

"Ribble," Webb said holding out his hands. "I know I was a shit better than anyone. But, pal, is it really any of your business?"

The man bristled. Hugo fidgeted but Webb threw him a warning glare. "Certain people have a right to be angry," Webb continued to the Havenite, coolly. "And I'll accept judgement from them. But not from you."

Ribble's face grew stormy and he glanced toward the witnesses. He snarled again and pointed a finger in Webb's face. "You were lucky, this time. But I'm going to make damn sure she knows you're back. Then we'll see…"

Ribble stormed away. The witnesses disbanded, muttering amongst themselves. Webb slumped and swore, touching his mouth gingerly.

"Who was he?" Hugo asked, watching the retreating figure.

"He's an Enforcer from Sector 2," Webb said, looking around and starting back off across the square. "An old buddy."

"'Buddy'?" Hugo said, hurrying after him.

"Well, you know," Webb hedged. "At one time. Come on, we're wasting time."

"Where are we going?"

"To a bar. Any bar," Webb said, glancing around then headed over to one of the buildings. He climbed some creaking stairs on the outside and Hugo followed. There was a door at the top, propped open with a crate and Webb paused for a moment to peer in then gestured for Hugo to follow and ducked inside.

Hugo stood blinking on the threshold to let his eyes get used to the dark. The door opened onto a large room, lit only by projections that scrolled on every inch of wall space, reeling numbers and charts. Hugo frowned at them, trying to figure out what the data was but it was like no feed the Service used. As they moved towards a manned bar, he remembered the fifteen-hour shift time structure and started to decipher that the figures were work timetables and maintenance schedules. Each of the four walls had its own sector on display.

Some of the patrons at the tables were huddled together over panels. Some had hard-copy schematics laid out in the meagre table space, weighted down by flasks at the corners. Even the ones laughing loudly with no work in sight were still dressed in coveralls and had wrist panels to hand.

"Work never stops here, does it?"

"Haven never shuts. Hey pal," Webb put his elbows on the bar, "Couple of whatever's on."

The man with a long ponytail and an eye missing filled a couple of metal flasks from a keg behind the bar and handed them over with a nod.

"Thanks. Say," Webb leaned over the bar, and lowered his voice. "It's been a while since I've been in these parts. Know where a welder could get hold of a Patch or two?"

Hugo clutched his flask tightly when the bartender's face flattened. "You're no good to your foreman laid out from a heart attack."

"It's just until I get used to the shifts again."

"Sure," the barman grunted, frown twisted by the scarring over his eye socket. "And you're not gonna have the Elders on my ass or nothing."

"Do I look like a rat?"

The man did a deliberate up-and-down of Webb. "Well you sure don't look like a welder."

Webb let out a noisy sigh, glancing about again. "Fine. They're for him," he jerked his head at Hugo. The man swivelled his calculating look Hugo's way, eye lingering on the brand at his neck. "Didn't want it getting about that I got my proby on Patches. But he's struggling."

Webb dug an elbow imperceptibly into Hugo's ribs. "The shifts are…hard," Hugo mumbled, not having to fake despondency.

"Friend, you can't handle shifts, you shouldn't be here."

"He's trying," Webb said. "He'll get there. He just needs -"

The barman held up his hand. "You guys finish your beer and go. I don't want nothing to do with folks cheating probation."

Webb ducked his head. "No problem, man. I understand. We'll finish these and be on our way."

The barman nodded and Webb led Hugo to a table.

"Don't worry," Webb mumbled into his flask as they sat down. "Just wait. Drink."

Hugo took a mouthful. It was beer, at a close approximation, but only just.

"What are we waiting for?"

"Trust me."

Hugo frowned and took another mouthful of his drink. He smoothed the grimace off his face when he noticed a young man at the bar watching him.

"Just relax," Webb said as the youth wove his way toward them, draining his flask as he came. He strode up to the table, glanced once back at the bar to make sure the bartender's attention was elsewhere, then leant and talked into Webb's ear, eyes fixed on Hugo. Webb listened and nodded.

"Stay here," Webb said to Hugo as the young man moved away.

"Where are you going?"

"Just stay here, will you? I'll be right back. Don't talk to anyone."

Hugo watched Webb follow the youth to a table in the corner where two men sat nursing near-full flasks and scanning the room. They looked up as Webb and the kid arrived and after they spoke for a moment they made a motion for Webb to sit. A glance or two slid Hugo's way and he felt his skin prickle. The barman was busy serving a rowdy group that had just come in, but Hugo still felt horribly exposed.

He was so busy trying not to meet anyone's gaze that he didn't notice someone had sat down beside him until she spoke.

"Hey there. You're Kaleb Hugo, huh?"

Hugo swung round, heart jumping up his throat. A woman a little younger than himself was sitting in the chair Webb had left, a broad smile on her mild face. She was slight but even sitting Hugo could tell she was tall for a Havenite. Her face was unscarred and her hazel eyes clear. Her sandy hair was cut short at the sides but long on top, styled back from her face. If Hugo didn't know any better he would say it was cut to look good, rather than be practical like every other worker he'd seen. Her clothes too, though faded and long-wearing, were not coveralls or utilities trousers but a well-fitted jacket over a shirt that didn't even look mended.

Hugo gathered himself, panic warring with anger as the woman kept smiling. "What did you say?"

"Oh, don't worry, I'm not a rat," her gaze flickered from Hugo towards Webb. Hugo looked in his companion's direction but Webb was sat with his back to him, still in earnest conversation with the men at the table. "Whatever you're doing here I'm sure it's none of my business."

"Who are you?"

"Old friend of Webb's. Been a while since I've seen him, mind. Nice look, by the way," she said, looking him up and down. "I honestly wouldn't have recognised you if you'd come in alone."

"How do you know who I am?"

The woman's pleasant smile widened but then Webb was back. "Jazz," he said, eyes wide as he took in the newcomer.

"Zeek," the young woman said, standing. "Long time no see."

"You heard from Ribble already?"

A small frown creased Jazz's brow. "Ribble? Not for a while."

"What are you doing here then?"

Jazz raised her eyebrows. "Since you're on my colony and in my bar, Ezekiel, I think that's my question."

"Your bar?"

Jazz nodded, folding her arms and glancing around. "A business deal fell through a while ago, you see. I had to find alternative investment."

Webb's jaw tightened again and a flush rode high on his cheeks. Hugo stood as well. "Webb, who is this?"

"Go on. Tell him, Zeek. Who am I?" Jazz wasn't smiling any more.

Webb stood in silence, the flush on his cheeks paling again. "Hugo, this is Jasmine...Jazz...Leon. A credit-broker from Sector 2."

"That's all I am, huh?" Jazz said after a pause, but there was no anger in her face. If anything, Hugo thought she looked disappointed.

Webb just stood there, jaw working, looking more and more uncomfortable.

"Well, luckily, I don't need him to introduce you," Jazz said, turning to Hugo again. "It's a pleasure to finally meet you, Commodore. Shall I call you Kaleb? No disrespect meant but I'm sure

Webb is right to try and keep you from being noticed as far as is possible. He can be forward-thinking. Occasionally."

"Alright, Jazz. Over here."

"What for? Not keeping secrets from your new partner, are you?"

"Enough," Webb growled and took her by the elbow to lead her away. Hugo watched them go, Jazz throwing an almost apologetic look over her shoulder as Hugo's worry was smothered with confusion. The pair stood out of earshot, heads bent together and whispering, Webb seemingly getting more and more agitated whilst Jazz stood with her hands behind her back, shrugging and replying coolly. Hugo frowned, trying to recall if he'd ever seen Webb truly flustered in this way before.

Just as he was wondering whether to intervene, Webb came back to the table and drained his flask. "Come on, Hugo, we're leaving."

"Who is she?"

"We're leaving," he repeated. "*Now.*"

Hugo followed Webb back out the bar, Jazz's cool gaze on them the whole way.

"She says she's an old friend."

Webb laughed bitterly as he clattered down the stairs. "Something like that."

"Is she dangerous?"

Webb stopped at the bottom to lean against the wall and rub his eyes. "Dangerous? No." He let out a breath that shuddered out of him and Hugo frowned.

"She's not going to break my cover?"

Webb shook his head, blinking out over the brightly lit square but not looking like he was seeing anything.

"Are you going to tell me what's going on, or are you just going to tell me it's not my concern?"

"Got it in one," Webb said, straightening up. "Come on. We better get ourselves to the yards."

He strode off across the square and Hugo fell in beside him.

"Did you actually find out anything useful in there?" Hugo said, increasing his pace to match the other man's as they turned right and left the light of the square behind them.

Webb nodded. "The guys I was talking to were Patch Dealers. Sol is ranging into their territory. They're not best pleased by the sound of it, but were more friendly in their bartering after I mentioned I might deal with him as I heard his deals were better."

"Is any of this relevant?"

Webb shrugged. "I don't know. Sol's Catiline. He gets labour for the bloodgrease refineries in payment for his Patches. Whether his interests range any further than his own security I doubt. But it gave me the chance to ask a question or two about what's happening with gangs doing off-colony trading."

"And?"

Webb shrugged again as they turned towards a shuttle stop. "Catiline seem to still be the same petty dealer-ring they've always been: they control a few refineries, their members fence bloodgrease and they have a lot of members working in the yards to control supply. They're not popular."

"No?"

Webb shook his head. "None of the gangs are. They act in their own interests and not that of the colony. But they keep themselves to themselves just enough that they're not worth the Elder's trouble."

"Did they mention any other trading rings? New ones?"

"Not exactly," Webb said as he stopped them by the shuttle rails under a floodlight. Half a dozen workers stood hunched nearby, not looking their way. Webb eyed them anyway and lowered his voice. "I asked, but they wouldn't answer me. Which is weird. People might not rat each other out, or not often, but dealers and fences aren't above smearing rivals for the chance of a sale. But those guys were definitely not wanting to talk about any new boys in town. Which proves one thing at least: there are some, somewhere. Though God knows what it is about them that's got those guys so twitchy."

A shuttle pulled in, rails rattling and engine coughing as it slowed. They boarded and when it pulled away Hugo watched as the light from the rec district faded into the distance. He held the hand rail a little too tight and was so lost in his thoughts that Webb had to repeat his question.

"Hey, Hugo, wake up."

"Huh?"

"What can you actually, like, you know…do?"

"What do you mean?"

Webb rolled his eyes. "We're about to try and get you some yard work. What can you do?"

Hugo rubbed his eyes, trying to think. "We did Engineering and Mechanical Theory at the Academy up to graduate level."

Webb raised an eyebrow. "But have you ever actually, you know, *worked*? With your hands?"

Hugo shook his head. "I was an officer."

"'Was'?"

Hugo looked back out the window and didn't answer.

Webb shook his head. "Whatever. Fine. We'll find something. Look," Webb sighed through his nose. "Just get through this first shift, ok? People need to see you working. We'll see what more we can dig up after that."

More and more people boarded the shuttle. Soon they were crushed against the window. Hugo could smell the sweat and engine grease in the work clothes around him. The light inside the carriage reflected off the glass, making it next to impossible to see out into the dark.

"You know where we're going, right?"

"All the shuttles go to the yards," Webb said, gaze distant.

Hugo hunched deeper into his jacket and stared through his reflection. He blinked and frowned, leaning closer and shading the glass with his hand. The nearest buildings showed up as black silhouettes against a distant, red glow. He could make out the colony ceiling daubed with its rust-coloured stain far above. A break in the buildings revealed a jagged construction hulking against the false horizon. It was framed in a hot red that drowned out the green of the track lights. Even at this distance Hugo could make out chimneys as broad as walkways branching from it and disappearing into the workings of the hull. There were no lit windows and as structures passed in between the shuttle and the factory, he felt more than heard a low thrumming in the air fade and strengthen.

"Bloodgrease refinery," Webb said in a low voice.

"There's no shuttle stop," Hugo said, peering into the murk.

"Refinery workers don't leave."

Hugo was glad when the shuttle rounded a bend and the refinery was blocked from sight. "We'll have to investigate."

"Not if I can help it," Webb said. Hugo was trying to find the words to argue but the shuttle ground to a stop and the surge of traffic disembarking swept them along.

There were a dozen more sets of track, each with a shuttle just arrived disgorging workers. The booming shift-end call rattled out from the shadows making Hugo flinch. Webb followed the crowd as they wove between the parked shuttles and swarmed over the tracks toward the shipyard, and Hugo followed him, spirits sinking.

VI

It wasn't until Webb plucked at Hugo's sleeve to urge him on that he realised he had stopped at the shipyard gate to stare. He'd been to a yard in the Sunside Strip before and remembered how the heat and smell and noise had made him feel like he could reach out and take handfuls of the atmosphere, if he didn't suffocate first. But that was nothing compared to this.

Craning his neck he could make out three towering scaffolds as tall as spacescrapers, supporting sections of unfinished spacecraft caught in webs of wires and metal. Around the scaffolds, the sprawling yard was a heaving mass of production lines, welding pits, storage enclosures and a million and one clusters of machinery and assembly points he couldn't even begin to identify. Workers swarmed over every inch, carrying, shouting, pushing, pulling, wiring, driving and gesticulating. The noise was like a solid thing pressing into his ears. Mopeds, lifters and cranes whizzed or lumbered amongst the melee, skirting around the pits and frames and mounted displays. No one even glanced up from their work as they passed, even when they went by with mere inches to spare, laden and at speed.

But it was the backdrop of open space through the biggest vacuum shield he'd ever seen that made the bottom drop out of Hugo's stomach. The vacuum shields on the larger docking bays at Service Command didn't reach even a fraction of the size. It made his bones feel watery. Stretching into the nothingness were miles of grid-ways, airlock tunnels and construction platforms framing the disjointed carapace of what looked to be the beginnings a long-haul cargo freighter. The flashes of a thousand jetpacks and construction tools rippled over its surface. Still further out, with its hull gleaming in the starlight, a half-constructed Service flagship sat like a monstrous sleeping sea-creature.

"The *Perseverance*…"

"What?" Webb had to shout.

Hugo blinked, the flashes of the construction around him showing red inside his eyelids. "It's the new flagship. The Special Commander commissioned her. I'd seen the specs but…"

Webb followed Hugo's gaze through the shield to where the *Perseverance* was being laboured on at the end of a hundred airlock tunnels and construction webs. "She's big," he said.

Hugo stood gaping until Webb pulled him on again. The booming shift call ended and workers started climbing off machines and laying down tools. Goggles and gloves were shed only to be immediately claimed by someone else waiting to take the spot. There wasn't even a lull in the noise.

"Now, Hugo…is your head fully out of your ass?" Webb said as they ventured further into the yard.

"What?"

"This is the part when the guy on probation would do anything short of cutting body parts off in order to get some work. I'm going to find a foreman. Get ready to act desperate. Think you can do that?"

Hugo clenched his jaw and nodded. Webb eyed him for a second before disappearing into the shambles. Hugo looked around for anything he might be able to do. Leaning to look at the controls of a nearby bolt cutter, he froze. The smell hit him just as he registered the thick, red liquid being syphoned into the engine of the cutter from a barrel held by two oil-grimed workers. They finished re-fuelling the machine and replaced the barrel of bloodgrease on a lifter, before waving at the driver who made an odd sign with his fingers and started up his machine.

Before the driver could leave, a wiry figure with thinning hair had sidled up to him and leant to talk in his ear. Hugo squinted at the lanky man. His eyes looked red and there were sores on his neck. He had a bruise over one eye.

Hugo realised with a start that it was the man he'd seen grappling with the Catiline Patch dealer. He stepped closer, keeping the bolt cutter between him and the lifter. The only person paying the man any attention was the driver. The worker nodded and the thin man took a seat next to the barrels. The driver started the lifter and steered them out of sight. Hugo swallowed. The metallic odour of bloodgrease was heavy in the back of his throat. He stepped around the cutter to follow them but then Webb was back and tugging on his elbow.

"Webb, over there -" Hugo began.

"Kaleb," Webb shouted over the noise, and Hugo turned to see he had returned with a stern-faced woman Hugo recognised, even with goggles pushed up on her forehead, ear protectors around her neck and hands in heavy gloves.

"Kaleb, is it?"

Hugo nodded. "You're Tag's mother."

"This is Foreman Michalski," Webb said. "She's in charge of the metal-beating lines."

"Can you pilot a basic five-six applied control panel?" she said, pulling back a heavy glove to check a chrono on her wrist.

"I can."

"Follow me."

Hugo glanced at Webb who urged him on with a nod. "I'll find you later."

"Webb, wait…"

"Go with the foreman," Webb hissed as she stopped to frown over her shoulder.

Hugo reigned in his temper, glanced once more between the production lines where the bloodgrease lifter had gone and followed Michalski.

"We've got no time to be training," Michalski said as she strode across walkways and between the wide maintenance pits that flashed with welding torches and the workbenches where people sat hunched over wiring, circuit boards and a million and one unidentifiable sensitive ship components. "You've got the next shift to prove you can do what we need. Don't screw up and I'll expect you back again at the beginning of the shift after next, clear?"

"Clear," Hugo said, hurrying to match her pace, one eye out for bloodgrease. Michalski led him towards a brace of holding frames. Workers climbed amongst ladders and gridways to get at every inch of the thirty-foot squares of unfinished bulkhead clamped in place. Some were running hand-held scanners over small sections, some were working on exposed wiring and connections. The air was filled with a deafening clanging from beating machines on risers that were pounding the raw bits of the metal into shape with blunted pistons.

Michalski paused to grab a pair of ear protectors off a workbench and thrust them at him. He put them on and she pointed to the next frame where there was only one beater being operated. Then she turned away and left him.

Hugo blinked around but when people started removing their goggles to peer at him he made his way towards the holding frame she'd indicated. The workers watched as he sat in the cockpit of the monstrous beater, a few waving in an odd way. Hugo nodded in return then frowned at the controls. The foreman was right: it was a five-six control panel, more or less, but so old-fashioned that a lot of the commands were manual instead of touch-screen. The pilot of the other beater gave him a doubtful look. Hugo shifted himself on the hard seat and then powered the engine.

Apparently Haven beaters had no need for guidance control or suspension of any kind. The thing juddered and lurched through its course so roughly that within fifteen minutes Hugo felt like his teeth were being rattled out of his head. The other pilot showed no signs of discomfort however and Hugo let the machine run along its program, adjusting occasionally to keep it from shuddering off-course and watched the piston beat the sheet of bulkhead into the desired curvature. Foreman Michalski came by once on a moped and flashed a lens-flare twice, apparently a signal since all the activity on his frame stopped. Hugo powered down his machine with the rest as Michalski produced a heavy-duty scanner from a compartment under the seat of her moped, ran it along the edge of their bulkhead section, checked the reading then waved and the work resumed.

When the beater was at its apex he had a good view of the surrounding yard but still no sign of the lifter full of bloodgrease, its driver or the thin Patch User. The noise, movement and bone-aching monotony dragged on.

Just as Hugo was feeling like he might either faint or vomit from exhaustion, a thin whistle cut through the pounding in his ears. When it sounded a second time Hugo paused his beater. A worker in the frame was using his free hand to catch his attention. He signed something at him and when Hugo just stared blankly, he pointed below. Hugo leaned out and saw the pilot of the other beater as well as most of the workers on their frame clambering down and gathering on crates and boxes at the base of the frame. Nutripaks and bottles of water were being handed round.

Hugo lowered his beater into its stowed position and clambered out on shaking legs. He dropped onto a crate and someone handed him water and food with a wary glance. Hugo downed the water, not caring that it tasted like metal. The other workers chewed on the paste from the Nutripaks and signed at each other or leant into each others' ears to shout their conversation. The few glances that came his way were guarded.

His shaking had almost subsided when the workers all stood as one as if on cue and went back to work. His fellow beater pilot gave him a smile that wasn't entirely friendly as he passed.

"Try and keep up, proby," he said as he started his engine. "We're on a deadline, you know."

Hugo held his tongue and climbed back into his machine.

The rations kept him alert for a while but soon the ceaseless noise and shuddering had his bones aching and his temper fizzling to a damp despair. The shift crawled on until he was pinching himself to stay focused.

Finally, the fifteen hour shift was done and the booming call, loud even through his ear protectors, rang out across the yard. Hugo climbed out of his beater and leant against it as the changing shift traffic swarmed past. It took almost more strength than he had left in him to raise an arm and pull off his ear protectors.

Webb appeared, scanning the crowds, hair swept back with sweat and goggle marks round his eyes. Hugo called out, voice croaking and Webb spotted him and gestured for him to follow.

"How you doing?" Webb asked once they'd left the beating lines far enough behind to be able to talk.

Hugo just nodded, wiping sweat off his face with his sleeve.

"Say it, I know you're thinking it."

Hugo glanced around at the incoming tide of workers as they left through the gate and approached the shuttle rails. "How do people live this way?"

"Like I said," Webb shrugged. "It's not about living. It's about surviving. But look on the bright side." He gave him a weak smile as they boarded a shuttle. "You have. Survived your first shift, I mean. It's longer than some people on probation have managed."

"I saw," Hugo coughed, throat raw from the fumes and thirst. "I saw...bloodgrease."

Webb gave him a tired look. "Of course there was bloodgrease. All these machines run on it."

Hugo shook his head. "There's something else. There was someone talking to the bloodgrease man. It was the worker from the street fight."

Webb frowned. "Sol? Here?"

Hugo shook his head again. "No, the other one. The one you said was just a User. He was here, talking with the bloodgrease trader."

Webb rubbed his eyes. "He probably works here, Hugo. Don't read too much into it. Now stir yourself. There's a faulty air filter waiting for us at Michalski's that I promised we'd get online before our next shift."

"You're kidding."

"We'll get some food and sleep first."

"And a shower?"

Webb patted him on the shoulder as the shuttle took off along the rails. "I'm sure that can be arranged."

"There's another thing," Hugo said.

"What's that?"

"People were signing at each other, with their hands…"

"Fingerspeech," Webb said around a yawn. "Even workers who haven't gone deaf can't hear each other over the machines. They talk with signs. I'll teach you. But not today."

Hugo swayed where he stood, unable to think of anything but the fatigue. The shuttle ride went by in a daze and soon he was following Webb through the familiar streets to the boarding house. He never thought he'd be so pleased to see the concrete steps of Michalski's building.

Webb trotted up to the door but Hugo paused, looking over to a darkened doorway opposite. A figure was standing in the shadows and he felt eyes turned his way. Hugo peered, trying to focus.

The figure stepped away from the doorway and into the light. He stood for a moment looking at him. It almost felt like a challenge. Or a warning. The man was small and slim, young-looking with striking features, but a cold expression. His sleek black hair was pulled back from his face in a tight tail. He wasn't in coveralls but black zippered jacket and gloves. One hand was in his pocket. The other arm hung stiffly at his side. Hugo was just opening his mouth to call out, when the man turned and seemed to melt away into the darkness.

Webb shouted his name and Hugo rubbed his eyes, swamped with weariness. He told himself to stop reading sinister meaning into every Havenite looking his way and climbed the steps.

Δ

"Ok, Hugo. Go and get some sleep before you face-plant the table."

Hugo blinked and pulled himself upright. He looked a little

more like himself after washing off the sweat and oil but the tiredness etched into his face looked alien. Webb watched his former captain glance around the dining room like he was struggling to remember where he was before his shoulders sagged. Webb swallowing another mouthful of noodles as Tag appeared at his side.

"Did you like it?" he said to Hugo. "I made it."

"*Hey,*" a girl a little older than Tag called from where she was collecting bowls at the next table.

"Well," Tag muttered, frowning at her. "Emm helped. But I did most of it."

"Yes," Hugo muttered when Tag didn't leave or look away. "Thanks."

Tag grinned and added Hugo's bowl to the stack he was carrying and disappeared through the kitchen door after his sister. Hugo's bleary stare followed the boy.

"Hugo?" Webb prodded again. "Go sleep."

"What about you?"

"I haven't finished," Webb said, pushing his food around his bowl.

Hugo gave him a baleful glance but then pushed his stool back and tramped between the tables to the door. A few of the residents clustered over their own meals watched him go. A couple more were watching Webb.

Webb sighed, making himself eat another mouthful. Weariness was like cement in his bones, but uncertainty had knotted his stomach and chased rest from his mind. He stared at the last of the noodles for another minute then pushed the bowl aside and left the dining room and passed through the hall and out the boarding house doors. He almost turned back twice before reaching the nearest shuttle bound for Sector 2 but made himself press on, forcefully unclenching his hands as he went.

He went over and over everything he could, should and wanted to say but when he found himself an hour later on a landing at the top of a large accommodation block, staring at a door with his hand hovering over the buzzer, everything was a tangled mess. He was so meshed in confusion that it was the familiar smell of disinfectant and orange oil and not the quiet footstep behind him that made him realise he was no longer alone.

"What are you doing here?"

Webb turned. Jazz stood with her keycard in her hand, blood on her medic tunic and a dark look on her face.

"Your doorman let me in."

"You know that's not what I was asking."

Webb rubbed the back of his neck. "Can I come in?"

There was a second when he was certain Jazz was going to refuse. But then her hazel eyes softened and she sighed before moving past him to unlock the door. Webb's chest tightened when he stepped into the apartment. Apart from another processor hooked up to the chaotic jumble of her heavy-duty workstation and some newer clutter overlaying the old, it was virtually unchanged from what he remembered. The familiarity of the battered but comfortable furniture, the worn rugs Jazz always kept clean and the broad view of the sector from the floor-to-ceiling windows set in one wall sent a shiver over his skin.

Jazz shrugged herself out of her tunic whilst Webb hovered by the door.

"Busy day at the clinic?" he asked, making himself make eye contact.

"What do you want?" Jazz said as she dropped the tunic in a washer set in the wall, though she sounded more tired than angry.

Webb shoved his hands deep in his pockets and felt his face grow hot. "Look, I'm sorry for being an ass earlier. I wasn't exactly expecting to stumble into you. I overreacted."

"Guilt'll do that to you."

"I'm trying to be reasonable here," Webb said as she strode across the apartment without looking at him. "I just don't know what else to say."

"I guess we're done then," Jazz said, seating herself at the work-station. "Now, if you don't mind, I have work to do."

"Look, I'm sorry I left," Webb blurted. "It wasn't personal. I just…changed my mind."

Jazz began scrolling through reams of data on the large display screens in silence. Webb ground his teeth together, shifting from one foot to another, fighting the urge to leave.

"Taking the ship," Jazz eventually said in a deliberately even tone, "*our* ship, and disappearing right before my meeting with the Apollos Outreach reps…that's not changing your mind, Ezekiel. That's running away." She finally looked over his shoulder. "I'm right, aren't I? You got scared that you might actually be building a decent future for yourself, turned tail and ran. Tell me I'm wrong."

Webb rubbed his neck again, feeling something crumble inside him. "I…"

Jazz sighed and got up. "Sit down, will you, before you strain something. I'll get us some beer."

Webb shouldered off his jacket and wandered over to the couch in a daze, perching on the edge of it and staring out the plexiglass window. The buildings, storage yards and shuttle rails of Sector 2 curved slightly down from this angle, lights blinking here and there in the dimness. The sight jolted something inside him and he couldn't even try and hold on to the pretense he'd gathered around himself like a shield. "I'm sorry," he said, his voice low.

Jazz came over with two flasks. "I know you are," she said, handing one to Webb and sitting next to him. "You're not really an ass, as much as you like to pretend sometimes. It's just…" Jazz paused and took a mouthful of her drink before settling a cool look on Webb. "I thought, really thought, you'd gotten through it. I thought we were *there*. But then you disappear and don't answer the comm or return my messages and the next thing I know it's a year later and I find you in a barhouse trying to score."

"That wasn't what it looked like."

"It doesn't exactly look good, Zeek."

Webb drank some beer, willing the trembling to leave his hands. "Maybe not. But I'm clean now. That much at least is true."

"Well," Jazz said after a pause. "As that former captain of yours was sat nearby, I was hoping that was the case."

Webb lowered his flask, frowning. "What has Hugo to do with anything?"

Jazz shrugged. "Well, whatever else he's done to your head, the good commodore does not strike me as the sort to sit by whilst you try and buy narcotics."

Webb frowned. "'Done to my head'? What are you getting at?"

"Well," she looked into her drink and not at him. "He's somehow convinced you to bring him here, and I don't imagine it was with his charm."

Webb took another mouthful of the beer to try to help frame his reply when he noticed high spots of colour on Jazz's cheeks. Despite everything he felt a smile spread over his face. "Christ Almighty, Jazz. Are you jealous?"

"You certainly think a lot of yourself," Jazz replied, taking a swallow, but the colour heightened.

"You are. You really are." Webb felt laughter rattle out of him. The broker's heavy frown just made him laugh more. "Lord above, Jazz," he said, when he had the breath to do so. "You think Hugo…and me? You think we…?" He wiped moisture from his eyes . "Jesus, you've got your charts upside down, honey."

"You've had relationships with men before."

"I…what?"

"There was that man, Paragon - "

"Jesus and Mary. How do you know about Paragon?"

Jazz gave him a measured look. "He called here, looking for you after you'd gone."

"That wasn't a relationship," Webb said with a shake of his head. "He was assigned to me when I did some systems work in the Storage District. He latched onto me for a few weeks, that's all."

"Well," Jazz continued, chin tilted up. "He certainly seemed keen to find you. And there was a time when you did nothing but track Hugo's activity on the Orbit newsreels. It seemed to be the only thing keeping you going. Is it such an absurd assumption that there was might be something between you?"

"Yes it is. My God, I wish Hugo had heard that. The look on his face, I can just picture it." He took a deep breath steady the last of the laughter whilst Jazz sat by, glaring. Before he knew what he was doing, Webb leant over and kissed her on the cheek. They stayed there, close for a second, Webb smiling whilst Jazz searched his face. Then he chuckled and pulled back. "Jesus, no, Jazz. Kaleb and I," he sighed, looking back out the window. "It's in no way like that."

"What is it then? What did you bring him here for?" Jazz said, still looking carefully neutral.

Webb felt his smile fade. The beer was better than that at the barhouse and he took another long draught. It was cold too. He savoured the taste for a moment before answering. "I don't think I can tell you."

"You don't trust me?"

"You're one of the few people in this miserable Orbit I think I *can* trust. But as that's such a rare thing these days, I wouldn't want to risk getting you involved."

"I think I already am. Or why are you here? It's not just to say sorry for running out, I'm sure, if that piss-poor attempt at an apology was anything to go by."

Webb let out a shuddering breath, closed his eyes for a long moment then heard himself speaking. "I'm helping Hugo hunt down a blade that someone hired to work over one of his officers."

"Why would you do that?" Jazz said after a silence but then paused. Webb opened his eyes to see her looking grave and still. "You're here after Ariel?" Webb felt the hair on the back of his neck rise and nodded. "You're crazy," Jazz said, standing. "Scratch that, you're suicidal. You helped Commodore Kaleb Hugo onto Haven to arrest a resident?"

"Hugo wants to arrest him," Webb said calmly, standing to make sure they were on eye level. "I don't."

"I don't understand," the broker said, her face a drawn with a mixture of concern and frustration. "You lived here for years knowing Ariel had a bolthole here and it never bothered you."

"Oh, it bothered me. But I was trying to forget. Now, it's different."

"Why?"

"Because Hugo's asked for my help."

Jazz let out a noisy sigh and lowered herself onto the edge of the sofa. "Explain this to me then, Zeek. And thoroughly, if you please. If you and Hugo aren't, you know, *involved*…what exactly is it about him that's worth risking all this for?"

Webb drank more beer and sat back down, looking back out the window. "Hugo is one of the very few people who knows… everything. About who I really am…*what* I really am."

"So?"

Webb shrugged. "He knows it all and still treats me as a someone. My own someone. Not a lookalike freak that stole someone else's life."

"Let me get this straight…" Jazz said, straightening her back and clasping her hands around her flask. "He makes you feel *real* enough that you'd risk your life for him, when you wouldn't even risk going into business with me?"

Webb winced. "I'm never going to be able to repay you for everything you've done for me, Jasmine. You saved my life and, believe me, I plan on feeling shit forever for running out on our deal. But, the truth is…if it hadn't been for Hugo, I wouldn't have even been around for you to save in the first place."

Jazz held his gaze. Her eyes ghosted with regret. "Then I guess we both owe him."

Webb snorted and patted her knee. "Just be careful what you

say to him. He's self-importance is healthy enough without any help from you."

"I agree. He doesn't sound like he calls in his favours cheaply."

"No." Webb sighed. "And I wasn't going to help him. I was going to run away and pray I never saw him again."

"What changed your mind?"

Webb finished his drink. "He did."

Silence strung between them and Webb tried to identify the emotions prickling through him.

"I'll help."

"Say again?"

Jazz's smile widened and her eyes had lost some of their bleakness. "I'll help you. You're obviously not getting anywhere on your own or you wouldn't be lingering in doorways mid-shift looking so pathetic."

Webb narrowed his eyes. "You'd help us smoke a Havenite out of sanctuary so a Serviceman can drag him to a trial?"

"No," Jazz said, gathering the flasks. "But I'll help *you* get the justice owed you."

"Why?"

Jazz moved to the kitchen. She took some time rooting through the refrigeration unit before coming back with their flasks refilled. "You have a right to make this man answer for what he did to you. However he pays is up to you."

Webb took the flask and drank. "You're far too good for this place, you know that?"

"I know," Jazz said, smiling again and resuming her seat.

Webb leant back into the threadbare cushions, looking out onto a spread of colony that didn't seem quite so dark any more. "If you mean it, Jazz...if you help...I think we might actually stand a chance of getting somewhere."

"Don't count on it," she said, raising her eyebrows. "Finding a blade's safehouse around here? You might as well try and find a particular grain of dust on the moon."

"Your confidence is inspiring."

Jazz shrugged. "Just wanting you to be realistic. Do you have anything at all to go on?"

"Nothing except Hugo thinks a gang dealing in bloodgrease are the most likely to have hired them for the job. He's stuck on the idea Catiline might be behind it."

"I doubt it. They're too wrapped up in keeping themselves afloat to be gambling on any schemes potent enough to be worth hurting a Service officer for."

"How do you know?"

"I know the guy who brokered for them."

"Catiline have a broker?" Webb blinked. "So they *do* launder credit?"

"Not anymore," Jazz shook her head. "The Elders found out and seized everything. They've spent the last year trying to claw back some control."

"So *that's* why Sol was dealing out of sector."

Jazz turned to him, a brighter smile on her face. ""This is why you were sounding out Patch dealers in that bar? You were looking for leads?"

Webb nodded and gulped down more beer, feeling the alcohol warm him inside. "Told you."

Jazz's smile seemed easier and Webb felt a warm one of his own spread over his face.

"Why did you go to Sector 4 anyway?" Jazz asked after they'd both drunk in silence for a time.

Webb looked away. "August Sinclair let Hugo on board. Thought we owed his sector our labour. And...I didn't think I'd be all that popular around here."

"You really do think a lot of yourself," Jazz said, but she was smiling.

"Well, Ribble agreed with me," Webb said, wincing as he touched the bruise across his jaw.

"Ah yes," Jazz said, smile taking on a satisfied edge. "He's been in touch. He asked if I wanted him to take you down. I said I'd get back to him."

"You did, huh?"

She nodded. "Don't think badly of him. He's a good Enforcer."

"Yes. Capable," Webb muttered, still rubbing his face.

"Do you want me to look at that?" Jazz said, eyeing the bruise.

"Nah. I'll live," Webb said, feeling his muscles relax and his eyes start to droop. The colony blinked outside the window and Webb fought to stay awake. The hum of the workstation, the smell of the citrus disinfectant and the steady blink of the pattern of lights through the plexiglass wrapped him in something that felt like comfort.

"I lied, you know," Jazz murmured after several minutes sat enjoying each other's silence.

"About what?" Webb asked around a yawn.

"That wasn't my bar."

Webb smiled. "It didn't exactly look your style."

"I'm glad you recognise that, at least."

"Why'd you say it was?"

"To try and wind you up."

"It worked," Webb said, draining the rest of his beer to distract himself from the memory of their angry words. "What were you really doing there?"

"One of the Sector 2 Elders has me keeping an eye on that Sol and a few others. Catiline won't be out of the dog house for a while."

Webb chewed his lip. "Have you heard of any new rings of bloodgrease traders setting up shop?"

Jazz's jaw hardened. "That's who you think really hired Ariel?"

"Not just me," Webb said, thinking of Hugo's words about Harvey's hunch. "Have you heard anything?"

"I've heard…well, I'm not sure what I've heard. Rumours. Whispers of something. Nothing solid. Which made me think that's all it was. Gangs don't normally keep quiet."

"If a gang was gathering real power, though," Webb mused. "Power enough to make the Elders concerned…they'd operate below the radar, wouldn't they?"

"If they knew what was good for them."

Silence resumed again. It was Jazz's turn to yawn and rub tired eyes. Webb looked at her properly and wondered if she were thinner than he remembered.

"I am sorry, Jazz."

"I know," she replied after a pause and put a hand on his knee. Her hand was warm. They both looked at it, then at each other. Webb wondered what else he could say but then Jazz said, "Your wrist panel's blinking."

Webb glanced at the time and swore. "I better get back. Hugo'll be having a fit."

"Zeek," Jazz caught his sleeve as he got up. "It's good to see you."

"Let's hope you feel the same way when all this is over."

"Where the hell have you been?"

"I can see you're feeling better," Webb said as he pushed past Hugo into their room.

"Webb…"

"Relax, Hugo," Webb said, dropping onto his cot and pulling off his boots. There were dark circles under his eyes. "I've got us an ally."

"You've what?"

"Jazz Leon is going to help us."

"That woman from the bar?"

"Yeah."

"The one that was angry with you?"

Webb frowned up at him. "Yes, the one that was angry with me. She's going to help."

"Why?"

"We go way back. Trust me. She's just what we need."

"She didn't seem all that fond of you, Webb. Are you sure this is wise?"

Webb's jaw tightened. "Yes. Trust me, will you? Why are you up anyway?"

Hugo felt his face flush. "I woke up. I thought you might be working on that air filter."

"Sorry. I should have sent a message to your panel. I'm beat, Hugo, I'm getting some sleep before the next shift. You should get some more too."

Hugo shook his head. "I'm fine."

Webb raised an eyebrow. "Really?"

Hugo shook his head again. "I can't sleep any more. You rest. I'll go fix the filter."

"Do you know how?"

"I can handle a poxy air filter," Hugo grumbled, pulling on his own boots.

Webb eyed him for a moment longer then shrugged and shouldered his jacket off. "Then knock yourself out. Hey…" Hugo turned at the door. "Don't go doing anything stupid, ok?"

Hugo ground his teeth and shut the door. He went downstairs and let himself into the building's maintenance room. He wrinkled his nose at the smell of rust and stale laundry fluid. Some of the industrial washers against the wall were rocking through their cycles. Hugo was standing looking around for the filter when a resident came in. He was bald, with scarring across his forehead. He startled to find the room not empty and blinked at him.

"You're new, huh? Proby?"

"Yes," Hugo said, eying the short man, trying to figure out if there was threat or just belligerence in his tone.

"Shouldn't you be at your shift?"

"This is my down shift," Hugo said, keeping his voice neutral. "I'm fixing the air filter."

The bald worker snorted. "Don't let me catch you slacking. Don't let anyone catch you slacking, understand?"

"I am not prone to 'slacking'," Hugo said.

The man scowled and stepped into Hugo's personal space. "I'll tell you this for free, proby. Lose the tone before you lose your pretty, straight teeth. Ok?"

Hugo didn't answer, but he didn't step back either. The man eyeballed him a moment longer, the lines in his scarred forehead deepening with his glower. He kept his eyes on Hugo as he grabbed a clean jumper from the neatly folded piles by the washers and left.

Hugo took a deep breath to let his temper cool. He was alarmed to discover the chill that rose in its place. He resolved to try harder to keep his tone in check, then turned his attention back to the room.

The filter was sunk into the wall in the corner. He hunted out a step ladder, climbed up and just managed to wrestle the casing off its rusted catches without cutting himself. His heart sank as he took in the state of the interior. He shifted carefully on the step ladder, the uneven legs wobbling under him as he fished out a lenslight to get a better look. Just like the lifter from the yard, the wiring was old and dusty, the controls and sensors mismatched and the small CPU ancient. His wrist panel had more processing power.

"Hey."

Hugo swore as the ladder wobbled under him. When he'd recovered, he looked down. "You should stop sneaking up on people."

"Sorry," Tag said, though he didn't look it. He stretched up to Hugo, holding out a small wrap of tools. "These are mine. Grandpa's aren't all that great. I keep telling Ma I can fix this thing but she won't let me on the ladder."

"She's probably wise," Hugo muttered, eyeing the bend in the metal halfway down. "Thanks," he added, taking the tools. He bent back into the filter. When he didn't hear the sound of Tag leaving he looked back down. "What?"

"I think I know you. Are you a pilot?"

Hugo blinked. "No. Not anymore."

"What happened?"

"You should be careful who you talk to."

Tag's eyes widened. "I'd love to be a pilot. Imagine being able to go anywhere you want in the whole wide Orbit."

Hugo bent further into the unit, unscrewing a burnt-out wire connection in hopes the boy would get the hint.

"Have you ever been to Earth? I've seen pictures of places covered in plants."

"Covered in…do you mean trees?"

"Uh-huh. And they say the air tastes so clean you don't even notice it."

Hugo leant back and blinked at the boy. There were freckles on his cheeks and his hair was an unruly mop of brown. There was also a small scar on his chin and his hands were bony and raw from work.

"Parts of Earth are…nice," Hugo murmured. "But a lot of it isn't."

Tag's face fell slightly but when he opened his mouth to reply the door swung open.

"Tag," Foreman Michalski entered in her house gown, brow clouding as she took in Hugo. In the interior light he could see she had brown hair like her son. She, too, had scars, one over her eye and an old burn on her neck. Her shoulders and arms were strong-looking under the thin gown but there were more lines on her face that Hugo suspected her age warranted. "How many times have I told you not to pester the guests?"

"But Ma -"

"Go back to the apartment. You should be in bed. Breakfast shift's in four hours."

Tag muttered something and trudged out. Michalski stayed, eyes hard. "I'd appreciate it if you wouldn't talk to my son."

Hugo frowned. "He's the one talking to me."

"I understand that," she said. "But I would like it if you didn't encourage him. Service idealism has no place here."

"Believe me, I'm not someone that's likely to impart it."

"That's not what I've heard, if you are who I think you are."

"I might be," Hugo said, keeping his tone cool to disguise the flush of worry he felt wash through his stomach. "But either way you heard wrong."

She stood there a moment longer. Hugo held her gaze, trying to figure out if she was offended or too drained to care. She broke the eye contact, stepping back towards the door.

"Thank you. There's new burn connectors out in the shed if you need them."

"Foreman," Hugo called.

She paused at the door. "Off-shift you can call me Lola," she said.

"Lola," Hugo said and came down the ladder. He clutched his lenslight in his hand whilst she stood weighing him up. "Can you tell me about bloodgrease?" he said, before he could stop himself.

She frowned. "Tell you what, exactly?"

Hugo glanced at the closed maintenance room door, feeling his heart rate creep up. "Can you tell me how you find the traders?"

Her frown deepened. "Why?"

Hugo made himself stand still and hold her gaze. "I could help them. On the outside."

She narrowed her eyes at him. "You could?"

"I know all about the new security measures the Service is using. And how to get round them."

She folded her arms. "Why in the name of hell would you want to help Haven off-colony traders?"

"They bring credit in, don't they? For the colony?"

"Yeah. Some of them."

Hugo managed a shrug. "This is my colony now. I want to help."

Lola was silent. Hugo felt his heart hammer against his ribs and willed his face to stay blank. "Have you asked your Sponsor about this plan?"

"He's being cagey."

"He's right to be."

"Look," Hugo said, fighting back frustration and willing his voice to be calm. "This is one of the few things I have. I want to be useful."

Lola weighed him up a moment more then sighed. "Bryce. There's a guy called Bryce. He runs a workshop in the grounds of Sector 4's refinery. All bloodgrease deals from there go through him. You can try your luck, if you're serious."

"What about at the refinery itself?"

Lola raised an eyebrow. "You really need to talk to your Sponsor more. No one goes in or out of a refinery. There's no one to deal with except the reps like Bryce. I'm done. That's all you're getting from me."

Hugo nodded. "Thank you."

"Don't thank me," she said, turning away. "Getting involved with the refinery dealings isn't something I'd thank anyone for."

He stood still after Lola had left, turning Tag's tools over in his hands. He shook his head and climbed back up the ladder and leaned into the filter. He put the tools aside and pulled out his computer panel, booted up Harvey's and the Service's reports on the investigation and searched for any mention of anyone called Bryce.

When nothing came up and the Analyst's case images of Harvey's injuries set his vision blurring, he put the panel away again and attacked the rusty connections until all the dead components were stripped away.

It was Webb's second shout of his name that pulled him out of his daze. He pulled his head out of the filter to find Webb stood propping open the door.

"How's it going?"

"I've got us a lead."

Webb frowned. "You what?"

Hugo came down the ladder, wiping sweat from his brow and stepped close to Webb. "I have a starting point."

"Hugo, I was talking about the filter. What the hell are you talking about?"

"How long until next shift?"

"We need to get on a shuttle within the hour. Tell me what you're on about first."

Hugo pulled Webb into the room and shut the door. "We need a shuttle stop near the refinery. I've found a name of a fence that deals for the bloodgrease refinery."

"Hugo…what have you done?"

"I talked to the foreman. She told me we need to talk to someone called Bryce."

"You did what?" Webb went pale. "Hugo, what did I say? What did I *specifically say* about you and doing stupid things?"

"Quiet," Hugo hissed as there was the sound of footsteps in the hall. They quietened down again and Hugo went to the door. "Come on, let's go."

"First, just, no," Webb said, grabbing Hugo's sleeve. "And second, have you lost your mind?"

"It's fine," Hugo growled, pocketing the tools. "I had a story. She doesn't suspect - "

"Not right now she doesn't. But what if she speaks to someone, who's spoken to someone else, who's spoken to someone more? You don't understand the way it works round here. People watch out for each other but keep a closer watch on everyone else."

"I'm not sitting by any longer without doing something."

"Yes you are," Webb hissed "Besides, I know that Bryce guy. He is not someone we want to be messing with. And either way, we're due on shift."

"If you think I'm slaving on a beating line for the next fifteen hours when I could be making headway - "

"Listen to me," Webb growled, leaning in close to his face. "You can't not show up for your second ever shift. Michalski will know and that will be us done here. Done. Deported. Or worse."

Hugo narrowed his eyes at the younger man but saw nothing but earnest concern in his face. The bald worker's words from earlier came back to him and he ran his hands through his hair. "Fine," he said through clenched teeth. "We'll go to the yard again. But after that, we go to this refinery workshop and see what we can find."

Webb rubbed his mouth. "Maybe."

"Maybe? Webb, we have nothing else to start on."

"Yes, we do. Jazz is meeting us here next down-shift. We're going to go through everything with her. And she, unlike you, soldier-boy, actually knows how to find shit out without landing in it. So wait, please. Listen to what Jazz says. Then, if we're still stuck, I promise, we'll check it out. Ok?"

Hugo scowled. "Fine."

Webb's shoulders tensed. "I'm not doing this to be an ass, Hugo. I'm doing it because this is the way it works. From the second we land to the second we leave, no one, and I mean no one, can know what we're really doing here."

"Except this Jasmine?"

Webb's face cleared. "We can trust her. But that's about it. Believe me. Now, come on, we better grab some breakfast before it all goes."

VII

If anything the second shift was even more soul draining than the first. Hugo got the same cranky beater and the same cracked ear protectors. It was the same pilot in the next machine. The only thing that was different was the section of bulkhead in the holding frame. Lola Michalski stopped by on her moped for a quality check and they stopped for a Nutripak and some water at the seven hour mark. And then it was back to the rattling, pounding, heat and noise.

He was wobbly again when he climbed off his beater as the shift-end call boomed out what felt like an eternity later. He met Webb near the shuttle rails, looking equally grimy and exhausted. They didn't speak as they joined the flow of workers heading back to the shuttle.

Hugo was trying to figure out how to broach the subject of Bryce again, when he felt eyes on him and paused. Someone grumbled as he blocked the way and people had to surge around him.

"Hugo?" Webb said, looking in the direction Hugo was staring. "What is it?"

Hugo stepped out of the flow of workers, but the figure he'd thought he'd seen by the gate, standing stiff, pale face with keen eyes turned his way, was gone.

"What are you looking at?"

Hugo shook his aching head and rubbed his eyes. "There was a man...watching us...there." He pointed toward the gatepost.

Webb followed his gesture. "There's no one there. You're seeing things."

Hugo didn't reply. He hoped Webb was right, but he still checked every face nearby as they all crowded onto the shuttle. No piercing eyes and neat, black hair among any of them.

He put the image out of his head and instead peered out the

shuttle windows to try to get a better look at the refinery as they passed, but it still looked like no more than a misshapen black cutout against a smudge of red light. He wiped his misted breath from the window and stared until it was out of sight, not liking the feeling that it looked as impenetrable as this mission was beginning to feel.

Webb checked his wrist panel as they stepped off at the shuttle stop. "Jazz'll be at the boarding house in an hour. I say we get some food -"

"Webb? Hey, Webb!"

They turned to see the broad-shouldered figure of Ribble in his dark coveralls bearing down on them through the departing shuttle traffic. This time he wore a belt with a large nightstick hanging from it and a knife holster strapped on his arm.

"Shit, Ribble, wait," Webb said, raising his hands. "Just wait a second, big guy."

"Relax, Webb," Ribble grunted as he drew level. "I've spoken to Jazz. You're off the hook. For now."

"Hallelujah," Webb tried for a grin but it looked haggard with the shift's dirt and weariness heavy on his face and the cut and bruise from Ribble's punch clear through it.

Ribble glowered. "That's not to say I'm happy, mind. But, either way…who's this then?"

Hugo clamped his mouth shut as Webb shifted slightly in front of him to block him from view. "My proby. What's going on?"

"I need you to take a look at something," Ribble said, dismissing Hugo and turning his attention to Webb. "We've had a death in one of my buildings. There's something weird going on. I need you to take a look."

"Why me?"

"Just come, will you? Need to get you in before Reclaim come for him."

"Webb, what is this?" Hugo asked.

Webb shook his head. "Damned if I know. Look, Ribble, it

makes me fuzzy inside that we're pals again, really. But I just got off shift -"

"Elders' orders, Webb," Ribble said, face darkening.

Webb ran a hand through his hair and sighed. "Anything for the Elders, I guess. Hugo, head back to the boarding house."

"Webb - " Hugo started to protest.

"I'm not arguing with you," Webb started but Hugo grabbed him by the elbow and pulled him to the side.

"We can't have any more delays," Hugo said in a low voice. "You said we'd meet Jazz and I'll meet her. But we're behind schedule as it is."

"I have to obey the Elders," Webb growled. "If we're to keep up appearances - "

"Damn keeping up appearances, already. What's this place done to you that you're so afraid of it?"

Hugo regretted the words the second they left his mouth. But the clone quickly recovered, smoothing away the tight look and hissed in his ear, "Do as I say, goddammit. I'll be quick as I can."

"What about Jazz?"

"Just tell her I'll be back soon. Go. Now."

Ribble was watching them. Webb gestured for the Enforcer to lead the way and followed him to a moped parked nearby. He climbed on behind the big man, throwing Hugo a warning look as he did so and then Ribble started the engine and drove them away. Hugo glanced around as the shift workers dissipated. None of them seemed to have noticed the exchange.

Hugo bristled as he made his way home to Michalski's, but remembered to keep his head down. His feet found the way on their own, skin crawling the whole way. It was difficult to know if he felt more exposed when the streets were busy or when they were dead. The doorway opposite the entrance to the boarding house was empty. He was too tired to decide if that meant anything so went to the shower room to wash some of the grime from his hands and face.

In the dining room a couple of the other residents nodded to him as he took the same stool against the wall as yesterday. The bald worker from the maintenance room was sitting with them but just gave him a long stare.

Tag brought him a tray of something unidentifiable in a greyish sauce. The synthetic protein was tasteless but hot and helped his belly feel less like a hard knot inside him. He finished quickly then plodded back to the room, trying to push his brain into planning his next move, but it refused to co-operate.

He didn't know he'd fallen asleep until a knock on the door woke him. He started up, cursing a crick in his neck. The knock came again, loud enough to bring him back to himself but quiet enough that it wouldn't be heard down the stairs. Hugo retrieved the Fourshot from his pack. He kept it behind his back as he opened the door a crack.

"Kaleb," the young woman greeted him with a warm smile. "Good, I got the right place." Hugo stood examining her a moment longer and her sandy brows drew together, though her smile never faltered. "Ezekiel here?"

"No."

She raised her eyebrows. "Oh. Well. He asked me to come by."

Hugo narrowed his eyes. "Who exactly are you?"

Jazz sighed through her nose. "I'm a friend, Commodore. I promise. Now, can I come in? It might be best if no one sees me."

Hugo hesitated but Jazz just stood there, head on one side, holding his questioning gaze calmly with her cool, hazel eyes. Hugo sighed, hid his gun in his waistband and pulled the door open. Jazz nodded and stepped inside, looking around the tiny room with the faintest trace of a frown on her face.

"You should have come and stayed with me."

"It didn't seem like Webb was hoping to see you," Hugo ventured, watching the broker closely as she looked around the room.

"Yeah, it seems he does that a lot."

"Does what?"

"Hides," Jazz said. She shrugged off her jacket and dropped it on the bed before leaning on the wall and examining the cracked ceiling tiles.

"You don't look like most of the other people I've seen here," Hugo said, pulling his t-shirt over the gun to better conceal it, but keeping his hand near it.

"I'll take that as a compliment."

"Why is that?"

"I work with computers. It means I do my shifts in my own apartment and I still have all my fingers."

Hugo searched her face for a while longer, feeling a question start to gather in his mind that he didn't want to ask. She put her head on one side again, questioning, perhaps seeing the struggle in his face. "Look, Miss Leon - "

"Call me Jazz. Leon was the ship I was born on. I don't own that name any more."

"Fine. Jazz…" He looked at the floor, rubbing his mouth a second. "I need to know something," he eventually said, looking up and watching her face. "About Webb…" She continued to regard him coolly. He continued, keeping his voice void of emotion. "I lost track of Webb after the Uprising. I know enough to know he's been on Haven, but he won't talk about what happened."

"Does he need to?"

"Whatever he's not telling me seems to be affecting him. I'm worried it might be impacting his judgement."

"I doubt that."

"You do?"

Jazz nodded. "Webb knows what he's doing. If his past is influencing your investigation it's because it needs to. He understands this colony, better than most other Outsiders."

"How much has he told you?"

"About what?" she asked, mildly, still watching his face.

"About why we're here?"

"Oh, I doubt he's told me everything. But he's told me you're after that blade, Ariel."

Hugo blinked. "You know about Ariel?"

"I know what he did to Webb. From the scars."

Hugo considered this a moment. "How well do you know Webb, exactly?"

Jazz hesitated before sighing and dropping her gaze to the floor. "He lived with me. Last time he was here. I took him in after…"

"After what?"

She paused a moment before continuing. "Just over two years ago I found him in an alley behind a barhouse in Sector 2, OD'ing on Patches."

Hugo straightened. It took him a second to find his voice. "He…what?"

The broker's face remained steady. Her voice was clinical but he could see pain in her eyes. "He'd been hooked for months before I found him. He was five minutes away from total respiratory arrest."

"Why…how did it happen?"

She shrugged one shoulder and finally let her gaze slide from his. "I don't know all the reasons. From what I've gathered, he drifted from one place to another after he left the Service, but couldn't find anywhere to…belong. It took him a long way down a dangerous road and he nearly didn't come back."

Hugo stood in silence, feeling a knot form in his gut. "What happened then?"

Jazz shrugged. "I managed to stabilise him…which he did not thank me for at the time, believe me. I took him home and helped him get through probation so he could stay."

"You're a medic?"

She nodded. "I volunteer at the Sector 2 clinic, but he wouldn't have made it there."

Hugo stood in silence again. Jazz stood by calmly and let him. "What was that argument at the bar then? If you saved his life?"

Jazz chewed her lip, eyes far away. "We didn't exactly part on the best terms. And, as I said, he wasn't exactly grateful to be saved at the time."

"But he's alive because of it."

Jazz smiled. It was sad. "He was a wreck, Hugo. He's kicked the Patches and seems to have found some sort of direction. But I don't know if he'll ever get his head round what he is."

Hugo froze. "You know?"

Jazz folded her arms and looked at the floor. "That he's a clone? Yes, I know. I think I'm the only one on Haven who does. Most people that knew the original Webb think he's the same person."

"It was that? It was knowing what he is…it nearly destroyed him?"

"The mother of all identity crises," Jazz said, looking back up with another sad smile. "I wouldn't be telling you any of this, except it's important you understand what exactly you've asked of him, bringing him back to the colony where he tried to lose himself…and nearly succeeded."

"He's getting paid," he muttered, swallowing the sickly feeling of guilt.

"That's not why he's doing it."

Hugo searched the broker's face for a moment, looking for something to say whilst trying to clear the emotion that fogged his brain.

"So," Jazz broke the silence and smiled again. "Why don't you tell me what you have so far and I'll see if you can actually be helped?"

Hugo shifted. "How exactly can you help us?"

"Are you always this resistant?"

Hugo ground his teeth and didn't answer.

Jazz shrugged and examined her fingernails. "I don't know that I can do anything. I live here. I hear things. I might be able to put some pieces together. But like I said to Webb: tracking down a blade's safehouse on his own turf?" She shook her head. "I don't like your chances."

Hugo opened his mouth for a frustrated retort when his wrist panel bleeped.

"Webb?" he said into the communicator. "Where the hell are you?"

"Is Jazz there?" came Webb's tinny voice over the panel speakers.

"She's here. What's going on?"

"Just both of you stay right there, ok? I'm on my way back."

The connection died.

"Where is he anyway?" Jazz frowned.

"Your friend Ribble took him away to look at something."

"Ribble? The Enforcer?"

"I guess so. Haven has Enforcers?"

"Of a sort."

"What sort?"

"The sort not to be messed with."

Hugo pushed buttons on his wrist panel. "He sounded like he was on the shuttle."

"I guess we sit tight then. I don't suppose there's any coffee?"

Hugo stomach clenched. "I've not seen any since I arrived."

Jazz sighed and sat herself on the edge of a cot. "Seriously. Next time, we meet at mine."

"You have coffee?"

Jazz's white smile flashed again. "I think I even have some blask tucked away. Heard you like that. It's amazing what you can get round here if you know who to talk to. So, Hugo," Jazz said, pulling a computer panel out of her pocket. "I'm curious. How does Haven hold up to the rumours?"

Hugo paced to the window. "The rumours don't even scratch the surface."

"Well," she said, booting up her panel. "Glad to know we don't disappoint."

Hugo watched what he could of the darkened street out the window as Jazz frowned over figures on her panel. Tiredness warred with tension and Hugo began shifting about the room, Jazz's eyes occasionally following him until they heard footsteps on the stairs. Hugo's hand went for his gun and Jazz straightened on the cot. Webb came in through the door, panting and flushed.

"What is it?" Hugo asked.

Webb shut the door and wiped sweat off his brow with his sleeve. "A Black Cross killing."

Hugo's spine stiffened. "You're sure?"

Webb nodded,

"My God," Jazz said. "Where?"

"Sector 2," Webb said, collapsing on the opposite bunk and pushing hair out of his eyes. "A residential block near your clinic. Messy."

"Are you ok?"

Webb nodded again, smiling at the broker. "Yeah. I'll not eat for a while, but yeah."

"What did they need you for?" Hugo said.

"Black Cross is a Lunar 1 thing and, as far as they know, I'm from there." Webb shook his head. "I don't know, I guess they thought I could tell why it was by done just be looking at it."

"Could you?"

Webb rubbed his eyes. "Of course not. Ribble's just desperate. No one's come forward to claim the body so they have no idea who he is, let alone why it happened or if it'll happen again."

"No one at all?" Jazz said, sitting up.

Webb shook his head. "The poor bastard's not even had anyone claim association."

"What exactly am I missing here?" Hugo put in.

"Someone dies," Webb said, "kin and associates claim the body and assets. Nothing goes to waste."

"There's normally too many people claiming what there is, body and all," Jazz said. "I've never known anyone to go unclaimed. What did you say to them?"

"I just told them the guy's pissed someone off bad, real bad, and that's all I could tell. But, Hugo..." Webb paused with his head in his hands, staring into nothing. "It was the guy Sol was fighting with."

"The thin man?" Hugo said, pulse quickening.

"What thin man?" Jazz asked.

"First night we were here, Sol was fighting with someone right out there," Webb said pointing out the window. "I figured he was just a Patch User."

"He's not, then?" Hugo asked.

Webb shrugged. "He's a User alright: skin sores and red eyes, the works. But he was also someone with no kin, no associates, nothing in his apartment linking him to anyone or any shipyard. I don't know, it was like he was..."

"A ghost?" Jazz asked quietly, something flickering in her eyes.

Hugo paced. "He's involved with bloodgrease, I'm sure of it. I saw him at the yard with a trader delivering it. Has anyone asked this Patch dealer, Sol, about who he was?"

"Ribble got Sol on the comm whilst I was there. He's saying the guy was just a customer, that's all he knew. I don't know, Hugo," Webb said. "It might be nothing. But this is someone with apparently no ties to anyone but has managed to bring a Black Cross down on his head?"

"This is the break we've been waiting for," Hugo said. "We need to get into that apartment."

"They won't let you in," Jazz said.

"Why not?"

Jazz gestured towards his neck. "Probation. They know you won't be kin."

"So we break in," Hugo said.

Webb shook his head. "There's nothing in the apartment worth breaking in for."

"They won't have looked to see if he has any credit records," Jazz put in after a defeated pause. "I'd wager on it."

"Can you do that?" Hugo asked.

Jazz smiled. "It's what I do. But we need to do it now. His assets will go to Reclaim if he goes another shift unclaimed. And someone who knows what he was hiding could show up any minute to make sure it stays hidden."

Δ

Webb and Jazz sat with their heads bent together on the deserted shuttle, muttering over something on Jazz's panel. Hugo sat on the seat facing them, trying not to glance around at the few Havenites that drifted on and off at the stops. He watched a different part of Haven roll by the window, blinking to keep his eyes open: more concrete, more metal. He glimpsed another shipyard between some of the buildings, again with a star-specked backdrop of nothing behind another huge vacuum shield which framed the bustling activity.

"If this guy is a member of a new, secret gang," Hugo mumbled. "What then?"

"Let's not get ahead of ourselves," Webb said, still with eyes fixed on Jazz's panel. "We don't even know what we're going to find yet."

"What are you likely to find on there?" Hugo muttered.

Webb frowned but Jazz just said smoothly: "I've found another reason why the Elders will be concerned."

"And what's that?"

She glanced around to make sure no one was looking their way then handed over her panel. It had a building schematic on the display and a list of the specifications down the side. "That's the building they found him in, in an apartment in the basement after an anonymous tip. You know where a worker lives, you can find out who lets it to him. From there, you can get where he works, sometimes who he deals with."

"And?"

"There's nothing," Jazz said, reaching forward and flicking the display through several pages that showed different floors of the building. "The building is mostly allotted to workers from the recycling levels. But his basement apartment was registered vacant."

"The guy really is a ghost," Webb said, then frowned as Jazz's face tightened. "What is it?"

"It's that word...ghost," she murmured.

"What about it?" Hugo said, handing her the panel back.

Jazz leaned forward, lowering her voice. "You asked about rumours of new gangs. I'm sure I've heard the word *Ghosts*."

Webb raised his eyebrows. "Do you remember what you heard, exactly?"

"No..." Jazz said. "But this whole situation is very strange. This man, he's...no one. It's like he never existed."

"Someone knew who he was," Hugo pointed out.

"Yes," Webb said, rubbing the back of his neck. "Or knew what he did."

"We're here," Jazz said, tucking the panel away.

Sector 2 was, if anything, even darker than Sector 4. The ceiling curved at a much greater angle so that none of the green glow from the track lights filtered down to street level. Floodlights illuminated the main avenues but the alleys and between-ways were so gloomy Hugo had to use his lenslight.

Eventually Webb stopped at a corner, waving at them to be quiet and for Hugo to shut off his light. They peered around the corner to another dimly-lit alley that looked the same as all the others.

Webb ducked back. "There's an Enforcer at the entrance," he whispered. "They can't know we're here. Follow me. Quietly."

Webb stepped out from their hiding place, checking the alley for a long moment before waving for them to follow. Hugo stuck close, staying in the shadows. He could just make out Webb's figure, hugging the wall below a garbage disposal that took up most of the alley mouth. Hugo stopped still when an Enforcer wandered into view, but he only gave the alley a glance before turning and pacing out of sight.

Hugo hurried on into the dark and felt someone grab his jacket. "Hush," Webb hissed in his ear. "Where's Jazz?"

"I'm here," Jazz whispered as she joined them. "You two have done this before, haven't you?"

Webb shushed them. Hugo held his breath. The silence stretched on.

"Why have we stopped?" Hugo murmured.

"We're being followed," Webb breathed in his ear. Hugo scoured the alley. All was quiet in the dark.

"Are you sure?"

"Jazz," Webb mumbled. "Watch the Enforcer."

"There," Hugo muttered, pointing towards a stack of crates. "I heard something."

"Jazz, go," Webb whispered and Jazz slipped past them. "Hugo, you go left. And stay quiet."

Webb began edging towards the crates. Hugo did the same from his side, pulling his gun out his waistband as he went, keeping it close to his body. There was a clink of something being knocked over and a shadow darted out from the shelter.

Hugo cursed and Webb gave chase. Hugo hurried after them and skidded around the corner to the sound of a scuffle and muffled cry. Webb was wrestling the smaller person against the wall. The light spilling from the alley mouth fell across her face as she struggled.

"Let her go," Hugo hissed, tucking the gun back out of sight before Webb saw. "Webb, let her go. Now."

Webb frowned, glancing at the stranger's scowling face, black eyes burning and close-cropped dark hair mussed, then released his grip on her jacket.

"Dana," Hugo spat, fury riding through him like fire. "What the hell are you doing here?"

"There's been a Black Cross killing, you moron," she scowled, straightening her jacket. "I'm investigating."

"Investigating what?"

"The same thing you are," she hissed. "Except I actually intend to get somewhere."

"Have you lost your mind?"

"Hey, hey," Webb hissed again, waving his hands and glancing back down towards the street. "Keep it down. What the hell? You know this girl?"

She bristled, turning her glare on Webb. "This is him, is it? This is Webb?"

"We're heading back to the shuttle." Anger made Hugo's words grind out. "Now."

Dana started hissing protests and Webb gestured for silence again.

"Tell me what the hell is going on here," he whispered fiercely. "Quietly, for the love of Christ."

"What's happening?" Jazz had come up behind them and took in the scene with a frown. "Who's this?"

Dana folded her arms and levelled her dark glare at them. "Midshipman Dana Hugo. I'm here ensuring justice is done for Marilyn Harvey."

Webb blinked, rubbing his eyes. "What…?"

"My sister," Hugo said, fists clenched.

"Your *sister*?" Webb gaped.

"If you can be here, so can I," the dark-eyed girl returned, burning gaze locked on Hugo.

"Actually," Jazz murmured, reaching out and turning down Dana's collar to reveal smooth, unblemished skin. "You can't."

Dana shrugged her collar out of Jazz's grasp with a glare.

"How did you even get on board?" Hugo growled. "Actually, I don't care. Webb, call dock control and tell them we're launching. We're leaving the minute we get her on board *Nod*."

"Hugo, this guy's assets could be seized any minute."

"I don't care. Dana is leaving. Now."

"I am not," she retorted. "If you can ditch all responsibility to get even, Kale, so can I. Except I might actually get something done since I've not got my head up my own ass."

"Stop smiling," Hugo growled at Webb. "And I didn't *ditch* anything."

"You left Marilyn to wake up alone in a hospital and try to piece together who she is."

"She's not alone. Rami - "

"Rami's her *doctor*," Dana snarled, leaning in closer. "She needs *you*."

"Christ in Heaven," Webb said, voice strained. "Look, this family reunion is touching and all, but we're under a little pressure here. She's coming with us, Hugo. Stow it," Webb held his hand up and Hugo clamped his mouth shut again. "Whatever shit you want to sort out you can do later. Unless you want to give this whole thing up?"

"No," Hugo and Dana said at the same time, before scowling at each other.

"I came to nail that blade to the wall," Dana said. "And I'm not leaving until I do."

"Zeek," Jazz murmured as she peered down the alley. Webb followed her gaze to where the Enforcer was standing, craning his neck and looking towards the noise. Webb swore under his breath.

"This way," he breathed, bending double and shuffling back into the deepest shadows. "Dana, you too."

Hugo held his tongue as his sister threw him a triumphant look and crawled after Webb. He cursed under his breath and joined them. They all crouched under a shuttered window and breathed in the smell of rubbish from the disposal for several minutes until the Enforcer moved on. Webb stood and checked they were clear before climbing on a crate and began fiddling with the catch on the shutter.

"Here," Hugo whispered, pulling Tag's tools from his pocket.

Webb raised an eyebrow but said nothing and used a screw-pick to work the catch open. He raised the metal shutter painfully slowly, pausing every time there was a creak. The patrolling Enforcer didn't re-emerge. When the shutter was up, Webb climbed through. Jazz gestured for Hugo to go ahead of her, but he instead took a moment to glower at his sister. She turned her back on them both and hauled herself through.

"Does the Special Commander know you're here, Midshipman?" Hugo said as he caught up with Dana in the corridor.

"Why should she?"

"You two," Webb said over his shoulder. "Quiet."

Hugo bit his tongue as they crept further down the corridor.

"This is it," Webb said when they reached a door with no number. He knelt to start picking the lock. Hugo kept his breath steady, listening for any movement but all was quiet around them.

"Webb?" he whispered as the seconds ticked by. "What's the hold up?"

"Keep your shirt on," Webb said, blowing into the keyhole and trying again. "It's been a while."

Jazz shook her head when the lock clicked and the door opened onto a set of stairs going down into shadow. "This is the sort of thing the Service taught you?"

"Hardly," Webb said, putting his lock pick back in his belt. "Webb learnt this on Lunar 1. Come on."

Jazz shook her head again and followed Webb through the door. Jazz led the way with a lenslight. There was another door at the bottom, also locked and again Webb picked it open.

The apartment smelt of damp and something sharp…chemical. It was unnervingly quiet. Jazz found the light switch and they all stood blinking around a small room with a bare concrete floor, one chair at a workstation in the corner, a side with a sink and a microwave and nothing else.

"No place like home," Webb muttered. "Jazz, think you can get in?" he said, nodding towards the workstation. "Looks like there's nothing else to search."

"I'll see what I can find," Jazz said, booting up the workstation and peering at the blinking screen.

"Where is he?" Dana said. "The victim?"

"In the bedroom," Webb said, nodding towards an open door.

"Stay here," Hugo said, moving past her.

"You don't get to order me around."

Hugo turned on his sister, face burning. "Yes I do. Of all the stupid things you've done, Dana, this is the most dangerous and the most stupid."

"Did you just call me stupid?" Dana said, taking a step closer, black eyes flashing.

"Guys," Webb growled. "Seriously?"

"And you can keep out of this too," Dana said, stabbing a finger at Webb. "You have no idea -"

"He knows enough to be my Sponsor," Hugo said. "He knows enough to have gotten us this far. I don't know how you've got here, but you have no idea what you're doing."

"You are so hypocritical you don't even know it."

"This is not a *game*," Hugo seethed.

"Game?" she returned. "Let's talk about games. Sure, I'm dodging the probation system, but I'm doing it to bring that blade to justice for *Marilyn*. *You* are screwing the system, and your supposed friend," she pointed at Webb again, "for your pride and nothing else."

"Children," Webb said, raising his hands. "This is not the damn time."

"Have you even told him?" Dana said, hands on hips. "This man who you've had risk everything? Have you told him *why* you're doing all this? Why you feel so guilty?"

Hugo ground his teeth. "He knows."

"Does he?"

"Hugo," Webb said with a frown. "What's she talking about?"

They all stared at each other, Hugo feeling his skin burn but unable to untangle his tongue.

"You," Dana said to Jazz who was watching over her shoulder. "Keep working." Jazz raised an eyebrow and turned back to the workstation whilst Dana faced the clone. "So, tell me, Webb. Did your captain tell you who gave Harvey this assignment? Who it was that *ordered* her to investigate bloodgrease traders?"

Webb frowned.

"She wanted to," Hugo said, voice cracking.

"She should have been given a team," Dana said. "She should have had Analyst input, armed backup, a partner, anything. But no. She was all on her own. So they came for her, knowing she was the only one who knew anything. That's why he got suspended. Gross Misconduct."

"I'm not justifying myself to you, Dana," Hugo finally loosened his throat. "I'm here, making this right. You've gone AWOL from the Academy and snuck aboard the most dangerous colony in the Orbit, without a plan and with no field experience. You do not get to talk to me like I'm the irresponsible one."

"The worst part is you can't even see," Dana said. "I bet he told you he was doing this for you, right? To give you a chance to get your own back?" Dana said to Webb who was looking pale. "Sorry, friend. He's appeasing a guilty conscience and a bruised ego. That's all that's happening here."

"Enough," Hugo said. "Webb -" he said as Webb turned away towards the bedroom. "Webb, don't listen to her," he said, hurrying after him "She's always twisting the truth."

"Must be a family trait," Webb muttered, stepping through to the bedroom and turning on the light.

Hugo stopped on the threshold. The thin man's body was on the bed, tangled in the sheets with limbs splayed. His skin was a sickly grey except where it was purpled with bruises from the struggle. His red-rimmed eyes were wide open and staring. His mouth hung at a broken angle. What was left of his throat was a tattered and bloody mess. The spray of blood went up one wall and spattered the ceiling over the bed. His face, nightshirt and bed clothes were saturated. The smell of old blood was cloying and cold. Daubed on the wall in thick black paint was a large cross.

"It looks…different," Hugo managed.

"The cross?" Webb tore his eyes from the body to examine the mark. "It wasn't a spray-and-run, like we did. They took their time. But whether it was before or after they cut him -"

"Before," Dana said as she joined them. She was a little pale as she took in the scene but kept her voice steady and her expression blank. "There's blood on top of the paint, there." She pointed.

"How did they paint the cross without waking him?" Hugo said.

Webb swallowed. "Very carefully."

"Or he was drugged," Dana murmured, leaning over the body and looking into the eyes.

"Hey," Jazz called from the next room, stopping Hugo from dragging Dana away from the dead man. "I think I've found something."

"What…?" Webb started to ask when they all stopped still. There were voices in the stairwell.

"Quick.," Hugo whispered, pointing to another door off the bedroom.

Jazz switched off the workstation as Hugo shut off the lights and Dana and Webb hurried through the door. Hugo and Jazz joined them in the tiny bathroom a second later and pulled the door to in the dark. Hugo held himself still and willed his breathing to calm. There was the sound of the apartment door unlocking and then voices in the apartment.

"…when can you take him?" a deep voice said, as the lights came on in the other room. The patrolling Enforcer stepped into sight through the bedroom doorway.

"I'll get a wagon over by the end of next shift. Poor bastard," someone replied whilst turning on the bedroom light. The man, stocky with some bruising on his brow and wearing grimy coveralls with a knife in the belt, came forward, shaking his head.

Hugo sensed Webb flinch in the dark .

"Isn't that Sol?" Hugo whispered as the man stepped towards the bed. Webb nodded.

Sol stood over the body, looking entirely too composed. "What a way to go. He should have stuck to dealing with me. I don't carve what's owed out of your neck."

"You reckon this was a bad debt then?" the Enforcer said.

"That's what I heard. Don't worry, I'll give him a send off and Reclaim can have his stuff."

"What should I tell my Elder?"

"Just tell him it's sorted."

The Enforcer grunted. "Fine. Get rid of him so we can reassign the apartment."

"Don't you worry," Sol said, following the Enforcer out of the bedroom. "I'll take the computer bit now and bring the wagon in the next few hours for him."

There was some shuffling in the next room during which they talked on about the disgrace of the unclaimed killing, then all the lights went out and the apartment door clicked shut.

"I have a real bad feeling," Jazz said as she pushed her way back out the bathroom and turned on the living room light again. "Yep," she said, examining the workstation. "He's taken the data drive."

"Webb," Hugo said, staring at the gap in the workstation's base unit. "I thought you said Sol knew nothing about this man?"

"That's what he said," Webb said. "He said the guy was just a User. I heard the comm call with me own ears. He swore he was nothing to do with him."

"Well, clearly, he was," Hugo said, kicking the workstation. "And just didn't want an Elder to know he was connected."

"Who was he?" Dana asked, looking at the door.

"Sol's no-one," Webb said. "He's a Catiline Patch dealer and a rat."

"It's been a few years since you knew him," Hugo said. "Do you think he's turned killer?"

"Why come back again for the data drive?" Jazz said.

"Sol's no killer," Webb mumbled. "He hasn't the balls for something like this."

"So he hears one of his Users is dead, waits for the hype to die down, then turns up saying he'll organise the Reclaim and takes the guy's data?" Jazz said, brows drawn together.

Webb shook his head. "This makes no sense."

"We don't care who killed this guy, or why Catiline want his data," Dana said. "We only care if this guy was a Ghost and, if so, how to use him to find Ariel."

"What did you say? If this guy's a what?" Hugo said, turning on his sister.

Dana folded her arms. "A Ghost. It's what they're calling the members of this new gang."

"I'd heard the word," Jazz murmured. "I didn't know what it meant."

"No one knows anything about them," Dana said. "What they call themselves, who they are, anything. But they're gaining power. And credit. Havenites are scared."

"How do you know all this?" Hugo muttered.

"Marilyn actually talked to me."

Hugo bristled but Webb stepped forward. "What did she find on them?"

"Not much," Dana said. "That's what scared her."

"What did you find on the workstation?" Hugo asked Jazz.

"It may be something. It may be nothing. But let's get out of here first."

Webb checked the stairwell and corridor before waving them out. They slipped out the open window and closed the shutter then slunk away through the shadows.

Hugo stopped at the first lit street they came to. "This is as far as you go," Hugo said, turning to Dana. "Webb, where's the nearest shuttle to the docks?"

She bridled. "I've already said I'm not leaving."

"This is an order, Midshipman."

"I don't have a rank here," Dana said "And neither do you."

"Kaleb and Dana, for the last time, shut the hell up," Webb said. "First thing's first, we're getting off these streets. We stick out a mile hanging around in the middle of a shift. Until we're out of sight, you need to stop drawing attention to us."

"This way," Jazz said, turning left. "My apartment's nearby."

Hugo followed Jazz, uneasily glancing up the streets that were still mid-shift ghost towns. Dana walked ahead, keeping her back to him. He fought the urge to grab her by the collar and drag her towards the shuttle stop. Webb wasn't looking at him either. Hugo swallowed his frustration, kept his head down and followed. Jazz turned off the main street. Steam was billowing from ventilation grids in the floor and there was a hum nearby of some unseen machinery.

Webb stopped so suddenly that Hugo nearly ran into him. "What is it?"

Webb shushed him, still peering into the steam gathered in a gap between the buildings.

"Webb?" Jazz whispered but Webb shook his head.

"Nothing. Let's get moving," he said and waved them on. Hugo passed the shadowy gap feeling a shiver run over his skin and hurried after Webb as he took the lead around the next corner. The clone pulled up short and flattened against the wall, waving them to get past. Even Dana obeyed, keeping still and quiet while Webb looked back around the corner.

"There's no chance any other family members might be tailing you, right, Hugo?" he murmured.

"What's going on?" Hugo breathed.

"Someone's back there."

Hugo scanned the dark alley but all he could see was the swirling vapour. "I don't see anything."

Webb stood a minute more, watching and listening before waving them on.

"You're paranoid," Dana muttered as Jazz took the lead again, but Webb ignored her, increasing his stride and stopped them at every junction to look around the corners. Hugo took up the rear, listening and checking every shadow and doorway.

"Quiet," he muttered, dragging Dana down a dark ginnel, shushing her protest. Jazz and Webb ducked in next to them, squashing single file in the narrow space that smelt like copper and smoke.

"You heard something too?" Webb muttered.

"Keep her here," Hugo breathed and padded back to the street, drawing his Fourshot. There was a sharp intake of breath from the others but he ignored it, tightening his hand on the weapon.

"Hugo," Webb hissed, scrambling after him. "Are you crazy?"

Jazz was whispering fiercely too but Hugo stepped out onto the street, weapon ready. He had expected the same small figure with fierce blue eyes that drilled right through him, even in his memory. But there was no one there.

"You idiot," Webb growled and hauled him bodily back down the ginnel. "A gun, Hugo? A *gun*?"

"Let me go," Hugo said, shrugging himself free of his grip. Webb's face was stormy but Jazz and Dana were staring at his gun with wary expressions. "Yes, I brought a gun. This mission is too dangerous and too important to be hindered by some primitive honour system -"

"Honour?" Webb said. "You think this is just about *honour*?"

"Commodore Hugo," Jazz said. Her voice was heavy, her expression grave. "You need to dispose of that immediately or I'm going straight to the Elders."

Hugo made a wordless noise of frustration. "I don't care what you do," he said, tucking the Fourshot back in his waistband. "I'm here to get a job done, I refuse -"

"Hugo," Webb snapped. "Just shut off your Service brain for a second and think. Why do you think they have the rule?"

"You said it was a justice thing," Hugo muttered, very aware of the loaded way Jazz was still looking at him.

Webb gave an incredulous laugh. "Yes, it's a 'justice thing'. If you want to hurt someone you have to get close, you have to look them in the eye and know why you're doing it. It also means you're only likely to take down the person you meant to and not any innocent bystanders."

"I'm a good shot," Hugo argued.

Webb rubbed his eyes and growled. "Hugo, what does this whole fucking colony run on?"

"What?

"Bloodgrease, Kale," Dana put in, voice full of disdain. "The life support, the yards, the recycling levels, the street sweepers, everything. You're never more than a few feet away from a fuel line or storage vat full of it."

Hugo went cold. He looked back at Webb who was watching his face.

"There, now you get it," Webb said. "One stray shot, just one, and you could take a whole street or, hell, a whole sector with you. So no guns. Ever. Now hand it over. We're getting rid of it before it gets you lynched or the entire district blown into drift."

Hugo went cold. The Fourshot that until a few minutes ago had made him feel like he had some measure of control, now felt heavy and chill against his skin. The look that was etched into Jazz's normally placid face was enough to make Hugo realise just how badly he'd blundered. He took out the gun and gave it to Webb who visibly wilted with relief.

"Jazz," he said. "What's the best way -"

"Give it to me," she said holding out her hand. She wasn't looking at Hugo.

Webb handed it over, looking drained. Jazz tucked it inside her jacket and brushed past them, back to the street.

"Jazz," Hugo said as he caught up to her. "I'm sorry."

She stared at him for a long moment as they paced along, then nodded and dropped her gaze. Hugo wished she'd say something but she didn't speak again. Dana managed to refrain from saying anything more but the looks she sent him were disgusted. Webb just appeared tired and followed on Jazz's heels, hands in pockets and head down.

VIII

More of Haven's dark streets went by in a blur. Hugo was just beginning to feel like he would go mad with the sameness of it all, when Jazz turned into some open doors on the ground level of a tall building. An Enforcer with no eyebrows, dark coveralls and a very large knife at his side was stationed just inside. His feet were on the desk in front of him and he was watching some monitors on the wall. He looked up as they came in.

"Ms. Jasmine," he nodded, looking over them all. "Mr. Ezekiel. You have guests?"

"Workers off-shift from Sector 4, Arn," Jazz said with a disarming smile. "Thought I'd treat them to a real coffee."

The man nodded and they carried on, though Hugo could feel the man's eyes all the way to the bank of lifts at the back of the lobby. He let go a breath he didn't realise he was holding when the doors shut and the lift juddered upwards.

They stood in silence. Webb stared at the floor. Dana leant against the wall and glared at the wall. A mix of hot anger and cold defeat were swirling in Hugo's gut. He bit the inside of his cheek to stop himself blurting the hundreds of frustrated things that were clamouring in his head. Jazz looked at no-one and the silence stretched on.

The lift seemed to take forever but then the doors opened and Jazz led them out and down a windowless corridor. She reached a door at the end and pulled out a keycard, opened it up and they filed in.

The apartment was more like loft space that had been filled with mismatched furniture than somewhere meant for someone to live. Broad plexiglass windows made up most of one wall and looked over the rooftops and gridded alleys of the sector. The dull green of the track lights gave everything a murky tinge, even after Jazz had turned on the lights. In the corner was a workstation the like of which Hugo had never seen, with four or five processors balanced on top of one another and half a dozen displays of varying sizes, ages and states of repair, all scrolling data in an endless stream. Jazz went to check the readings as Dana stared around and Webb shrugged himself out of his jacket.

"Right, back to business," Dana started, turning to Jazz. "You found something on that computer. What was it?"

Jazz raised her eyebrows, glancing at Webb who was refusing to look at any of them. She sighed, seemed to make up her mind about something, took off her jacket, checked the gun in the pocket and shut it away in a cupboard.

"Not much, exactly," she said. "He didn't seem to have any credit of his own hidden anywhere. But he did have some authorisation codes and passes in his software that are usually used to access the Elders' inter-sector credit flow system. He wasn't a broker, I don't see why he needed that sort of software."

"Unless he was a fence for bloodgrease traders," Hugo mumbled.

Jazz shrugged and nodded. "It's a possibility. His last log-in had him accessing the system used to manage the yards' supply budgets."

"The shipyards?" Hugo asked and Jazz nodded. "Why would he be checking that?"

Jazz shrugged again. "I can't tell."

"Could it have something to do with Apollos Outreach?" Dana asked.

Jazz shook her head again. "I honestly couldn't tell you. All I can tell you is he was able to see where credit was going around the colony. No one except a broker or an Elder would have reason to do that."

"So we have no proof that he was a Ghost, or even if he had anything to do with…what are you doing?" Hugo growled as his sister, who had a panel out of her pocket and was tapping commands into it.

"None of your business," she said. "Webb, what was the name of that Catiline member that took the processor?"

"Sol," Webb said, staring at nothing.

"And where does he live?"

"Stop," Hugo ordered. "Just stop, now, Dana."

"I'm not stopping," she said coolly, pocketing the panel again. "Webb. Tell me where I can find that Sol."

Hugo stepped between her and the door. He was trying to decide what to say first when Webb slammed his hand down on a tabletop.

"This all stops. Now," the younger man said. "Whatever's between you two, I frankly could not give less of a shit. But we're all mixed up in this together now, whether we like it or not. We either finish the job or we all leave."

"I have every intention of finishing the job," Dana said, jutting her chin. "Tell me what I need to know and I'll be off to do it."

"Not a chance, Hugo Junior. It's bad enough having one of you running amuck on this damn colony. We stick together."

Both Hugo and Dana started protesting and this time Webb kicked the table. Jazz pursed her lips but didn't say anything.

"No brand, no say," Webb said, pointing at Hugo then his sister. "I'm taking no more shit off either of you."

Dana's face was flushed and she looked like she might explode. Hugo felt the same heat riding up his spine but his belly was knotted with guilt. Webb's pale eyes were angry and slightly pained. He looked at him for a long second then stormed out of the room. The silence he left in his wake was thick. Jazz pursed her lips and moved to follow but Hugo held up a hand.

"Let me go," he said.

He found Webb in a store room at the end of the apartment's narrow hallway. He sat in the light from the single window which reduced the piled-up furniture and disused computer equipment to shapeless bundles in the dark. He sat with his feet up on a crate, staring out across the colony cityscape. His face wasn't angry any more. He just looked tired.

"I'm sorry," Hugo said, stepping into the room.

"Which screw up are you apologising for?" Webb mumbled, not looking up.

"You're angry with me. I understand that. But what Dana said, back at the Ghost's apartment -"

"She reminds me of you," Webb said.

Hugo clamped his mouth over his first response, shifting from one foot to another. "She's always been…impetuous."

"She's a lot younger than you," Webb murmured, still not looking up at him.

Hugo took a step closer. "There are six of us," he said.

"And she's the only girl?"

Hugo nodded. "Not counting Catherine."

"The oldest?"

Hugo nodded. "She died during the McCullough's Revolution. Dana never knew her."

"It's tough to live up to a dead person," Webb said, examining his fingernails.

"Webb," Hugo said, taking another step closer.

"Was she telling the truth?" Webb said, finally looking at him.

"Marilyn came to me. She had leads on Orbit traders buying bloodgrease. She wanted to find enough to shut them all down. I assigned her the mission."

"With no team or backup?"

Hugo clenched his fists but then felt his strength rattle out of him and slumped onto a crate. He clutched his head in his hands and closed his eyes. "She didn't want to work with anyone else in case she turned up evidence that the Service could use against Haven," he whispered. "But I should have insisted."

There was a moment of silence then he heard Webb shifting. "Harvey was never one to be talked out of something," he said quietly.

Hugo clutched at his head tighter. "It's my fault. It's all my fault."

Webb didn't say anything.

Hugo sat with his head in his hands, breathing heavily. After a while, he found the strength to sit up. He blinked at the wetness in the corners of his eyes then met the clone's heavy gaze even though there was still a darkness in his expression that unsettled him.

"And I'm going to make it right," he finally said, voice low. "Whatever it takes."

"Whatever the cost?"

"Yes. But not just for me. For both of us. Dana was wrong about that."

Webb nodded and looked away. "She doesn't seem to like me much."

"She doesn't like anyone much."

The shadow's shifted around Webb's face as he nearly smiled. He heaved a sigh and stretched and Hugo heard his joints click. "Well, won't this be fun together? One big, happy, screwed-up family."

Hugo massaged his temples. "Great."

"Come on," Webb said, standing. "Let's see if Jazz will make us some coffee."

Hugo's mouth started to water and he suddenly realised how tired he was. "I think we'll need it."

He followed Webb back to the main room. Dana was standing at the window with her back straight and a stony expression on her face whilst Jazz moved around the kitchen unit. They both looked up as Hugo and Webb came back in.

"Kale, tell this woman to let me go."

Hugo frowned.

"I've locked the door," Jazz said as she started a machine in the kitchen that whirred and released the deliciously rich smell of coffee.

"I'm not working with you two - " Dana started but Hugo cut in.

"Dana," he snapped. "You don't know the first damn thing -"

"It seems to me," Jazz put in, raising her voice enough to quiet them all as she fetched mugs from a cupboard. "That none of you really has any idea what you're doing."

Doubt dampened Hugo's palms and he saw Webb's jaw tighten, though Dana visibly bridled.

"Who are you anyway?" she said. "Why is this anything to do with you?"

"I've been asking myself the same thing," Jazz said, pouring the coffee.

"Let me out, already. I got this far on my own -"

"Dana," Hugo warned.

"How did you manage that, anyway?" Webb asked.

"None of your business," she growled. "Marilyn trusted me with her secrets, just like she can trust me to get the bastard who hurt her."

"Can she? When you're still going about this in all the wrong ways?" Jazz asked. She offered a mug to Dana.

Dana was frowning heavily but inhaled and then took the coffee. "And how exactly are we going wrong?"

"You won't find what you need by talking to people," Jazz said. "You need to *listen*."

"Jazz is right," Webb said as he took his own mug. "It's what I've been trying to say all along. If we want to track Ariel down, it's going to take time. Time with open ears and eyes and with our heads down. We go questioning Sol or Bryce or anyone, word will get round fast that we're up to something."

"Bryce?" Dana asked. "Who's Bryce?"

"A fence for the refineries," Hugo muttered.

"He must know all of their business," Dana said, face brightening.

"Only what they want him to know," Webb put in. "And we can't ask him, so don't even think about it."

"Webb -"

"I'm telling you, he's dangerous, Hugo. Talking to him is the quickest way to get us all deported."

"Whoever that Black Cross victim was, he's tied up in the yards and in bloodgrease."

"Maybe," Webb said, tipping his head back and draining his mug. "But if he's a Ghost, or even if he's not, or even if they exist at all, we're only going to find out by getting people to trust us and include us in the gossip. That goes for you too, Mrs AWOL."

Dana scowled and slammed down her mug. "This is bullshit. God knows how long that will take."

"We have to listen to them," Hugo said, staring into his coffee. "This is their world, not ours." The silence that followed was charged and he felt three pairs of eyes on him but all he did was drain his coffee and head to the door. "Webb, come on. We've got a shift." Webb weighed him up a second before nodding and grabbing his jacket. "Jazz," Hugo said. "Will you carry on listening for us too?"

Jazz nodded. "If I hear anything that will help, I'll be in touch."

Hugo clenched his teeth as the returning tide of futility threatened to sweep him under, but nodded. "Dana, do you having boarding?"

She nodded. "I'm secure."

"Get to it, then. Keep out of sight. Let's sync our communicators," he tapped a few commands into his wrist panel and Webb and Dana did the same. "Keep in touch. And don't do anything stupid."

Dana narrowed her eyes, sighed and shifted her glare to Jazz. "Can you let us go now?"

Jazz spent another second looking between them all, looking vaguely pitying then moved to the door and unlocked it.

"Webb," she called after them as they left. Webb returned to the apartment door and a few quiet words were exchanged. What Hugo could see of Jazz's face looked worried. What he could see of Webb's looked resigned.

"Kale," Dana hissed in his ear.

"What?"

She glanced at Webb and Jazz to make sure they were still engrossed then pulled him further down the corridor. "You know where to find this Bryce guy?"

"You heard what Webb said."

"I heard bullshit," she said. "He's afraid. This could be a real lead."

"What's to say he'll talk to us? I'm on probation and you're an illegal alien."

"He doesn't need to talk to us. One dig through his systems could give us everything we need. We could have Ariel in our hands by this time tomorrow."

A surge went through Hugo at the thought. He hesitated, looking back to Webb stood with his head bent close to his friend's. "Webb can't know," he whispered and Dana nodded.

"I'll send you co-ordinates for a rendezvous," she said. "Meet me on your next off-shift. Be there, or I'll tell him everything."

Hugo ground his teeth but then Jazz was closing the apartment door and Webb was joining them again.

"What was that about?" Hugo asked, quickly schooling his features as Webb glanced between them suspiciously.

"She was just reminding me not to get myself killed."

Δ

"No, you're putting too much angle on the thumb," Webb said wearily, showing Hugo the hand-sign for a greeting yet another time. "Try again." Hugo attempted the sign again but Webb shook his head. "You just told me to bring you a spanner. Again."

"This is a waste of time."

"Coffee worn off?" Webb said with half a smile.

Hugo grumbled as the shuttle rattled over another bump in the rails, causing him to stagger. He looped his arm tighter around a pole and attempted the hand-sign one more time.

"Better," Webb said, around a yawn. "Again."

"Remind me of the point of this," Hugo said as he tried again.

"Everyone will expect you to be picking it up," Webb said, shifting as he was jostled by a worker attempting to get a better handhold next to him. Webb leaned closer and lowered his voice. "Besides, it's easier to eavesdrop with your eyes than with your ears."

"What's the sign for Ghost?"

"Shh," Webb hissed, glancing again at the worker closest but he was staring out the dark windows with a vacant look in his red-rimmed eyes. "I'll teach you that later," Webb said in a low voice. "Now, the greeting again. There's still overtones of 'spanner' in your pinky."

Hugo did it again and again on the ride to the shift until Webb was happy, then he started him on practicing the sign for blood-grease. Hugo tried to sink himself into it and didn't meet Webb's eyes once on the ride, afraid the clone might be able to read the guilt in his face.

He pushed aside that feeling. No matter what he planned to tell their mother as soon as this was over, Dana was right. Bryce was their best bet and the possibility of tracking down Ariel direct without having to wait for crumbs of clues from potentially non-existent gangs burned fiercely enough in his mind to sear away his reservations. Webb was seemingly too tired to notice Hugo's tension, but Hugo still got himself away from his friend as soon as they stepped off the shuttle before he could pick anything up.

The shift was, again, like the last: nauseatingly exhausting, loud and long. He watched out for signs exchanged amongst the workers, picking up a few favoured expressions and the greeting he had learned, but a lot of it moved too fast for him to even be sure he was seeing anything. He let the hope that he would not be here long enough to need to learn any more grow inside him as his beater juddered again on another course.

Foreman Michalski came by for her usual quality check just

before the shift's half-way break and Hugo had to tell himself that the look that she seemed to let linger on him was probably just his imagination. He earned himself a piece of dried fruit by being able to sign his thanks during the break and he gobbled it down, surprised to realise how much he'd missed food with flavour.

He couldn't quite pin down how he felt when the shift-end call finally boomed out. Tired, yes. More so than he could ever remember being. Sore, too, from the worn padding on his seat as well as the rusted suspension on the beater. But woven through his physical discomfort was a thread of anticipation.

Webb looked worse than he felt when they boarded the shuttle and he remembered with a new stab of guilt that his friend had yet to sleep from the shift before. The taller man's shoulders were slumped and his hair was slicked back from his forehead with dirt and sweat. He blended in almost completely with the other workers who stood around staring at nothing, bent and dirty.

"They had me on an assembly line today," Webb said as the shuttle pulled out and the yard noise died away. "Near the storage pits. I saw some guy deliver some bloodgrease but no one did or said anything unusual. You?"

"I didn't hear anything."

"What is it?" Webb muttered when he saw Hugo looking at him.

Hugo took a breath. "Don't get lost, Webb."

"Huh?"

Hugo searched for words. "You've got your own reasons for being here. But I'm aware you're still doing it because I asked you to. Don't let it...I mean..."

"What are you getting at?"

Hugo paused then made himself say it. "I talked to Jazz...about how you met."

"You did, huh?"

"I needed to know."

"Yeah, well," Webb said, not looking at him. "That's just one side of the story, Hugo."

"You should tell me your side."

Webb looked back at him, tiredness gone from his eyes to be replaced by a sharpness Hugo wasn't sure he preferred. "I'm not going to start Using again, if that's what you're worried about."

"It's not."

Webb was tense the rest of the trip back to the boarding house and Hugo couldn't think of anything to say to make it better.

They ate their dinner in silence. Even Tag seemed to sense their mood and brought them their Nutripaks without a word. Webb went to the room ahead of Hugo and by the time he had showered off all the grime and returned to the room, Webb was already asleep. Even poking at his past apparently couldn't keep the clone awake after that shift.

He got into his cot, making sure it creaked as he did and made himself lie there for a full hour, Webb snoring away in the dark, before getting quietly up again, grabbing his remaining weapons, pulling on his cap and leaving. He didn't like to think about how hard it had been to pull himself from those threadbare blankets. Fatigue weighted him like lead. But he spurred himself on with the thought that if they could get what they needed from Bryce, he could very well be on his way home by the end of next shift.

Away from Haven, with Ariel in the brig ready to face tribunal. Heading home.

Home to Harvey.

He quickened his step, keying a message to Dana as he went. A set of co-ordinates came back in seconds and Hugo turned down another street to head vaguely towards the rec district.

Dana was waiting in the shadows under a bridge which branched over another nameless, dark street. Hugo found himself having to reign in his temper again at the sight of her: she was too young to have done anything but field exercises, but here she was in Haven coveralls with the collar turned up to hide her lack of brand. She was too busy consulting her panel to notice and didn't even look up as he arrived.

"I wondered if you'd actually come."

"Less talk," Hugo said. "Let's get going."

"Don't talk tough with me," Dana said, pocketing her panel. "I'm only bringing you along because you know where to find this fence. And I know you're only bringing me along because I'm the only one with a hope in hell of being able to hack into his systems quick enough to not get caught. So less of the tone."

"Let's go," Hugo repeated, swallowing the flare of anger and striding off. Dana had to run to catch up with him. They walked in silence as Hugo steered them towards the nearest shuttle stop.

The shuttle, just like all the others, eventually turned onto the main bank of lines heading towards the shipyard. They got off at a stop just as the red stain of the refinery appeared ahead.

For a while all they did was stand on the platform and stare at the black outlines of the nearest buildings framed against the red light from the refinery. Hugo could smell it already. It clung to his throat like the smell of blood.

"This way," Hugo eventually broke the silence and picked a way towards the light. They padded between dark buildings, barely daring to breathe it was so quiet. As they got closer, a red stain overlay everything like rust. They turned a corner and were faced with a rift in the floor, ten feet wide and dark as space. A thin rail stopped them stepping straight into it. On the other side was a high wall and beyond that there was nothing but shadows and the distant sound of heaving machinery. The hull overhead was glowing deep, dark red.

"Over there," Dana said, pointing. Hugo wondered if he imagined the change in her voice or whether she really was as unnerved as him. He followed her gesture and saw a bridge spanning the fissure to a gate in the wall.

Hugo took the lead. The quiet was so complete that they both jumped when something rattled down in the fissure. When all was quiet again they moved on.

"Wait," Dana whispered as reached the walkway.

Hugo saw the eyes of cameras set in wall over the gate. He tapped some commands into his wrist panel. It beeped then displayed an electronics scan of the glowing power lines that fed the cameras.

"They're active," Hugo mumbled, backing away from the bridge.

"Over here," Dana murmured and stepped behind a lean-to, pulling out her panel. Hugo watched over her shoulder as she began to run scanning and infiltration programs. It showed the wireless signals going to the cameras as red threads on the schematic. Hugo couldn't follow his sister's fingers as they triggered queries and commands, gaining control of the stream.

"The Academy taught you that?"

"No," she replied, clicking the last command that broke the cameras' feeds. "Rami did, last summer."

Hugo made a mental note, not entirely sure he was pleased, then crossed the bridge. The gate was fastened with a manual lock. Neither his wrist or Dana's computer panel picked up any electronic alarms but Hugo left the handle alone anyway.

"Here," he said, getting on one knee and making a stirrup with his hands. Dana gave him a dubious look. "When you get over, don't move, understand? No arguments," Hugo snapped as a frown gathered on her face. "Systems might be your area but infiltration is mine. Do as I say."

Dana clamped her mouth shut and pocketed her panel. She braced herself on Hugo's shoulders and stepped into his linked hands. He stood and boosted her up. She grabbed the top of the gate, scanning about for a minute then pulled herself over. Hugo jumped, grabbed hold and pulled himself over.

The smell was even stronger and the light even redder. There was still no sound apart from the clunking heartbeat of unseen machinery. Dana stood against the wall, staring. All Hugo could make out were the vague shapes of outbuildings, jagged heaps of abandoned machinery and a web of pipes of all sizes sprouting from the floor, the buildings and each other. They joined and split like metal veins for as far as he could see. They curled along the floor and climbed up into the air. They all ran into a structure that towered over the rest. Hugo had to crane his neck to see where the top was framed against the red light above. Sprouting from the apex were dozens of chimneys that fed into the colony hull far above.

It made no visual sense. It was like a nightmare jumbled with the industrial designs of a madman.

"Where now?"

Hugo shook his head to bring himself together and glanced around. "Foreman Michalski said Bryce's workshop was somewhere along the boundary," he said and set off along the wall. They had to clamber over pipes and hatches and skirt round unmarked pits. Some of the pipes were cold, others were scalding. He kept their pace up, scouring everything in the rusty light for any sign of a workshop, straining his hearing for anything other than the humming and creaking of the refinery.

An exhausting scramble later, Hugo spotted a different sort of light ahead. He could hear voices for the first time in what felt like hours. He gestured for Dana to get behind him and they eased along the wall, sticking to the darkest shadows.

When they came within sight of the source of light they slowed to a crawl and peered between a tangle of pipes. A two-storey building stood in a cleared square. Electric light poured from all the windows and a door at the front stood wide open, spilling more light onto the concrete. Through the doors they could see a wide workshop floor with workers moving about. There were shouts and the clank of tools.

There were two barrels propping the doors open and on each barrel lounged a man on watch. They chatted but their eyes were watchful and the knives at their belts clearly displayed. A third guard stood at another gate in the boundary wall, this one open, chewing and staring out into the sector.

"So what now, oh great infiltrator?" Dana muttered.

"Can't your panel access his systems from here?"

Dana rolled her eyes. "I checked already. He's on a closed, wired system. I need to get to a workstation or a terminal."

"*Quiet*," Hugo hissed as the gaze of the guard by the gate swung their way. He crouched out of sight, pulling Dana with him. "This way," he said, after the guard had turned away again. He moved quietly, bent double, Dana at his heels. Ignoring Dana's muttered protests about time, he swung them in a staggered arc around the workshop, keeping behind the scattered outbuildings and screens of tangled pipes.

He finally stopped when he spotted a side door propped open with a block of concrete. The glow of a computer display reflected off the walls inside. They kept motionless for five minutes before Hugo was satisfied there was no one around, then made a dash for the door.

The room was empty of people. Two interior doors were closed but there was a window overlooking the workshop. The glass was grimy, but he could still make out at least a dozen people at brightly-lit benches, clicking keyboards at workstations, sorting scrap or bent over broken equipment. Distaste surged through him when the small figure of a child, about Tag's age, made his way across the room, pulling a heavy barrow of scrap.

He made himself step back from the window and take up post in the corner where he could watch all the doors. His fingers itched for his gun.

Dana was already at the workstation, plugging her panel into one of the ports. The room was small, with racks of machine parts in various states of disrepair filling the walls. Apart from the one Dana was trying to hack into, there was another display on the opposite wall displaying camera feeds of the workshop floor and corridors and other rooms.

"We need to hurry," Hugo said. "This must be the foreman's

office. He could be back any minute."

"Then shut up and stop distracting me."

Hugo reigned in his temper and crossed to the camera feed display to see if he could make out anyone heading their way. He frowned. The larger windows showed angles of the workshop, the space in front of the building and the gate. Minimised down one side were a number of other feeds, all reeling footage so dark and grainy it was hard to make out. He checked the door again, and on Dana who was still typing feverishly on the main workstation, then tapped in commands and expanded the minimised windows.

He squinted at the dark footage. It was showing somewhere too large to be anywhere in the building. The camera was somewhere high up and the feed quality low. He could just make out great vats, spills, filters and fires, all shuddering, flashing and glowing red and black. The scale could only be guessed at since the darkness and the lumbering vats obscured the distance but swarming over everything were workers. They looked like ants scurrying amongst the straining machines. Men and women and smaller figures of children too, all either stripped to the waist or wearing nothing but worn vests and cargo trousers. The few that had hair long enough had it plastered to their scalps with sweat. Every one of them was filthy and moved like every inch of them ached.

"What the...?"

Dana's muttered words pulled him from his trance and he turned away from the display with a shudder. "What is it? Have you found Ariel?"

Dana shook her head. "No," she turned in her seat and caught sight of the other display. "What's that?"

"I think it's the refinery," Hugo said. "What have you found?"

Dana opened her mouth but they heard voices approaching from outside.

Hugo cursed, looking around. "Quick," he said hauling Dana from her chair by her coveralls. She grabbed her panel just in time then he was dragging her to a door, opening it a crack. It was dark and he ducked through, pulling Dana with him and clicking it shut.

Voices came through the door. His pulse thundered in his ears. He looked around for any clue as to where they were but it was too dark. They waited, blinking in the gloom and heard the sound of another door opening and then shutting again. Hugo put his hand out to hold Dana still for a further ten heartbeats before letting her open the door a crack. The office was deserted again.

"Time to go."

"For once I agree," she said and they made for the exit.

The man that stepped into the doorway just as they reached it was about twice as big as Hugo around the chest and had a knife the length of his thigh slung at his belt and a look of surprise on his face that was quickly melting into anger.

IX

"Who the hell are you?" the guard said after he, Hugo and Dana had stood blinking at each other for an excruciating second. Hugo glanced at his sister, waited for the man to shift his gaze to her then charged forward, shouldering him against the doorjamb.

"Dana, *run*."

The big man's splutters died away as they tore around the corner and scrambled over the first tangle of piping in their way. Hugo paused to help Dana climb over the top, then they were running blind, deeper into the clutter of the refinery yard.

"There," Hugo called when they rounded a corner to see the boundary wall ahead. The pipes arched up almost to the top. Hugo skidded to a halt and got down on his knee to vault Dana up just as shouting and running footsteps got closer. Hugo was so busy watching out for pursuit that when Dana cursed and stumbled in his grip, he lost his balance and they crashed in a tangle on the concrete.

"What happened?"

"The pipe's hot," Dana panted, hissing between her teeth and clutching a scalded hand. They got to their knees just as three figures hurtled from around the nearest outbuilding, wielding industrial lenslights that blinded them. Dana and Hugo scrambled to their feet but the workshop guards were quick and seized them both. Hugo struggled and reached for Dana who was kicking and spitting curses at the woman holding her but the man holding him jerked him back by his collar, cutting off his air.

"Foreman wants a word with you," he grated and then they were being hauled back toward the workshop.

They were dumped on the floor of the foreman's office. Hugo got to his knees, rubbing his neck and blinking back dizziness from the stranglehold. The woman who had held Dana was closing a blind on the window that looked out over the workshop whilst someone was bellowing for Bryce.

Hugo got to his feet and looked around desperately but each of the three figures blocked all the doorways. Before he could begin to think of a plan, someone was slamming through the door from the workshop. He had large shoulders and had once been tall for a Havenite, but now his bent back made him shorter than the others in the room. He had some mean scarring up his neck and head. His left ear was a pale ruin of flesh and no hair grew on that side of his head. His jaw was large and he had it clenched tight and anger burned in his black eyes.

"What the hell is all this?" His voice was raspy, like soldiers Hugo had known who had survived gas blasts.

"Looks like these two hacked into the computer system, Foreman. Cowards tried to run."

The scarred man's heavy scowl landed on Hugo. "And who the fuck are they?"

The man who had spoken shrugged and Bryce's eyes blazed still hotter. He shambled forward, bent close to Hugo's face. "Who the hell are you and what are you doing here?"

"What do you know about the Ghosts?"

"Dana," Hugo hissed.

The foreman snapped his attention to Dana, jaw bulging. "You don't ask me questions, little girl," he grated. "You are in my workshop, at my workstation messing around with my systems. You are not asking anything. You are telling. And now. Who the fuck are you?"

The door from the workshop opened again and a worker in grimed overalls staggered in, panting. "Foreman?"

"What is it?"

"There's someone here," the newcomer said between breaths, taking in Dana and Hugo. "Says you have his probys. They're trying to hold him..."

"Who is it?"

The worker shifted on his feet, looking uncertain. He opened his mouth, but turned when there was a commotion in the work-shop and then Webb was elbowing his way past the worker with a drawn knife.

"You," Bryce spat.

"Let them go, Foreman."

"Webb," Hugo began.

"Quiet," Bryce thundered, scarred face twisting with fury. "You've just made the second biggest mistake of your miserable life," he said to Webb. "You say these sneaks are…" he trailed off, blinking then peered back at Hugo. Hugo held himself tall and tried not to shift on his feet. Dana watched everything with nar-rowed eyes. "It's you, isn't it?" Bryce said. "You're that Serviceman they're all talking about?"

Something went through the room. The guards muttered. The worker by the door gaped. Webb stiffened.

"Bryce -"

"Shut it," Bryce thundered. "You," he snapped at the two guards closest to Dana and Hugo. "Get them into the workshop and lock them in. Use your sticks if you have to. You," he yelled at the worker who jumped. "Go and get the Enforcers. And not on the comm, either. Go and *physically* get them. Now. Tell them I have thieves to punish and I want official witnesses."

"Bryce," Webb started again as he tried to shrug off the hold the nearest guard had taken on his jacket.

"Stow it," Bryce said. "It's finally time for you to pay, Webb. You have no pet Elder around to save you this time and no one is going to cry innocence for you when you've snuck a pet Service captain aboard to spy on innocent civilians."

Hugo tried to pull away as a guard laid hands on him. Dana was shouting as another did the same to her and they started to wrestle them toward the door.

The hot, iron smell of bloodgrease was heavier in the workshop, along with the smells of oil and sweat. Men, women and children were straightening up from benches to gawp. The guards holding them shouted for everyone to get out and tools were dropped and machines abandoned in the mad scramble for the doors.

"That's more lost work hours. As if you didn't owe me enough already," Bryce growled as he locked the door behind him. More doors were shut and locked around the room and more large guards came to help hold them whilst Bryce yammered orders into a wrist comm.

As yet another man got a grip on Hugo and forced him to hold still, Webb managed to tear free of the man holding him and stumbled to a stack of bloodgrease barrels in the corner, fumbling in his pockets.

"Bryce!" he yelled and everyone stilled. He was holding a cigarette lighter over the barrels. In the heavy silence the lighter clicked and everyone stared at the flame.

"You don't have the spine," Bryce hissed, but he'd gone pale under his scarring.

Hugo held his breath and searched Webb's face to try and figure out if his friend was bluffing but he barely recognised the cold mask that Webb wore.

"Don't I?" Webb didn't speak loudly but as everyone around was stock still and silent he didn't have to. "Getting blown up or letting you get even," Webb gave a tired sort of shrug. "At least exploding would be quicker."

"You'd take out a whole sector rather than take what's owed you?" Bryce took a step toward Webb and the hands holding Hugo twitched. "You're not only a thief but a coward too."

Webb stiffened and lowered the lighter toward the barrel. A couple of the guards shouted but then Bryce bellowed for silence. His meaty fists clenched and unclenched at his sides.

"Get out," he hissed after another swallowing silence. "All of you. But, Webb," he took another step closer and Webb's hand holding the lighter twitched though his pale eyes remained locked with Bryce's. "I'd run bloody far bloody fast."

The air crackled as Webb and Bryce glared at each other. Hugo almost saw the decision to drop the lighter flicker through Webb's eyes but then he blinked.

"Hugo, go," he said. Hugo didn't think, grabbed his sister's elbow and ran. A guard scrambled to unlock the door for them. They tore out through a cluttered entrance hall, one or two workers staring after them as they went. Webb caught up with them as they reached the door outside.

"I've locked them in but it won't hold them," Webb said as they skidded out into the yard. More workers stood around looking lost and confused but none moved to stop them as they ran for the gate.

They hit another bridge running and their footsteps rattled the metal. When they reached the other side they all skidded to a halt together, panting. The beams of lenslights cut into the gloom ahead in the direction of the shuttle rails. The worker who had been sent to get the Enforcers rounded a corner, talking over his shoulder to people following.

"This way," Webb hissed and ran in the other direction. Hugo hated the gloom and darkness they stumbled through, once again on the run, fighting a tide of despair threatening to take him under. The second time Webb stopped at an empty intersection of streets, panting and looking lost, Hugo realised for the first time just how much trouble they were in.

"Do you know where we are?"

"We need to get off the streets," was all Webb could answer.

"This way," Dana said, checking their location on her wrist panel and ran down the street to the left.

"Where are we going?"

"Less talking more running," Dana said, ducking down another alley and scrambling over piled-up trash boxes. The smell made Hugo's eyes water. Unable to stop them, memories of sprinting through the alleys of Lunar 1 after the Splinters with Harvey and Webb ghosted through Hugo's mind. Then there was darkness, fear and desperation also, but it was different then. There'd been a purpose. They were sure they would achieve something.

And Harvey had been there. And the real Webb.

Hugo choked the emotion down and took the hand Webb's clone offered to get him over a crumbling wall. He risked a glance at his partner's face but the younger man didn't meet his eye.

"There," Dana suddenly called and pointed ahead. A small on-street parking pool was crowded with mopeds. She skidded to a halt next to one and pulled out some start keys.

"I assume you can get one of your own?" Dana said, nodding towards the other mopeds whilst hers coughed to life.

"Where are we going?" Webb demanded, bending over another moped and fiddling with the starter. Hugo stared at the little vehicles, starting to feel sick. There was still an hour until shift change but there were lights on in some of the buildings and the sound of voices where doors to dining and rec rooms were propped upon.

"Far away and fast, just like he said," Dana said. There was a grunt and a whine and the engine of the moped Webb had chosen spluttered to life.

"Hugo," Webb prompted. "You remember how to do this, right?"

Hugo just nodded and bent over a moped. It took far longer than it should have to hot-wire it because his hands were shaking and vision blurry. Finally, it started and Dana wheeled her machine round and sped off down the street just as someone leaned from a door and shouted after them. Hugo and Webb followed, the angry worker's yells dying away.

Dana was going too fast. She ignored Hugo's shouts of warning. Time was an unreal thing. It felt like he'd been trying to overtake Dana for hours, but she kept just ahead of him, taking corners stupidly fast and dodging the increasing street traffic by taking them through darker and narrower passes than he would have dared.

Finally, she pulled around a corner and braked, wheeling her moped under a sheet-metal lean-to hidden between two storage units. Webb and Hugo's brakes screeched as they careened in after her, avoiding piling up only by spinning their mopeds around each other. They cut their engines. The only sound was their breathing. Dana climbed off her bike and snapped at them to hurry as she pulled a clattering screen across the entrance and squeezed through a gap at the back.

"Where are we?"

"I haven't the faintest idea," Webb said, hurrying after Dana. "But she does."

"We're getting under cover," Dana murmured as they sprinted around a corner. "Now come on, will you? Someone might be able to track the stolen mopeds."

"Webb, wait," Hugo said and grabbed his friend by the elbow. The man stopped but didn't look at him. "You could have destroyed the sector. Hell, that close to the refinery... you could have breached the hull..."

"It doesn't matter any more," Webb said, voice lifeless and face blank.

Hugo shook his head, confusion reeling with fear. "I don't understand."

The shift call boomed out and stopped Webb from replying. He turned and went after Dana. Hugo stared then hurried after them, a heaviness in his stomach.

They caught up with her in a narrow space between two concrete walls. She slowed down, appeared to be searching about then crouched on the floor.

"What the...?" Hugo leaned round Webb just as there was a faint click and Dana hauled open a grate set in the floor, almost hidden by the dark. She sat on the edge of the opening and then climbed onto a ladder in the shadows below. Webb went next and then Hugo took a breath and followed.

"Shut the grate," Dana hissed from somewhere beneath him and Hugo pulled it closed after him. The air was still and stale, with the faint odour of oil and refuse. The noise of the other two descending the ladder echoed off unseen walls.

Hugo began to climb. The ladder was sturdy enough but they climbed until the light from the slatted grate had shrunk to almost nothing over them. It was pitch black.

"Where the hell are we?" Webb asked once, only to be hissed into silence by Dana. At one point a humming sound grew and then faded again. When Hugo was afraid his strength was going to fail, there was a mumbled warning from Dana and muttered curses from Webb as they reached the bottom. Hugo's arms were aching and he stumbled when his feet finally connected with solid ground. The grate was a pinprick like a single star overhead. There was no sound apart from the faint humming somewhere above and the smell was stronger than ever.

When Dana clicked on a lenslight, both men swore at the sudden brightness. She didn't pause and shouldered past them to follow the narrow passage.

"Don't talk until we get inside," she whispered.

"Inside where?" Hugo muttered only to be shushed again. The passage was so narrow they had to walk single file. Hugo felt like the air was thin. The passage narrowed and widened with no discernible pattern and at times the ceiling was so low they had to crawl. Dana didn't walk them far but by the time she was kneeling and spinning an old-fashioned code-wheel on a hatch at ground level, Hugo felt like they'd been wandering around in the silence and the dark forever.

There was a click and the hatch creaked inwards and Dana was crawling through the gap. The two men followed her, Webb cursing as he bent his tall frame through the tiny space and stood up in the small room just as she was powering up a free-standing lighting panel. Hugo blinked in the sudden light. The chamber was small, barely bigger than their room at the boarding house. There was a fan turning sluggishly in a vent in the ceiling but the air still smelled close and rusty. There was a pallet against the wall and a workstation in the corner, the connections hard-wired into the wall. Against the other wall was a stack of shelving made from different sized sheets of metal and breeze blocks which held a jumble of tools, med kits, wrist panels and boxes vacuum-sealed Nutripaks. There was also a bank of mismatched lockers shunted in beside them. One locker hung open on broken hinges and he could see more equipment, batteries and Nutripaks piled inside.

Dana had gone straight to the workstation and plugged in her panel but Webb stood blinking around.

"What is this place?" Hugo asked.

"Bolthole," Dana said, fingers flying over the keys. "There's a few in the betweenways around here."

"Betweenways?" Hugo asked, still staring round.

Dana made an impatient noise. "Marilyn really didn't tell you anything, did she?"

"I chose not to ask," Hugo ground out, trying to convince himself it was true.

Dana sighed, peering at data. "They're from when Haven was just a bunch of long-range freighters welded together. The betweenways were made so people could get about. They run through the foundations of the whole colony. Mostly they're abandoned now, or only used by maintenance or recycling level workers. But some people use them when they're running from something."

"And who keeps them so lovingly stocked?" Webb asked, pulling open another locker to reveal shelves of belt knives and night-sticks.

"Haven has its own fugitives," Dana muttered. "Some folk take advantage of them rather than reporting to the Elders. If you know who to talk to…and you've not done anything too bad… you can find somewhere to survive."

"Survival is big business," Webb murmured, almost to himself, pulling one of the knives from its sheath and examining the keen edge.

"So this is where you've been living?" Hugo looked at the rumpled palate with a raised eyebrow.

"At least I don't have to beat metal for it," she muttered.

"Will you two stow it, just stow it already?" Webb said, slamming the locker door shut.

"Webb -"

"We need to act quick," Webb continued, ignoring him. "Shut off your wrist panel."

"What?"

"Just do it," Webb said tapping commands into his own. "Plenty of folk have the comm number for mine and if they have that they can get yours and they can track us. Shut it down."

Hugo watched the fevered way Webb powered his panel down and did as he was told.

"Aren't you being just the tiniest bit paranoid?" Dana said.

"Paranoid?" Webb let out a bitter bark of laughter. "Don't you get it? It's over. It's all over. We are officially screwed."

"No we're not," Dana said, face set as she worked through more data on the workstation.

"You don't even have the first damn clue how much trouble we're in, do you?" Webb said. "Bryce will tell the Enforcers. *Everyone* will be out for our skin. We can't go back to the boarding house, we can't go back to the yard. All we can do is try and get to Nod and get the hell away."

"I don't understand," Hugo said, keeping his face blank though the sinking feeling inside him was as powerful as a vacuum.

"You've never understood," Webb said, rubbing his temples. "That's the problem. Don't you see? Your little stunt at the workshop? A crime. Me getting you out of it? Another crime. Walton Bryce now has a right to our necks. If we're lucky enough for him to aim at the neck first, that is."

"You're scared of that creep?" Dana snorted.

"Yes I am," Webb said, exasperated. "He's a *citizen*. He is owed justice and will fucking get it unless we run. Run fast and run now."

"I'm not going anywhere," Dana said.

Webb threw his hands up in the air. "Fine. You two stay and get your asses handed to you if you want. I'm done."

"Webb," Hugo said again, reaching to stop him heading for the hatch but the younger man shook him off.

"I mean it, Hugo. It's over. When I agreed to this whole poxy venture it was because I thought you were actually going to listen to me."

"I did -"

"You did? When? Ok, I might have expected this sort of stunt from her," Webb pointed at Dana. "She thinks she knows what she's doing because she's gal pals with Harvey. Though if Harvey really gave a shit about her she would have warned her off ever setting foot in this place." Dana made an outraged noise but Webb wasn't stopping. "But you?" he glowered at Hugo. "You heard everything I said, I know you did. You saw that User getting what he owed beaten out of him by Sol. You saw Ribble nearly taking my head off for welching on Jazz. This is Haven justice, Hugo, and it's out for us now. All three of us. And there's no getting away unless we escape the whole damn place."

"I'd heard enough about you to know you were reckless and short-sighted," Dana said after a long pause. "But I'd never pegged you for a coward."

Webb went very still. "Little girl, the amount I care what you think of me would not fill a blask glass. I only wish I knew as little as you seem to, then I might actually think I stand a chance of getting the hell away in one piece."

"*Dana.*" She had opened her mouth to speak again but Hugo's barked command stopped her. "Dana Hugo," he continued in a low voice. "You don't get to say anything more here. Webb is right. The mission is over and it's our fault."

He could see his sister's anger war with her doubt in her face. Her anger won. She span back to the workstation with a huff. "So the Enforcers will be on the watch for us. So what? Not like I was planning on introducing myself to them anyway."

Webb laughed again. "If you think you're going to find anything on the Ghosts or Ariel now, you're a spanner short of a toolkit. We'll be blacklisted. Our faces will be reeling across all the comm and embargo boards right now. No one will talk to us or even see us without yelling for the Enforcers or trying to drag us to Bryce themselves."

"How does he know you?" Hugo asked.

"Who?" Webb said, rubbing his eyes.

"Bryce."

The younger man's look slid to the wall. "Webb…the original Webb screwed him over good."

"How?"

Webb's expression softened. "Kinjo. Remember Kinjo?"

Hugo blinked. He remembered the midshipman from the *Zero*. She was small but fierce, with earnest eyes, and a good heart despite everything she ended up doing. Devoted to the original Webb. Irrevocably crushed when they lost him. "She was from Haven…"

Webb nodded. Hugo saw him glance at Dana who was pretending not to listen. "Her father worked in the yards. He died in debt. Bryce took Kinjo as payment."

"To work in the workshop?"

Webb nodded. "She was five years old. Her family let him take her."

Dana's fingers stilled on the keyboard. The only sound was the fan creaking in its vent.

"I…he…" Webb shook himself, looking pained. "Webb stole her away when he was at the workshop trying to make a deal for an engine part."

"He rescued her," Hugo murmured.

The clone shrugged. "Not in Bryce's eyes. Not in the colony's eyes, either. When I first came here I made damn sure to stay out of his way. But now," Webb straightened himself. His look was steady but grim. "Busting you guys out of his workshop has put the last nail in my coffin as far as Walton Bryce is concerned. I can never come back to this colony, do you understand? Never."

"I'm sorry."

Are you, Commodore? Oh, well that's alright then."

Hugo flinched.

Webb made a dismissive gesture at them both. "Good luck, guys. I'm outta here."

"I don't think you are," Dana said softly.

"What do you mean?"

She turned the display of the workstation round. Webb took a step closer to the screen, face falling. Hugo's heart sank further. Dana had hacked into a camera feed from the docks. Nod was berthed in the left of the shot. Enforcers hung round her, conversing with some dock workers who were consulting panels and checking the ship's reg-strip. There were two technicians working on the door lock.

"They're impounding her," Webb muttered.

"They're what?" Hugo peered closer just as the technicians got the door open and the Enforcers pushed past them into the ship. "They can't do that."

"Yes they can. You've violated your probation and I helped you. We're officially blacklisted. I just didn't think the word would get to the docks that quickly."

"What does that mean?" Hugo said.

"We're fucked."

"No we're not," Dana said coolly, going back to typing.

Hugo could see Webb struggling to come up with a curse foul enough and stepped between them. "We are not arguing again. We need to think of a plan of escape."

"I told you, I'm not leaving without that blade," Dana said. Hugo started to argue, but she talked over him. "When we have Ariel, I can get us out of here."

"Oh, everything's ok," Webb muttered. "Hugo Junior has a plan."

"How can you get us out?" Hugo asked his sister.

"On the *Phoenix*."

Hugo blinked. "You have Marilyn's ship?"

"Uh-huh," Dana smiled over her shoulder. "And she's not in any public dock either. She's safe and won't be found. I will be using her to get away, but only when I have that blade hog-tied in the brig. So you can either help or you can hang around this bolthole until I'm done. Your call. I honestly couldn't care either way so long as you don't get in my way."

"Dana," Webb said. "Where's that ship?"

She looked at him calmly. "I'm not telling you. It will leave when I leave. That's the end of it."

"Damnit," Webb shouted. "I saved your life back there."

Something flickered in Dana's eyes a second then they hardened again. "We'd've escaped somehow. It was your choice to come after us and antagonise someone Webb had already made an enemy of and then threaten to blow everyone up."

"Listen," Hugo stepped up to his former commander before he could respond. "Webb, I'm sorry," he said in a low voice. The burning eyes swung to him. "I'm sorry we did this. You were right, I have been listening but I haven't been thinking. Marilyn...I mean Harvey...I've been trying...but she's all I can think of."

Webb's face softened.

"We're going to find this man," Hugo continued. "He's hurt too many people I care about. Stay here if you want, I won't think any less of you. Dana and I will -"

Webb shook his head. "You idiots won't last ten minutes now you're blacklisted."

"We'll manage," Hugo said. "I'm sorry I got you involved. I may have been...short-sighted," Webb rose his eyebrows but Hugo dogged on, "but I need to do this. We - " he said, glancing at his sister whose jaw was set in a way he knew his was when he was determined, "- need to do this."

Webb looked defeated. The anger had evaporated from his eyes to leave an emptiness and something Hugo thought might be hurt. It cut Hugo like a knife but the fire of purpose was starting to burn inside him again and he clung to it.

"You'll get me out of here?" the clone asked Dana quietly. "Once it's done?"

She turned in her chair and met his eye. "I will."

Webb closed his eyes. His fingers instinctively went to touch the scars but he visibly stopped himself and rubbed his forehead instead. Hugo tasted guilt again but held his tongue.

"Fine," Webb said. "We'll need some sort of miracle to find the bastard now. But the quicker we do the quicker we're out of here."

Hugo nodded, spirits lifting. "Dana," he said. "Did you get anything out of Bryce's systems?"

Dana didn't look at them but he saw her fighting a smile. "I just might have."

"What is it?" Hugo said, coming over and looking at the data on her screen for the first time.

"Credit records," she mumbled.

"Bryce doesn't use credit," Webb said, coming forward. "He's never left this colony in his life."

"He might not," Dana continued. "But the bloodgrease traders do. And it appears he likes to keep tabs on their accounts, just like our unfortunate friend in the basement."

"He'll just be tracking it to make sure he gets what he's owed in labour and luxuries," Webb muttered.

"He could be using it to get haemorrhoid cream for all I care," Dana said. "All that matters is that he was monitoring all bloodgrease traders' credit streams and one of them has to be the Ghosts."

"Which one?" Hugo prompted, peering at the data as she scrolled through it but unable to see any patterns.

"Well I don't know, do I?" Dana retorted. "I'm not a broker.

I can see that he was dealing with at least three different rings," she pointed at a loose grouping of numbers then two more. "And some of these are account codes…I think," she said, pointing at yet more numbers. "From what Harvey said, the account codes will be able to tell us more than anything else."

"Webb," Hugo said, looking up at the clone who had gone very quiet. "You think Jazz might be able to make something of all this?" Webb was still peering at the screen. "What is it?"

"Part of this account code," Webb said, pointing. "That's our yard's ID…Sector 4's shipyard."

Dana shrugged one shoulder. "I guess yards need credit to trade off-colony for materials."

"Yeah," Webb said. "But these are Sectors 2 and 3's accounts," he pointed to some more streams. "Notice anything?"

"I'm not a poxy broker," Dana snapped again and Hugo put a hand on her shoulder to quiet her.

"The amounts are larger in Sector 4. Much larger," Hugo said. Webb nodded.

"But what does that mean?" Hugo said.

Webb shrugged. "I don't know enough to tell you."

"We need Jazz," Dana said.

"And how exactly can we speak to her now that you have so conveniently got us blacklisted?"

"She wouldn't turn you in," Dana said giving him a narrow glance.

Webb frowned. "I don't know what you think you know, but un-think it. Jazz is a citizen, one who has probably done too much for us already."

"She cares for you," Hugo put in mildly. "She would want to help."

Webb gave him a searching look and Hugo kept his face blank. Webb heaved a sigh. "Fine, I'll try and get a message to her, but it will have to be next shift, she'll be at the clinic now. And if she tells me to get fucked I will be doing just as she says."

"We're getting close," Hugo said.

Webb held up a hand. "Don't get ahead of yourself, Commodore. We don't know what Jazz will find or even if she'll look. But we can try. And in the meantime, I'm beat. We should rest."

Δ

Webb knew he would dream of black eyes in a pale face that night, but even knowing it would happen didn't stop him sitting up in the dark, sweating and breathing like he'd done the run from the workshop all over again. The lighting panel was turned down to its lowest setting and he could only just make out Hugo and Dana's forms huddled in blankets on worn pallets in the dark.

He took a moment to get his breathing under control then lay back down, pushing his sweaty hair back from his face and listening to the whirr of the fan. He rubbed his brand absently, wondering whether it might be worth trying to get it lasered off now it was useless.

Then he remembered how his skin didn't seem to respond to the lasers and turned over to try and get away from the thought. He reached out in the dark and touched his fingertips to the wall, imagining he could feel all of Haven pulsing behind it. He hated the place, he was sure of it. The memories he'd inherited were not happy ones and his own were even worse. But now he was facing exile…he realised how he'd come to think of this place as home. In an Orbit in which he didn't feel like he could ever belong, this colony had given him the chance to scratch together some semblance of a life. He admitted to himself now that when he'd run away and left Jazz before they'd closed their business deal, he hadn't wanted to leave…his fear had just overridden everything else. He'd done nothing but drift since.

He chewed his lip. When Hugo had turned up at his door, deep down, he had been secretly pleased for a direction.

He sat up with a sigh, knowing there was no point in trying to go back to sleep while his head was in this place. He peered at the chrono on the workstation and figured Jazz should be back from the clinic. He grabbed one of the disused wrist panels off the shelf and eased himself out the hatch as quietly as he could. Neither Hugo nor his sister stirred. They both talked tough, but this had to be taking it out of them.

He pushed those thoughts aside, determined to stay angry with them and straightened up in the dark passage outside the bolthole. A shiver ran over his skin but he made himself take a few paces down the silent betweenway before booting up the wrist panel.

The light made him blink and illuminated a little of the ancient passage. The screen was cracked and the display took a few determined jabs to get it to obey. Either he'd picked a very old panel or Harvey's friends didn't care much about keeping the bolthole well stocked.

Eventually he found the old hardware's equivalent of a communicator and punched in Jazz's code from memory. It flashed *'Connecting'* for long enough to convince him Jazz was either asleep or not answering the unidentified number when the flash faded to a steady green light and Jazz's voice came from the tinny speakers.

"Who's that?"

"Jazz, it's me."

"Ezekiel? What the hell? I've been trying to get you for hours but your comm's off. What the hell has happened?"

"Yeah, sorry," Webb said, wondering where to start. "Something…kinda…came up." He was so familiar with Jazz's silences that he could tell the one that met this comment was a disdainful one. "Look," he began.

"Don't," the broker said, then, after a sigh. "Don't explain. You don't have to. But I will let you know that your little stunt at that workshop is all over the newsreels. They've put up pictures too. Whatever you were planning, you should give it up and run."

Webb chewed on his lip. "They've impounded *Nod*."

Another silence. "That's not good."

"No. No it's not. Look, Jazz, I agree with you. We should run. But we can't so…we're not. Not yet."

"Zeek," Jazz began, a warning in her tone but Webb cut her off.

"Hugo is determined. I still owe it to him and his fruit-loop of a sister to try and help them survive this idiotic venture. Plus, Dana is now my only way out of this colony with my neck still in working order."

She sighed. "What are you going to do?"

Webb hesitated. "Bryce had trader data. Account data by the look of it."

"Is that so?" Jazz said a little too casually.

"It might be the key to finding the Ghosts," Webb said, trying to sound more hopeful than he was. "Would you take a look at these numbers, see if they tell you anything?"

There was another long pause and Webb wondered whether he could sense more of their friendship crumbling away. "I can take a look, if you really think it will help."

"If it doesn't," Webb said after a shaky breath. "Maybe I can convince the Hugo duo to give this up and we can get out of here."

"You'll be gone for good this time." It wasn't a question.

"Where should I meet you?" Webb asked after an awkward silence.

"I'll come to you. It's safer. Where are you?"

Webb frowned and stared around the dark passage. "Do you know I haven't the faintest damn clue. I'll see if this wrist panel can tell me," he said, looking at the old locater without much hope.

Another sigh from Jazz. "I'll find you. Keep that panel on. My tracker should be able to find it. But we'll have to be quick because I'm due in the clinic again next shift."

"Great. And…Jazz?"

"Yes?"

"Thank you."

She sighed again. "Just try and not threaten to blow anyone

else up before I get there, ok?"

Webb smiled as the connection cut then rubbed his eyes, took a breath and ducked back in the bolthole.

"Rise and shine," he said, keeping his voice clipped.

"Wha?" Dana grumbled, sitting up and blinking.

"You wanted progress," Webb said, flicking the switch on the lighting panel and flooding the room. "Jazz is on her way to see if this data of yours is actually going to help us any."

Dana muttered darkly and shoved back her blankets. Hugo had already rolled his up and was putting them away in one of the many cupboards. As soon as Dana had shoved hers away she resumed her place at the workstation.

"Harvey never told me about these betweenways," Hugo murmured as he pulled open a door next to the lockers to reveal a cramped washroom.

"Maybe you should have asked her more questions," Dana said.

Hugo glared at his sister and shut the washroom door behind him.

"Hey, Dana," Webb said after a moment. "Your brother's a good man, you know. You should cut him some slack."

"You think you know him. You don't. He's just like the others."

Webb gave it up and helped himself to a Nutripak, slumped cross-legged on the floor and tried to see what sort of specs the wrist panel had. Hugo came out of the washroom with the ends of his hair still damp and stood over Dana to watch her work, his face clouded. Webb was momentarily startled by how similar they looked when they were concentrating.

He shook his head and turned his attention back to the wrist panel. He was just beginning to suspect that it didn't have a range wide enough for Jazz to be able to track them down when it beeped.

Webb activated the comm "Jazz?"

"Zeek? My tracker says I'm right on top of you. Where the hell are you?"

"What can you see?"

"I don't know…relay sheds? Storage bunkers?"

"Sit tight, we'll come get you."

"I'll go," Dana said, already heading for the hatch. "You'll only get lost."

Webb and Hugo didn't say anything and barely looked at each other until Dana climbed back through the hatch with Jazz in tow. The broker blinked around the bolthole, but Dana ushered her straight to the workstation.

"It's all there," she said.

Jazz threw Webb an unreadable glance then sat at the workstation and started typing. He came and leaned over her shoulder as she frowned at the numbers.

"Does it mean anything to you?"

"Yes," Jazz said.

Hugo came forward with Dana crowded around the screen too.

"What do you see?" Hugo asked.

"Is Sector 4 looking weird to you?" Webb said.

"It all looks weird to me. The refinery shouldn't have this much credit. And there's no legitimate reason for them to transfer it to the Sector 4 shipyard."

"That's what they're doing?" Webb asked.

Jazz nodded

Dana straightened up. "Why wouldn't a refinery have credit? Don't they deal the bloodgrease?"

"Not for credit," Jazz said. "Refineries don't need credit. They only deal on-colony."

"Or are supposed to," Hugo said. "This must be illegal credit from the traders selling it in the Orbit."

Jazz shook her head in disbelief. "If the Elders knew about this…"

"They don't? Surely they know people trade this stuff off-colony?" Webb said.

"They do," Jazz said. "And they let it happen since the traders normally give them their fair cut. But I've never seen Orbit bloodgrease trade rack up these sorts of amounts. And none of it is going to the Elders."

"Bloodgrease traders with more credit than they should have…" Dana said. "This is what Harvey found."

"We don't know that yet," Webb said.

"This is big," Dana said, looking at Jazz's face. "No one steals or lies round here. Smuggling credit? And lots of it?"

"It's big," Jazz said.

"We may have stumbled into some serious shit here, guys," Webb said into the silence that followed.

"Can you tell anything else?" Hugo asked, light back in his eyes. "Who in the shipyard the credit has gone to or why?" Hugo asked, still peering at the numbers like he was forcing them to make sense.

Jazz shook her head. "I can't. But to shift this kind of money with no one noticing? They'd need a broker. The broker would know everything."

"Can you tell who the broker is?"

"I already know who it is. I can tell from the transfer signatures."

"Who?"

Jazz looked between them all. "She's a friend."

"So?" Dana said.

Jazz's face hardened. "So, it's bad enough that I've found this out. I'm not going to drag her into some Outsider's crusade."

"Jasmine," Hugo began and Webb could see him fighting to keep his voice calm.

Webb held up a hand. "Hang on," he said. Both Dana and her brother were standing with shoulders tensed and arms crossed, determination etched into their faces. He wondered if they knew how alike they looked then shook it away. "Just, back off you two, ok? Jazz?"

"Zeek," Jazz said, keying in commands and the screen went blank. "I think you'll agree I've risked a lot already."

"We just want to talk to her. That's all. She doesn't even need to know you're involved."

"We're not going to report her to anyone," Hugo said.

"No, but I should." Jazz said, staring at the blank screen.

Webb chewed the inside of his cheek. "Just let us speak to her. You don't know, maybe someone's got a hold on her and is making her do all this. Maybe we can help her."

Jazz's usually calm face was drawn. "Fine," she said eventually. "She's called Celeste. We'll talk to her. But I'm taking you to her to speak in person. Nothing's going through comms that can be tracked."

"No problem," Webb said. "Anything you say."

"And if I want you to leave," Jazz said. "You do it. Or I'll turn you in myself."

"Whatever you say," Webb said again, keeping his face blank, despite the claw of hurt that hooked itself inside him at the look in Jazz's eyes. "Consider us at your mercy. Right, guys?"

Dana and Hugo nodded.

"Thank you," Hugo said, already going to the lockers to retrieve his cap and weapons.

Dana didn't say anything and Webb wasn't sure he liked the calculating look in her eye.

X

Dana led the way back through the labyrinth of dark between-ways. Jazz followed her and Webb followed Jazz. He could tell even in the near dark the broker was tense. Hugo was close on his heels, hurrying them on with muttered orders.

Even Webb had to admit this felt like they were finally on to something, but when they had returned to the gloom of Haven, he was taken over again by the sensation that time didn't pass on this colony. The light stayed the same, the smell stayed the same and every shift was followed by another.

Hugo telling him to hurry snapped him out of his thoughts and he trotted to catch them up. They returned to where they'd left the mopeds. Webb examined the two they'd stolen and removed the only part of their electronics he thought could be tracked, grinding the microchips under his boot heel. Hugo started his moped without flinching but as Webb sat on his own with Jazz climbing on behind him, he couldn't completely suppress the wash of guilt.

"You're already blacklisted, Webb," Dana said, looking at him with an arched brow. "Stealing that thing's hardly going to make a difference."

"This could have been someone's livelihood," Webb said, fighting to keep his temper.

"Shall we go?" Dana said, infuriatingly calm.

Webb refrained from answering, not even mollified by the warning glare Hugo shot his sister. He turned on his engine and followed the Hugos out of the lean-to. It was mid-shift again and mercifully quiet in the twisting, narrow streets.

"Will this broker talk to us?" Dana called to Jazz but Webb shushed them.

"Let's just try and get there without getting spotted first, shall we?" he called over the whining of the engines. Jazz directed them with instructions muttered into his ear. Her arms were warm around his waist but he felt too guilty to enjoy the feeling.

It was almost two hours before Jazz was tapping his shoulder and saying in his ear to slow down.

It was brighter here. He blinked and looked up and was startled to see they had come right up to the outskirts of the Planning District. Spires and towers, all illuminated in a bright, even green, reared up ahead. Some stretched almost to the hull and were shaped a dozen different ways but all uncharacteristically elegant. He'd never seen it up close before. It was like something from another colony…another world even.

The light from hundreds of windows on dozens of floors, intersecting walkways and banks of floodlights pooled for miles, showing up the harsh lines in the concrete and metal structures around them. He saw for the first time in weeks just how dirty his clothes were.

They left the mopeds behind a storage shed before skirting around the edge of a busy industrial lot, crowded with small stalls surrounded by people bartering or searching through cast-off computer parts. There were buckets of wiring, tables of monitors, displays, stacks of drive housing and circuit boards and memory films everywhere.

"Where's all this come from?" Hugo asked.

"There," Jazz said, indicating the tall buildings. "The Planning District."

"This is the Planning District?" Dana said, looking ahead and eyes widening.

"Not yet," Jazz replied. "Follow me."

"She lives here?" Dana asked in an awed voice as they hurried around the edge of the lot and made for a broad avenue that ran towards the towers.

"She's done pretty well. Officially, she brokers commissions from the Orbit," Jazz said. Webb thought she still looked drawn. "Big ones."

"Why is she involved with the likes of bloodgrease traders?" Hugo said.

"That's what I want to know," Jazz murmured.

The noise of the industrial market place died away as they passed under the first of the brightly-lit spires. Webb watched Hugo and Dana staring upwards as they moved through the towering structures.

"I saw these," Hugo murmured, "from the shuttle when we first arrived. I couldn't figure out what they were."

The district was heaving with people. Nearly all of them wore dark jackets that zipped up to the chin, rather than the coveralls and work-suits of the yard workers. A lot of them were absorbed in hand-held computer panels or the huge street displays reeling yard reports and work schedules. But one or two glances came their way and Webb's skin crawled.

"Stick to the edge," he said as they turned onto another avenue swamped with floodlights. Webb kept them tight against the walls, steering them away from the main body of foot traffic.

"They look…different," Hugo said, looking around at the passersby.

"Less scarred and more awake you mean?" Webb muttered.

"It's amazing," Dana breathed again and took a step out to stare up at the glowing spires, but Webb grabbed her elbow.

"We're not tourists," he said. "And our names and faces will be on those displays so we best stay out of sight."

"What happens here?" Hugo said as they followed Jazz towards a busy intersection.

"Planning," Webb muttered, keeping their pace up.

"These are the shipwrights," Dana said, voice still hushed. "And the systems experts. This is where everything's designed."

Hugo raised his eyebrows but didn't reply. Dana didn't seem to notice, she was too busy trying to catch glimpses into the lower level windows.

"Dana," Webb snapped again. "Stay away from the glass. There are cameras around here."

"I know," Dana snapped. "I'm not an idiot."

"What do you mean, you know?" Hugo said.

"Marilyn told me. This is one of the only two sectors on Haven with integrated, Elder-maintained surveillance."

"What's the other?"

"The Storage District, of course."

Hugo shook his head and Webb couldn't tell if he was impatient or a little impressed.

"But this," she looked around again, eyes shining, "Kale, this is the heart of the colony. This is where everything is dreamt up. Some of the greatest minds in the Orbit are in these buildings."

"You think it would be more organised," Hugo muttered, looking around at the mismatched buildings, open walkways and high-quality but purely functional street displays.

Dana shook her head impatiently. "You still don't understand. They don't need conference halls and banqueting suites like in Sydney. They don't even get paid. They do it for the love of it." Webb stole a glance at Dana and was taken by surprise at the thought that she looked like a completely different person with her face open and her eyes wide in admiration. Webb shook himself and hurried after Jazz.

The broker pulled them up short when the entrance of one of the buildings came in sight, guarded by two Enforcers. They were keeping back several shipwrights who were thronging around looking anxious.

"She's on the fifteenth floor," Jazz murmured.

"Why are there Enforcers on the door?" Webb said.

Jazz shook her head. "I don't know. Maybe she's been found out."

"Can you get us in?"

Jazz didn't answer right away. Webb put a hand on her shoulder, making her jump. "Yes," she said, shouldering herself out of Webb's grip. "This way."

"Will she be expecting us?" Hugo said as they crossed the street and ducked into the shadows down the other side of the building.

"I'm going in alone," Jazz said. "At least to begin with. I might be able to convince her we don't care about the credit, just whose it is."

For once, it only took a look from Webb to convince the Hugos not to argue. Jazz kept her gaze locked ahead as they came to a closed door tucked away between a couple of relay sheds. The buzzing of the electronics inside was loud enough for Webb to almost feel the power in his skin. He watched Jazz type codes into the door's keypad. The door clicked and Jazz pulled it open and the followed her through. The passage beyond was well-lit and Webb again felt himself twitch at the feeling of exposure. He couldn't see any cameras however and followed Jazz as she turned one corner and then another.

They paused when the passage opened into a wider walkway. Windows on either side looked into computer labs with ranks and ranks of workstations with shipwrights and technicians at every one of them. Webb peeked out from under the brim of his cap, despite himself. There were displays of every shape and size, most bigger even than Jazz's, as well as simulators, processors and other top-of the range equipment that all looked custom-made. They rushed by towards a bank of lifts, keeping heads down but all the shipwrights were so absorbed in their work they didn't look up. The ones in the corridors were too busy rushing or checking data as they moved about to spare them a glance.

"They must not check the blacklists here much," Hugo mumbled, though he still kept his head down and his own cap low on his face.

"Don't count on it," Webb said, restraining from fidgeting or glancing into the nearest labs as they waited for the lift.

Finally the doors opened and they hurried in, though he had to hiss at Dana again who was trying to get a better look at a 4D design simulator that took up most of the floorspace in the nearest lab.

The doors opened onto a much quieter level with fewer doors, all numbered. Residential level, Webb guessed. Jazz went straight down the passage to an intersection, looked round the corner, started and pulled back.

"What is it?"

"Get back," she said. "There's more Enforcers at her door. Something's happened."

"We should get out of here," Webb said.

"No way," Dana said. "I've not come all this way to let a lead slip by."

"The minute they see you, you're all done," Jazz said.

Hugo clenched and unclenched his fists. "This can't be it. There must be a way," he crept to the corner and peered round. "There's only two," he said, ducking back out of sight. "We could take them down."

"No," Jazz said, so loud that Webb flinched. "No," she repeated, quieter. "We don't hurt them. They're just doing their job. Look," she said, pinching the bridge of her nose between her thumb and forefinger. "I might be able to get them to leave. Stay out of sight and wait for my signal."

Webb waved Dana and Hugo back and Jazz went round the corner. Webb edged as close to the corner as he could and tried to listen to the conversation between Jazz and the Enforcers but couldn't make out what was said. Soon there was the sound of boots heading their way and Webb shuffled further back towards the lifts. The Enforcers strolled by the junction but didn't look their way and disappeared around another corner. There was a bleep on Webb's wrist panel and the word *clear* flashed up.

Webb still glanced up and down the length of the corridor before waving the other two to follow him and they rounded the corner. His heart fell into his boots. The apartment door was daubed with a black cross. Rivulets of still-drying paint ran down it like oil on the clean white varnish.

Jazz met them just inside the apartment. She was calm but her face was very pale, her hazel eyes heavy. They were stood in an impeccably neat living area, with stylish furniture arranged around the room precisely and with care. There was no clutter on the surfaces and the equipment in the kitchen unit was neatly aligned and sparkling clean. A workstation with a series of gleaming, high-tech displays dominated the room. The keyboards were all arranged by function with no exposed wiring or loose memory films anywhere.

There was a single half-drunk glass of red wine on a table next to the sofa. The rest of the bottle was smashed on the floor, leaving an ugly stain on a rug. The red wine mingled with a trail of blood that started at the sofa and ran to the bedroom door. Bloody handprints were smeared up the jamb like someone had scrabbled to get away. The door was ajar. It was very still, the noise from the district not penetrating the wide plexiglass windows. No one spoke for a few minutes.

"They've cleared the whole floor," Jazz said, words dropping like stones in the silence. "No one's claiming kinship or association, though shipwrights are queuing up to bargain her equipment from Reclaim. The Enforcers have given me a few minutes to try and find them any clues that might be in her systems."

"Is she…?" Dana began, eyes locked on the bedroom door.

Jazz didn't say anything, just stood there looking ashen.

Webb forced himself to move across to the door. He took a breath and pushed the door open with his boot to avoid touching the blood and stepped through. Hugo came up behind him and they both stood still, not breathing.

The cross on the bedroom wall was daubed in the same thick, black paint as on the door. It stretched the whole length of the wall over the bed. The sheets were rumbled and tangled and stained red, but Celeste's body was slumped in the corner of the room, eyes wide open and staring right at them. She was in a nightshirt and house gown. Her hair had been very fair so the blood from the stab wounds made it hang in coppery ropes about her face. Webb could still see a little red wine on the corner of her mouth. He turned and left and Hugo followed him out.

"Don't," Webb said softly, blocking Dana's way. A spark of defiance flashed in Dana's eyes for a minute but then died when she took in the look on her brother's face. She nodded.

"This can't be coincidence," Webb found his voice.

"We should go," Hugo said.

"No," Dana said, but softly. She rubbed her mouth and took a breath and tried again. "No, we can't. Please. We have to see what's in her systems. Can't you see?" she looked between them all. Webb rubbed his damp palms on his trousers and looked longingly at the apartment door. "This is all linked. It has to be. Illegal credit brokering, new bloodgrease trader rings with too much cash and someone going after the people involved?"

"Ariel's not doing this," Webb said, not recognising his own voice as he glanced at the stains of blood where Celeste had been dragged from the sofa. "This is not the work of a hired blade. This is something else. Something personal."

"It has to be connected," Dana said, voice firm. "There's a big secret here, a nasty one. They tried to silence Harvey, now these people. We find the secret…we find the traders…we find Ariel."

Jazz glanced at the workstation then at the floor.

"I'm sorry," Dana said as she turned to Jazz. "I know you knew this woman. But, you do this one last system check for us and we'll not ask anything more. We'll disappear and you won't hear from us again."

The look Jazz sent Webb's way was like a knife in his belly. "I believe you," she said.

Webb pulled off his cap and ran a shaking hand through his hair. He could feel Jazz's eyes on him and the others' glancing between them both. "You want us gone, Jazz. No matter what you might think. You need to free yourself of me. Please."

Jazz's lips pressed together. Sadness was heavy in her eyes.

There was a moment when Webb felt as lost as he'd felt those awful days when he'd first come to Haven with nowhere else to go. But then Jazz turned towards the workstation and the moment was broken.

She sat down and booted up the machine.

How much time do you need?" Hugo asked, glancing at the door.

"Not long."

"I'll keep watch," Hugo said and went to stand by the door. Dana stood at Jazz's elbow, eyes following the numbers that started to appear on the screen. Webb stood in the middle of the room, trying to not look at the blood.

"This place doesn't look right," Dana murmured as she looked around the new and neat furnishings and equipment.

"This is the place of someone who has credit and ways to spend it," Jazz said. Her voice was flat, either defeated, angry or both.

"Someone's coming," Hugo breathed some moments later and stepped back from the door.

"Quick," Webb said, waving to the bedroom door. Hugo and Dana followed him through to the bedroom and they pushed the door to. Webb put his eye to the gap just as Jazz looked up and an Enforcer came into the room.

"Got anything?"

"Maybe. I need a bit longer."

"There's someone else here," the Enforcer said pulling the apartment door open and a stout figure shambled into the room with grubby coveralls and an uneasy smile.

Webb swore and ducked out of sight. Dana was standing with her back to the corpse looking pale. Hugo frowned.

"Sol," Webb mouthed, then listened as more soft words were exchanged. When the sound of the apartment door shutting behind the Enforcer was heard, Webb flung the door open.

Sol turned at the sound, eyes widening. "What the...?"

"Sol," Webb said. "What the hell are you doing here?"

Sol's face flattened in recognition. "Webb? Ezekiel Webb?" He glanced around the room, taking in Jazz's mild look and Hugo and Dana emerging from the bedroom and moving to block the exit. "I thought you were dead."

"Surprise," Webb said. "Now spill. What are you doing here?"

"What's it to you?"

"Never mind that," Webb said. "You're obviously mixed up in some neck-level shit here, Sol. Don't make it any worse. Tell us what's going on."

A shudder ran over the man. "How much do you know?"

"Just that two people have died under a Black Cross and you've turned up at the scene both times to hurry the Enforcers into closing the case," Hugo said.

"How do you know that?"

"It doesn't matter how we know," Webb said. "Start talking."

Sol shook his head and backed away. "This is none of your business. Believe me, you don't want to…" he frowned again. "What are *you* doing here, anyway?" He glanced over at Jazz who was watching everything silently. "You know each other? And you…" he jabbed a finger at Hugo. "I recognise you. What the hell is going on here?"

Webb folded his arms. "That was my question."

Sol froze. "It's you isn't it? You're the killer from Lunar 1."

"We've not killed anyone," Dana said, coming forward. "What about you?"

"No," Sol, barked, raising his hands. "I ain't touched anyone. I…" He made a wordless noise of frustration, caught sight of the blood and looked away, rubbing his red-rimmed eyes. "You don't understand. Let me have her data drives and I'll be on my way. You can have the rest, I don't care."

"What do you want her data for?" Jazz asked.

"I can't tell you," Sol said, starting to sweat. "I can't tell anyone…not until I have more."

"More what?"

Sol growled and lunged towards the workstation but Webb grabbed him and held him back. Hugo was across the room in a second and helping Webb wrestle the man away from the workstation.

When he went still in their grip he was panting. "I don't know why you're here," he said. "And I don't give a damn. You want to get mixed up in this Ghost crap that's your death wish. Just let me get what I need."

"Ghost?" Webb asked.

Sol's eyes widened. "I didn't say that. You didn't say...you don't know..."

"He knows," Dana said, coming across the room to look him in the eye. "He knows what's going on."

Sol shook his head. "No," he said, voice now shaking. "I don't know. Not enough. Not yet. Let me go, Webb, for the love of God. I need more information...for the Elders...."

Webb glanced at Hugo but his face was a blank mask. "Who are the Ghosts? A new gang? They are, aren't they? *Tell us.*"

"I'm not saying another word," said Sol. "Either let me go, or throw me out the window because it's more than my neck's worth to tell you anything more."

"Webb," Jazz said, standing from the workstation. "I think I have everything we need."

"You found something?"

Jazz nodded.

Sol went pale under the sheen of sweat. "What did you find?"

"Don't tell him," Dana snapped and came forward, drawing her knife.

"What are you doing?" Webb said as Sol again tried to pull away.

"He's seen us here. We have to silence him."

"Whoa, whoa," Webb said, giving Sol over to Hugo and stepping between him and Dana. "Not so fast."

Dana glanced at the door. Everyone froze at the sound of boots in the corridor. They all held their breath, but then the sound faded away again.

"Out the way, Webb," Dana said. "We need to get this done now."

"We're not killing Sol."

"He's here to try and cover all this up," Dana said. "Just like he did in Sector 2. He's involved."

"*I'm not,*" Sol pleaded, still trying to pull out of Hugo's grip. "I swear I'm not. And you thinking that just shows how much you don't know."

"Then tell us," Webb said, turning back to the dealer. "Tell us what's going on. We need to know."

"Why?" he cried. "How do I know you didn't kill these people? Or that the Ghosts didn't send you in to destroy all traces?"

Dana muttered but Hugo shook the man. "Silence, everyone. Dana, back off. Webb, you know this man, yes?"

Webb nodded.

"Do you trust him?"

Sol's imploring eyes locked on Webb's. Webb shook his head. "No. He's a Catiline gang member. But," he said, as Dana twitched. "I believe he's telling the truth. He's scared. He's not here to cover anything up."

"I'm here to find proof," the Patch dealer said, voice steadying.

"Proof of what?" Dana said again.

"Dana," Jazz said softly. "We have enough of our own to go on. We should leave. Whatever this man's business is, it's his own."

Sol straightened and shouldered out of Hugo's grip. "That's right. Get out of here, the lot of you. Leave me to my affairs and I'll leave you to yours."

Hugo looked to Webb and Webb, after a second, nodded. Hugo stepped back.

"No," Dana protested. "We can't trust him. He could ruin everything."

"You're not from here, are you?" Sol asked, eyes narrow and

voice suddenly low and cool. Dana scowled. "I thought not. You," he looked at Jazz. "I don't know how you got mixed up with these Outsiders but if I was you I'd walk away from them and don't look back. They haven't the first clue what they're getting caught up in and they'll drag you down with them."

Jazz didn't look at them. "What are you trying to do? I might be able to help."

Sol sighed, looked at the workstation and brushed a trembling hand over his worried forehead. "I can't tell you. Not yet."

"Good luck to you then," Jazz said and Sol nodded. She turned to Webb. "We're leaving. Now."

Sol stood staring after them as they left. Jazz checked the corridor then waved them out. The Enforcers were stepping off one lift just as they ducked into another. A couple of confused glances was all they got from them before the doors were closing.

"I can't believe we left him alive," Dana said. "He could tell anyone."

"He won't," Jazz said. "He was telling the truth."

"What did you find?" Hugo asked the broker but she shook her head.

"We need to get away from here first. Sol's not going to say anything, but if he was able to find out about this killing, others will, including whoever Celeste was working for."

"If they didn't kill her themselves," Webb muttered.

"They didn't," Jazz said, meeting Webb in the eye. "Not with thc Black Cross. Like you said, this is personal."

Δ

Jazz hurried them to the rear entrance of Celeste's building, then took them a different way back out of the district. She managed to find a way that avoided the wide and teeming walkways, but that did require them to clamber over more relay sheds, duck below ground floor windows and use Webb's multitool to get them through a locked gate or two. It took them a lot longer but Jazz was stiff and the look on her face meant no one argued with her.

Finally, they were back at the mopeds.

"I'll tell you what I found, then I have to go," Jazz said. "I'm already late for the clinic."

"Jazz," Webb started.

"You were right, Webb," she said coolly. "And so was Sol. This is as far as I can go with you. And you promised it would be all you would ask me for."

Webb throat tightened but he nodded.

"What did you find?" Hugo said, not seeing or choosing to ignore the strings of tension tightening in the air.

Jazz broke her locked look with Webb and glanced back at the bright spires of the Planning District. "Celeste was brokering credit that she shouldn't have been. With what you found at Bryce's I'd say we're looking at a ring of bloodgrease traders, though that's more credit than I've ever known anyone make from bloodgrease alone."

"Can you tell what was going on from the credit transfers?"

Jazz shook her head. "All I can tell you is where the credit was going. That might be enough for you to find out everything else you need."

"Where was it going?" Dana said. "Sector 4 shipyard?"

"Not just the shipyard…" Jazz said. "The *Perseverance*."

"What?" Hugo said. "The Service flagship?"

Jazz nodded. "Celeste has it all well coded, but the credit, along with a lot of other information and communication, was all going to Sector 4 yard workers working on the *Perseverance*."

"The workers?" Webb frowned. "Workers don't use credit."

"These ones do," Jazz said, glancing at the chrono on her wrist panel. "And that is already far more than I wanted to know."

"They're Ghosts," Dana breathed. "They must be."

"Thank you," Hugo said to Jazz, face grim but hand outstretched. "I do understand how much you've risked for us."

"I don't think you do," Jazz said, not taking his hand. There was no malice in her face or tone. Just regret. "But I hope you never have to. One last word of advice…" she looked at them each in turn. "That man, Sol, is doing the right thing. He might be involved, he might be scared, he might know too much…but he's trying to find enough evidence to bring whatever is happening here to the Elders. I hope he manages it, though he's in more danger than the rest of us put together. But either way, you need to watch your step. He's doing it for the colony. You're looking into this for yourselves." She held up a hand as Dana bristled and Hugo stiffened. Webb was just cold with guilt. "I'm just warning you. No one will care about your vendetta. They *will* care that you got involved for your own reasons. Get what you need and get out as fast as you can. Whatever is happening under the surface here will break eventually and when it does, you do not want to be in the blast radius."

"We know," Webb said, before the Hugos could say anything. "Thanks, Jazz. For everything."

She pressed her lips into a thin line for a moment then nodded. A hundred things clamoured in Webb's head but he couldn't bring himself to say any of them, especially with Hugo stood by with his eyes narrowed and his sister visibly itching to go.

He sighed and took Jazz by the elbow and stepped her around the corner. She just looked at him.

"I didn't mean for this to happen."

Jazz shook her head. "You've always made your own choices, Zeek."

"You think they're bad choices."

The edge of a smile turned up the corner of the broker's mouth. "Yes. Some of them. Ok, most of them. But a pilot has to chart his own course."

Webb nodded then leant forward and kissed Jazz on the cheek. He ignored the catch in his chest at the familiar smell of coffee and citrus and pulled away with his eyes on the ground. Jazz grabbed his hand before he could go. When Webb looked back, the calm mask had slipped and there was pain clearly burning in her face.

"Just…survive this ok?" she asked. "And get that Ariel off my colony."

Webb felt a thin smile pull at his mouth. "That's a promise."

Δ

Webb looked flushed and pained when he came back round to Hugo and Dana at the mopeds. Hugo heard Jazz's footsteps fade away.

"Are you ok?"

Webb looked at him a moment as if trying to remember where he was then his jaw tightened. "We've got work to do."

"Finally," said Dana. "Come on. We've got to get out to that flagship."

Δ

Hugo let Dana pick their route back, trusting to Webb to call her up if she took them close to well-lit or busy areas. Webb was sombre and the set look on his face brooked no argument when he did. Despite the delays, Dana seemed to be in better spirits, face still grave but her eyes bright.

Hugo was sure his sister felt what he did: that they were getting closer. But, unlike him, she was clearly enjoying the ride.

When they were finally back in the bolthole, they rummaged through the storage lockers for different coveralls, kerchiefs and goggles. Dana took charge, insisting Webb looked too distinctive in a cap and helping him tie a stained dust scarf over his long black hair. Hugo was allowed to keep his cap but given welder's goggles and a scarf to hide the bottom half of his face. They all pulled on gloves.

Dana zipped up a welding tunic over her coveralls and wrapped a kerchief around her neck to hide the lack of brand. Hugo took a couple of disposable lenslights, though he wasn't sure they looked up to much. Webb supplemented his own knife assortment with a nightstick he slung at his hip inside his coveralls.

Dana insisted on checking over them all before they headed out and carried on muttering at them to slump more and not look so tense. Hugo ignored her, knowing she was mainly issuing orders as a way of keeping herself calm. It was something he knew he used to do. Webb ignored her too and they got back on the mopeds without even an exchanged glance. They struck out back the way they'd come from the refinery - back towards Sector 4.

They had to loop round through narrow alleys away from the main thoroughfares and once stop and haul the mopeds over a fence to avoid getting too close to the refinery. Hugo had to shake away the images of blood and black crosses the whole way. He thought of Celeste in her house gown, enjoying her wine before starting at the sound of someone picking her apartment lock.

He shook it away and told himself again that the killings were none of his concern. He was not the only enemy these people, these Ghosts, had made. He remembered the way Webb had talked about the Black Cross on Lunar 1:

"The Black Cross is a symbol. For revenge. For retribution. For the punishment of a grievous and personal sin."

He remembered the eyes of the people he'd killed under it when they'd realised what was happening. Another image, stronger than any other, rose before his eyes. Webb in Doll's basement flat on Lunar 1 before the last war. The original Webb. That day his commander had been angry and scared and determined. His face, normally so quick to smile, had been bleak and his eyes hard with purpose. He'd had a wrong he needed to right. Vincent Marlowe had to die under a Black Cross, by his hand, and know why.

That man was dead now, but his clone carried those same memories and determination. They both knew what they were looking at when they saw a Black Cross. Someone, like them, was out for revenge. They just had to get to the heart of the secrets before the killer finished their work and silenced everyone who could tell them where to find Ariel.

"Pull over here," Webb said and slowed his moped, steering into the thick shadows behind a wall near the shuttle stop for the shipyard. When they cut their engines they could hear the muted roar of the yard and the rattling of shuttles on old rails. The vacuum shield was visible, the stars distant and cold in their spread of blackness.

Hugo swung himself off his moped and they clung close to the wall, flattening themselves into shadows whenever a worker passed within sight. Dana got them right up to the shuttle rails without having to go out into the main walkways. Hugo breathed in the smells of oil, metal and bloodgrease and wondered at how familiar it was.

A shuttle was just pulling away with a heave and a shudder when Hugo grabbed Webb's elbow.

"What?"

Hugo peered into the shadows behind them, holding his breath.

"What is it now?" Dana said.

"There's someone back there," Hugo said, fingering the hilt of his knife. "Stay here. Dana, silence."

They obeyed though Dana twitched with impatience and Hugo crept back along the wall, not letting his steps make any noise. He got to the corner and held his breath, listening hard but all was quiet again. When he dared a glance around the corner there was nothing but shadows and billows of steam stained green from the glow of the track lights.

"Anything?" Webb said as he appeared at this elbow.

Hugo shook his head. "No. But I definitely heard someone."

Webb scanned the alley. "That's the second time it's felt like someone's been tailing us."

"Third," Hugo murmured.

"Third?"

Hugo turned to him. "When we got back from our first shift there was a man stood outside Michalski's, watching us. I thought I saw him at the gate of the shipyard once too."

"What did he look like?" Webb said, visibly trying to hide his growing concern.

Hugo closed his eyes, tried to bring up the vision of the man with the sharp eyes. "Short. Black hair. Not a worker...though I think he had something wrong with his arm."

Webb's face tightened a moment before he shook his head. "That could have been anyone. Still," he said, glancing around the drifting steam and shadows. "I don't like this."

"Me neither. We need to hurry."

He heard nothing more, but that didn't stop him checking over his shoulder several times as they made their way back. Dana stood poised in the shadows, arms folded.

"Right, let's get on that flagship," Webb said, voice tight and eyes scanning the teeming activity of the yard.

"We're just going to walk right through the yard?" Hugo said doubtfully.

Webb nodded, pointing to the section of colony hull next to the vacuum shield which was bristling with ladders, platforms and windowed hatches. "The only way onto the *Perseverance* without a suit is through those airlock tunnels. We don't have drift-work passes so we need to look like we belong with the air-lock teams long enough for me to hack our way through a quiet access hatch."

"And you can definitely do that?" Dana muttered.

"No. But if you've got any other ideas, I'd love to hear them."

Dana scowled but said nothing and then Webb was taking a breath, tucking his hair in his headscarf and striding out over the shuttle rails. Hugo gathered himself and hurried after him.

XI

The foreman at the edge of the welding pits was too absorbed in his quality check to notice three figures slipping through the gates mid-shift. Webb skirted around the edges of the pits and then through the production lines, sticking to the busiest thoroughfares.

"We'll stick out more sneaking around the edge," he muttered in Hugo's ear when they got caught in a bottleneck of workers queuing for access to the airlock tunnels. "Just relax."

Hugo gave himself a mental shake but then cursed and pulled Webb by the elbow to jostle them deeper into the crowd.

"What?" Webb said,

"Lola."

"Who?"

"Foreman Michalski," Hugo clarified. She was barely five feet away, climbing off a moped, hands flicking fingerspeech at a pit worker.

"Shit," Webb said, looking about. "Quick, this way."

Hugo hung his head and followed Webb as he elbowed his way out of the crowd towards the vacuum shield.

"This is too exposed," Dana said as they stepped onto the platform in front of the shield.

"Just keep moving," Webb replied and they followed him along the platform. Giant displays suspended from a series of frames hung between the shield and the yard, scrolling schematics and production figures. Workers hurried back and forth with hand-held panels, making notes and blinking in the starlight reflected off the metal platform. The ship skeletons hung in space, silent and huge against the yawning backdrop outside the shield. The *Perseverance* dominated them all, her hull gleaming silver and her bulk impossibly large against the half-constructed freighters and spaceliners around her. The airlock tunnels anchoring her to the colony branched off her hull like parasitic worms.

Hugo risked a glance back towards the pits and stiffened. "Michalski's looking this way," he said, forcing himself not to break pace.

"Almost there," Webb said, not looking up as they tagged onto the end of a knot of technicians moving toward the airlocks. "Can you see what she's saying with her hands?"

Hugo glanced back as casually as he could. "She's gone."

"Christ Almighty," Webb muttered as they slowed their pace and allowed the technicians to drift ahead. "That could cost us."

"Relax," Dana said. "Even I don't recognise you in the stupid head scarf. Just keep moving."

"We have to get back in the queue," Webb muttered as they drew closer to the lines of workers. "Keep an eye out for Michalski."

"Wait," Dana said as they passed one of the access ladders, reading the information display. "This tunnel goes to the *Perseverance*."

"It's locked," Webb said, pointing at a warning on the display. "Out of order. Come on, we're going to be seen."

"Wait," Hugo said, peering at the little display and then up the ladder to the windowed airlock hatch. "The lights are on in the tunnel."

"So?"

Hugo frowned at Webb. "So, if you were accepting illegal credit for something to do with the construction a ship, wouldn't you want your own way to access her that no one else would be using?"

Webb frowned. "I don't know…"

"He's right," Dana said, looking around. "For once. Quick, while there's no one looking."

"No," Webb said, but Dana was already climbing. Hugo followed. "Hugo, wait! This isn't a good…aw, damnit, I swear you Hugos will be the death of me. Again."

Hugo ignored the comment, satisfied to hear the younger man start climbing behind him. He surveyed the other ladders and platforms, teeming with workers, that fed the honeycomb of air-locks. The workers kept to their ordered lines, made way for each other and barely looked up. He felt like any moment everyone in the yard might turn and see them, but they somehow reached the top without incident. The platform felt even more exposed than the ladder but he concentrated on looking like he was meant to be there by keeping his shoulders loose and his eyes turned away from the yard. Dana examined the dark display next to the door.

"I'm telling you, it's bust," Webb said, peering through the window set in the hatch. "The gravity could be offline. Or it could be breached. We open this hatch, we could be sucked straight into drift."

"The filters are open," Hugo said, pointing at an open grid at the base of the door.

Webb blinked and bent down to put his hand in front of the grid. "Air flow. Weird."

"It's fine," Dana said, still prodding at the panel on the display. "The levels are all normal."

Webb clattered across the platform to peer at the readings. "Son of a bitch," he muttered.

"Where does it attach?" Hugo asked.

"One of the aft shuttle bays," Dana said.

"Get it open."

"Webb," Dana said, stepping back and gesturing toward the control panel. "This is your chance to impress me."

Webb shook his head and set to work on the control panel. Dana bent over his shoulder to watch as Hugo tried not to shift on his feet. He peered out over the shipyard from under the brim of his cap, watching for any goggles or visors turned their way. Finally, the hatch shuddered and opened.

Hugo all but ran through. The air in the tunnel was cold and he shivered, calling at the others to hurry over his shoulder.

"Ok, you were right," Webb said as he trotted to catch him up. "No breach."

"No, no breach," Dana said as she overtook them. "And gravity's on. So why was it locked?"

"Be careful," Hugo said as he increased his pace to match his sister's. He shivered again. The air tasted thin as well as cold. He blinked in the strong light from the ceiling panels and tried to convince himself the growing prickle of nervousness was coming from the low quality air.

The tunnel stretched on and on. They picked up their pace, their boots rattling on the metal flooring in otherwise utter silence. There were viewscreens every few feet and he could see the ships caught in their webs of wires and airlocks and crawling with workers jetting around in drift. The gleaming hull of the *Perseverance* soon started to dominate the view.

Dana was ahead and stopped them once, waiting and listening at a bend in the tunnel, but no one came.

"The tunnel might be empty but there may be workers in the ship," Dana said as they kept going.

"Just remember to act like a worker and we'll be fine," Webb said. "We'll just pretend we took the wrong tunnel."

Finally, they turned around one last bend and saw a hatch into the ship up ahead.

"Wait," Hugo said as they got closer. "Careful." He edged up to the hatch, hand automatically going to his knife and peered through the small viewscreen.

"See anything?" Webb said.

"It's dark," Hugo replied. "Wait... get down." He ducked and the other two dropped with him. He held his hand out for stillness and silence, heart thudding in his chest.

"What?" Webb mouthed, glancing at the hatch.

"Someone's coming..." Hugo said. They all looked around but there was nowhere to hide. Hands went to weapons and the seconds ticked by. Sweat broke out on Hugo's forehead. Another minute passed. No one came through the hatch. Hugo slowly straightened and checked the viewscreen again.

"Quick, Webb. Get this open before whoever it is comes back."

Webb got to work on the control panel whilst Dana and Hugo hovered.

"Any idea where we should even start?" Webb muttered as he worked. "Hell, we don't even know what we're looking for."

"The reason Ariel was hired is on this ship somewhere," Hugo said. "We find that, we find him."

"Get ready," Dana said and there was a hiss and a gust of even colder air and the hatch opened.

They hurried through and it slid shut behind them, plunging them into dimness. The only light was what bled in through the hatch viewscreen. The air tasted crisp and Hugo took deep breaths to clear his head.

"Wait," he muttered as Webb pulled out a lenslight. "Someone's just passed by here. Let's get away from this hatch before we use any light. This way."

Hugo turned to the right, moving as quickly and quietly as he dared, one hand on the metal hull on one side to keep him orientated. His boots thudded on solid metal and he sensed more than saw an open space on their left.

"Where are we?" Dana said.

"Aft engineering," Hugo replied.

"You sure?"

"I approved her specs," Hugo muttered. "Keep quiet."

A dull light was bleeding from somewhere, now picking out the edges of the walkway and some of the hull above them. They rounded a bend and stopped to listen again. The quiet was unbroken apart from a low thrum of air vents somewhere in the dark around them.

"I think we're on our own," Dana muttered.

"Then why is the life support on?" Webb said.

"Quiet," Hugo said again, feeling his heart alone was making enough noise to give them away. "There's light ahead."

They turned another corner and a square of illumination hung ahead. Getting closer, he made out a viewscreen in a door. He held his breath and approached, feeling Dana and Webb keeping close behind. He reached the window and peered through.

"What's through there?" Dana said.

"Shuttle bay," Hugo said. "There's light."

"Workers?" Webb asked.

"No. It's empty."

"Come on then," Dana said. "What are we waiting for?"

Hugo took a breath. "We move in silence. Keep the lenslight off and be ready."

There was mumbled agreement and then Hugo hit the door control. It opened without so much as a whisper and they stepped through into more shadows and sharp air. The shuttles hulked like giant insects in dark. The ceiling was lost in the gloom but the weak light revealed offline control panels and workstations positioned at intervals around the bay. The light was coming from the last shuttle berthed to starboard.

Hugo picked a path towards it, keeping away from the open space in the middle of the bay. A clatter broke the silence and Hugo froze. A muted mutter followed and then the sound of boots.

He ducked down, Dana and Webb doing the same. They crushed themselves behind a workstation as the footsteps approached. The light from a lenslight bounced off the new metal around them and Hugo crouched lower, Webb's elbow digging into his side. The footsteps passed by and Hugo breathed again. He craned his neck and caught a glimpse of a slight figure, white coat back lit with a lenslight, disappearing through the door they'd come through.

They sat in silence for several heartbeats until Webb unwound himself and got to his knees to scan the bay. "Clear," he whispered.

Hugo scrambled up, peered around the stillness and the dark, took another breath and continued toward the light.

They rounded the last shuttle in the row to see its main hatch was open and light was pouring out. The mounting ladder was down.

"What the…?"

"Stay here," Hugo cut Webb off. He made a conscious effort to keep his breathing level as he approached the opening. He felt horribly exposed as he moved into the light, but there was no sound.

He blinked. The shuttle's storage bay was lit by uniform paneling in the bulkheads. He waited but could only hear the steady bleep of equipment. He climbed the ladder, stepped into the shuttle and frowned, a strong smell causing a chill to blossom in his belly. Memory tugged at him. The smell was sharp. Acidic. A workbench with displays and lab equipment that had not been in any shuttle specs was installed along the port bulkhead. A large refrigeration unit was standing against the hatch to the engine room. Displays over the workbench blinked numbers and indecipherable diagrams. A digital microscope was set up at one end, a stand of samples to its side and a clutter of hand-held panels, test tubes and a silver tray of scalpels, tweezers and syringes took up the rest of the workbench. The door to the small surgical bay in the stern was open. The gurney was empty and clean and white, but all the monitoring equipment was on and blinking.

"Hugo," came Webb's whisper. "What's going on?"

Hugo shook himself. "All clear."

Webb and then Dana climbed up and joined him, staring round. Dana's nose wrinkled. Webb had gone pale, his eyes fixed on the tray of surgical equipment.

"This isn't a shuttle…" Dana said.

"Not any more," Hugo said.

"Someone's put a lab in here? Why?"

"Not for anything good," Webb said, voice low.

"I know that smell," Dana muttered looking around.

"Phozone," Webb said

Hugo jolted. "For preserving organic samples…" he said. His mission on Earth with the original Webb all those years ago came flooding back. "It can't be…"

"What?" Dana said. "It can't be what?"

"Relax," Webb said, taking a step towards the workbench and peering at one of the displays. "Your brother's just being paranoid. Plenty of labs use it."

"But *why* is there a lab in this shuttle? And what sort of lab is it?" Dana said, wondering up to the surgical bay and peering round the blinking monitors.

"Got me," Webb said narrowing his eyes at one of the diagrams on the display. "Biology was never Webb's strongest subject."

Hugo suppressed a shudder. The clone's whole stance had changed. He was standing stiffer and his face had taken on a hard edge.

"Keep looking," Dana said, pacing around and pulling open lockers of equipment.

Webb's gaze had once again fixed on the tray of scalpels. Hugo shook himself, unclenched his teeth and forced himself to look around. He crossed to the refrigeration unit and pulled it open.

"Hugo?" Webb's voice sounded from far away. "What is it?"

Hugo didn't reply. His knuckles burned from the tightness of his grip on the handle. He felt Webb come up behind him and look over his shoulder.

"What the…?" Webb said. "Is that…are those…?"

"What?" Dana hurried over then stopped. "Is that… is that a *heart*?"

Hugo swallowed. His throat had gone very dry. "This one's a liver," he said, pointing at one of the other transparent cases containing a dark lump of glistening tissue. "And this is a lung."

"Organs?" Webb said. "Human organs? Are we really seeing this?"

"They look real," Dana said, leaning in.

"They are real…" Hugo said.

"This is it," Dana said, voice quickening. "This is what the Ghosts are hiding."

"*What* is it?" Webb stammered, looking around the lab again. "Why the hell is there a fridge of lungs on this damn shuttle?"

"Who are you?"

They all span round. A slight, oriental man in a white lab coat stood in the hatchway, eyes and mouth widening as he took them in. Hugo stood rooted to the spot for a broken second, recognition teasing the edge of his awareness, but that second was all it took for the man to turn and scramble back down the ladder.

"Get him," Hugo shouted and Webb sprang after him, Dana at his heels. Hugo's boots hit the deck just as Webb threw himself on the stranger and wrestled him to the ground. There was scuffling and curses then Dana was on them and helping Webb drag the man to his feet.

"Release me," he barked. "Help," he yelled at the top of his lungs. "Help, intruders!"

"Silence him," Hugo shouted and Webb clamped a hand on his mouth. They dragged him back towards the shuttle and slammed him against the hull.

Hugo pulled his knife. "You'll be quiet, understand?"

The sweating man's eyes widened. He breathed heavily through Webb's hand and nodded. "Who the hell are you?" Hugo growled.

Webb took his hand away and the man took a couple of panicked breaths then his face twisted with anger. "Let me go now," he demanded. "Or you will regret this."

"Holy shit," Webb said, his own mouth dropping open. "It's Yoshida."

"Who?" Hugo frowned, peering again at the man's face.

"Dr. Yoshida," Webb croaked. "LIL's cloning researcher."

Hugo stared. Heat surged through him and for a moment all he knew was the feel of it. When he could focus again, Yoshida's eyes were flicking between them all then fixed on Webb.

"Oh my God," he breathed. "It's you... it's you isn't it?"

"No questions from you," Dana said, shifting her grip on the researcher's coat and pulling out her own knife. "Just answers."

"Dana, wait," Hugo said. "Get him back in the shuttle. Before anyone sees."

Dana and Webb bundled Yoshida up the hatch ladder and onto the shuttle deck. Hugo followed and punched the control. The hatch hissed shut and he stood over the cowering researcher, breathing heavily through his nose to try and keep himself restrained.

Yoshida got to his feet, hands working together and sweat gleaming on his forehead, but the whole time his eyes were glued to Webb. The clone had taken a step back, arms folded and a dangerous look on his face.

"Dr. Yoshida Jun," Hugo ground out, not recognising his own voice. "You are a registered fugitive." The shaking man's eyes finally turned to him. "You are wanted for war crimes."

"War crimes?" he said, straightening himself, though his voice shook. "I am a scientist."

"You're a criminal."

The small man drew himself up. "I advanced genetic science to levels never before imagined. I achieved what no one before me had. I made *him*," he pointed at Webb who stood there in stony silence, pale apart from two high spots of colour on his cheeks. Yoshida paused and took a step closer to Webb, drinking him in. Webb stiffened. "You...I can't believe it's you. Let me look at you..."

"I wouldn't get too close," Webb muttered.

"You were my triumph," Yoshida breathed, not listening, eyes shining.

"I wouldn't go that far," Webb muttered. He tapped his temple. "You screwed up in here, remember?"

Yoshida reached out a hand but Webb tensed, raising his chin and the man let it drop and instead rubbed his palms on his lab coat. "I didn't think I'd ever see you again. How do you function? Do you -"

"Enough," Hugo thundered. "Get away from him."

"None of this matters," Dana spat. "His friends could turn up any second. You," she said, pointing her knife at the researcher, "tell us what's happening here."

Yoshida backed against the hatch, taking quick breaths and watching Dana's knife.

"Answer her," Hugo said.

The researcher's shaking stopped and emotion loaded his face. "*You* dare come here and demand answers from me? You're Kaleb Hugo. You took away everything I worked for. I'm now having to continue my work in this hell hole, begging funding from the worst kind of people and hiding my lab in a construction site."

"These Ghosts are funding you, aren't they?" Hugo said.

"I'm not telling you anything. You can't touch me here, Serviceman. You have no power here."

"Your illegal cloning experiments are taking place on a Service flagship, Doctor."

"This is neutral space," Yoshida said. "You can do nothing."

"Don't be so sure," Hugo said, voice low.

"You lie," the researcher replied. "This is not your world, Commodore. You should leave. Now. Leave me in peace to continue my work."

"Your work being cloning organs for a Haven smuggling ring?" Webb said, quietly. Silence rippled about them a moment. Hugo saw Yoshida swallow.

"You wouldn't understand. You can't understand."

Hugo felt his fingernails digging into his palms. "Who's paying you, Yoshida? The Ghosts?"

Yoshida's jaw tightened. "They are not to be taken lightly. And they are here on this ship, with me along with my own personal guard. You should act with more caution, Commodore."

Dana shifted, hand working the handle of her knife. Yoshida's eyes flickered to Webb once more. There was an open, almost hungry look in his eyes. Webb shifted and glared.

When Hugo looked back to the researcher he realised, too late, that his hand had slipped in his pocket and he was clicking something.

The hatch opened and the researcher hurled himself out before Dana could grab him.

"*After him*," Hugo called. By the time Hugo was down the ladder, Yoshida had picked himself up from the floor and was running across the bay. He had a head start this time and was outstripping them, shouting into a wrist panel as he went.

Dana and Webb were ahead but the fire of fury burned in Hugo's gut and pushed him faster and he was soon at their heels. The researcher had ducked between the berthed shuttles and fled into the dark. Dana yelled and Webb overtook her, skidding around a workstation and pulling out a lenslight.

Hugo caught up just in time to see the researcher's coat disappear through another door. They pelted after him. They tore through the door into another cavernous space, pitch black apart from low light from a number of muted displays and the beam of Webb's lenslight. It flashed off towering metal cylinders and stretches of dark control panels and a rigid web of anchor cables keeping the giant structures in place.

"Engineering deck," Hugo called. "How does he have the run of the place?"

No one answered as their boots rattled on a walkway that spanned the dizzying space, casting about for any sign of Yoshida. They all scrambled to a halt, breathing hard and Webb flashed the lenslight around.

"Where did the little weasel go?" Webb panted.

"There," Dana called and took off along another walkway. They ran after her and Webb's light picked out a darkened exit. "He went down here," she called. "Come on."

They picked up their pace and hurled themselves through the

exit only to skid to a halt as three men with lenslights and grim expressions rounded the corner ahead. They were all badly scarred, one was missing an ear and they all had the same nothing-to-lose air about their movements. One shouted and pointed then they were running towards them, pulling weapons as they came.

"Ghosts," Webb cried. "Fucking *run*." He turned and did just that. Hugo swore and followed.

"Split up. Webb, that way," Hugo called as they reached the walkways over the yawning engineering levels. "Dana, follow me." He turned to the left and heard Webb's boots rattle in the other direction. He risked a glance over his shoulder and saw his sister was close behind.

"Get the tall one alive," Yoshida's shout could be heard from somewhere behind them. "Kill the other two."

"Kale, go left again," Dana called as they came to another junction.

"I'm not leaving you," he growled.

"You got any better ideas?" she said then skidded off to the right and started climbing a ladder to another level in the web of walkways.

"Dana," Hugo called but then a lenslight flashed in his eyes and one of the Ghosts was bearing down on him. He bolted left, found another ladder and scrambled up it, his pursuer cursing at his heels. There was a clang as a night stick crashed into the rungs just below his ankles.

He hauled himself onto the next level and ran, trying to picture the ship's engineering schematics. The Ghost was catching up. The beam from the light sliced holes in the darkness and illuminated the bulkhead blocking his way. He skidded to a halt, breathing heavily, looked around and climbed up on the walkway's railing. There was an angry shout as his pursuer reached him, then Hugo flung himself into the darkness.

As the seconds and cold air sped by and his reaching hands grabbed nothing, he panicked that he had miscalculated, but then with an almighty wrench, he caught hold of an anchor cable. His sweaty hands almost slipped but he gathered all his strength and flung one elbow over, then another. He dangled there over nothing, trying to get breath into his lungs and make the black spots stop dancing in his vision. When he could see again he looked around. The Ghost was cursing from the walkway, scanning around for a way to reach him. For the first time Hugo was grateful for the no-guns precedent.

"Dana," he cried, seeing her on the level above. A Ghost was closing in behind her but she was concentrating on staying out of reach of his long knife and didn't see the one who had broken off his pursuit of Webb to lurk in the shadows near the next ladder.

Webb's warning rang out, but too late. Dana cried out as the hidden Ghost grabbed her. The one chasing her caught them up, bringing up his knife. Hugo felt himself go cold and time slow down. A lenslight lit up Dana's terrified face and the blades of the Ghosts' weapons.

Hugo called out again but then there was a confused mess of shouts and clangs of metal on metal and Webb's voice rang out above it all. In the fractured light, Hugo just made out his tall frame dropping from a walkway above into the scuffle and then there was a wild yell as the man with the long knife was heaved over the railing. Hugo got a knee over the cable and started scrambling hand-over-hand toward the nearest platform.

The commotion continued along with the sound of running as the remaining Ghost converged on the struggle. Hugo reached the platform and scrambled on. He didn't pause for breath but raced towards the nearest ladder.

He reached the walkway just as the Ghost with no ear reached it too. Hugo flung himself at the broad-shouldered man, using all his weight to pin him against the railing. He managed to get a grip of the Ghost's weapon-hand and pulled his own knife. The man wrestled his free hand up and got a crushing grip on Hugo's throat. He tried to use his knife but his knees buckled. His vision swam but then Dana yelled somewhere far away. He pulled together some strength and plunged his knife into his assailant. He wasn't even sure where the weapon had bit, but the man loosened his grip with a cry.

Hugo ran as soon as he was free. Everything had gone very dark with only one lenslight glowing somewhere along the walkway. Hugo pelted toward it, heart thumping, breath heaving and praying. He staggered over a man crumpled on the floor then came up on the crouched figures of Webb and Dana.

"What's happened?" he said.

Webb was slumped against the railings, half supported by Dana who was scrabbling for the lenslight that had rolled away.

"Webb's hurt," she muttered and Hugo felt his heart come into his mouth. He dropped down next to his friend. The younger man's breathing was pained. Dana found the lenslight and brought it up. Webb was grey-faced, a hand clutched at his side just above the hip. Blood soaked his clothes and hand and dripped onto the walkway.

"Shit," Hugo said, fumbling through the pouches on the cargo suit but finding nothing to help.

"Keep watch," Dana snapped, pulling the kerchief off Webb's head and lifting up his hand to press it to the wound.

Hugo grabbed the lenslight. He stood and scanned around the engineering deck but everything was motionless. "No sign of anyone. No sign of Yoshida either."

"We need to get him out of here," Dana said. "Help me."

Hugo pushed aside the wash of fear when the lenslight shone on the amount of blood that had pooled on the walkway and bent to get Webb's arm over his shoulder.

"Shut the light off," Webb bit out between gasps. "They'll see us a million miles away."

"Quiet," Dana scolded, getting her shoulder under Webb's other arm and helping get him to his feet. "Kale, keep this pressed hard."

Hugo felt Dana's hand, slick with blood, find his own and press it to the wad of sodden fabric at Webb's side. Webb hissed and swore as Hugo took a step, helping Webb along.

It was painfully slow going. Every step was accompanied by a hitched breath from Webb and the echo from his dragging feet. Once they heard voices somewhere behind them and a light sliced through the dark, but they managed to stagger behind one of the towering reactor chambers before they were seen.

He turned them down the first corridor they came to and closed his eyes to try again and remember the layout.

"Hold on," Hugo muttered to Webb as he staggered again. "Just round this corner."

Sure enough weak light greyed the darkness ahead and the entry hatch to the airlock tunnel came into view. Hugo crept ahead then softly called the all clear. He took up Webb's arm again and pushed the non-coded internal hatch control. He kept their pace as fast as Webb could manage down the airlock tunnel, listening for any sound of pursuit, but they reached the end unmolested.

"All clear," Dana muttered after peering out the viewscreen. They got the hatch open and were swamped with the constant clamour and oily smell of Haven.

"Careful, just take it slow," Hugo said as they got Webb to the ladder. His skin had taken on a sickly sheen. Hugo deliberately didn't look at the blood but helped his sister manoeuvre Webb onto the ladder.

It took an age to get back to the deck and Hugo was sweating from climbing with one hand, taking Webb's weight and straining to keep watch to see if they were noticed. Webb stifled a cry as their boots hit the floor. Hugo's pulse thundered in his ears in time with the heaving groans of the shipyard as he scanned around for a way through.

"This way," Dana said, edging Webb along to the vacuum shield platform again. "I think there's a way into the between-ways on the other side of this yard."

"Stay where you are!" Hugo felt the bottom drop out of his stomach. He watched in slow motion as two Enforcers in dark coveralls closed in on them. Hugo untangled himself from Webb who staggered just as he recognised the small but determined figure of Simone Sinclair stepping on to the platform with two more Enforcers who closed in and surrounded them. They all had their nightsticks drawn. Simone's face was grave as she took them in.

"You two, go and get more men," she snapped and two of the Enforcers threw them poisonous glances and paced away.

The two remaining flanked them, their expressions dangerous. Workers from the nearby welding pit pushed up goggles to stare.

"Foreman Michalski recognised your Service-walk a mile away," Simone said, bitterness sharp in her voice. "I told her you wouldn't have the gall to come back to your own yard after what you've done and yet here you are."

"We should secure them, ma'am," one Enforcer said.

"Simone," Webb croaked, trying to take a step away from Dana and buckling.

Simone's eyes widened as they took in Webb's blood-soaked clothes. "What's happened here?"

"He's hurt," Dana began, but Webb cut her off.

"We can't tell you," he said, wincing, but drawing himself up and looking the Elder in the eye. The two Enforcers shifted on their feet, exchanging glances. "Simone, please, you have to listen to me."

Heat had flushed her face but it looked equal parts pain to anger. "No, Ezekiel, I don't. We trusted you. August trusted you. You have abused that trust and betrayed this colony. All three of you," she pointed at each of them in turn. "One of you is an illegal immigrant. You have abandoned your shifts, attacked citizens and stolen property. You're lucky we didn't find any black paint in your boarding house or we'd be having a hanging here and now."

"That wasn't us. You don't understand," Hugo said.

"I don't have to understand," Simone said. "You are traitors and you will face justice."

"We're after our own justice," Webb pleaded, taking another shuffling step and a hitching breath.

"Webb, stay still," Dana said, but the clone ignored her.

"We can't explain it all, Simone. Not yet. And it may be that we end this owing you more than we can repay…but you trusted me before. You have to trust me now."

"You're after recompense of your own, is that it?" she said, folding her arms. "What for?"

Hugo clenched his jaw, searching Webb's face. Dana's looked almost desperate but Webb shook his head.

"Don't be an idiot, Webb. Tell me."

"We can't," Webb said, voice tight with regret. "The colony can't know about this…until it's over."

"If you won't tell us why you're doing what you're doing, we can only judge you on your actions, which make you a criminal. God help you when August gets here," she said, shaking her head. Webb kept his face blank but Hugo could see pain wash through his eyes.

"I will explain when it's over," he said. "Please, Simone. You know me. Would I be doing this if it weren't for something serious?"

Simone's hard glance softened, doubt creeping into it for the first time and Hugo felt hope begin to flicker.

"Ma'am," one of the Enforcers said, craning his neck to look over the increasing numbers of workers gathering below in the pit to gawp. Some were muttering and pointing at them. Others were fingering tools.

"Get them back," Simone said. "Keep order here."

The Enforcers looked uneasily between the workers and their prisoners, but Simone barked her orders again and they moved into the crowd, brandishing their sticks and shouting for the workers to step back. With a start, Hugo saw Lola Michalski was on her moped at the far end of the pit. Her goggles were up on her head and she was staring at him. A tightness wrapped around his chest at the cold anger in her eyes.

"Lady," Dana suddenly said as Webb gasped and buckled again, jerking Hugo's attention away from the foreman. Simone swung her heavy gaze to Dana. "He's hurt. Either take us away right this second or let us go so we can get him help. Do whatever, but do it now."

Simone's jaw worked, her glance flicking between them all, lingering on Webb's grey face and the increasing ruckus in the pits.

"Get them out of this yard," someone yelled. "Drift them. Get them off the colony!"

"Traitors! Scum! Outsiders!"

Dana had to stagger to the side with Webb to avoid being hit by a spanner flung at her head. The Enforcers voices raised over the increasing noise and Simone stood rooted to the spot, watching the crowd with uncertain eyes.

"Simone," Hugo came forward. Her jaw tightened and her eyes flared. "Let us go. This is not a Service matter. I didn't lie about that. It's personal. And it could help us get to the bottom of something that's a far bigger threat to your colony than us."

Defiance hardened Simone's face for a moment more. But then she looked back at the swaying Webb and Dana whose eyes flashed fury and hands were coated in blood.

"Get him out of here," she hissed, glancing down at the Enforcers breaking up the melee and calling out to their colleagues arriving at the yard gates. "Now. But Hugo," Simone called as Webb and Dana began to shamble away. "You will not get away a second time."

Hugo nodded, let out a shuddering breath and ran after his companions as more shouts rose behind them. They finally staggered around some towering scaffolding, blocking them from the view of the pits.

"Where are we going?"

"There," Dana panted as they shambled along, hauling Webb

with them. They rounded another corner into a narrow gap between the scaffold and the hull. She propped Webb up and dropped down, feverishly working at a grate in the floor locked with bolts. Hugo bent to help his sister throw back the bolts and heave the heavy grate open.

"Quick," Hugo said as the noise from the yard gathered in volume. "Webb," he snapped. "Stay with us."

Webb nodded, breathing shallow.

"Kale, look fast," Dana said, then scurried down a creaking ladder into darkness. Hugo followed. The ladder was short and he shuffled in beside Dana in the narrow dark space as she was calling up to Webb. The clone moved slowly and Hugo resisted the urge to hurry him. He sat on the edge of the hatch and fumbled his way down, Hugo and Dana catching him as soon as he was in reach.

"That way," Dana barked, waving off down a gloomy passage before scurrying back up the ladder to close the grate.

Hugo shuffled off down the passage with Webb. There was the clang as Dana shut the grate and they were plunged into darkness. The air smelt dusty and stale. It was very cold and, above their shuffling steps and heaving breaths, eerily quiet.

"Quick," Dana said, taking the lead and switching on the lenslight. "It's only a matter of time before they figure out where we've gone."

They came to a junction of three corridors, all identical and dark and Dana turned them left. "Hurry," she said.

"He can't hurry," Hugo said as Webb stumbled.

"Yes I can," Webb said, attempting to get his feet under him. "Keep going."

Dana cast about at the next junction they came to. The ceiling was lost in darkness and a clanging echoed down the corridor on their left. A dull light shone from the one ahead. Dana took them right.

"Where are you getting us?"

"Lost," she said.

She always chose the dusty corridors and tried only the rusted and creaking hatches and doors, only some of which opened. She tutted and cursed over rooms and sheltered sidings. They turned away from light and sound and passed over abandoned work pits and storage areas. They even passed through a rusting cockpit that must have belonged to one of the original vessels that first made up the colony, until Webb was sagging on Hugo's shoulder.

"Here," Dana said as she came back out from yet another darkened room. "This one's safe. The hatch still locks from the inside."

"Thank Christ," Webb groaned. They helped him over the threshold. Dana propped the lenslight on a shelf and it lit the interior of the narrow, dusty room. There were broken storage shelves against one wall, some sacking in the corner and no ceiling, just a tangle of cables ranging from pencil-thin to the width of Hugo's arm. A faint buzz was the only thing that indicted they were still active and Hugo eyed their cracked casing warily.

They eased Webb down onto the sacking. He muffled a cry as he collapsed and Hugo felt his chest tighten as he rubbed blood off his hands.

"Get the light," Dana said as she knelt next to Webb and eased his clenched hand away from the wound in his side. Hugo shone the light on it as Dana worked at Webb's belt.

The clone gave a strangled laugh. "Hugo, your sister is taking my pants off."

"Quiet," Dana snapped and pulled his coveralls open at the hip. Webb hissed but made no more sound.

"Damn," Hugo muttered and knelt beside his sister. The stab wound was ugly, and deep, stretching from Webb's hip bone up to his ribs.

"It doesn't look like they got the artery," Dana said, voice shaking only slightly as she covered it back up, pulled off her scarf and pressed it on.

"He's lost so much blood," Hugo muttered. "He needs a medic."

"We'd never make it to a clinic," Dana said. "Even if we did, they'd turn us in as soon as they recognised us."

"Webb," Hugo said, shaking his friend's shoulder as his eyelids fluttered. "Stay awake."

"Go away, Hugo. I'm tired."

"Stay awake," Dana snapped and pinched his good thigh.

"Ow. You little -"

"We have to think of something," Hugo said as Dana flipped the scarf over as it soaked.

"Jazz is a medic," Dana said.

"No," Webb croaked.

"Webb, this..." Hugo rubbed his mouth. "It's not good."

"We can't ask her," Webb said, sounding defeated. "She won't come anyway. Not now."

"Is there a medkit back in that bolthole?" Hugo asked Dana.

She nodded. "But it's a two-hour moped drive away, or a four hour stagger through the between ways. He'll never make it."

"You go," he said. "Find help. Steal a medkit from a yard, anything."

"Hugo," Webb grated.

"I'm on it," Dana said, getting to her knees.

"Use the betweenways," Hugo said. "Stay out of sight."

"It's what I've been doing since I got here," she said, with the start of a smile. "You," she said to Webb and poked his stomach. "Stay awake." Webb cursed and muttered but shouldered himself up a little more against the wall. "I'll be quick," Dana said, standing and wiping blood on her coveralls.

Hugo made Webb take a firm hold of his compress and followed Dana to the hatch. "Be careful," Hugo called after her as she disappeared into the darkness, closed the hatch and swung the locks home.

XII

"**S**he's so much like you it's scary," Webb mumbled as the sounds of Dana's footsteps faded to nothing.

"Keep quiet," Hugo said, dropping next to his friend and readjusting the compress.

"Keep quiet, stay awake, lie down," Webb grumbled. "It's like being back at the youth unit."

The silence that followed was thick. Hugo knew they were both thinking that this man had never lived in a youth unit. A rush of anger rode through him.

"I'm going to kill him."

"Who?" Webb said, voice tired.

"That researcher. Yoshida."

Webb groaned. "You and your murderous temper. Yoshida's not the bad guy here. He's just an obsessive crank."

"How can you say that?" Hugo said, keeping his voice steady with an effort. "He's cloning human organs."

"We don't know why."

Hugo made a wordless noise of frustration. "I don't need to know why. That bastard and his experiments. If it wasn't for him, there would never have been a need for Webb to have been killed."

Webb shook his head. "Yoshida won't be the only one who could do this. It might have taken longer, it might have been different, but Pharos was determined. She'd've found her man. And, besides, if they'd used a more competent scientist," Webb tapped his temple again. "Maybe this would have been empty as they planned and I'd've led the revolution. And if that had happened," he grinned, though his head lolled against the wall. "They might have won."

Hugo muttered, willing himself to unclench in case he press on the injury. "I don't understand you. You're still getting screwed and still shrugging it off."

Webb sighed. "And when exactly have I done that?"

"Professor Spinn on the *Zero*," Hugo said the name through clenched teeth. "He lied to you your whole life. He took you away from Doll, the one person who could have been a decent parent to you and kept you a political prisoner without you even knowing it. I wanted to dump him on the nearest asteroid and you wouldn't let me."

"I knew..." Webb stopped and sighed. "Webb knew Spinn better than you did," the clone said. "He might have had secrets but he was a good man. He did what he believed was right."

Hugo snorted. "His secrets could have saved Webb. His secrets nearly destroyed you. Don't you have any anger about any of it? Any regret?"

"Yes," Webb said softly after a pause. "Hurting Kinjo."

Hugo shifted. "She betrayed you too."

Webb let out a shuddering breath. "Webb made her a promise. She was never supposed to have to be scared or alone again. He promised her that when he took her away from Bryce. Whatever she did, it was because of anger and fear. I don't blame her for either."

Hugo was silent, his own anger flagging but refusing to burn out completely. "Making cloning illegal was the one thing I managed to do," he said, voice strained. "It was the only thing..."

"The only thing, what?"

Hugo face felt hot. "It was the only thing I could do to make it up to you. To him."

"You didn't kill him, Hugo."

Hugo found himself talking without being able to stop. "Everything and everyone else in his life had failed him. I had the chance to save him. And I couldn't."

Webb shifted on his sacking. "Kaleb Hugo, you are many things, stubborn asshole being top of the list. But you did not dream up that insane cloning plan, nor did you put the contract out on his life. The people that did I killed myself."

Hugo was glad the darkness hid his face. "I don't care. I was supposed to make a difference. I was supposed to change things. It's the only reason I stayed in the Service. But it's all been for nothing. Nothing's changed and I'm still losing people…" Hugo swallowed, throat dry and without any more words. He stared into the shadows feeling his eyes prickle and his chest tighten. "I've failed. I failed Webb, I've failed you. And now I've failed Harvey."

Webb's silence stretched on so long Hugo reached out to shake him, fearing he'd lost consciousness. But Webb grabbed his wrist.

"Hugo," he said, voice firm even with the edge of pain. "Whoever I am… whatever I am. I'm not your responsibility."

"But you're my friend." A grey bleakness filled Hugo and he slumped, blinking into the dark. "I was supposed to help you. And now look at us."

Webb gave a weak chuckle. "We always end up bleeding in the dark, huh? Look, man. This is all very touching and all, really, it is. But each poor bastard born into this shitty world is in charge of his own course. You no more got Webb killed and cloned than you are responsible for what happened to Harvey. I've known her longer than you… technically," he added with an awkward shrug. "Webb knew her well, you know. She understood what she was getting into when she started work on those traders better than you did. All she saw was a chance to shut down people taking advantage of Haven to make credit. As hopeless or foolhardy as that might seem, it was a chance she had to take, and all the risks with it. The same as you trying to straighten out the whole damn Orbit with your own two hands." He shook his head. "You two are made for each other, really. Idiots, the pair of you. But tough-assed and well-meaning idiots."

Hugo sighed and closed his eyes. "Do you think it was Yoshida and the cloning? Do you think that's what Harvey found?"

Webb winced as he tried to shift again. "Maybe. Whether she

did though or not, I'd say that was what they were afraid she might have found."

Hugo checked his wrist panel, but it was dark. He prayed Dana was being smart. "I say we get you fixed up then get out of here."

"What?"

"I'll make Dana take us out of here as soon as you can walk to wherever she's stashed the *Phoenix*."

"Hey, hey, hey," Webb said, propping himself up in his elbows. "Not so fast. What, a little stabbing's scared you off?"

"'A little stabbing'? You could have died. Still could."

"No," Webb shook his head. "They don't take me down that easy. This isn't over. Not after I've said fifty-fucking-thousand times we should give it up and go and you told me to shove it. Now I'm telling you to shove it, Captain."

"Commodore."

Webb croaked another laugh. "Fine. Commodore. They've drawn first blood. I'm not leaving this damned colony without that blade. He's the only one that will have enough information to get the Service moving against all the crap-weasels that have hired him. We leave without him, I might as well have carried on trading contraband in the Lunar Strip and stabbed myself in the groin to save the Ghosts the hassle. No. This ends with Ariel or it doesn't end at all."

"You can't ever come back here after this. Jazz, your chance at a life here...all gone."

Webb shrugged. "I'm not convinced it was ever meant to be. Clone or not, drifter or not...Haven is for the lost and those with no choices left. I'm not sure I'm either, any more."

"Trust you to have your life-changing realisation when you're bleeding to death in some abandoned hole in the underbelly of a dead-end colony."

Webb laughed then groaned. "Shut up, Commodore. Your sister better be back with that medkit soon or I *will* go and die on you and leave you with another bucket of guilt and self-loathing to carry about with the two-dozen others you've already filled."

Hugo smiled, turned the compress over again and shone the light on it. The wound was still bleeding, but keeping him lying down seemed to have slowed the flow. "Keep still."

"Like I have a choice," Webb muttered and laid his head back and closed his eyes. Hugo contemplated prodding him awake but his breathing was steady and Hugo decided rest was probably what he needed.

He sat and stared at the wall, cables humming overhead, checking his dark wrist panel every few minutes. Whenever Webb groaned or winced he had to stop himself from calling Jazz, but he stayed firm.

"What exactly is your relationship with Jasmine?" Hugo muttered aloud without realising.

"Huh?" Webb murmured, voice thick.

"You. And Jazz. She obviously cares for you a lot."

"I'm not entirely sure that is any of your business," Webb said.

"Dana is starting to like you."

"Huh? Say again? The blood-loss must be affecting my hearing."

"She likes you," Hugo said again. "Don't give her hope if there isn't any."

Webb mumbled a few beginnings of words but was cut off by the bleep of Hugo's wrist panel.

"Hold this," he ordered Webb, placing his hand over the compress then pressed a button on the wrist panel. "Dana? Are you on your way back?"

"I have her." The voice was a woman's. It was hard and edged with menace. "She is safe. For now."

"Who is this?" Hugo demanded. Webb was trying to sit up.

"I'm sending co-ordinates. Come alone." She had a trace of an American accent. "You have one hour."

The connection cut and some co-ordinates flashed up on the little screen.

"Lunar 1," Webb said. "That's a Lunar 1 colonist talking."

"Stay put," Hugo said, blood pounding in his ears as he got to his feet.

"What, you're going?"

"Here," Hugo pulled off his dust scarf and handed it over. "Keep the pressure on."

"Hugo, wait."

But Hugo had crossed to the hatch and was already throwing back the bolts. He slammed it on Webb's protests, not able to think about the fact that he was abandoning him, wounded and alone, only of the murderous certainty in that tinny voice.

He checked his panel for directions and set off, next to blind with anger and fear, but running as fast as he could. The passages were narrow and dark, some pitch black and he was forced to slow to a walk and feel his way along, having left the light with Webb, but his heart never slowed its fevered pounding. The distant roar of machinery sounded down other corridors and he passed over more than one echoing chasm without daring to look down.

Odd smells assaulted him, sewage, bloodgrease and sometimes burning. Twice he had to duck back out of sight as workers came into view, pushing barrows or lifters or working on the subterranean machinery.

He took several wrong turns, almost coming up on the co-ordinates several times only to find himself forced to turn away or climb to another level in the maze of passages. Finally, there was a dull light ahead and a steady thunk of something huge moving close by. He came to a doorway, wrist panel flashing as he finally reached the co-ordinates. He passed through and found himself in a large, round chamber with a walkway running around the wall. Choppy light flooded the room, flashing as a giant fan spun somewhere out of sight below. There was the rush of moving air and the smell of oil. He dared another step and saw Dana crouched on the walkway on the other side of the chamber. Her wrists were secured to a railing by wire and she was cursing and pulling at her bonds, blood already thick on her wrists with her efforts.

He ignored all his instincts and training, called her name and rushed to her. She looked up, face white, mouth open and tear tracks through the dirt on her face.

"Kale, no," she called just as a bone-jarring clang sounded behind him.

He span. A woman, taller than him, in black clothes and spacer boots had stepped out from a doorway and sunk a machete into the railing. The weapon was almost as long as his arm, heavy-looking with an edge that flashed in the shifting light. Her hair was a shocking red and pulled tight back from her face. She stood there, staring out at him with eyes like flint from the black cross painted on her face.

Hugo felt cold fill him.

"Who are you?" It was the voice again, low and loaded with anger.

Hugo stood straighter, fingers itching for his own weapon but the woman's gaze pinned him still.

"You're the Black Cross killer?"

She pulled her weapon from the railing and stepped closer. "I know who I am. Tell me who you are."

Hugo took a step back, making sure he stood between the woman and Dana. "Who we are doesn't matter. We're nothing to do with you."

"You've dogged my every step."

"We weren't after you," Hugo said, keeping his voice under control and making himself meet her eyes. "Your grievance is of no interest to us."

"I don't believe you. You're sided with them."

"With who?"

"The Ghosts."

Hugo shook his head. "We're nothing to do with them. We're after someone else."

"Who?"

"Someone… someone they've hired."

She halted. The machete spun as she shifted it round and round in her grip. Her sharp eyes flicked from him to Dana and back again. "You've turned up at two of their apartments and you tell me you're not one of them?"

"We're not. We're using them."

"How so?"

"Kale, don't say anything," Dana said.

The woman moved. Hugo ducked to the side but she was fast and strong. The blade sunk into the wall just above his head and she pinned him, hand at his throat and face inches from his. The painted face was twisted, the eyes danced with madness. "All Ghosts will die by my hand. And so shall their friends."

"We're not their friends, you mental bitch," Dana snarled.

The woman swung another sweep, weapon clanging off the railing inches from Dana's hands. Hugo went for her, but she was too quick. She swung the weapon and he had to spring back to stay out of reach. He stood, every muscle tense as she stood with her feet apart and the machete in a two-handed grip, glaring at him. Strings of her blood-red hair were plastered to the black paint on her face.

Slowly, she straightened and stepped round Dana. His sister tried to wriggle away but the woman grabbed a handful of her collar and pulled it tight.

"Let her go," Hugo said.

"You want me to believe you're not one of them?"

"We're not," Hugo said.

"Convince me." She raised the blade.

"We're not even Havenites. We're on the blacklist."

"Why?" she asked with narrowed eyes.

"Kale," Dana warned but was choked off as the woman shook her.

Hugo took a breath. "We're after a blade they use."

The woman lifted her head, peering at him with narrowed eyes. Dana sat still with eyes clenched shut. The weapon dangled by the woman's leg. Hugo's fingers went to his knife hilt but just rested there as the woman watched the movement.

"What's the name of this blade?"

"I can't say. We can't let him know we're coming."

"You're lying," she said, tightening her grip on Dana and lifting her machete. "Cowardly lies to protect yourselves."

"Ariel," Hugo blurted, stepping forward. Dana's eyes flew open. The woman paused. "His name is Ariel," Hugo repeated, quieter.

The fan below spun on. The sweat on Hugo's brow was chilled in the breeze. He clenched and unclenched his hands, tacky with Webb's blood, but all he could see was his sister staring at him.

"I know that name," the woman said a pained eternity later. Her grip on Dana eased ever so slightly.

Hugo nodded, put his hands up and took a step closer. "He's involved with these Ghosts. We're trying to find him. For our own reasons."

"You're Service, aren't you?" The woman hadn't moved but she suddenly looked dangerous again.

Hugo shook his head. "Not any more."

The woman lifted her machete and pointed it at him. "I knew I recognised you. The Special Commander's hero son, isn't it? Not looking so grand now, Commodore."

"Our friend is hurt," Hugo said. "Please. Let us go so we can help him. We won't interfere with your vendetta, whatever it is."

The woman nodded, though it wasn't in agreement. A cruel smile had spread across her face. "'*Whatever it is*'. Yes, that's as little as you care. That's as little as anyone cares."

"Listen, lady," Dana growled. "*No one* cares. That's the truth. No one cares about my friend lying broken in hospital on Earth because of them, or the one who's bleeding out in this rusted hole. Let us go so we can get our revenge for someone no one cares about and you can do the same."

The woman was staring down at Dana who was glaring right back up at her. Hugo wasn't sure but he thought he saw wetness in the tall woman's tortured eyes. Hugo was about to reach for his knife when the woman sheathed her weapon and pulled a multi-tool out her belt. Her face was blank as she cut the wires holding Dana.

Dana scrambled away as soon as she was free and Hugo rushed to her and helped her to her feet.

"This blade. Ariel? I take it he's worked on people you know?"

Hugo looked up from his examination of Dana's wrists, which weren't cut too badly, to meet the newcomer's difficult gaze again. "That's right."

"Under instruction from the Ghosts?"

Hugo nodded. "We believe so."

The woman looked at the ground, clenched her fists then looked up. "Take me to your injured friend."

"Why?" Dana said, eyes narrow.

"I can help."

"I'm not impressed with your brand of kindness to strangers so far," Dana said.

"You can't look me in the face and say you wouldn't do the same if you thought someone stood in between you and your goal."

Dana scowled but didn't answer.

"How can you help?" Hugo said.

The woman patted her utility belt. "I have medical supplies."

"You're a medic?"

She shrugged. "Not officially. My sister got very ill. I looked after her."

"And did she survive your care?" Dana said.

The woman stiffened. Her hand went to her weapon again. "You have no idea what you're talking about." She looked to Hugo. "If you want my help, I suggest she keeps her mouth shut from now on."

Dana's face contorted but Hugo cut her off.

"Dana, quiet. We've got no choice. Webb needs her. What's your name?"

A corner of a smile pulled at the stranger's cruel mouth. "Webb. Nam Webb."

"Lunar 1?"

She nodded. "As is your friend?"

"Yes," Hugo said, checking his wrist panel for directions back the way he'd come. "And he's badly hurt. We have to hurry."

Δ

"I don't trust her as far as I can spit," Dana hissed in his ear.

Hugo winced but Nam's brooding silence remained unbroken. "We have no choice, Dana. And besides…" He glanced over this shoulder at the tall woman pacing a few feet behind them, eyes fixed ahead and blank. "She's after the Ghosts. She might know something that can help us."

Dana shook her head and increased her pace. "Webb better live through this," she mumbled, almost to herself. "If she hurts him -"

"I won't hurt him." Nam's voice wasn't loud but it shut Dana up mid-mutter.

Hugo increased their pace. When they finally found the room again, Hugo pushed the rusted hatch open, calling Webb's name.

There was a groan and shuffle in the gloom and then the len-slight flicked on and pointed at them.

"Shit," Webb said, trying to get up, eyes riveted on Nam's face paint. "Christ, Hugo, look out."

Hugo glanced back at Nam as she straightened inside the room, blank eyes staring about from under her paint.

"Calm down," Hugo said, going to him and taking the light off him. "She's going to help us."

"Are you fucking kidding me? Her? She's the killer…"

"What's the damage?" Nam said, coming forward and kneeling next to Webb, taking in his blood-soaked coveralls with an empty glance.

"Stab wound to the side," Dana said, voice clipped and reached to peel Webb's hands and saturated fabric from his hip.

"Are you all shitting me?" Webb panted, voice thin with pain and panic. "Get the psycho the hell away from me."

"Be still, you're pulling on it," Nam said as she started taking things out of her belt.

"Hugo, what's going on here?" Webb spluttered.

"Your enemy is my enemy," Nam said, unfolding a light pole she'd pulled from one of her deep pockets, setting it on the floor and flicking it on. They all cursed and blinked in the sudden light. Hugo felt his throat tighten when he saw how pale Webb was. There were dark shadows under his eyes and he was soaked with sweat. "Keep still," Nam ordered again then laid out sterilising pads, a surgical stapler and syringes.

"Oh good Christ in Heaven," Webb moaned.

"You," Nam said to Dana as she loaded a syringe from a vial. "Hold his head. Keep him still."

"Oh, Holy Mother," Webb said. "Not me, why me? Why is it always me?"

"Shut up and grow a pair," Dana grumbled as she shuffled up to Webb's head, but Hugo could see the strain in her face. She ignored his protest and shifted him into her lap so she could support his head and shoulders.

"What should I do?" Hugo said.

"Thread a needle," Nam said as she dragged the lighting pole closer and started wiping blood away with the sterilising pads. Hugo found the needle and thread in sealed pouches in the med-kit and set about trying to thread the needle with shaking hands.

"Hugo, I'm going to kill you," Webb growled. "You too, Dana. If she doesn't kill me first, I'm killing you both."

"Shush," Nam said and injected him in the hip as he muttered incomprehensible curses. "Hold him," she instructed Dana as Webb's mumblings quietened and his eyes fluttered. Then she took up the surgical stapler. "Commodore. Hold it closed."

Hugo winced as he shuffled closer and attempted to press the edges of the wound together. Webb whimpered but Nam reached around Hugo and stapled the injury in three places. Webb cried out and Dana cursed and held his head, brushing hair out of his face even as she mumbled to him to grow up.

The staples held the wound shut. She waved Hugo away and took up the needle.

Hugo stared, belly threatening to heave, as the woman stitched the torn flesh together. The stitches were fine and even and she called for a pad every few seconds to wipe the skin clean. When she was done, she dressed the wound with bandage and gauze. Webb had gone still.

"Webb?"

"He's fine," Nam said after a quick glance at his face and a check of his pulse. "Keep the wound clean. He will need to rest a few days and make sure he eats. There's a supply bunker under a yard office three blocks hubwards that's not well guarded."

"Thank you," Hugo said and Nam nodded. She glanced at Webb again and reached up. Dana tensed but all Nam did was turn back his collar to expose more of the thin scar that ran from behind his ear down to his collar bone.

"This Ariel's work?"

Hugo nodded. Dana was staring at the scar like it was the first time she'd noticed it.

Nam sat back on her heels, wiping the blood off her hands with more pads.

"Maybe we're even more alike than I thought. We're all after people who have hurt us. Good luck to you."

"Nam, wait," Hugo said, getting to his feet as Nam did. "We should work together."

Nam shook her head. "I'm not after this blade. You'll only get in my way."

"Hey," Dana said, shifting a moaning Webb back onto the sacking and standing. "You're the one who came after us."

"When I thought you were Ghosts," Nam said. "You turned up at both their places, I know I was watching."

"You were the one following us..." Hugo said, realisation dawning.

Nam nodded. "I wasn't sure. But then you turned up at the broker's apartment too."

"You killed Celeste?"

"She was a Ghost," Nam said. "They will all die by my hand, under a Black Cross. The world will know that they were evil."

"Nam," Hugo said, taking a step toward her. She stiffened and stepped away but he moved between her and the hatch. "At least let's exchange information. Tell us what you know about the Ghosts."

"I know nothing about them except what they took from me." Her voice was thick with emotion and the blankness of her face shifted a second to reveal a twisted mask of fury and pain that she looked down to hide.

"That sister you mentioned. They killed her, didn't they?" Dana's statement was not voiced kindly and she stood with her arms folded and her gaze watchful.

Nam looked back up. The burning agony was now only evident in the thin press of her white mouth. "No. Much worse."

"We are not going to stand in the way of you avenging the wrong done to you but..." Hugo took a breath. Dana was wary and Nam was staring at the wall like she could blast a hole through it with her look alone. "But if you tell us all you know, it might help us. And, in exchange, we will tell you where their lab is."

Webb blinked his eyes open, dazed, winced and muttered something. Dana just took on a frozen look but didn't say anything.

Nam tore her gaze from the wall and it hit Hugo like a blow. "They have a lab?"

"Yes."

"Tell me. You tell me now." She advanced a step and Hugo took a step back.

"Kale," Dana warned but Hugo held up a hand.

"Dana, be quiet. Nam. We will tell you -"

"Hugo," Webb started to protest from the floor, voice thick from the drugs.

"Quiet," Hugo snapped again. The woman stood over him, hand on her machete handle again, her other fingers twitching. "We will tell you what we know, if you do the same."

Her jaw worked, her eyes burned and the knuckles around the handle of her weapon were white. The edge of madness was bright in her eyes again and Hugo found himself glancing over his shoulder to check how far he was from the hatch should he need to make a move.

When she still didn't say anything, he took a breath, closed his eyes and the words fell out of him. "They didn't kill my fiancée either. They set Ariel on her." He opened his eyes. "She lost our child. But she doesn't remember. She doesn't remember anything. I was supposed to marry her and now she doesn't know who I am."

The woman started to tremble. Something went out of her eyes then she covered her face with her hands and stepped back, out of the pool of light from the lighting pole and crumpled to her knees, shoulders shaking though she made no noise.

Webb grunted as he tried to sit up. Dana threw a wary glance at Nam then went to help him. Hugo stayed where he was until Nam dropped her hands. She had chased all emotion from her face: it was set under the smudged black paint. Wetness stood in her eyes but when she spoke her voice was steady and hard, like it had never known laughter.

"I'll tell you what I know, though I don't see how it can help you."

"Anything might help," Hugo encouraged.

Nam stared at the wall, hands clenched together and eyes far away. "My sister and I scavenged wreck sites on Lunar 1 for scrap but we weren't turning a profit any more. We were desperate and Magdalena grew reckless. She went to the sites that were still dangerous."

"She did?" Webb said.

Nam looked at him as if suddenly remembering he was there. "You're a Webb too," she said. Webb nodded. "You know then. I knew, too. Even Magdalena knew about the chemicals left from the war, even if she called it lies. She said the nuns were just clinging to the past, that the older generations just wanted an excuse not to have to revisit those places. So she went."

"She got the wasting sickness?" Webb said softly.

Nam nodded. "Her liver was failing. The clinic kept her sedated. They said it was only a matter of days."

"I'm sorry," Webb said.

"Don't be," Nam said, pointing at him, eyes flashing. "Not for that. That was Magdalena's fault. She knew it might end her but she went anyway. She didn't care about leaving me alone."

"What happened?" Dana's voice was hushed now.

Nam took a few deep breaths, like she was trying to contain something inside her. "I was in her clinic room, screaming at her for being stupid and selfish."

"Wasn't she sedated?" Dana said with a sardonic look.

The look Nam threw back at her was black. "She could hear me. I know she heard me. But…" she closed her eyes and bit her lip. She crossed herself, a gesture that made Webb flinch. "So did someone else."

"Who?" Hugo asked.

Nam's eyes swung his way but looked right through him. "He had one arm and a nice smile. A smart suit. A panel full of diagrams. He said he knew someone who could save her. Someone that could give her a new liver and new blood and flush the wasting sickness away."

"One arm?" Webb asked. Hugo looked at him. His face was

grave under the sheen of pain.

Nam nodded, not looking up. "I signed over my trading post as collateral. My ship too.

"She disappeared from her room that night. The medics didn't know where she'd gone. All the surveillance footage was wiped. I searched on the solarnet for days, trying to find out who the man was. Then I went to my trading booth in Houston Block and it was locked and barred. The level manager showed me the exchange papers with my signature on. My storage units in the basement levels were locked too and my ship had gone from its berth. They'd taken everything."

"What about Magdalena?" Hugo asked.

"Her screams woke me one morning a few days later. She'd been dumped at the doorway of my boarding pod." Nam started rocking back and forth, hands clasped round her knees. "I don't know what they did to her. I still don't know. She had incisions in her back but she didn't know how they got there. She wasn't dying any more, but she was in agony. I tried to take her back to the clinic but she just screamed and screamed and wouldn't go near anyone in a medic tunic. I stole some sedatives to try and keep her calm but she never truly stopped hurting, moaning and whimpering all night and day. She couldn't move, she couldn't eat, she couldn't cry. She begged me to end her suffering, begged and begged until…"

"Until you did," Webb finished after the pause had stretched on painfully long. His face was grim.

Nam stared into space again. When she spoke her voice was hard again. "I finally found out who the one-armed man was. I found out he came from Haven. I found out he worked with a gang called the Ghosts. Then I came here… searching."

"For him?" Hugo asked, voice far-away sounding in his own ears.

"For him and them. For his organisation. For everyone involved in making me have to kill my sister."

"And how exactly did you do that?" Dana said, still disdainful though there was a catch in her voice. "It's next to impossible to get information on this damned colony."

Nam's wide, empty eyes turned her way. "You need to know your enemy's rivals."

"Catiline?" Webb ventured.

Nam nodded. "They know more than they let on. They gave me names. And now, all the Ghosts are mine."

Silence filled the room like a vacuum. Hugo felt heat in his face but his body was chilled. He tried to rope together a coherent thought but his mind was a cold, aching blank.

Nam broke the spell by sweeping to her feet. "Where's the lab?"

"Sorry?" Hugo blinked, shaking himself.

"You said there was a lab. Where is it?"

"Hugo," Webb warned.

"I'm not leaving until you answer me," Nam said, drawing her machete again. "I can always re-open his flesh if you need convincing."

Dana scrambled to her feet and moved between the tall woman and Webb though the clone did nothing more than keep his warning glare on Hugo.

"She has a right to know," Hugo said. He turned to Nam, ignoring the doubt that had started his nerves twitching. "It's on the Service flagship being constructed by Sector 4's shipyard. The Ghosts are on the work crew and they've modified a shuttle on the aft deck. They probably plan to steal it and make a getaway once the ship is launched and through the blockade."

"They want their lab mobile," Nam said, face darkening. "To trade in the whole Orbit."

"Don't let them," Hugo said.

Nam blinked in vague surprise and for a moment, looking almost normal. Then she shifted, sheathed her machete and the mask was back in place. "Keep the lighting pole. Make sure he eats and rests. Good luck to you."

"And you," Hugo said, surprising himself with the sincerity in the words.

Nam held his gaze a long moment whilst Dana and Webb were silent. "We've helped each other today. But I repeat: I will not stand anyone getting in my way."

"Neither will we," Dana replied. The two women looked at each other, two sets of eyes blazing. Then the red-haired woman turned and left through the hatch. Hugo bolted it after her, then leant his forehead against it.

"Ok...so maybe Yoshida isn't as harmless as I thought. But I still don't know if telling her about the lab was the best idea."

Hugo ignored Webb, keeping his forehead pressed against the pitted metal. He could smell the rust, coppery like blood.

"Kale?" Dana's voice held just a hint of concern.

Hugo turned on them both, mastering himself with a deep breath. "She has her way of making sure no one else gets hurt. We have our own."

"We know that," Webb said, wincing as he propped himself higher up on one elbow.

"Then what's the problem?"

"I just thought you'd prefer Yoshida in a court facing a Service judge, not having his throat hacked open in the shuttle bay of the *Perseverance*. My mistake."

"Yoshida is not the target here."

"So it's ok for that crank to get served Nam's brand of personal justice, but I'm not to lay a hand on the man that tortured me?"

"When we find Ariel, which we will," Hugo said, voice like ice, "he will be taken back to Headquarters to stand trial. Not because I wouldn't rather put a bullet in his head myself. But what he might know is too valuable."

Webb rolled his eyes and looked at the wall. Hugo strode across the room and dropped beside him. Webb flinched away, but Hugo put his hand behind his friend's head and pulled him forward to press their foreheads together.

He'd last done this when they'd stood on the command deck of the *Resolution* as it plummeted towards the moon's surface. If anything, the fear and desperation that pumped through Hugo's veins now was even more intense.

"Please," he breathed. "I've failed at everything else. Help me do this and do it right."

Webb let out a shuddering breath. "Ok, Hugo. I'm sorry." Hugo felt him pat him on the shoulder. "You can let go of me now."

Hugo broke away then rocked back on his heels, angrily swiping at his stinging eyes.

"Jesus, it's no wonder people think we're sleeping together," Webb muttered.

"What?" Hugo and Dana said at the same time.

Webb laughed. It was a weak and tired sound but it gladdened Hugo to hear it all the same. "Never mind. Can I go to sleep now?"

XIII

Webb had never known exhaustion like it, in either of his lives. It sucked at him like a black hole. And yet even as he lay there in the darkness and the quiet, he did not sleep. He drifted between awareness of the raging wound in his side and a place where he forgot what that feeling meant, but he never truly slept.

Nam's words went round and round in his head. When he shut his eyes he saw her sister as he imagined her, crawling over the Lunar 1 blast sites, scavenging for anything that might make a sale. Then he saw her with her skin clammy and yellowish, eyes red and hair coming out in chunks. Webb had seen people with the wasting sickness before. The thought of being denied the release of death but still having to live with the symptoms made him go cold.

When he managed to push aside those visions, there was a pair of black eyes in a pale face and the glint of light off a scalpel waiting to take their place.

He would sit up sweating then curse as he pulled at his injury. Then he would breathe in the smell of the sacking, the dust and the antiseptic and swear to himself all over again that he would do as he had promised. Ariel was the end to all this, one way or another. And Webb would make sure it ended.

Time was an even more inconstant thing here in their hiding place than it had been in the colony above ground. The cables buzzed but otherwise he never heard another noise. He could have been sprawled in the dark for days or weeks.

There were times when Dana and Hugo were there. Dana would bully him into sitting up and swallowing protein shakes and Nutripaks, which he managed to keep down most of the time. Hugo would pace, brood, or both. If anything the pair of them exhausted him more than the blood loss.

"This supply bunker must be getting pretty empty," Webb

mumbled as Dana handed him a clean shirt after her latest supply run.

"We've found another. And been back to the bolthole," Dana said. "Now, are you going to wash or do you need me to do that for you too?"

"No thanks," he grated. "I think you've already seen more of me than your brother is comfortable with."

Dana pressed her lips together and Webb hoped it was the poor lighting that made him think he saw a flicker of hurt in her eyes. Hugo didn't appear to be listening. He was bent over a computer panel, the light from it washing his face a sickly green.

"I don't know what you're expecting to find," Webb said wearily as he crawled over to the bowl of clean water and washrag Dana had put out for him.

"We're still on the blacklist," Hugo said.

"Of course we are," Webb said, wincing as he shouldered himself out of his coveralls. "We won't be cleared off it until Haven thinks it's been made right."

"Until we're dead then," Dana muttered as she sorted through their supplies.

"Or worse," Webb said then swore as he pulled his old shirt over his head. "Have you tracked down Sol yet?"

"No," Dana said, dusting off her hands. "He's vanished. You need to give us the name of another Catiline member."

"Even if I had another, no," Webb repeated, utterly tired of this line of badgering. He soaked the rag and wiped his hands and face. A shiver ran over his skin but he had to admit the cold, clean water felt good. "Nam may have got her information from them, but we're not as kamikaze as her. Not yet, anyway. Sol is the only one I would even think about asking about Ariel. And there's nothing to say he'd help anyway. Ariel's not a Ghost. For all I know, Catiline use him too."

Dana grimaced at that. "So we just sit here and wait?"

"Wait for news," Webb said, gingerly peeling back the bandaging to clean the wound. "See if Nam's vendetta flushes any more information into the rumour boards."

"We've been on this damn colony for weeks without so much as a peep about Ariel from anyone," Dana growled. "What makes you think anything will happen now?"

Webb sat back on his heels and closed his eyes as he pushed back a wave of dizziness. When he blinked his eyes back open Hugo was glancing away, hiding his concerned look and going back to the panel.

"I don't know if anything will happen," Webb said, squeezing out the rag and watching the water go murky with old blood. "But Ariel knows who we are. The blacklist will have told him we're here, if he didn't know already and, for all he knows, we're here doling out Black Crosses. He'll be looking to get us before we get him. He's probably looking to get us before we get him. If we're careful, canny and patient, he will come to us."

"With his own personal band of Enforcers with very large knives, most probably," Dana muttered.

"Which is why we need to be careful," Webb said, keeping his voice mild. "Now I know you're just arguing with me because you're bored, Hugo Junior. So why don't you make yourself useful and pass me the gauze?"

Dana muttered something profane and grabbed the medical supplies and paced over to him. When he reached for them she batted his hands away and knelt next to him and started cleaning the stitches with a sterilising pad. Her face was dark with frustration as she glowered over her work but her touch was gentle and Webb felt himself relax despite himself.

He settled himself in a better position as Dana cleaned and bound the cut then cast a wary glance Hugo's way, but his former captain wasn't even looking at them.

"So, your brother and Harvey. Engaged, huh?"

Dana winced. "Sort of."

"What do you mean, sort of?"

Dana looked her brother's way then turned her attention back to the bandaging. "Well, does it count if she doesn't remember it happening?"

"Ah," he said, lifting his arm to let Dana wrap the bandaging around his waist. "She'll remember, though. She's a tough one that one. What is it?"

Dana smoothed the look on her face. "It's nothing it's just…" She looked Hugo's way again but he was still frowning at the panel. She lowered her voice anyway. "He applied for the marriage license weeks before it happened. But it never went through."

"Why not?"

"She didn't sign it."

Webb blinked. "How come?"

Dana shrugged and dropped her eyes back to her work. "I think she thought he was married to his rank."

Webb chewed on the inside of his cheek, a fluttering in his chest he was uncomfortably aware of as pity. "That's not true is it? Or at least, not any more?"

"Maybe. But it might be too late now."

Webb looked at Hugo again. His face had taken on a harder set than usual. "Hugo? What is it?"

"There's been another."

"Another what?"

"Another death," Hugo said, passing the panel over.

Dana cast aside the soiled bandages and took it. Webb peered over her shoulder. There was a picture of another concrete apartment block with two stony-faced Enforcers stood in the door. The article was only a couple of sentences long with no names.

"I don't care what you say," Webb said in a low voice. "That woman's deranged."

"Is it any wonder after what happened to her?" Hugo said.

"You don't end up that self-destructive without a hefty cargo of nutbars in the hold to begin with," Webb said.

"You did," Hugo said. His voice and face were calm.

Webb frowned. "That was different."

"How?"

"Shut up, Hugo," Webb growled. "Marlowe was part of a mission."

"I wasn't talking about Marlowe," Hugo replied.

"Makes you wonder what they get out of all this," Dana said quietly before Webb could think of a suitable retort.

"Who?" Webb asked instead.

She started, like she was just realising she'd spoken out loud. "The Ghosts. It says here that no one is saying they know this victim, either. They don't even protect their own or come forward when they're being hunted down, and for what?"

"Credit," Webb answered, pulling on the new shirt.

Dana snorted. "Ridiculous."

"You're speaking as someone who's always had it." Dana turned a burning look on him and he held up his hands. "Hey, I ain't judging. Just saying."

"Well don't."

Webb shrugged. "Ok then."

Hugo took the panel back and started scrolling through the article again. Dana went back to the supplies. Webb tried not to wince as he scraped his hair back from his face and tied it in a fresh tail. It snagged and pulled on his fingers and he dreaded to think how filthy it must be.

He got gingerly to his feet and was just about managing to climb into a cleaner, if not newer, set of coveralls, with Dana pointedly not offering to help, when there came a tap on the hatch.

They all froze. Dana was closest. She looked to Hugo who gestured for silence as the tap came again, louder this time. Hugo signed for them all to be still and got to his feet, pulling his knife. Webb fumbled for his own amongst his old clothes just as Hugo reached the hatch and pressed his ear to it.

"Commodore Hugo?" a small voice came from the outside. "Are you in there, sir?"

Hugo pulled the hatch open, fury and confusion contorting his face. "Tag?"

The boy stood blinking in the light from their lighting pole, face smudged and grubby. He clutched a holdall in his hands. "I found you!" he cried, a grin spreading over his face. "I knew I'd find you."

"How did you find us?" Webb said but Hugo held up a hand.

"Not how," he growled. "Why?"

Tag blinked between them, smile faltering. "I brought you your stuff."

He held up the holdall. Hugo snatched it off him, face like thunder. "What are you doing here, Tag?"

"Hey, easy, easy," Webb said, limping forward as the boy's face fell.

"Get him in here and out of the corridor," Dana said and Webb waved him in.

"Come in, kid. Don't be scared."

Tag took in Hugo's stormy look again and stepped over the threshold. Hugo slammed the hatch shut making them all jump.

"Explain yourself," he said.

"I, I," Tag fumbled, looking to Webb. "I heard you'd gone into the betweenways. Stuff's been going missing from a yard near here. I figured - "

"Again," Hugo said. "Not how. Why?"

"Hugo," Webb said, "Calm down, will you?"

Tag sniffed back angry tears. "I wanted to help you. I know you're not what they're saying. They say all Servicemen are scum, but I know you're not like that, sir. I've read all about you. I know you're a good captain and I wanted to help."

Hugo's eyes blazed.

"You did good, Tag," Webb said, patting the lad on the shoulder. "Well done. And thanks, we need this stuff," he added, indicating the holdall. "It's just…"

"It's dangerous here," Hugo said. Tag looked at him. The fire in Hugo's eyes died. He rubbed his mouth and got down on one knee to be on a level with him. "Thank you, Tag. It means a lot that you believe in us. More than you know. But tracking us down is a very dangerous and foolish thing to have done."

Tag folded his arms and glared. "You grown-ups are all the same. You think I can't do anything. Well, none of them have found you, but *I* did. None of them understand what you're doing but *I* do."

"We're grateful, kid," Webb said before Hugo could respond. "And impressed, quite frankly." Tag sniffed, scowling at the wall. "Seriously. All the Enforcers on the colony are out for us and you're the only one that's found us."

"So far," Dana muttered from her corner, eyeing the boy suspiciously.

"No one followed me," he said. "I swear!"

"It's ok," Hugo said. Webb could hear the effort to stay patient in the commodore's voice. "We believe you, Tag. And you are right. You might be the only one on Haven that understands what's going on here."

"That's what I said," he said, gap-toothed smile widening. "I am, aren't I? I'm right, aren't I? You're the good guys?"

Webb felt his throat tighten at the hopeful look on the child's face. "Sure, Tag. We're the good guys."

"And you're going to save the day, aren't you? You're going to stop the killings and bring the Service to Haven?"

Webb raised his eyebrows. Hugo and Dana exchanged an unhappy look.

"You want the Service here?" Webb asked carefully.

"Sure. They make sure everyone has food and safe work and school, don't they? They make sure trade is done right and everyone has credit."

"In Sunside maybe," Dana muttered but Webb shushed her.

"The Service can do good," Webb said. Hugo's jaw was clenched. "But it's not that simple most of the time, kid."

Tag blinked, mouth turning down.

"What we are doing," Hugo said. "Is making sure someone who is hurting people doesn't get away with it any more. That's what we're here for."

Tag looked up. He pursed his lips, considering, then nodded. "That's good," he mused. "Yes, that still works. You're good guys and I was right. That's all there is to it."

"You got it," Webb said, managing a smile.

"In that case," he said, paused, took a breath and apparently came to a decision. "There's a guy looking for you."

"Someone in particular?" Hugo asked carefully.

Tag nodded. "He's looking for you, really," Tag said, pointing at Webb. "He's another good guy. I think."

Webb felt himself pale. "This guy…he approached you?"

"Uh-huh," Tag said, smiling now. "He came to the boarding house. He said he could tell I knew more than all the grown-ups in the building put together."

"What did he say?"

Tag shrugged. "Just that he was looking for you. And if I find you, I should bring him to you. Do you want me to?"

"What's his name?" Webb said, not looking at the expression that had stolen over Hugo's face.

"I don't know. He said he couldn't tell me."

"What did he look like?" Hugo said, voice careful.

Tag rubbed his chin. "Ur, tall, like you," he said nodding at Webb. "Old. Really old. Beard and hair all grey, though he wore a hat and visor. I couldn't see much of his face."

Webb frowned, scratching his head.

"Who's that?" Hugo asked.

"I haven't the faintest fucking idea. Sorry," he said when Tag giggled. "The faintest idea."

"Don't bring him to us, Tag. And don't tell him where we are," Hugo said.

"Hey, hang on," Webb said. "We don't know who it is. He might be someone who could help."

"He said he wanted to help," Tag said. "He seemed like a nice guy. He said to say to you...urm..." Tag's face crumpled in concentration. "He said to say 'tell Webb I know where to find the man he's looking for.'"

The cables buzzed overhead in the stunned silence that met Tag's words. Hugo was staring at him and he could feel Dana's eyes on him too.

"What shall I tell him?" Tag said.

"Where is he?" Webb asked.

Tag shrugged. "I dunno. He said he'd come back to the boarding house to find me after I'd found you."

"Hugo," Webb said, nodding to the hatch. "A word."

Hugo nodded, opened the hatch and stepped out into the corridor.

"Stay with Dana, ok?" Webb said to Tag and followed Hugo.

Hugo helped him pull the hatch shut then he leant on it, looking him up and down and taking in the way he bent to favour his side.

"Are you in pain?"

"I'll live," Webb said. "I think. Hugo, we need to meet whoever this guy is."

Hugo stood silent, face unreadable.

"You want to as well," Webb said. "I can tell."

Hugo frowned at the floor, thinking hard.

"Come on," Webb insisted. "We can't risk not speaking to him if it's the truth."

Hugo's jaw worked. He looked back up but Webb got the feeling he wasn't seeing him. "It could be a trap."

"Tag's not lying."

"I'm not saying he is," Hugo said. "But this man might be."

"We can't ignore this. He's either genuine, or he's dangerous and we need to meet him like he wants. To get Tag out of the equation."

Hugo blanched at that.

"You know I'm right."

Hugo let out a gust of breath and rubbed his temples. "What I wouldn't give for an Eclipse team on our side right now."

"You've got better than that," Webb said, attempting a smile. "You've got us."

Hugo dropped his hands and gave him a baleful glance.

"Look, we'll plan it. We'll get Tag to give us a signal when the guy turns up. He needs Tag to lead him, so you tail them from the boarding house and me and Dana will be here, ready. If he tries anything funny, the three of us will be more than a match for him."

Hugo nodded grimly.

"We'll find out what he wants," Webb said. "Then we ditch this place so he can't bring anyone down on our heads."

"Are you able to move elsewhere?"

Webb straightened, suppressing a grimace at the bloom of pain. "I'll manage."

Hugo stared at the wall for a painful minute. Webb held his tongue with an effort. The curiosity was almost enough to over-power the tendrils of uncertainty that were still threaded through him, making his skin itch. He pushed aside both sensations and waited for Hugo to admit to himself this was the only chance they were likely to ever get.

"Fine. We'll bring him here, whoever he is. But if he hurts any of you, including Tag…" Hugo's face was dark.

"If he does, we'll set Nam on him," Webb said.

The shadows of Hugo's face shifted and Webb dared to think he might have been smiling, but then he pushed the hatch open and went back in. Tag was sat slumped against the wall, idly turn-ing the locked computer panel over in his hands. Dana stood on the other side of the room, arms folded and watching him uncer-tainly. They both looked up as they came back in.

"Ok, Tag. We're going to meet this man," Hugo said. "You can bring him to us."

"He wants to see Webb."

"He can see Webb," Hugo said and, when Dana started to protest. "Providing he's safe. Now, Tag," Hugo went forward and sat on the floor with the boy. He took the computer panel out of his hands and made sure he was paying attention. "You've been a great help but this is it now, ok? No more helping."

"But -"

"No buts," Hugo said firmly. "This is not a negotiation. You're brave. But this is too dangerous a situation."

"Hugo's scared, Tag," Webb said, leaning down to look Tag in the face. "If anything happened to you, your mother would slaughter us."

He snickered. "She might do that anyway."

"That she might," Webb said. "So let's not give her any more ammunition, ok? Do as Commodore Hugo says and bring us this stranger when he turns up, then you go home and stay there, ok?"

Tag stuck out his lower lip but he nodded. "Fine," he said.

"Good," Hugo said, rooting through the holdall and pulling out a small comm link. He pushed a few buttons then handed it to Tag. "When this man shows up, you push this red button in the middle, ok? I will come and follow you, to make sure it's safe. But don't tell him I'm there."

Tag's eyes brightened. "Ok." He pocketed the comm link. "I won't let you down."

"I know you won't," Hugo said and Webb thought he saw warmth creep into his features.

Webb ruffled Tag's hair. "Now, scram, kid, before your mom notices you're gone."

"Don't worry, I can handle Ma," Tag said, scrambling to his feet.

"Then you're even tougher than we thought," Webb said, but Tag was still gazing at Hugo who'd crossed the room to open the hatch.

"Good luck. Be careful," he said.

"I will, sir," Tag said, beaming, then scurried away.

"This is crazy," Dana muttered. "We're getting help from children and mystery old men."

"And psychopaths," Webb said waving a finger in the air. "Don't forget the psychopaths."

Dana rolled her eyes and sat back down on the floor, leaning against the wall and closing her eyes. Hugo retrieved the computer panel and went back to his corner and set to work again. Webb sighed and lowered himself carefully onto the piled sacking and closed his own eyes.

For the first time in a long time, he fell into a deep and restful sleep.

Δ

Webb felt his strength return the more he rested and ate, but with it came impatience. His injury at once itched, ached, stung and throbbed and Dana's snapping at him to stop whining did not improve his temper.

Hugo had stopped pacing but this just meant there was room in the chamber for Webb to start pacing himself. Hugo's other comm link was sitting on a shelf where they could see and hear if it went off but it didn't stop them checking it every few minutes.

The hours and shifts rolled by, broken only by Dana making a trip for more charges for the lighting pole. Nothing more turned up on any of the sites and networks Hugo checked so religiously. Webb refrained from telling him again that it was useless to check them anyway. He knew Hugo was only doing it as a way to keep his mind off everything else and Webb bitterly wished he had something similar to do.

So he slept and ate and complained until one quiet hour, like the dozens preceding it, was broken by the bleeping and flashing of the comm link on the shelf.

All three of them stared at it a second before Hugo shut it off.

"Arm yourselves. Be ready."

"Get on your wrist comm if anything goes down," Webb said as he shambled after Hugo toward the hatch.

"Likewise," Hugo said and was gone.

Webb stopped himself from pacing with an effort and took up position in one corner as Dana did so in the other. She had a knife in her hand and her eyes locked on the hatch. The wait might have been one hour or ten but when they heard Tag's voice and footsteps in the corridor, his heart hammered against his ribs and he willed himself to be calm and ready.

Dana's grip on her weapon tightened and she shut off the lighting pole, plunging them into pitch blackness. Webb pulled out a lenslight and they heard the hatch open.

"Webb?" Tag called. "You in here?"

Webb flicked the lenslight on and shone it toward the hatch. Tag blinked and threw his hand up to shield his eyes as did the man behind him.

"Alright," Dana said, coming forward from her corner. "Tag, go. Go now."

"But - "

"*Now,* Tag."

Tag and the man jumped at the sound of Hugo's voice behind them. Tag peered into the light a second longer then nodded and slunk out. They heard his running footsteps fade away.

"Get in," Hugo ordered and the man, who was still shielding his eyes, shuffled further into the room and Hugo shut the hatch.

"You wanna get that out of my face, lad? You're gonna blind me."

Webb lowered the light, gaping. "Mac?"

Dana turned the lighting pole back on. The man looked between them all, a wary look on his face. It was the lined face and white beard Webb remembered from the cottage in the highlands, but there the similarity ended. He stood differently, looking taller and his ice blue eyes, always piercing, were now also measuring, taking in their hiding place, their weapons and their expressions with a swift, assessing glance. He was dressed in combat trousers and military issue boots, a black cap pulled down low on his face and a long black coat over everything, concealing a belt that held no weapons but lots of empty clips and sheathes.

"I'm unarmed, lad," he said, pulling back his coat to show the rest of his empty belt. "I ain't here to hurt you. You should know that."

"You know this man?" Hugo said, frowning hard at Mac's face.

"Yeah," Webb said, coming closer. "What in the name of Christ are you doing here?"

"I came to see you."

Webb opened and closed his mouth a few times, "Don't say that like it's no big deal. Let's forget the giant fucking *how* and start with the giant fucking *why*?"

Mac shifted and glanced at Hugo and Dana who were both still stood, weapons in hand, staring at him like they were trying to figure something out. "Can we talk in private, lad?"

Webb blinked. "Uh…sure, I guess."

"No, Webb," Hugo said.

"Relax, Hugo," Webb said, limping to the hatch. "He's not gonna hurt me."

"Wait," Dana said as Webb pulled the hatch open. "Who the hell is he?"

Mac slid a glance Webb's way and raised his eyebrows.

"It's a long story," Webb said. "I'll explain when I get back."

Mac stepped into the dingy corridor and Webb pulled the hatch closed with a curse as his injury strained. He almost buckled but Mac caught his elbow.

"God, lad," the older man, said, helping him straighten. "What's happened to you?"

Webb frowned, the emotion in Mac's voice firing his confusion. "Same old, same old, Mac. You wanna tell me what's going on here?"

Mac's face was pained as he looked him up and down. He stared hard at his face then released his elbow, hesitated, then put a hand on his face. The roughened skin of his palm was warm on Webb's cheek. "What have they done to you, boy?" he breathed. "And it's not…it's not even really you, is it?"

Webb quailed. "What did you say?"

Mac dropped his hand. "I know what you are."

Webb couldn't untangle his tongue to ask any more than, "How?"

Mac shrugged one weary shoulder. "You were all over the newsreels after your little *Resolution* stunt. I recognised you as the lad I'd caught stealing apples from my kitchen and looked you up using certain…unofficial channels."

Webb leant against the wall, pulse thundering his ears, trying to pick apart the sorrow and regret he could read in the older man's face.

"You know what I am?"

Mac nodded.

Webb rubbed his temples. "Ok then. Let's skip over what a mind-fuck that is and get to the real issue. What are you doing here?"

"Like I said," Mac said with a drab smile. "To see you."

"Ok look, old man," Webb managed. "I admit, yes, you saved my bacon after the whole cloning thing and I'm grateful. It's actually kinda touching you've taken such an interest in me. Really. Slightly obsessive and a little creepy, maybe, but, yes, still…nice, I guess. But, seriously, guy…we only met once."

"Twice, now."

Webb rolled his eyes. "Ok, twice. But even so. You trailed me to Haven? What in the Orbit for?"

Mac heaved a huge sigh. His broad shoulders rose and fell and he slumped a little more. He stared at his boots, seemingly chewing over something, then raised his head and looked him in the eye. "I'm yer daddy, Ezekiel."

Webb blinked. It was all he could think of to do. In the light from the lenslight a sad smile played on Mac's weathered face. Webb shook his head in an attempted to get some thoughts moving again.

"Ur…" He made a sound, something between a laugh and a snort. "Look, fella. I don't know who you've been talking to…or what you've been smoking. But you're not my dad. Trust me."

Mac looked around. "Shall we get out of this corridor? Then I can explain."

"No," Webb straightened up, flinching and staggering as the stitching in his side lit with flame. Mac reached for him again but he pulled it away. "No more talking. I'm sorry you've come all this way and I'm sorry you've got this ridiculous idea. But my dad… he was…someone else. Now, if that's everything, you should go. Now. We're kind of in the middle of something."

"Ezekiel." Mac hadn't moved. Webb stood staring past his shoulder, waiting for him to move. "Ezekiel," he said again, quieter. "It's me. I'm…him."

The rushing in Webb's ears got louder and louder until it seemed to fill his head. His vision went blurry. It was almost a conscious effort to pull his breath in and out. It felt like the colony was crumbling apart around him.

He brought the light up again. Mac allowed himself to be examined. Now he was thinking of it…the set of the jaw was familiar. Take away the beard and a few decades from his face… replacc thc wcary sadness in his eyes with the determined fire he remembered from the newsreels.

"Shit a brick," Webb breathed.

Mac snorted. "Well, it's not what I expected you to say, but, frankly, it's better."

"You're…you're Duran McCullough."

Mac winced. "That used to be my name. I've kinda gotten used to Mac now, if you don't mind."

"Mind?"

"Listen, lad -"

"No, no, no," Webb shouldered past him. "No, you don't. I'm not listening to any more of this."

"Ezekiel, wait."

"No," Webb snapped. "This is…just…" he made a wordless exclamation. Mac's heavy expression and pleading eyes swam in and out of focus. He shut his eyes and took a breath, forcing his coherency together. When he opened them again Mac was still there, still looking sad and questioning. "Get your ass back in here. Now."

Mac shrugged and reached to help Webb with the hatch. Webb shouldered him out of the way, heaved it open, ignoring the flare of pain it caused and flung himself in.

"Hugo…Hugo," he said. Hugo was stood in the middle of the room, clearly broken off mid-pace.

"What is it?" Hugo said, taking in Webb's manic air and the tense look on Mac's face as he came into the room.

"He's…fuck…he's…"

"Now, lad," Mac said. "Just hold on a sec before you blow a blood vessel."

Webb slammed the hatch closed and pointed a finger in the old man's face. "You…you…"

"Webb," Hugo said, looking alarmed. "Calm down. What's going on?"

"He's Duran fucking McCullough."

Hugo's mouth opened, Dana scrambled to her feet from her spot in the corner.

"What?" she stared at him. "Webb, have you been at the painkillers?"

"It's true," Webb said. He clutched at his head and took a couple of deep breaths. "Just look at him. Look at him!"

Hugo and Dana stared at Mac, again, like wheels were turning in their heads.

"I can't…" Webb fumbled, turning away. "I can't even…"

A warm hand rested on his back. "It's alright, lad."

"I respectfully disagree," Webb said. He didn't want to, but he turned and looked at the older man's face in the light from the light pole. Now he knew, it was impossible not to see.

"You're supposed to be dead," Hugo said.

Mac tore his focus from Webb and smiled. "Not just a pretty face, eh, Commodore? Glad someone here's keeping their head." Webb sputtered but Mac talked over him. "In all seriousness though Commodore Hugo, I feel I need to say, that whatever Pharos was wrong about…and she was wrong about many things… she was right to invest in you. Probably more than she knew."

"Did she know?" Webb asked, voice gaining pitch. "Did she know you were alive and hiding in the Highlands?"

"Yes. It was her idea."

"Highlands?" Dana said, coming forward. "What do you mean?"

"That's where I met him," Webb said, still staring at the man's face and trying to pull himself out of the sucking vacuum of confusion and anger that had opened inside him. "Before I knew anything…when I woke up in the Medic Centre, I ran away into the woods and he saved me."

"I swear, lad, I didn't know anything then." He lifted his hand as if to touch Webb again and then dropped it. "I had nothing to do with Pharos's plan. She…she didn't even tell me."

"She said…" Webb felt his mind reeling back to the *Resolution* and the image of Pharos glowering at him down the barrel of his gun rose in front of his eyes. "She said it was her idea to hide me…the real me… on Lunar 1, but your idea to bring me back?"

Mac nodded. When he spoke again his voice was thick. "You were our lad. I wanted you watched. I'd never even seen a picture of you…" Mac's eyes began to swim. "When I thought I knew you…at the cottage. It was because you reminded me of a younger me. I should have known then. I should have thought…"

Webb took a shuddering breath, reached inside past the seething emotion he didn't want to think about, but all he found was more questions. "The *Zero* was your idea?"

Mac rubbed his bearded chin, looking at the wall. "No. The ship and the assignments were not my plan. I just didn't want you left unguarded on Lunar 1. I was afraid of what might happen if anyone found out who you were. It was my idea to keep it a secret from everyone, including you. But she just said she would take care of it and I was better not knowing the details. I agreed, though I never stopped thinking about it. But I never dreamt... I never even thought that she'd..."

"She killed him." It was Hugo that spoke. "She had your son killed because he wouldn't dance to her tune. Your tune."

Mac didn't flinch. He didn't shift or start. His face didn't move but Webb saw a gulf opening behind his eyes. "She did."

"Then I killed her," Webb said.

Mac nodded. "I know."

"How, exactly, do you know all this?" Dana said after a long silence in which Webb's head span and his eyes stung.

"I still have contacts," Mac replied smoothly. "And ways of finding things out. They couldn't cut me off completely."

"And who exactly is 'they'?" Dana asked with folded arms.

"The Service Commanders that know about me. Pharos arranged the cottage for me in the Highlands. She arranged that I be watched and not let near the spaceport in exchange for their silence, though very few involved knew the whole truth. I was just a political prisoner with some benefits. After the first war had burned on for so long, she convinced me that a staged assassination was the best way to end the crushing reprisals the Service was laying on the Lunar Strip."

"A staged one? Why not a real one?" Dana drove on mercilessly.

"Because she loved me," Mac said. "She believed in me. She was the only one in the Service that had the chance to influence me and she did. She convinced them to let me live and she convinced me that the revolution had failed and to let it die."

"Your revolution," Hugo said.

Mac met Hugo's black glare with a calm one of his own. "Yes, my revolution. I was a different person then. I believed things could change."

"You should have listened to Doll," Webb said. He had balled his fists to stop his hands shaking. "She was your wife and a better person than Pharos ever was."

"I know," he replied. "There's many things I know now that I didn't then."

"Including that your psycho lady-friend killed your kid because he wouldn't play Happy Rebellion Families, then had him cloned to take your place?" Webb wasn't sure who his anger was truly aimed at, but he couldn't staunch the flow. "Oh, and that that experiment fucked up and now this poor bastard has to live with all this in his head, knowing it was all for nothing?"

Mac's face bled pain. "Yes."

Webb's shaking limbs suddenly stilled. The tearing war of emotions dissipated to a grey, shapeless nothing. He groped about inside him for anything at all, some of the anger, resentment or self-pity that had threatened to pull him under and drown him before Jazz found him. But there was nothing there. He turned his back on the three of them, hobbled to the wall, slid down it and sat on the floor, staring at nothing.

"Why have you come after him now?" It was Hugo's voice. Webb closed his eyes, trying to believe he still wanted answers to the remaining questions but all he could think about was the ache in his head and the burning wound in his side.

"Or at all?" Dana said. Her voice dripped acid. "Too little too late doesn't even begin to cover it."

"I have not come for forgiveness," Mac said, squaring his shoulders. "I have come for you. For him."

"Explain." Hugo again. Webb looked at him. He stood with his head up, arms at his sides, back poker straight. Even with the dust and grime of Haven caked into his skin and clothes, he was still every inch the Service commander. But what was flaring in his friend's face was anything but professional.

"When I saw the three of you flag up on a Haven blacklist I thought well, what links you three and this colony?"

"Ariel," Dana said, stepping forward. "You know about Ariel?"

Mac inclined his head, face grim. "I know the Lunar Independence League hired him during their last revolt. And I know what he did." He looked at Webb who repressed a shiver as imaginary fire burned along the scars. Mac turned back to Dana. "You're right, lass. 'Too late' doesn't even come close to what I am. But I want to help."

"How?" Dana demanded.

"I can tell you where to find him."

"Where?" said Hugo and Dana at once but Webb scrambled to his feet.

"Wait, wait, wait," Webb said, getting up limping forward. He fought down the rush emotion that threatened to pour out of him as either curses, tears or vomit. He took a breath to get control before continuing. "Why?" he breathed. "Why are you doing this? Is it just to make yourself feel better? Because I'm not him, you know. I'm not the one you failed."

Dana and Hugo didn't speak. They watched Mac with blank faces.

"You can't understand what it is like to know that everything you cared about has been tortured and destroyed because of you," Mac said. Hugo's face flickered. "There is nothing, *nothing* I can do that will undo everything that's happened," Mac carried on, not looking at anyone but Webb. He took a step up closer, looking into his face. Webb noticed for the first time they were exactly the same height. "But this is something I can do…the only thing I can do. So I am doing it."

Webb took a minute to make sure he could stop his voice from shaking. "Ok. Where is he?"

Mac held his eyes a moment longer, searching for something in Webb's face. "Storage District," he finally said, pulling a data thumb from one of his pockets. "There's a few off-the-radar types who have fashioned some sort of stronghold in one of the bunkers and holed up together there. But be careful. They're there because they don't want to be found. I don't know what lengths they'll go to, to stay hidden."

Webb took the data thumb. The sick feeling was still there but he couldn't figure out whether it was regret for what had happened already or regret for what would never be. "Thank you," he managed.

Those two words appeared to stabilise something in the older man. He nodded and smiled. A genuine smile. "I'd stay and help if I could, but I now have some highly trained Service Analysts and Eclipse tracking teams on my trail. Besides," he looked around the dusty chamber. "It seems you have everything under control."

Webb snorted. "No less than usual, anyway."

Mac's smile widened. He glanced back at Hugo and Dana who had already booted up the computer panel and were bent over maps, then turned back to Webb. He hesitated, then reached out and put his arms around him. Webb stood stiff for a minute then returned the hug. He felt himself start to tremble and tried to stop but the effort made his injury throb and squeezed wetness from his eyes.

"I don't even know what I'm feeling," he whispered. "These are his feelings. Not mine."

Mac's embraced tightened for a second then he pulled away and held Webb at arm's length, looking into his face. "Do what you have to, lad. Get your revenge for both of us and I hope it's worth it. But I want no more of that." He gave him a gentle shake. "Everything that made up him makes up you. Whatever happens, you're my lad and I won't have you doubt that. And anyone lays a finger on you again, they'll have to answer to me."

Webb swallowed against the choking feeling, but nodded.

"Whatever you say, old man."

"Hey," Mac pointed in his face. "Less of that 'old man' crap. Right, Commodore. Midshipman." Hugo and Dana looked up from the panel, Dana clearly nettled. "I have a date with a deep-space freighter. Good luck to all of you."

He moved straight to the hatch and left without looking back.

XIV

Webb stared at the closed hatch in silence for a long time. A million things swirled in his mind like detritus after a hull breach, but none of it obliged him by ordering itself into anything useful. Pain blurred it all together, and he didn't know which part of himself it came from.

"You ok?"

Dana's question broke the spell. He took a breath and blinked. She had that pinched look about the mouth he'd figured out was her being worried and trying to hide it. Despite everything, it warmed something in him.

"Oh, I'm peachy," he said, rubbing at his aching eyes. "Just golden. Hey, Hugo?" Hugo blinked. He'd been staring at the hatch too. "You with us?"

"Yes."

"You sure?"

Hugo shook his head, still staring blankly. "That was Duran McCullough."

"Yeah," Webb said, rubbing his neck. "Ain't that a kicker?"

Hugo examined him a moment then held out his hand. "What's on that data thumb?"

Webb passed it over. "Stuff on Ariel's pad, hopefully. Just do me a favour: if there's any info on me being related to any more genocidal assholes or dead people who are actually alive, keep it to yourself ok?"

Webb had hoped Hugo would smile but if anything his frown got heavier. Dana took the panel off Hugo and plugged in the thumb.

"It's schematics of the Storage District," she said. "Restricted ones."

Hugo frowned "Restricted?"

"The layouts and security systems in the Storage District aren't public," Dana said, eyes widening as she flicked through. "I guess there's no need for Havenites to know about the colony's wealth. But it's all on here. And it looks like Mac's right: someone's managed to barter storage and accommodation space for private use in there."

"Why would the Elders allow that?" Hugo asked, eyes flicking as they took in the data.

"If you bring enough wealth and business to the colony," Webb said wearily, limping over to look over Dana's shoulder, "there's a lot of perks to be gained. Look at Celeste's apartment."

Webb only realised he was staring at the hatch again when Hugo put a hand on his shoulder. He started. Hugo didn't say anything but Webb could, for once, read everything he was thinking in his face.

"My God," Dana said under her breath, starting them both out of their reverie. "This is it. This warehouse here." She pointed, grinning. "We've found him. We've really found him."

Δ

"Hugo? Will you say something? You're making me nervous."

Hugo didn't look up as he helped Dana pack everything into a holdall. "We will have to move fast. Are you going to be able to keep up?"

He heard Webb sigh. "Yes. I'll keep up. Am I allowed to know what's happening?"

"You know what's happening," Dana said, loading a pack onto her back.

"I know we're going after Ariel. I don't know what you two seem to be able to know without saying anything to each other. Is that a Service thing or a brother and sister thing?"

"Here," Hugo said, handing more dust scarves out from the hldall. "We need to keep our faces covered."

"Hugo," Webb snapped as he snatched the scarf off him. "Tell me the plan."

"No plan yet," Hugo said, not meeting his friend's look. "For now, we're just relocating to the Storage District."

"I still think we should take the mopeds," Dana muttered.

"Negative," Hugo responded, hefting his own pack onto his back and checking his knives. "We don't go above ground unless we have to. Is everything ready?"

"Medkit, weapons, tech, panel, comms," Dana reeled off, checking her belt and pockets. "All set."

"Dana, you're scaring me too," Webb mumbled as he gingerly wrapped the scarf around his face. Hugo watched the clone's stiff movements with uncertainty.

"You're scared of everything," Dana replied. "Do you need me to take some stuff out of your pack?"

"I'm *fine*," Webb said, adjusting the straps but Hugo could tell he was hiding a grimace behind the scarf. "Shall we get going?"

Hugo nodded. "Dana. You have a route?"

Dana tapped her temple. "All up here. It will take us the best part of a shift to get through avoiding inhabited and active areas."

"I trust you," Hugo said, earning raised eyebrows from both of them. "Lead the way."

Dana's surprise melted into a look of suspicion but her glance at Webb only produced a shrug from the younger man. Then she nodded and headed for the hatch.

Hugo took up the rear. As he shut the hatch on their dusty, cramped hiding space he'd never felt gladder to leave something behind. With the buzzing of the cables gone and his blood moving as they marched along the passage, his mind felt balanced. Even the contorted muddle that was Mac's revelations didn't penetrate. He felt like he was sailing on top of it, with a clear heading and control of the vessel. At last.

Finally, he had a plan. He knew the others were not going to like it. But he told himself that didn't matter.

This was going to end his way, and soon.

Δ

"Oh good. Another dirty, rusty hole."

"I want a weapons check, a tech check and everyone to eat," Hugo said, ignoring Webb's complaints. He could tell his friend was in pain. The slog through the betweenways had taken even longer than they'd expected. Webb had kept up for the most part but it had cost him. Dana had insisted they stop every few hours. The last time she had checked his bandaging the bleeding had started again.

When they finally called a complete stop and Dana was arguing with Webb and making him change his dressings, Hugo went through their packs and started to lay everything out.

"Why this place?" Dana said, looking up at the towering chimneys that dominated the space they were in, disappearing somewhere in the dark above them. They were silent and cold, rusted through in parts, but still felt like a solid presence in the otherwise empty chamber. "We're still ages away from the Storage District."

"This is outside the District's surveillance nets," Hugo repeated. "And it's the first place we've found where the door locks."

Dana glanced doubtfully at the heavy metal door with its rusted lock-wheel. "It might have locked once. It doesn't look like it will now."

Hugo left the tech spread on the floor and went to the hatch. His heart pounded and he hoped his guilt didn't show on his face. It locked with a fierce spin of its wheel, confirming to Hugo that neither his sister nor Webb in his injured state would manage it on their own.

"It locks," he said, managing to keep his voice steady, then went back to their equipment. Webb was drinking a protein shake and watching him but Hugo kept his eyes on his work. They finished the checks in silence and then Dana handed out Nutripaks and water. Hugo put his water bottle aside unopened.

"Are we going to make a plan, then?" Webb said as he tried to make himself comfortable against the wall. "I'm willing to bet

Nod that that son of a bitch knows we're coming by now. He'll be prepared."

"Soon," Hugo said, packing the last of the gear away. "Rest first."

The sounds of them swallowing water filled the echoing silence for a moment. Both Dana and Webb were looking tired, gazing at nothing. Hugo concentrated on his tech check rather than wonder what they were thinking.

"You know where I'd like to go when all this is over?" Webb murmured after a time, staring at his Nutripak.

"Where?"

"To the Highlands."

Dana wrinkled her nose. "What, the Academy?"

"No," Webb said with a yawn. "Mac had a cottage there, right on the loch shore. I'd like to go back."

"Why?"

Webb frowned. "I don't know. It was… peaceful."

Dana looked sceptical and took a bite of her food. "If you say so."

"It was," Webb insisted. "You don't get these things if you're born on Earth. But just the water and trees and…I don't know. It felt like an escape."

"I know what you mean," Hugo said quietly. "There's a lake outside Sydney. It used to be a reservoir but it's been landscaped and is now in a protected area. No buildings. When you're there it's like…" He closed his eyes saw himself there, walking along the sand with Harvey, the wind tugging at her curls and the breeze flushing her cheeks. "It's like the rest of the Orbit doesn't matter. You're in your own world."

"Sounds great," Webb said.

"You two are weird," Dana grumbled. "Earth's a dump."

"Enough talk," Hugo insisted. "Sleep."

Webb yawned in answer and Dana's eyes, too, were heavy, though she shook herself and pulled out the computer panel. Hugo took it off her and put it in his pack.

"I want to go over the entries and exits again," she moaned.

"Tomorrow," Hugo said, zipping up the pack. Dana glared, but tiredness robbed the look of any power. "Go to sleep," he insisted.

His sister yawned, finished off her water then nodded, defeated. She pulled out the three blankets they'd brought with them and curled up in one of them. Webb was already asleep, propped up against the wall. Hugo shuffled over and covered him in a blanket then shut off the lighting pole.

He waited until both his companions had been breathing steadily and evenly for a several minutes before slipping out and locking the hatch behind him.

Δ

He didn't let himself think about how easy it was to set the guilt aside as he scurried through the betweenways, guided by directions he'd loaded into his wrist panel. Maybe that was because he didn't feel very guilty. Webb was hurt and Dana was too impulsive. He was better on his own.

It was well over an hour's scramble from where he'd left his companions to the Storage District. He rounded a corner and a breeze was gusting from somewhere and the passage, though dusty, was lit with the sound of voices not far away. He knew he should waste no time, but he still stood staring up at the vent he knew would take him into the District for far more time than was sensible.

He tried to decide if he was scared. But that wasn't it. It wasn't fear of facing Ariel and his stronghold alone. It wasn't about getting hurt or not knowing what he would do when he was finally looking this man in the face. Those things didn't scare him.

But there was something else under all that. And with a start he realised what it was. It was the thought that even if he found Ariel, took him down and managed to smuggle him out of his stronghold, past the blockade and back to the Orbit to stand trial...what he succeeded in all that but Harvey still looked at him with empty eyes?

Mac's words came back to him again.

…you can't understand what it is like to know that everything you cared about has been tortured and destroyed because of you… this is something I can do…the only thing I can do.

Hugo closed his eyes and shook his head. His eyes prickled. We swiped at them with his sleeve then strapped on his hand-grips, clenching his teeth together and taking deep breaths through his nose.

This was something he could do. So he'd do it.

He focused on that thought, glanced about one more time to make sure he was alone, then touched the grips to the metal wall and felt them take hold. He climbed up to the vent, levering off the grid with a multitool and crawled into the narrow space, leaving the grid swinging behind him.

The air vent, like so many others he remembered crawling down during his missions for the *Zero*, was dark, cold and cramped. He felt his way along. When it started to climb, he knew he was heading the right way.

Finally, it lightened and he reached a junction with another grid that looked down over an empty yard, walled in on all sides by tall concrete. He unscrewed the grid and took a full five minutes checking there was no one around and that none of the area's cameras were anywhere in line of sight before shuffling out feet-first and dropping to the ground.

He scanned around. Ahead was the wall of a featureless building. Behind him and on each side were the District's high boundary walls. In the distance he could just make out the blinking tops of the Planning District towers.

Hugo couldn't help but feel the vent had been a little too conveniently placed. But then, looking around at the rest of the fortifications, he figured that whatever these Havenites were worried about keeping out, it probably wasn't one man and his multitool.

He took another check of his position on his wrist panel then ran across the yard and around the side of the building, heading deeper into the District. He kept away from the broader avenues that ran between the clusters of windowless buildings, but the further he went the more unsettled he became. It was like whenever he thought he had his head round this colony, he discovered a new place or turned another corner and he was right back to feeling lost and disorientated. The buildings were all large but in a dizzying array of shapes. Some towered up into the shadows, some seemed to sprawl for blocks. The access avenues between them converged on wide squares. Innumerable lifters, from little hand-carts to the industrial-sized cranes, were parked up and stored in many of these open spaces, but there was barely a soul around.

Many of the buildings had huge rolling doors, all closed, all locked. Some had platforms and doors on other levels high above his head with walkways between them, supported on metal and concrete pillars that split the colony's dull green light into green bars flung across the miles of empty accessways. He occasionally heard voices, engines or machinery in the distance and the throb that was the constant sound of distant yards and refineries, but he only had to duck out of sight of a real person once. The cameras and motion sensors were concentrated around the boundaries and avenues so even they were easy to avoid.

The few noises faded as he approached the cluster of buildings that Mac had highlighted as those that had been bargained off the Elders. If anything, it was even more spartan than the rest of the district. Most of the doors had been bricked up or welded shut. There were no lifters in sight, though he did see parked mopeds and a couple of old but serviceable flyers. Floodlights had been installed and washed everything painfully bright after the gloom of the rest of the District. The black eyes of camera clusters dotted most corners and walls.

He sunk into the shadows of a blocked doorway when he heard voices. Two men, big enough to be Enforcers, though they weren't in the ubiquitous dark coveralls of the colony's official security, came round a corner. One had burn scars twisting up one side his face. The other walked with a heavy limp. They were talking but they were watchful, checking between the buildings and looking over the square.

Hugo held himself still until they moved past and continued on their patrol. He paused there for another ten heartbeats until their footsteps had faded away before risking another look. He recognised the building across the square as the one that Mac had marked as Ariel's stronghold. There was nothing to tell it apart from any other buildings or to even indicate that it was used at all. If he hadn't loaded the co-ordinates into his wrist panel he would have thought he'd made a mistake. What had once been a door big enough to fit several industrial lifters with cargo was now a series of iron seals barricading the entrance. Once again, there were no windows and no other visible way in. However, as he padded closer, he made out a watch tower and communication rigs on the roof.

Something almost like excitement, but colder, buzzed through him. He ducked back down the way he'd come, to approach the building from the shadows of its neighbours. He began a circuit of its cluster of outbuildings, relay sheds and storage bunkers, looking for a way in.

He found side doors, but they were all sealed or guarded. He was beginning to feel a nagging doubt that perhaps he wasn't as well-prepared for this as he thought, when he heard the whooshing sound of ventilated air somewhere nearby. Looking about, he spotted an open shaft in the concrete over his head. It was far too high to reach and his grips wouldn't work on concrete so he began a tentative search of the storage bunkers for something to stand on. Most were locked or empty but the last one he checked yielded a rusted sit-on sweeper, some piles of unidentifiable tools and two empty bloodgrease canisters.

He winced at the noise the canisters made as he dragged them back to the vent. He paused to catch his breath and listen. He heard radioed orders and information exchanged between some of the guards echoing off the tall walls, but nothing close by. He stacked the canisters beneath the vent. They wobbled as he clambered up. He stretched. His fingertips just brushed the lip of the vent.

"Hey, you!"

His heart leapt into his mouth. He span and just had time to take in a startled-looking guard before the canisters toppled. He sprang free as they fell, landing with a roll and then was up again and running, shouts and the clattering of the canisters following him.

His heart pounded. He steered away from the light, not letting himself consider the sucking despair that threatened to swallow him whole. The sounds of shouting and running could be heard behind him and then the cough and whine of mopeds being started up.

He skidded round a corner, glancing over his shoulder as he went and so didn't see the hand-lifter blocking the way until it was too late. With a crash and a shout of surprise and pain, he went over, spilling the lifter's load of cans and drawing spluttered curses from its driver.

Hugo lay dazed on the concrete, the green murk of Haven's hull spinning far above him. The cans rolled about and bumped into his legs and the worker bent over him.

"Hey, you ok?"

"There he is," someone shouted and Hugo scrambled to his feet just as two guards on mopeds rounded another corner. He turned and ran, though there was nowhere to go. They caught up and outflanked him. He skidded and jumped back as they braked in front and behind him. He pulled out both his knives and spread his feet, trying to blink away the spinning in his head.

"Put your weapons down," the guard in front of him ordered.

Hugo tightened his grip on his knives, a million and one ideas racing through his head and getting rejected one by one.

"Hey, I recognise him," the other guard said as he sidled closer. "He's the one the bosses said would come skulking."

"Grab him," the other man said and made a swipe.

Hugo sidled out of reach then lunged. The guard ducked the blow and Hugo staggered, turned and threw his knife at the second man. It caught him in the shoulder. He and his moped went sprawling, but the first one had recovered. He leapt forward, ducked Hugo's stab and shouldered him in the solar plexus, taking him down. Hugo hit the concrete hard and gasped, winded. He lashed out blindly and tried to roll away but the guard's weight was on top of him and he pinned his knife hand to the floor.

Something cold and blunt pressed into his neck, cutting off his air. He coughed and shifted as his vision steadied.

"You keep yourself fucking still, hear me? Or I'll blow your head off."

Hugo tilted his head to try and free his windpipe from the crushing press of the gun at his neck, still dazed enough to not be able to make sense of what was happening. With his other hand the guard tightened his grip on his arm.

"Drop it."

Hugo choked and dropped the knife.

"Get up," the man ordered, standing up and dragging Hugo with him by a handful of collar.

"Blood and sand, Art," the wounded guard cursed as he scrambled to his knees. He'd pulled out Hugo's knife and had a hand clasped over the bleeding in his shoulder. "Put the gun away. There's a worker right over there."

The guard holding Hugo paled and looked over to the worker with the overturned lifter, who was stood gawping. The guard called Art put his gun away and pulled out a short stick-knife to take its place at Hugo's throat before his fractured awareness could take advantage of the break.

"Leave the scoots," Art muttered. "Can you walk?"

"I don't walk with my fucking shoulder, do I?" the other

growled, wincing as he pulled out a knife of his own with his other hand. "Come on, let's get him locked away so I can get to a medic."

"You going to tell us who you are?" Art said as he twisted Hugo's arm up behind him and wrestled him forward.

"Don't talk to him, you idiot," the wounded guard hissed. "Let the bosses handle it, like they said."

Hugo managed to take a breath, and a degree of calmness stole through him. He assessed both guards and the surroundings, even as they manhandled him across the square and called for backup on a wrist comm. Neither of these guards limped but the one he'd injured had one milky eye and the one holding him definitely had one weak wrist. Ghosts, he wondered? The men on the *Perseverance* had all been visibly scarred or limped. He wondered whether they chose this life because the yards had left them crippled and bitter, but then he forced himself to focus.

Hugo tested the man's hold again. Whilst he was distracted by his pulling, Hugo slammed his head back into the man's face. There was a sickening crunch and a bubbling cry and Hugo was able to wrench himself free.

He ducked the injured man's knife and took out his legs with a sweeping kick. The man went down, taking Art with him and whilst they were cursing in a tangled heap on the concrete, Hugo took off towards the nearest gap between the warehouses.

He'd gone down one alley and was skidding toward the boundary walls when the first spatter of silenced gunfire cracked into the ground at his heels. He looked back, made out more men on mopeds bearing down on him, handguns drawn, barrelled around a corner and right into the arms of three more men. He heard someone shout an order not to shoot before something cracked into the back of his skull and everything went dark.

Δ

The first thing Hugo became aware of, some indeterminable time later, was a pounding in his head and a metallic taste in his mouth.

After that, it was the coldness of the floor and the awkward angle of one his arms. He took a breath and opened his eyes, blinking away stars. He tested his limbs. All worked, though everything ached.

He eased himself up of the floor, fighting back a sweep of nausea. He was in a cold, windowless room, lit by some dingy lighting panels in the ceiling. There was no furniture and nothing on the walls, though marks on the floor and walls suggested heavy objects had been stored here. He peered about but saw no cameras.

He touched a finger to his forehead and it came away bloody. A careful probing with his tongue confirmed a split lip also. Everything else felt sore and bruised. He got to his feet, leaning against the wall a moment until the ringing in his ears eased and his vision stopped swimming, then he went to the door.

The handle on the inside had been snapped off. There was an electronic lock but no panels or controls on his side. He gave the door an experimental kick but it didn't budge. His attempts to shoulder it open only succeeded in increasing the ferocity of his headache.

He slid down the wall and sat on the floor, closing his eyes to ease the pain and cursing himself. His weapons, wrist panel and tech were all gone. He crossed his legs, closed his eyes and rested his head against the wall. All there was to do was wait.

He purposely did not think about Webb and Dana trapped underground, or about the fact that he could be anywhere on Haven, held by anyone. He could be in one of the Elder's holding cells, about to be handed back to Bryce.

He breathed deep, wiped his mind clean and waited.

He didn't realise he'd fallen asleep, or passed out again, until the sound of shouting outside the door and the lock opening jerked him awake. He was on his feet in an instant, ignoring the protest from his pulled muscles and throbbing head and put himself in the middle of the room so he couldn't be cornered.

His heart dropped like a stone when he heard Webb's raised voice. The door scraped open with a hideous noise and the clone was bundled in. The door was hauled shut again and the lock buzzed and clicked.

Webb got himself to his knees, swearing and holding his injured side. "Oh, hey Hugo," he said through gritted teeth. "So that's where you'd got to."

"What the hell are you doing here?"

"That was my question," Webb said, crawling to the wall.

"Where's Dana?"

Webb groaned and shifted to lean against the wall. "Hopefully somewhere doing better than us."

"What happened, how did you end up here?"

"How did *you*?" Webb countered. "Jesus Christ, Hugo. When we woke up and I'd calmed Dana down, I told myself you wouldn't have bolted unless you had some sort of kick-ass plan. Did you even have *any* kind of plan?"

"Yes. Did you?"

Webb shook his head and kicked his heel into the floor. "Christ in Heaven, I don't believe you. After everything that's happened, you ditched us? Hell, even your pain-in-the-ass of a sister didn't deserve that."

"Do you know where we are?"

Webb blinked. "They hit you hard, huh? Good."

"Where are we?"

"One of the privately-held strongholds," Webb muttered, looking around at the dingy room. "No thanks to you. You know, if we'd planned this together this wouldn't have happened."

Hugo clenched his mouth shut, closed his eyes and tried to think.

"Hugo," Webb said, getting to his feet. "Hey, Commodore. I'm talking to you."

"Shut up," Hugo gritted. "I'm thinking."

"Hey, hey, hold up," Webb raised his hands. "*You're* mad at *me*?"

"You were supposed to stay put."

"Why?" Webb tried to sound angry but the hurt wasn't entirely hidden from his voice.

"Because you were right, ok?" Hugo deflated and clutched at his forehead. "You were right, right from the start. I've used you, even though I said I wouldn't. And it got you hurt."

"That's why you ditched us?" Webb said, folding his arms.

Hugo ground his teeth together. "I told myself that as long as I got Ariel, it didn't matter how I did it. But I was wrong. I didn't want you to get hurt again."

Webb's face was rigid but then he looked away. "Well I'm telling you now, Dana has more than a few select words stored up for you. But whatever, we're here now. What do we do?"

Hugo chewed the inside of his cheek, staring at the door again. "I don't know yet."

"He knew we were coming, just like we said," Webb said after a defeated pause. "The bastard's got this place tied up tighter than a ship's hull and they've got guns. *Guns*, Hugo."

"I know," Hugo said, running a hand through his hair, wincing as he hit the bruise blossoming across his scalp.

"Well, shit on it," Webb sighed. "Two different plans and neither of us even got close. We've fucked this, haven't we?"

"No," Hugo said, going to the door and feeling round the seams "We're not fucked until we're dead."

"If you say so."

"I do," Hugo said, rounding on Webb. "Ariel is in this building somewhere."

"We don't even know that."

"He's got to be. 'Let the bosses handle it' is what the men that jumped me said. He knows we're here by now and he's not getting away. We get him off this colony or we kill him."

Silence spun on as Hugo realised what he said.

"You've changed your tune."

Hugo clenched his teeth, kicked the door and swore.

"Alright, alright, don't have a fit," Webb said, getting to his feet and pulling Hugo away from the door. "We've done this before. Keep calm. We just need a new plan."

"Where's Dana?"

"Don't worry about her. She's more capable than you give her credit for."

"I know she's capable. She's also reckless."

Webb cracked a crooked grin. "Must run in the family."

Hugo rubbed his face. "This isn't helping."

"No, right, ok. First question, then. Ariel must have recognised us from the blacklist. He must know why we're here. He's set and armed his guards ready…"

"So why are we still alive?" Hugo finished.

Webb scratched his cheek. "And why do I get the feeling we don't want to know the answer?"

Hugo's mind skidded about like a marble in a bowl then there was the sound of voices and footsteps outside the door.

"Get back," Hugo said and they both fell in next to each other, the wall at their back and their eyes on the door. The lock buzzed and the door was heaved open.

In stepped a man, short even by Haven standards with dark hair pulled back from his face and tied in a short tail at the back of his head. His eyes were a very pale blue, startlingly so, and if it weren't for the extremely unpleasant expression on his face, Hugo would have considered him handsome. Beautiful, even.

Hugo started. It was the man he'd seen spying on them at the boarding house. He watched the man register his recognition and straighten his shoulders in response, scorn clear in his eyes. He carried no obvious weapons but by the way he held himself, as well as the two large guards standing at his back, he clearly did not feel the need.

"Paragon?" Webb said, face stricken.

"You know him?" Hugo asked.

The short man's icy eyes darted over both of them as he sneered.

"Always knew I'd see you again someday, Ezekiel," the man's voice grated, like he had a throat problem. "And somehow I always knew it wouldn't be a joyous reunion."

"What's going on?"

Hugo saw Webb swallow. "I…we…"

"We were close, for a time," the small man said as he looked Webb up and down. "Very close."

"Don't flatter yourself," Webb said. "I knew…I knew there was something weird about you. You were spying on me?"

"What, you thought it was your sparkling personality that kept me around?" The man snorted, pulled back his sleeve and pressed a command on a top-of-the-range wrist panel. Hugo noticed his left arm moved with the slight stiffness of a synthetic. The skin didn't quite match his other hand, either.

"The one-armed man," Hugo muttered but Paragon was already talking. Webb didn't appear to be listening though Hugo could see him making the connections.

"You were right sir," his rasped into his communicator. "Our lanky friend is back. And he brought the bulky, angry-looking Serviceman, the one that was involved with that Eclipse agent."

"And the girl?"

The high-quality speakers on the panel meant the voice that replied barely had any distortion, but it was thin and flat, slightly high-pitched and controlled to an almost painful degree. It put Hugo in mind of the simulant technology he'd been shown on his last official tour of the research and training vessel, *Endeavour*. The researcher had said that the androids were more likely to end up being engineered for domestic and retail markets than the military, but their blank eyes and empty voices had set his flesh on edge.

A glance at Webb showed that the voice had even more of an effect on him. His jaw was tight, his skin pale and he wasn't blinking. He was staring at the Havenite's wrist panel like he had seen the devil himself.

"No girl," Paragon went on, examining Webb's reaction closely, the beginnings of a cruel smile playing about his mouth.

"Very well. Bring them to me in the Conference Suite."

"Sir," he began to protest. "I think we should keep them locked up. They're slippery, these two."

"I'm not moving for them, Paragon. We employ guards, don't we? Use them."

The Havenite looked angry for a moment, then he schooled himself and transferred his angry look to the guards. "You heard him. Get these two up to the Conference Suite."

The two men nodded and drew their guns. One stepped forward, reaching for Hugo.

"Come on, you."

"And what if we're quite happy here?" Webb muttered.

"Shut up and move," the guard snapped and hustled Hugo out as the second man came in for Webb.

They marched down a wide passage with bare walls and a series of reinforced doors. They marched in silence and Hugo spent the time trying to set aside the growing feeling of unease that sprouted from the disorientation and Webb's reaction to the voice on the comm.

They turned a corner and climbed a flight of stairs. Hugo's mind went through a dozen possible ways to overpower the guards as they climbed, using the steps to their advantage. However, the guard in front kept checking over his shoulder as if he knew his thoughts and whenever he glanced back to try and catch Webb's eye, his friend didn't look like he was entirely with them.

The sounds of clattering of metal, running water and chattering voices gained volume as they climbed. They stepped through a door into a hot, steamy space. The air was heavy with cooking smells that made Hugo's stomach clench. Half a dozen cooks stopped in their work around the clean and expensively-fitted kitchen to stare as they were hustled through.

They were marched through carpeted hallways. They went past

wide arching doorways looking onto luxurious rooms with deep couches, high-quality displays, book shelves laden with hard-copy volumes of books as well as small statuary and ornaments. There were real as well as digi-prints hung on the walls and Hugo struggled to fight off the disorientation that swamped him after the bare corridors.

He started to put serious consideration into whether they might have somehow been taken off-colony, but then they passed rooms in use. There were men and women, all well dressed, sitting at the tables and watching newsreels or films on the displays, making calls on the comm units or leafing through books with glasses of wine to hand. Some were obviously Havenites, short and dark-featured and more often than not badly scarred or missing digits or limbs.

A few people amongst them wore flight suits and spacer boots. He recognised some of their arm-patches as the logos of smuggling ships Eclipse had under surveillance. They were looking at figures and prices on the displays with the Havenites. The bits of conversation he overheard sounded like trade deals and negotiation. Knowing what they were bartering for made Hugo go cold.

Some looked up as they passed, but most didn't. What looks they did draw were knowing and disdainful.

"Ghosts," Webb muttered in Hugo's ear before he was grabbed and pulled back.

There were still no windows anywhere. To reduce the risk of intrusion, Hugo wondered, or to add to the illusion that they weren't on Haven?

Paragon barked at them to hurry. They were led around another corner and ushered into an express lift. The machine made no sound above a purr as they moved up. The bright lights showed Hugo how dirty and dishevelled he was, especially next to Paragon.

The lift doors slid open onto dimness and they were shoved out and onto thick carpet.

XV

Hugo blinked in low light. The room was large and open, lit by some floor-level lighting panels installed behind a black boarder that merged with the thick carpet. A large fireplace and mantel dominated one wall and a simulated fire burned in the grate. The room was warm from its hidden chargers and the light it gave off flickered and pulsed.

A large table took up almost half of the room, dark displays in its surface as well as mounted on the wall above. A large desk and comm-unit was built into the corner. Hugo could tell just by looking at it that it was more advanced even than the ones on Command. In contrast to the sleek, hard lines of the table and workstation, deep, soft chairs and sofas were clustered around the fireplace.

The green glow that bathed everything came from the walls that were made entirely of plexiglass that overlooked the vast spread of Haven. The spires of the Planning District rose in the distance, casting their green light on colony around them like an Emerald City from the books he'd read as a child.

He wondered if the man in the armchair by the fire had the lights off and the vast view on display in a deliberate attempt to overwhelm them. He had an open book in his lap and his legs crossed. His light suit was tailored to his slim body. His tie against a white, white collar was a deep charcoal, as were the fine gloves that covered his hands. These colours only made his white skin and hair seem even more uncanny. His hair was tucked neatly behind his ears but was so fine that strands floated free. The light from the simulated flames lit it up like threads of fire.

Set in the pale face was a pair of the blackest eyes Hugo had ever seen. They weren't just dark, they were cold, empty and deep as space. One look at them was all Hugo needed to know that this man tortured people for money.

He said nothing as Hugo and Webb were shoved closer toward him. Hugo risked a glance at his friend. Webb was holding himself tall, his shoulders square and his back poker-straight. He was staring at the man like it was only force of will that was stopping him either leaping on him to beat him senseless, or fleeing the room.

"You managed to get them from the detention room to here without losing them, then," Ariel said, glass eyes sliding to Paragon. "From what you were saying I thought they might manage to kill all three of you, break through the walls and fly away."

Paragon stiffened but visibly bit back his response and stood with this hands clasped behind his back. "You remember them now, sir?"

Ariel raised one fine white eyebrow. "No, not really. It's you that's been obsessed with this one," Ariel said, idly indicating Webb. "Not me."

"I thought…" Paragon flushed, straightened himself and tried again. "I thought it best to keep an eye on him, sir. What with his connections."

Ariel sighed, looking them both over with a bored air. "I suppose you might have been right, by the looks of it."

Hugo felt Webb shift next to him. His own palms were beginning to sweat and every inch of his skin tingle with the proximity to the blade. He tried to ignore the pounding of his heart and concentrate on assessing the positions of the guards and their attentiveness to their weapons.

When his eyes came forward and met Ariel's dead-on, Hugo was once again assaulted by the feeling the man was looking right into his head.

"You can try if you want, Commodore," Ariel said, standing in one smooth motion and straightening his suit. "But, I'm curious. After managing to grab one of the guns, shooting both me and Paragon and my men…where exactly do you plan to go?"

Hugo bristled, fists clenching at his sides. He refused to give Ariel the satisfaction of having him glance around the room. He already knew there was no way out apart from the lift back into the stronghold.

"Yes, be sensible," Ariel said as he stepped towards them. "If there's one thing I can't abide, it's foolishness."

He went right up to Webb and stood toe-to-toe. He reached out and folded back the younger man's collar. Webb clenched his fists. He seemed to stop breathing and stared at the wall, sweat standing out on his skin. Hugo was convinced his friend was about to faint when Ariel made a musing noise, pulled off one of his gloves and ran his bare fingers up Webb's throat. The clone took a sharp breath and finally blinked.

"Yes, I do remember you now. The clone, of course. LIL, wasn't it? And their little plan for Orbit domination," Ariel murmured, leaning in for a closer look at the scarring. "I see you've tried to have these lasered off. It hasn't worked, has it? How interesting." He straightened and pulled his glove back on, examining Webb's face like he was an object of mild curiosity. "I imagine your physiology is quite unique. What a shame we aren't on better terms. I do believe there might be quite a lot to be gained from studying you. Paragon, come here."

The short man stepped up next to his master, distaste clearly written in his face.

"Observe," Ariel said, gesturing airily towards Webb's neck. "The healing here is abnormal. Take a closer look -"

"I'm telling you now," Webb ground out. "The shrimp touches me, he's going out the window."

Paragon bridled, but Ariel just gave a tired sigh. "Brutish threats. You're all the same, you Outsiders."

"Whereas you're like nothing else in existence."

"I take that as a compliment. Now. Both of you," he looked at them each in turn, eyes dark as pits. "Paragon informs me there's another. Where's the girl?"

Webb glared, jaw working. Hugo glanced about the room for anything that give him an advantage but still found nothing.

"Come on now," Ariel said, putting his hands behind his back and rocking on his heels. "We don't have all shift. You've failed. If you possess even half the intelligence I suspect you do, you know that by now. Tell me where the other Hugo is and we can put a lid on this ridiculous affair."

"Go fuck yourself," Webb said. He was frighteningly still, the sort of immobility Hugo recognised as coming from someone stopping themselves from shaking.

Ariel tutted. "You've said that to me before, young man. It didn't succeed in rattling me then either, did it? Now, as you might guess, Paragon here is a sort of apprentice of mine," he laid a hand on the shorter man's shoulder. Hugo didn't miss his involuntary flinch making his synthetic fingers tic. "His work has a different style, but is possessed of its own sort of finesse." A slow smile started to spread on Paragon's face. "He's handled some lucrative contracts already, so I have no qualms in handing you over to his capable care. He can extract the answer with very little effort I can assure you. But," Ariel checked his fine old-fashioned watch. "We are due on a conference call with a client. So, it would really help everyone involved if you just told us where to find her."

"The minute you know you'll kill all three of us," Hugo stated.

"Well done, Commodore," Ariel said. "You are intelligent, after all. And that being so, you should know that I can't have vengeful vigilantes running about my colony. It's unprofessional and frankly, rather embarrassing."

"If you think I'm here to listen to anything you have to say," Hugo said. "You grossly misunderstand the situation."

Ariel sighed and looked at the ceiling. "Honestly, you do irk me. None of what I've done is personal, Commodore, Commander, or…" he frowned slightly at Webb and then waved impatiently. "Or whatever you are. I was hired for those jobs. I was selling my skills, nothing more."

"You're a psychotic freak," Webb said.

Ariel looked almost pitying. "If it makes it easier for you to think that, go ahead. I really couldn't care less. But you'd be a lot less troubled if you understood the reality. You and that Eclipse agent: you were just job numbers to me. And a complete waste of resources, that job turned out to be," he said, almost as an afterthought. "She didn't even know anything about the Ghosts' little organ-trading project. They can be quite amateurish at times with their concerns."

Hugo had gone white with rage.

Ariel heaved a sigh. "Honestly, Commodore, this behaviour is most unbecoming. If anything you owe me. I left your officer alive, didn't I?"

They both jerked at once but Hugo got to his guard first. Blind with anger, he didn't think and threw his whole weight, shoulder-first, into the man's solar plexus. The man grunted and Hugo reached to wrench the gun, still an unfamiliar object in the man's grip, out of his hand. The man stumbled back and Hugo pulled the weapon free, but then the guard got a hold on his arm and pulled him off balance. He went down and the man was on him in a second, kneeling on his back. He twisted Hugo's arm up behind him whilst slamming the other wrist on the floor until he dropped the gun.

The guard straightened, pulling Hugo onto his knees. Ariel's only reaction had been to take a step back. Paragon hovered behind him, surprise melting into a smirk as he watched Hugo being hauled to his feet. The other guard was holding a tousled Webb and scowling with a rapidly swelling eye.

"I'm going to kill you," Webb said, straining against his captor's grip. "I'm cutting you into a million pieces myself."

Ariel used his thin fingers to rub his temples. "You are so tiresome."

"Blade known as Ariel," Hugo growled, standing tall despite his screaming in his shoulder as the guard bent his arm up further.

"You are under arrest. You are to accompany me back to Service Headquarters for formal charges and questioning."

Ariel laughed. It was a horrible noise. Paragon sneered. Hugo had already noticed the man's fingers were twitching again and he was looking at him with a greedy glint in his eyes.

"This is my colony," Ariel said. "You're the criminals, here."

"Yeah, Haven treats you good, alright," Webb said, with a pointed look around the room. "Though I don't think the Elders would be so acrimonious if they knew the whole truth."

"If you're referring to the regrettable use of firearms," Ariel replied smoothly, "it is hardly my fault the witless wonders that pass for Elders these days are unable to keep the riffraff at bay."

"And shacking up with the likes of the Ghosts?"

Ariel's face went still. "We're business partners. They sometimes require my services. I need somewhere to live out of reach of prying Outsiders. What they do outside this colony is none of my concern."

"You're on borrowed time," Webb said, face grim. "If I don't get you, Haven will."

"These are my people, young man," Ariel murmured. "And this is my home. And you have outstayed your welcome. Tell us where the other one is and now. I grow tired of this game."

"They're not going to talk, Master," Paragon grated in his creaking voice. "Let me get started on them. We can have the girl by next shift."

Ariel heaved another sigh. "No, Paragon. I don't think we have time."

"But sir," Paragon said. "She could be cleverer than these two."

Ariel gave a delicate snort. "That's hardly an achievement. Put them back in their cell. If they aren't ready to give us what we need by tomorrow, you can see what you can get from them then."

"Yes sir," Paragon said. "And you know what," he added, nodding at Hugo. "This one's a high-ranking Serviceman by all accounts. There's probably all sorts of stuff this one knows that might be of value."

"Indeed," Ariel said. "Make sure to record everything you extract. I'll expect a report when it's done -" Ariel broke off when his workstation started bleeping in the corner. "Get them out of here," he said, striding over to answer it.

"You heard him," Paragon said, waving toward the lift. "Get them back to the detention cell."

"You're a pair of fucked-up freaks," Webb said as the guards started to drag them back to the lift. "Both of you."

Paragon sneered again. "Bitterness doesn't suit you, Ezekiel," he said. "I shall look forward to tomorrow."

The guards grunted at them to move and prodded them with their guns back to the lift. Webb continued to curse all the way down in the lift until his guard gave him a violent shake to shut him up. Hugo heard a joint pop and Webb swore once more but then fell silent. They were taken back through the corridors and kitchen and locked again in the dim cell. Hugo leant against the door, staring at the pitted ceiling.

"He was right," Webb said as he slid down the wall to slump on the floor. "Even if we'd managed to overpower the guards, there's nowhere to go."

Hugo closed his eyes. "There's nowhere left to go."

"Hey, hey, hey, what happened to the 'we ain't fucked until we're dead' business?"

Hugo kept his eyes closed and didn't say anything.

"Good God, Hugo," Hugo heard Webb get up. "I know he's a freaky bastard, but you can't let him get under your skin now... excuse the phrase."

Hugo opened his eyes. Webb was still pale. He was leaning against the wall, his hand clasped to his injured side.

"Do you actually believe in God, Webb?"

Webb blinked. "Huh?"

"I think your original did. Do you as well?"

"Why?"

"It's a simple question."

"Some might say a personal one."

"Well?"

Webb ran his hands through his hair. "You want to have a theological debate….now?"

"No," Hugo said, pulling himself up off the door to stand in front of his friend and look him in the face. "I'm just asking you."

"Again," Webb said. "Why?"

Hugo shook his head. "I don't know. I'm just wondering… it must be nice to be certain of something. Anything. That no matter what happens, to have something that keeps you going."

"And you think God does that for me?"

"I don't know. That's what I'm asking."

Webb chewed on his lip, worry clear in his eyes. "Look, Kaleb," he said. "I know we're cruising right up shit creek right now with no paddle in sight, but hold it together, ok?"

"He's putting you back on the table tomorrow," Hugo said. He watched something crawl over Webb's face and felt it like a kick in his own stomach.

"It won't come to that," the clone chose to say. Hugo didn't believe him, but didn't say so. "Listen, man. You are not to give up. Understand?"

Hugo didn't reply.

"I'm serious, you pig-headed ass," Webb snarled. "We are not fucked. Not yet."

"You thought we were fucked already."

"Ah yes, but that was before."

"Before what?" Hugo asked, rubbing his eyes. His head was pounding and everything ached. He just wanted to curl in the corner and forget everything.

"Before we knew for sure the freak was in this building." When Hugo raised his gaze and saw Webb was smiling. "He's not scared of us. But he should be."

"Why?"

"Because we have something he doesn't."

"What?"

"Balls," Webb grinned wider. Hugo just raised his eyebrows. "I'm serious, Hugo. Did you hear him talk? I swear the man's a robot. I don't think he understands just what a human being can do when he's really, really pissed."

Hugo looked at the wall.

"Come on, you know I'm right. I've seen you storm a flagship just for a chance to kick my butt."

"I was only able to do that because you made a hole in the side of the damn thing first."

"Bull," Webb said, going to the door and starting to feel at it. "You'd've found a way. Come on. We are not going to be beaten just because this nutcase hired guards with guns."

Hugo pressed his lips together, doubtful. But Webb's face was earnest. He felt the start of a smile creep across his face.

Webb clapped him on the shoulder and got down to his knees and put his eye to the door seam. He patted his pockets and cursed.

"They took my multi-tool. There's got to be…" He sat back on his heels and looked around. His eyes landed on Hugo. "Give me your dog tags," he said, holding out his hand.

"Why?"

"Hugo, we've got a precious few hours before the shrimp comes back to practice on us. Do you want to waste time on stupid questions? Hand them over."

Hugo felt something in his chest clench and he clutched at the metal through his clothes. There was sympathy in Webb's glance but urgency too. Hugo lifted the chain over his head, throat tight and held them out.

Webb was just reaching for them when all the lights went out.

"Shit," Webb cursed in the dark. "What the hell…?"

"Quiet," Hugo said, fumbling his dog tags back on. He listened. There was a muffled shout and some very distant noise, so dampened by the layers of concrete around them it was impossible to make out.

"What's going on?"

"The power's gone," Hugo said. "Listen."

Webb went silent again. More voices and hurried footsteps were heard somewhere above their heads, followed by a crash. But other than that… silence. No humming of generators or wires or breath of ventilation.

"Christ. Do you think it's the whole colony?"

"Let's hope not. Move back."

"What are you doing?" Webb asked as Hugo groped in the darkness and pushed his friend back from the door.

"These locks are electric. Maybe we can force it now there's no power."

Hugo felt for the door then took a step back and kicked. He paused to listen but the only noises were still indefinable distances away so he kicked again and felt the metal give.

"Move over," Webb said and Hugo made room. They held on to each other in the dark and got into position.

"One, two, three," Webb counted and they both pounded the door with their booted feet. The metal groaned.

"Again," Webb said, bracing against him but then Hugo grabbed him to still him. "What?"

"Shh," Hugo hissed and felt his way to the door, listening.

"Kale? Webb?" The voice came from somewhere.

"Dana!" Hugo cried.

"Shit, is that her?" Webb scrambled to join him at the door.

"Kale?" she called again.

"Dana," Webb bellowed, pounding on the door. "We're in here."

They heard boot steps and then a light shone under the door. "Webb, is that you?"

"We're both in here," Webb said. "Christ Above, it's good to hear your voice. How did you find us?"

"No time for that now," Dana snapped. "We need to get the hell away from -"

She was cut off by a deafening blast that shook the walls around them.

"Jesus," Webb cursed. "What the hell is going on?"

"Dana, can you get the door open?" Hugo said.

"Yes, just hang on, will you? Oh for the love of… which genius has been kicking at the door?"

"What's wrong?"

"The manual release is all bent. Stand back."

They heard the straining of protesting metal. More shouts echoed in the building, closer this time.

"Can you do it?" Hugo called through the door as Dana paused.

"Will you just leave off nagging me?"

"Don't worry, Hugo," Webb said. "Your sister is freakishly strong. How do you think we got out of that room?"

Hugo didn't have time to process that because with a scrape and a clank the door was released and Dana was shining a lenslight in his face.

"You," she snapped, pointing at him.

"Dana, honey," Webb said, stepping between them. "You can tear your brother a new one when we get out of here, ok? First, let's move."

"What happened?" Dana said, keeping the light on Hugo's face.

"It's nothing," Hugo said, swiping at the dried blood on his face with his sleeve. "Was it you that cut the power?"

"No," Dana said, something creeping into her voice. "You won't believe what's happening."

"No time," Webb insisted, shouldering past her and into the passage. "Quick, Dana, where's the way out?"

He halted when another crash echoed through from outside and the ground trembled under their feet.

"Dana, explain what's happening," Hugo said.

Dana gave the empty corridor a nervous sweep with the lenslight. "It's the Havenites. They're storming the District."

"They're doing what?"

Her eyes were wide. "Hundreds banded together and stormed the walls. I think someone's tipped the Elders off about what the Ghosts have been up to… and they're saying they've got guns."

"It's true," Webb said.

"They're mad," Dana said. Even in the poor light of the lenslight she looked pale. "What's even madder: the Ghosts are fighting back. I was able to slip through in the confusion."

"We need to get the hell out of dodge," Webb said. "We do not want to be in this building when the colony takes it."

"No," Hugo said. Webb and Dana looked at him. "This is our chance."

"Hugo," Webb pleaded. "We're caught in the middle of a civil uprising here, both sides of which want us dead."

"I don't care," Hugo said. "Ariel is not prepared for this. This is how we take him."

"He's right," Dana said, drawing herself up and throwing Webb a defiant look. "This will be our only chance."

Webb threw a glance to the ceiling. "Jesus, Mary and Joseph. God save me from Hugos."

"Come on," Hugo said, taking the light from Dana and starting up the corridor. The others followed, Webb still muttering. Hugo paused at every corner to listen and look for light, but they encountered no one else and moved quickly. He chose the way from memory and eventually came to the stairs up to the kitchen.

The beam from the lenslight showed the kitchen had been hastily deserted. Food was left steaming on rapidly cooling heat pads and half-prepared on chopping boards. He moved across the room to the knife rack and started grabbing what he could, shoving a long blade in his belt and a smaller one in his boot.

Dana was next to him doing the same, examining the edges as best she could in the poor light.

"Webb," she snapped.

Hugo shone the light back into the kitchen as Webb moved

away from the fridge, stuffing the last of something into his mouth.

"Shut up, I'm starving," he mumbled around his mouthful.

"Focus," Hugo said and Webb mumbled something profane, wiped his hands on his clothes and cast his eyes over the knife rack. When he'd also armed himself, they left and found themselves in the carpeted hallways between the rec rooms.

"Shut the light off," Dana hissed and Hugo did. They stood flat against the wall in the solid dark. There were high-pitched voices not far away and the beams from lenslights and torches cut through the darkness in the direction of some of the rooms. There was the frenzied chatter of people talking into wrist panels and comm links and getting brisk, panicked replies.

"They have no idea what they've done," Dana breathed.

"Oh I think they do," Webb said, a grim satisfaction in his tone.

"Their whole colony's turned against them," Dana said.

"They turned on it first," Webb muttered.

"This way," Hugo said and they felt their way along in the dark.

"Do we even know where to find him in this place?" Dana whispered as they rounded a corner. Hugo clicked their light back on, sweeping it over a wide open space with game tables with cards and panels abandoned in drifts across their surfaces and bar dotted with half-finished drinks spanning one wall.

"There," he said as the beam lit up an ornamental building plan on the opposite wall.

"This is so the jerks can find the bathing suites and the dining room," Webb said, glaring at the plan as Hugo examined it, getting their bearings. "I can't believe the Elders have let these weasels live like this."

"They can't have known the whole truth," Dana said.

"Quiet," Hugo hissed and they heard voices approaching.

"Quick," Webb said and ducked between one of the game tables and the wall.

They all crouched in the narrow space and held their breath.

There was a whine as someone forced an electric door open and then hurrying footsteps and bobbing beams of lenslights.

"Get more men to the central boulevard," someone was barking. A harried reply came from wrist panel speakers. "I don't give a shit," the man replied as his and his companion's lenslights flashed off the walls over their heads. "They break through there, the south entrance is theirs. Get back up -"

"They've broken through the boundary wall," his companion muttered. "Shots were fired. The gatehouse on the port side is a pile of smoking rubble."

"Fuck. Pull away from there. Fall back to the stronghold."

There was silence again as they passed through another door and the room was dark and empty again.

"Shit," Dana murmured in the dark when none of them had moved. "This is serious."

"A private army with guns versus a million pissed Havenites," Webb said. "This is not going to end quick or easy."

Hugo didn't speak. He stood and flashed his light around. It landed on some of the abandoned panels on the smooth green of the gaming table. He scrambled over, grabbing a panel and turning it over and over to try and find the power button.

"This is not the time for cards Hugo," Webb muttered as he and Dana shimmied out.

Hugo found the switch, booted up the panel and handed it to Webb. "Can you hack this thing to connect to the solarnet?"

Webb took the panel and frowned at the simulated game of Dead Man's Candle on the screen. "These things are very basic..."

"They should still have solarnet connections," Dana said. "To download the latest game software."

"Get it connected. We're sending a message out."

"To who?" Webb asked.

"Anita Rami," Hugo said.

"Why?" Webb's voice was heavy.

"One way or another, this is ending today," Hugo said, feeling a shiver run over his skin as he said the words. "And we're going to need help getting away."

"The Service won't help us," Dana said, looking equal parts wary and bitter.

"Rami will," Hugo said and turned away. "Get working on it, Webb. I have the secure comm numbers when you're ready."

Webb looked uncertain but when Hugo said no more, he shrugged and started tapping at the screen. "If you say so."

"I trust you can work and run?" Hugo said, starting for the door.

"Where are we going?" Dana panted as she drew level with him.

"Ariel only hurts people when they're tied to a table," Hugo said, keeping his pace up. "He's a coward. We'll find him in the safest place here."

"The Conference Suite," Webb agreed. "The elevators won't be working, though."

"This way," Hugo said, turning across an empty hallway and scanning around for the service door he'd found on the plan.

"Should we try and get some guns?" Dana asked as more muffled shots were heard.

"The last thing we want right now is to be caught with guns," Webb said, voice starting to sound strained.

"Kale, wait," Dana commanded, stopping where they were to take Webb by the shoulder and spin him to face her. "Are you ok?" she asked.

Hugo felt a stab of guilt and angled the light so that Dana could better examine the clone. His skin was pale and he was breathing through his teeth.

"I'm fine," he grunted, lifting the panel again and trying to carry on but Dana stepped in his way.

She grabbed Hugo's wrist and angled the lenslight down to Webb's waist. "You're bleeding again."

"It's kind of tough cheese," Webb said. "Come on, there's no time."

"Kale," Dana pleaded.

"Hey," Webb snapped. "Can we keep focused? I'll be fine. Let's go."

Hugo nodded. "Webb's right. We keep moving."

Hugo turned and carried on. The service door was up ahead, painted to match the walls. Hugo didn't stop to look at the lock but kicked at it. The fine wood splintered and gave way to his boot and then they were climbing metal stairs in a narrow space with bare concrete walls.

"This comes out on the roof space," Hugo said as they climbed past more service doors. "There will be no cover. But if that plan was right, the lift shaft up to the Conference Suite has an external access hatch…"

"Less talking more climbing," Webb panted from behind.

The noise from outside gained volume as they climbed.

"Alright Hugo, let's have those numbers," Webb said as they reached the top. Hugo reeled off Rami's secure connection code and the clone's fingers flew across the screen.

"Done," Webb said, pocketing the panel. "Let's hope Anita's checking her messages."

Hugo nodded. "She will be. She'll be here in ten hours. Twelve at the most."

"And she'll really help us get Ariel away?" Dana asked.

Hugo nodded, hoping he was right.

The door at the top was also locked and sturdier than the last. Dana growled at Webb to stay back and she and Hugo shouldered at it until it dented enough for them to force the bar lock and shove their way through. They ran out onto the open roof space, blinking in dull light and shivering in the chilly air.

Hugo stopped and stared. Webb walked in a daze to the edge of the roof. The Storage District was in total darkness. The maze of warehouses and avenues were misshapen hulks and hollows in the colony's dull green glow. Below there were the flashes of torches and lenslights, hand-held flood lights and the sweeping beams of head-torches. The noise was like nothing Hugo had ever heard. The only large-scale combat Hugo had ever seen had been in space. The clamour aboard a fighting ship during or after a battle was nothing like this.

This was primal, ferocious and racked with fury. Gunfire and screams punctuated the seething, continuous roar of people tearing each other apart. There was crashing, bangs and the wining of moped and low-flyer engines. It all ebbed and flowed like an ocean as units of the Ghosts' defence pushed forward or were pushed back from the stronghold. His brain could not make sense of the clashing of hand-held weapons, the strangled noises and the cries of the injured and dying.

"Ariel's army is already beaten," Dana breathed as she stared out over the darkness full of fighting.

"They're going to take as many people with them as they can." Webb's voice was flat.

Dana shook her head and Hugo felt his gut surge with the pointlessness of it all. But he shook himself and stepped back.

"We need to hurry. They're almost at the building."

Webb and Dana nodded and Hugo turned back to scan the roof space. It was wide and open with many outcroppings that housed the building's electric relays, ventilation, cooling and heating systems, all now eerily quiet. The comm rigs were mounted on frames, stretching the aerials and dishes up toward the hull. Behind them were more built-up and windowless levels that had clearly been added since its construction, with the lift shaft jutting from the side. Craning his neck, Hugo could make out the background illumination reflecting off the plexiglass of Ariel's Conference Suite at the top.

"Be careful, they'll be on watch," Dana said, slinking up to one of the outbuildings and hugging the wall tight. She led the way to the shaft, running the open distances with light feet and taking them on a round route to a relay house near the lift shaft.

Hugo stepped to the edge and peered round and up. The plexiglass room was almost directly above them. There was no light from inside. Doubt nagged at him but he pushed it aside and searched the shaft for the access hatch.

"There," he said, pointing.

"Looks too thick to force open," Dana murmured.

"I can probably get that open with a knife," Webb said. "Hugo, what's the plan when we get up there?"

"Plan?" Hugo said.

"You still don't have a plan?"

"I'm making this up as I go," Hugo muttered.

"Jesus, now you tell me."

"Relax," Dana said. "We'll think of something."

"Did either of you even attend Strategy classes at the academy?" Webb muttered.

"Yes," Hugo replied shortly, rolling up his sleeves and checking his boot knife. "But you didn't and you're the best strategist of all of us. Now stay focused and see if you can come up with something."

Hugo didn't leave Webb time to protest but ran across to the lift shaft, the others in tow. Webb pulled out one of the smaller kitchen knives and started work on the lock in the beam of their light as he kept up a continuous stream of indignant mutterings. Hugo exchanged a brief, amused glance with his sister over his head. He was struck again by how the softening of her face made her look like Catherine, their sister who Dana had never even met. As if reading his thoughts, her expression hardened and she turned back to watch Webb.

A few more clicks and curses and the door swung open. Hugo leant into the shaft.

"The car's above us," he said. "At the top level. The only way into the room will be through it."

Dana took the light and leant through the opening, craning her neck up. "There's an emergency hatch in the car," she said. "Webb, how are you at hacking a lock when hanging over a chasm?"

"I guess we're about to find out," he said, zipping up his coverall.

Hugo glanced at the dark patch at his side.

"I'll be fine," Webb murmured, following Hugo's example and rolling up his sleeves. "I'll have to be. Someone just hold the light steady for me, ok?"

"I'm on it," Dana said and climbed through.

"Be careful," Hugo said.

"Quiet," Dana's command echoed down and Hugo took a breath, nodding for Webb to go next.

Webb climbed after Dana and then Hugo went after him. His sister was already further up, heading for the car. She had the light tucked in her sleeve and was moving swiftly and surely, using cable housing and structural supports as hand and foot holds. Hugo scanned around again but the only ladder was on the side closest to the internal access hatches. Webb followed Dana, though he moved slightly slower, stretching with one arm more carefully than the other. Hugo winced in sympathy then got a grip above him and started to climb.

It was eerily quiet with the shaft blocking most of the noise of the battle. Hugo concentrated on pulling himself up after Webb and holding himself still as his friend shimmied up next to his sister. He got as good a hold as he could and leant out to work on the hatch in the base of the car. The only sound was the blade of the knife on the release mechanism and Webb's heavy breathing.

With a click, it finally opened. Webb leaned out further, Dana keeping a fierce hold of the back of his coveralls, and swung the hatch up and into the car. He hung there a moment, staring up into the black space, before shaking himself and hauling himself through. He reached down and helped Dana through then Hugo climbed up himself.

Webb gently clicked the hatch shut again once they were all inside the lift. Dana shone the light on the dark controls but Webb signed for silence then reached and shut the light off.

They were plunged into complete blackness. Keeping still and silent, Hugo became aware of soft noises. He heard Webb take a step forward and did the same, pressing up against the door and listening. Lowered voices were murmuring to one another. One of them grated and rasped.

"Paragon," Hugo breathed.

Webb didn't answer. Hugo felt Dana come up behind them and leaned in close.

"Ariel?" she whispered.

They all kept motionless and listened for several more minutes. There were grunted commands, the heavy tread of a guard and a burst of panicked reply over a comm, but they couldn't make out any words. Then silence again.

Hugo felt Webb tense in the dark beside him and felt frustration coursing through his own body.

"There's no way to tell if he's in there," Hugo murmured.

He heard Webb swallow. "We'll just have to go for it."

They all stepped back as one and there was the whisper of fabric and metal as knives were drawn. He heard Webb step up to the doors and took up position behind him. Dana was at his shoulder. He felt and heard the clone release a shuddering breath and then there was the toothy noise of a knife blade being forced between the lift doors.

XVI

Webb could taste his own terror. He hated himself for it so much that is almost choked him. His palms sweated around the handle of the long-bladed knife as he jimmied the lift doors open. When Hugo shouldered in next to him to force the doors, some of Webb's terror fled, though not all. He shut away what was left and heaved.

Shots were already firing their way. Someone was shouting orders but it was too dark and too muddled to tell how many Ghosts there were. Webb let his instincts take over, diving for the cover of the conference table. Whoever had the guns had fallen back behind the furniture at the fireplace. Shots buried themselves in the lift doors and ploughed into the soft carpet and finally a shot went through the plexiglass.

Either Ariel and his buddies had never expected to defend themselves against bullets up here, or, more likely, whoever constructed the window presumed the same thing, because it wasn't bulletproof and the great sheet shattered in a glittering mass with a noise like music exploding.

Webb covered his head with his arms as glass rained down on him. Someone on the other side of the room was screaming with fury but was ordered to silence. A great draught blew through the room and the noise of the riot filled the air.

Webb got to his knees, glittering debris falling to the floor. He whispered a prayer of thanks that the blade had gone for a great, solid slab of simulated marble for his conference table. He held his breath and peered between the chairs just as someone ignited a lighting pole and flung it into the middle of the carpet.

Webb barely had time to make out the tops of Hugo and Dana's heads ducking behind a sofa when the two guards fired their handguns again.

"Hold your fire." Paragon's rasping shout was almost choked by his rage. "Save your ammo, you idiots."

"You can fuck off," one of the Ghost guards with a bald head and a wonky jaw answered, voice strangled with panic. "I'm not being taken alive to the Elders."

"You will do as I say," Paragon growled. "Keep your weapons ready but hold your fire until I say. Ok you lot," Paragon raised his broken voice. "You can't win. Either leave the way you came, and quickly, or we'll end you all."

"It's over, shrimpy," Webb called. The Ghosts, eyes wide and hands shaking, span in his direction. Paragon hung behind them, trying to peer through the gloom. "Your whole game is up. Haven's out for your head."

"It's the clone," he hissed. "Kill them," he shouted at the guards. "Kill them all, now."

The firing broke out again. Webb scurried to the end of the table as the glass and rock exploded over him. He sat with his back against a chair, took a deep breath and pulled one of the kitchen knives from his belt. He sent up another quick prayer, took a hold of the blade between his fingers, flung himself to his knees, took one precious second to aim and threw it.

There was a scream and the shots stopped. Someone was gibbering, saying his friend's name over and over as a gurgling noise ceased. Webb shut his eyes against a rush of guilt. These men weren't soldiers… just desperate enough to get out of the yards that they'd accepted anything they were offered, illegal weapons and all.

And under all that lurked the black fog of realisation: he hadn't heard Ariel's voice.

Paragon was muttering furiously. Webb peered between the chairs. The lighting pole showed the bald man bent over the downed one, Webb's knife protruding from his ribs. Paragon stood over them both, perfect skin flushed and strands of hair worked free from its tail, hanging about his face and stuck to his forehead.

His voice cracked with panic and frustration as he rallied the remaining Ghost to his defence.

Webb was just trying to assess another throwing angle when there was a flurry of movement. Hugo was over the sofa, across the carpet and bowling the other guard to the floor. Dana wasn't far behind him and was going for Paragon, knife drawn.

Ignoring the pull on his injury, he ran to join them. When he reached the struggle, Hugo was burying a knife up to the hilt in his man's neck and Dana was wrestling Paragon for the downed man's gun. Webb dived at Hugo's man, who, not releasing he was as good as dead, was using his bulk to roll Hugo under him. Webb ploughed bodily into him, side screaming, and the three of them tangled on the floor.

By the time Webb had shaken the stars from his vision, the guard was dead and Hugo was trying to wipe blood from his eyes and scrabbling for the other gun.

"Get back," Paragon growled so loud that Webb froze. Dana was getting to her feet, bloodied about the nose, lips split, with her knife held out to the side. There was a terrible moment of silence when they all panted and stood crouched over the two bodies of the guards. Paragon had both guns, one under one of his boots and the other aimed at Dana's head. There was nothing left in his handsome face but terror and fury.

"Where's Ariel?" It was Dana that had spoken.

Paragon's face contorted and the gun in his grip started to shake. "You bastards," he said, sounding almost pityingly young. "They'll make me go back to the yards."

"No they won't," Webb said, surprised at finding his voice steady. "They'll lynch you. Or drift you, maybe. And your master."

As if to back him up, there came a surge of noise from outside. There was the sound of more shattering glass and groaning metal as well as continuing crashes and shouts. Paragon's eyes widened and shone with terror.

"Come with us," Hugo said. His voice was husky with exhaustion, but the words were calm even as his eyes never left the weapon aimed at his sister. "We're taking you and your master for trial. You'll live. That's the best I can offer you. You won't get any such offer from your own people."

Paragon gave a cracked noise like a sob and swung the weapon round at Hugo. "You," he croaked. "You've destroyed everything."

"Not us, sunshine," Webb said. "You're the one that helped the Ghosts screw over Haven."

Paragon shook his head. "You don't understand. Ariel is a visionary. You are all heathens. Outsiders. Scum." He choked and coughed, bending with the force of trying to get air into his damaged lungs.

Dana took the moment and lunged, shouldering Paragon against the wall. They struggled. Hugo and Webb rushed forward to help. A single shot rang out and then there was the clattering of the gun against the fireplace. Dana yelped in pain and Webb saw nothing but red until he was standing over the crumpled form of the apprentice blade, Dana with blood on her knife and Paragon clutching at his stomach and sobbing into the carpet.

Webb breathed until the rage subsided. Pity, regret and hatred fought for supremacy in his gut and it made him sick. He looked to Dana who was looking at the downed man with exactly the same war of emotions playing out on her face.

She looked up and met his eyes. She opened her mouth to speak but then her look slid past him and widened.

"Kale," she cried and shoved Webb out the way. "Kale, please, no."

Time slowed down. He turned as Dana threw herself on the floor next to her brother, but to Webb it seemed she took an age to reach him. Hugo was on his back, staring up at the ceiling with a slightly confused look on his face. His hands, gloved in blood, were fumbling at his chest.

Webb blinked. He was suddenly somewhere else. He could

smell rock dust and iron. Mining machinery surrounded him and Kinjo was screaming somewhere close by and there was a crushing blackness in his chest.

He shook his head, tried to pull in a breath to bring himself back from the ghostly memories. He was on his knees next to Hugo, helping Dana pull at his clothes.

"You stay with me, Kale, do you hear?" Dana was saying, though her voice was thick. "You do as you're told for once."

"Dana, give me a knife," Webb said, surprised at how calm he sounded. Hugo's face crumpled as he watched the knife blade get close to his skin. Webb sliced through his shirt with one quick movement. He used a scrap of the fabric to wipe away as much blood as he could.

"There's no bubbles," Webb said, unwinding his scarf. "That's a good sign. Here, press on this." He placed Dana's hands over the scarf. "Press hard, like you did with me. It doesn't matter if it hurts him."

"I know," Dana spat. Her eyes were brimming and furious. She leant into the compress and looked around the room. "We have to get him out of here."

"Stay there. Keep that pressure on."

"Where are you going?"

Webb got to his feet, wiped Hugo's blood on his clothes and looked around. Reality folded itself into a series of unimportant elements: the commotion outside, the flickering light of fire somewhere in the distance, Paragon curled on the floor panting and moaning with his synthetic hand twitching, the smell of blood. He went to the shattered window and scanned the roof space below until he found what he was looking for.

"I'm going to get the elevator working," he called over his shoulder as he forced the lift doors. "Keep him alive, do you hear?"

The doors snapped shut on her shouted response. Webb forced himself not to think about the expression on her face but clutched the lenslight in his teeth and threw back the floor hatch.

He climbed down to the opening onto the roof as if in a dream. His side was on fire and felt sticky. He shoved this all away, staggered through the hatch and hit the roof running.

He didn't stop to look at the lock on the electric relay house door but kicked it down. The wood was old and the lock rusted. It was dark and dusty inside. For a horrible moment he thought the shed might be disconnected, but he closed his eyes and forced himself to dredge up his electronics knowledge anyway, knowing he didn't have a choice. A vision rose before him of Rami leaning over his shoulder to point out the finer details in some relay circuitry displayed on one of the *Zero*'s workstation screens. He shook the wave of bitterness that threatened to take him down with it and just concentrated on the knowledge Webb had gained that day.

He cast the light around, grabbed a pair of cracked rubber gloves off a hook in the wall and set about searching for any labelled links to any sort of back-up power.

"There is always some back-up somewhere," Rami's voice, along with the smell of her hair, wafted through his mind. "No matter how old or how small the building: if it's on a colony, there will be a back-up power, even if it's just there for the atmosphere controls. You can rewire anything to get even part of the building back online, at least for a while."

Webb started to sweat as he opened every fuse box and lid in sight. Wires upon wires upon wires swarmed around switches and control boxes. It all blurred in front of his eyes until he found the box he was looking for, tucked in a corner under some thick bundled cables. He read the text on the door, sweat starting to gather in his collar, forcing his brain to do the calculations Rami had taught him from the numbers listed in the faded paint.

There might just be enough… if the generator, wherever it was, still worked.

He wiped sweat out of his eyes, glanced around the dusty room, gripped the lenslight in his teeth and wrenched open the front of the box. He took a breath then made himself work and not think, pulling out and reconnecting the wires. The tiny numbers on the connection points were faded or rubbed away. But he didn't think. Rami's voice and numbers flashed through his brain. He looked at the colours and thicknesses of the wires and blinked liquid that was either sweat or tears of frustration out of his eyes whilst reading from the tiny, scratched schematic on the inside of the housing.

It took an age. Hugo must have bled out by now. There was no point. He might as well give up.

He ignored the thoughts and pushed aside the extra wiring that now dangled loose about the connection switch, took a breath and flicked it on. The wires sparked.

He didn't stop to think but got up and ran back to the lift shaft. He let out a strangled laugh when he saw it was lit up from within. He made it back up to the car so fast he thought his lungs and muscles might burst, climbed into it and laughed again when the lighting panels and controls of the lift were all evenly lit. He pushed the button and the doors slid open. They paused part way and the lights flickered off then on again. He ran for Dana, still bent over her brother on the floor.

Hugo lay still, blinking slowly, hand resting on his sister's as she clutched at his chest.

"Come on," Webb said and stooped to get an arm under his former captain. Hugo cried out when they pulled him up into a sitting position. "It's a good sign," Webb said to Dana, trying to believe it himself. "If he can feel things, it's a good sign."

"Wait…please wait," Paragon's rasping voice was weak. He was still curled on the floor, darkness pooling on the thick carpet under him, with his real hand stretched out toward them. His eyes flicked around, unseeing. His skin was white. "Ezekiel, please. Take me with you."

"Not likely, asshole," Webb ground out, shifting himself to get Hugo's arm over his shoulders.

"I'll tell you everything," the young man choked. "I'll tell you where Ariel is. I'll stand trial and tell you whatever you want to know. Just, please. Help me."

Webb panted with the effort of getting Hugo upright. Dana was under her brother's other arm, face a rigid mask. Paragon seemed to focus on them for a moment and shook with pain. His face pleaded as his breath rattled in and out of his body.

"Too late, friend," Webb answered. "Far, far too late."

They turned away from his whimpering and staggered with Hugo to the lift. Hugo looked around at the lit car, dazed. Dana hit the button for ground and the doors shut. The lift shuddered and the lights went. Webb crushed his eyes shut and prayed and they flickered back on. The lift started down.

It wasn't smooth. The power he'd found was not meant for this and wouldn't last. Dana stared at the numbers counting down and mumbled under her breath.

"Stay with us, Hugo," Webb said, hoisting the heavier man further up onto his shoulder.

"Keep still," Hugo gasped.

"That's better," Webb said, but then his stomach dropped into his feet when the car ground to a halt and the lights went again. As the sounds of the mechanism died, a riot of noise filled the air.

"Shit," Webb said. "Dana, what floor are we on?"

"Almost ground level," she said and he heard her boots shift. "Take him."

Hugo grumbled and Webb staggered as all of the commodore's weight was shifted to him.

"Be careful," Webb said. "Sounds like there's some serious shit going down out there."

Dana didn't reply. He heard the sound of her forcing a knife blade between the doors. She made a wordless noise of effort and then there was a creak and a streak of dull light fell in. Dana got her shoulder in the gap and she used her whole body to force the doors apart. Webb muttered more curses as he registered they were several feet from the ground.

"Quick," she said, using her boots and elbows to keep the doors apart.

"You ready, Hugo?" Webb said. "We need to get down off the elevator, but we can do it if we take it slow ok? Just take it easy."

Hugo didn't answer. Webb didn't allow himself to spend too long examining his friend's sweat-covered face but got to his knees and helped Hugo do the same. They scrambled to the edge of the car, shimmying under Dana as she held the doors open. Webb looked around the storage bay the lift had opened on with its stoved-in hanger doors and ground strewn with bodies and groups of workers attacking each other with tools and night sticks, then jumped down and eased Hugo down after him. He wobbled on his feet but stayed upright. Dana landed down beside them.

The thunder of a shot rang out from somewhere to be replied by a cry and a roar of collective anger. More people, men and women, labourers, Enforcers and refinery workers, streamed in through the ruins of the hanger doors, silhouetted against the green of outside. There were more cries and more shots as the knots of resistance that were all that remained of the battered and dwindling Ghost army were overwhelmed.

"Stick to the edges," Webb said, starting to hurry Hugo along. They staggered together, all three of them, weaving around the stacked-up crates and bays of machine engines that made up the stronghold's property stockpile. No workers they passed, running, fighting or tending the wounded, gave them a second glance. The few Ghosts that were left had their hands too full to notice them.

Hugo stumbled more than once and Webb felt his heart begin to pound as the man got weaker and weaker. Webb pressed the scarf more firmly against his friend's ribs and was rewarded by a weak hiss of pain.

They reached the doors and hung back in the shadows, waiting for a break in the onslaught of Havenites scrambling through.

Webb panted in the dark and stared at them coming in an endless stream, some wounded or bloodied but all armed with knives, axes, tools, bars of metal and a unity of purpose that Webb hadn't seen the like of, even in the fighting units of the Service. Most wore night-vision goggles that blanked out their eyes and increased the eeriness of their appearance.

It left him with a chill that went right to his bones.

"Go," Dana snapped and Webb shook himself and realised there was a break in the charge. They hurried Hugo through the twisted doors.

As his eyes adjusted to the dim light outside, shapes in the shadows slowly took form as bodies and wreckage. Overturned mopeds lay abandoned amongst the dropped weapons and crumpled figures, some still twitching. Dust and shrapnel was scattered about. A monstrous crane, its head still buried in the remains of the stronghold doors, had been run right up against the building. Its great arm was twisted and hanging at a drunken angle. There were the sounds of struggles elsewhere, but the square in front of them was clear of anyone upright.

"This is nearly over," Webb said, voice low.

"There," Dana cried, relief lightening her voice. "A low-flyer. It looks like it might be working."

The machine was shouldered up against the side of a building, hastily abandoned and still attached to a lifter full of cargo. The control panel was lit. Dana made quick work of uncoupling the lifter and then she was helping Webb get her brother into the back seat and checking his pulse and eyes.

"Keep him breathing or I'll kick both your asses," Webb said and climbed into the pilot seat.

"Where are we going?"

"The only place we can," Webb said and fired the engine. He pushed the thruster controls forward and the flyer took off down the boulevard. Some straggling rioters dove out of the way and someone fired at them once, but they soon saw the boundary wall ahead. Webb took a breath. A huge section of it, gatehouse and all, was now a slump of rubble across the gateway. The metal gates were bent under the mound. Teams of workers had cleared a path for the people on foot and some cranes and movers were working at the bigger rubble, but there was no room for the flyer.

Webb cast his eyes over the controls, clenched his teeth and punched in a couple of commands and pulled the stick back.

"Webb," Dana warned, but he was already diverting all the power to the thrusters and pulling the craft into a climb.

"This thing isn't meant to fly," Dana cried.

"It just needs to get us to the next sector," Webb ground out. The control lights flickered but he punched the panel and they came back on. They gained enough height to pass the rubble and kept climbing. People stopped in their work, pointing as they sped past, but Webb kept them crawling up and the noise soon died away.

He got them above the levels of the buildings and steered so the Planning District was to starboard and coaxed more speed from the engine. He didn't look in the mirror and shut his ears to Dana telling her brother over and over that it was going to be ok.

Δ

"What the hell? Ezekiel, this is not -"

It was the first time Webb could recall seeing Jazz flustered. She stopped talking as she took in his blood- and dust-stained clothing then leaned out her apartment window further, took in the low-flyer dropped at an angle on her the block's roof and her eyes widened further.

"Please, Jazz," Webb said, desperation creeping into his voice. "Hugo's been shot."

"Shot?"

Webb nodded and Jazz's face went grim.

"Is this anything to do with what's happening in the Storage District?"

"I'll tell you anything you want to know. Just please, help him first."

She pressed her lips together, considering him for a long moment. He shivered in the wafting air and tried to figure out what was happening in her eyes but then her face softened and she scrambled out onto the ledge next to him and hurried to the flyer.

Dana was holding herself together with a visible effort. Her eyes were dry but her breathing was ragged and she was clutching at Hugo like drowning woman clutching at wood. Hugo was very pale, grey under his eyes which were only half open. If he was breathing at all, Webb couldn't tell.

"Dana," Jazz said after she'd taken in the whole situation with just a glance. "There's a chair-bed in the back room. There's antiseptic in the hallway closet, and sheets. Get it all ready, please. Go now."

Dana looked at her with empty eyes then nodded and scrambled out of the flyer towards the open window. "Ezekiel, you help me. Don't make him take his own weight. See if we can lift him."

Webb hurried to straddle the front and back seats of the flyer, Jazz's calm commands helping him bind together his flagging resources. He got his arms around Hugo as she did the same on the other side and they lifted him clear of the flyer. The Serviceman made a noise but was otherwise a dead weight.

They carried him down the ledge and into her apartment. They found Dana spreading a sheet out on the tilting chair-bed in the gloomy back room, movements jerky and eyes hard and distant. The air smelt of antiseptic. Jazz and Webb laid their burden down as Dana tied knots in the sheet at the base and head to keep it steady.

"Dana, get some lights. Zeek, my kit and my scanner-panel from the store room, please. Bring me a tunic and a box of gloves too. Hugo, can you open your eyes for me?"

Webb stumbled down the corridor as Dana ran ahead to find lamps. He collected the medkit and other items without really seeing or thinking. When he returned, Jazz had already pulled off the remains of Hugo's clothing, making Dana keep their futile compress in place as she did so. She wiped her hands on her trousers then pulled on the tunic and gloves, talking to Hugo the whole time. Webb looked at the amount of blood smeared across his friend's chest and belly and the grey tinge to his skin and collapsed against the wall.

"I'm going to put you to sleep," Jazz said soothingly as she filled a syringe. "Everything's going to be ok, alright? Just relax."

Hugo gave a shudder, like he had let something go. Watching him slacken as Jazz injected him was almost more than Webb could bear to see. The broker checked his pulse and leant in over his mouth to listen for breathing then waved to Dana.

"There are utilities in the hall closet," she muttered as she started laying out surgical plates, tongs and scalpels from the kit. "You two get cleaned up and changed and get some food from the kitchen. There's nothing more you can do for him."

"Jazz," Webb tried.

"Go now," Jazz said, face blank with concentration as she pulled an Energy Patch out of its packet, wiped a spot clean on Hugo's chest and applied it. Hugo's body gave a twitch then lay still. Webb took Dana by the hand and led her out of the room.

Webb swallowed a foul taste in his mouth and stared into Jazz's hall closet. Dana had to reach past him to grab what she wanted. He woke himself up enough to direct her to the bathroom. She went in without looking at him and shut the door.

Webb sat on the hallway floor with his back against the wall and his arms around his knees, listening to water splash in the bathroom. Dana came out some time later that might have been minutes or hours, hair wet and hands and face red from scrubbing. Her eyes were puffy. She'd left her coveralls crumpled in a heap on the bathroom floor. Jazz's faded t-shirt and trousers were too long for her and brought out how pale she was.

"Go find something to drink," Webb said as he got to his feet. He laid a hand on her shoulder, making her shiver. She still didn't look at him.

He went into the bathroom, locked the door and leant against it, staring at the ceiling and feeling his pulse pound in his ears. The worry, fear and anger had deserted him. He felt sore, dirty and so very, very tired.

He made himself move. He stripped and got in the shower, turning the water up to the hottest setting. He peeled away the stained dressing on his wound and flinched as the hot water ran over it, washing away crusted blood. He made himself examine it. Nam's surgical staples were holding. It was red and painful but not hot to touch.

He washed it thoroughly then pulled the tie out of his hair and plunged his face under the steaming stream, wishing he was could just flow away with the water. Despite everything, the feel of the dust and dirt of the last few days rinsing out of his hair and off his skin felt good.

He shut the water off when his skin was starting to sting with the heat and dried and dressed in what he had grabbed from the closet. He realised with a pang that they were his own clothes from when he'd lived here. He didn't let himself think about that too hard and just pulled on the cargo pants and t-shirt, enjoying the feel of clean fabric against his skin.

He gathered up their filthy coveralls and paused, patting at something solid in one of the pockets. He pulled out the hacked gaming panel, its screen dark. A quick boot up revealed no re-plies to his message and he sighed and pocketed it, then padded through to the living room, hair hanging in wet ropes down his back. He took the coveralls straight to the disposal and forced them all in. The mechanism whined and belched as it shredded the thick fabric but he kept shoving until the scraps that were left had disappeared down the chute.

"You seem to know this apartment well." Dana didn't look up as she spoke. She sat cross-legged on the couch, staring into space, a glass of black liquid in her hands. There was another on the counter. The smell of the blask was sharp in the air and made his mind skip over some unwelcome memories. Still, he took the glass and sat next to Dana. There was an open Nutripak on the table in front of her, but she'd only taken a bite and laid it aside.

He tried to think of something to say but couldn't. He took a sip of the drink instead. It burned in his throat and something inside him strengthened. He set the glass aside and took her hand. They sat there like that, staring at the doorway to the hall, hands clasped together.

They finished their drinks and managed a Nutripak each before they heard a door open and shut and Jazz emerged. They both got to their feet as she came into the room, pulling off her blood-spattered tunic. She crossed to the washer and dropped it in, then came and stood in front of them with her hands pressed together.

"It's not good, I'm afraid," she said. Webb felt his stomach drop again. Jazz held first his then Dana's gaze as she talked. "I've removed the bullet. It missed his lungs and wasn't a direct hit on his heart…but there is tissue damage. And he's lost a lot of blood."

"What does that mean?" Webb said, once he found his voice. He could already see on Dana's face that she understood what it meant, but he needed to hear it.

"He needs transfusions," Jazz said. "And specialised surgery. But even if we could get it for him…which we can't…I suspect the damage to his heart isn't repairable. The Patches are keeping it going at the moment, but they won't for long."

Webb put a hand out for anything to steady himself on but there was nothing. He sat down heavily on the edge of the couch. Dana stayed standing. Her eyes were swimming.

"I'm very sorry," Jazz said.

"Can I see him?" Dana didn't sound like herself.

Jazz nodded. Dana drifted toward the hallway. Webb rose to follow. Jazz stopped him with a hand on his shoulder. She kissed him on the cheek, skin warm against his face then turned back and disappeared down the hall. He heard the bathroom door shut.

Eventually, he managed to put one foot in front of the other and made his way to the back room. Jazz had pulled a blanket over Hugo. He was still unconscious. He didn't look asleep and he didn't look peaceful. He was frowning and his breathing was thin and pained. She'd cleaned him off as much as possible, but his hair was still caked with filth and dust. There was blood on his skin and the sheet around him. Dana stood staring like she was afraid to touch him.

"This is my fault," she said, after they'd both stood there in silence for the longest minute of his life.

"It's not your fault."

"Of course it is," she said with a huge sniff. She wiped her eyes on the hem of her t-shirt and suddenly looked terrifyingly young. "I always screw everything up."

"Not true..."

"Shut up," she cried. "You don't even know me. You don't know..." she dissolved into wordless emotion, stepping up to her brother with her hand clenched over her mouth. Her strength visibly crumbled away and she bent over him and buried her face in his neck and shook.

Webb stayed where he was. He almost turned away and left them alone, but he couldn't make his feet move.

"You're right," he said softly when Dana's breathing had levelled out. "I've not known you long. Him either, really. But I can tell you this for sure: your messed-up family is not only the most stubborn and bloody-minded bunch of Service stuck-ups I have ever met...you also have a hugely screwed idea about what is your responsibility."

Dana raised her head. Her eyes were swollen, dark hair dishevelled and her fingers dug into her brother's skin.

Webb took a step closer. "It's great...amazing really...that you all feel this need to go out and make the world a better place. It's even more amazing that you never stop trying, even after you get knocked down. And I've tried to explain this to your stubborn-assed brother I don't know how many times and I'll try and explain it to you too. Not everything is yours to fix."

"If I hadn't come - " Dana started but Webb pulled her into his arms before he knew was he was thinking. She shuddered against him. She smelt like tears and soap. Her arms went round him and she clung on tight enough to hurt, but he didn't care.

"If you hadn't come, Dana, you wouldn't have been here to help me get him out of there." She gave a choked sound. "And either way, it wouldn't have stopped him plunging into gunfire for a chance at Ariel. Trust me. He doesn't need you around to be an idiot."

"That's just you, then?" She said dredging up a watery smile.

Webb shrugged a shoulder, felt his chest tighten and his smile become harder to keep in place. She stepped out of his embrace. He felt colder for it. He looked at Hugo's still form and felt it all come up his throat in a rush. The urge to reach out and shake and shout at his friend swept through him but he managed to keep his arms at his side.

"Mother won't cope," Dana said in a small voice. "Not again."

Webb searched her face, trying to think of something reassuring to say.

They both jumped at a commotion from the living room. They exchanged a confused look and rushed toward it, shutting the door on Hugo and hurrying down the corridor. Webb made out a banging noise along with a raised and angry voice. They skidded into the sitting area just as someone hammered again on the apartment door.

"I know you're in there," the high and angry voice wailed. "Let me in or I'll break in."

Jazz hurried into the room, hastily buttoning a clean shirt and staring at the door. "What is that?"

"It's Nam," Webb said.

"Who?" Jazz asked.

"Don't let her in," Dana said, staring at the door. "She's a maniac."

"I can hear you, little girl," Nam called. A louder crash of a boot against the handle rattled the whole door.

"Who is it?"

"The Black Cross killer," Webb said.

"She'll get in either way," Jazz said, moving across the room though her face was grim.

"No, wait," Webb called but Jazz was already pulling the door open.

Nam shoved past her and stood trembling in the middle of the room. She looked even taller than Webb remembered. Her red hair hung in flaming strands around her face. Her knuckles were white around the handle of her machete. The blade was dark with old blood. There were new stains on her black clothing. Jazz stared at the Black Cross painted on her face in horror.

"You," she hissed, raising her weapon and levelling it at Webb's face.

Webb held up his hands and took a step back. "Now just hold on, lady. I don't know what your problem is, but we're having a pretty rough day here already."

"You lied," she spat, advancing on him. Dana stepped between them but she reached and shoved her away. Dana staggered and fell and Webb glared, fists forming.

"You touch any of my friends again," he glowered, stepping up so the blade pressed against his breastbone. "Then you and me will have a big fucking problem, understand?"

"You lied," she said again. "There was no lab."

"What?"

"You said their lab was in a shuttle on that flagship," she growled, giving the machete a twitch against his skin. "There was nothing there."

Webb blinked, trying to process it.

"They must have moved it," Dana said, getting back to her feet and glaring daggers.

"Or you lied to get information from me."

"Listen to me, Nam Webb," Webb growled. "I'm going to say it slow, so listen. *You are fucking crazy*, ok?"

"Webb," Jazz warned, coming round the other side of the sofa.

"You're messed up, woman," he said, holding a hand up to Jazz but keeping his eye on Nam. "No great wonder. What happened to you would mess anyone up. But, listen to me on this one, *we are not the enemy, understand?* That lab was on that ship. I'm sorry if they've moved it but that really isn't our problem."

Nam's face crumpled with fury but he could see he'd reached her. She let out a cry and raised her blade. Webb ducked but Nam just buried it in Jazz's coffee table. Then she fell to her knees, buried her hands in her hair and rocked back and forth, wailing.

Jazz watched all this with raised eyebrows and a bewildered expression which she then levelled at Webb. Webb shrugged apologetically, throwing a worried glance over his shoulder toward the hallway. He looked to Dana for inspiration and saw her face bright with dawning realisation and a flicker of hope.

"What?" Webb mouthed but all Dana did was reach out and put a hand on Nam's shaking shoulder.

"Nam?"

Webb started forward but all the woman did was look up through her tear-streaked paint.

"Nam," she said again, still softly. "We might be able to help you find the lab."

"How?" Nam sniffed.

"They moved the lab, I'm sure of it," Dana said. "But you can't just fly a Service-standard shuttle through Haven and find somewhere to berth it." She threw Webb a significant glance. "And besides, there was a lot of specialist equipment on there…as well as the cloned organs…" Dana let that hang in the air for a second. Understanding hit Webb like a fist. Jazz was looking at him with an alarmed expression. "They would need to move and store it carefully. For that kind of operation, they would need to use lifting equipment and rent some space. I would say that credit will have changed hands somewhere and Jazz here is a broker."

"You are?" Nam said, getting to her feet and looking at Jazz. "That means you can track credit?"

Jazz caught Dana's glance and nodded. "That's right. I should be able to help you find where it's gone."

Webb knew she was talking to everyone in the room.

Nam looked between them like she could sense there was more happening here than she knew. "Do it then. Now."

Jazz nodded and went to her workstation.

Nam glanced between them all again. "Where's the other one? The Serviceman?"

"He's out," Webb said quickly. Jazz was already scrolling through data and tapping keys. Dana was at her shoulder, scouring the display. "Tell me, Nam," Webb continued, trying to keep his tone light. "How exactly did you find us this time?"

Nam glared at him. "Why should I tell you?"

"Drop that attitude, ok?" Webb grumbled. "We're helping you, aren't we?"

"Yes and I don't know why." She spun the blade in her hand. Webb watched it, rubbing his sternum where the razor edge had bit at the skin through his t-shirt.

"Because we need you to believe us," he said. "We've got... plans of our own and we could do without you interfering again."

Her jaw hardened and she stilled her weapon but he could see she understood. "There's a roof you can see this apartment from," she said, finally, nodding out the window. "I tracked you here after the first time you came snooping about and I came back to watch for you."

"You saw us land?" Webb asked carefully, making himself not look at the hallway to the back room.

Nam frowned. "Land? No. I saw you through the window. You

flew here?"

"It doesn't matter," Webb smoothed over, relief calming his heart again. "Jazz, any luck?" He tried not to sound too keen. Dana had her hand on Jazz's shoulder and he was sure he could almost see her trying to convey things to the broker without speaking. Nam was watching them too.

"I think so," Jazz said. Her fingers stopped typing and she pointed at a string of numbers. "This account that looks like a dummy to me was used to secure a loan of an industrial lifter and some storage on the edges of Sector 4's shipyard."

"Where?" Nam said, coming forward and frowning at the numbers. "Tell me. Tell me now."

"Here," Jazz tapped a couple of things and then pulled out one of the dozens of data thumbs that were plugged into her processor and handed it to Nam. "These are the co-ordinates. It's as sure as I can be."

Nam clutched the data thumb and spent a long time staring between them all. Webb prayed silently and didn't dare look at the others. He kept his face as calm as possible.

"Ok, are we done here?" he said, trying to only sound irritated.

Nam's jaw worked. She stared at the data thumb then at his face. She threw one more narrow glance at them all then turned and stormed out. Webb waited until her hurried footsteps had faded away then scrambled over the sofa to slam the door.

"Quick," he said. "Dana, we need to move. We'll take the flyer. We can get Hugo to Yoshida before she finds him."

"Relax," Jazz said getting to her feet and folding her arms. "I gave her fake co-ordinates."

Webb's heart sank.

"You didn't find the shuttle?" Dana said, despair painted clearly on her face.

"Oh no, I found it alright," Jazz said. "I just sent that one in the wrong direction. I don't understand everything that's happened here…but I think I've guessed a lot of it."

"Jazz, you are and always will be our saviour," Webb laughed, coming around the sofa and throwing his arms around her. "Thank you."

"If you're planning what I think you're planning," Jazz said patiently, pushing Webb gently away. "You need to hurry. You might not meet Nam there, but he doesn't have long."

"Thank you," Webb said again. "I mean it."

"Stop prattling," Jazz scolded, waving them through to the hallway. "Get your boots on and take jackets. But go now."

Dana gave both him and Jazz an uncertain look then rushed to the hall. Jazz watched after her with a slightly sad expression.

"She likes you, that one," she murmured softly.

Webb rubbed the back of his neck and felt himself blush. Jazz put a finger under his chin and made him meet her eyes.

"Look after yourself, Ezekiel. And let yourself be happy. That's all I've ever wanted for you."

"I really am sorry," he whispered. "About everything."

"Get yourself out of here and get yourself a future and you will have more than made everything up to me," she said with a warm smile. "But Zeek," she said with a more serious expression. "I want you to be prepared. He may be too far gone already."

Cold threaded through his veins and he shook his head. "I can't believe that."

He hurried after Dana. She was folding the blanket back from Hugo. He saw her averting her gaze from padding taped on his chest and the Patches stuck around it, the skin reddened around them. Webb's breath caught in his throat. He could see the shuddering beats of his struggling heart through his skin.

"See if you can find something for him to wear," he said. Dana nodded and went to move past him. He grabbed her by the arm and made her look at him. Tiredness, confusion, fear and hope all warred in her face. "Listen to me. It's going to be ok. Alright?"

Dana hesitated before she nodded and swept out.

Webb adjusted the chair-bed and eased Hugo into a sitting position. His skin was hot to touch. Dana returned, arms laden and Webb rooted through until he found an old sweater, loose with a thousand washes. Dana helped them get it on Hugo and then he grabbed a worker jacket for himself, probably one of his old ones from the yard he did his probation in, and pulled on his boots.

The boots were uncomfortable to put on again so soon and full of dust and a stickiness he didn't want to think about. He straightened his aching back, resisted rubbing the itching stitches in his side and got his arms back under Hugo.

"You didn't re-dress your cut did you?" Dana muttered as she got her brother's arm over her shoulders.

"Big picture, Dana. You ready for this?"

Dana nodded. "Let's go."

XVII

The flyer choked and lost power way before they reached Jazz's co-ordinates. They dumped it and carried Hugo between them the rest of the way. A report on the flyer's short-wave radio seemed to suggest that the chaos of the Storage District had sent waves through the whole colony. It wasn't clear what was happening now, or what the Elders' plans were to handle it, but it was clear that it wasn't over yet.

They both stilled when their names and descriptions were reeled off, along with the promise of a reward for reports of their whereabouts.

"Don't they have bigger problems?" Dana had muttered.

Webb found he had no trouble forgetting everything else and just staying focussed on the task in hand. Soon they shambled into a deserted lot at Jazz's coordinates. There was a single squat building with wide gates, locked and barred but recently used judging from the scratch marks in the concrete.

"He chose a good spot," Dana muttered, glancing around. They were shouldered right against the colony's hull. The nearest floodlight was several streets away and there was no indication that any of the other buildings around them were being used.

"Shit," Webb said as Hugo started to make low noises. "Is he waking up?"

Dana touched a hand to his forehead and cheek. His eyelids fluttered. "I don't know. But he's burning up."

They hitched Hugo up between them and hurried across the dusty lot to the building. Webb scanned the huge gates in despair. It was all silent inside.

"There," Dana said, and started pulling them towards a smaller door in the wall. Webb worked the lock in a time he was even impressed with, especially with the dim light, then helped Dana carry Hugo through into a dim corridor.

"Webb," Dana said, voice strained. "He's not breathing."

"Keep moving," Webb ordered and elbowed them through the first door they came to. They stumbled through into a high and wide hanger, lit only by the glow from the interior of a Service shuttle in the middle of the storage space, loaded on an industrial lifter. They approached in silence, though Webb was sure the thudding of his heart was audible for miles. He could hear someone moving around inside the small ship, then the hiss of sliding doors and footsteps on the deck.

Yoshida came into sight just as they came forward into the light pooling on the floor from the open hatch. They all stood and stared at each other.

"You are going to keep your mouth shut and listen," Webb said. "His heart is damaged and you are going to save him. Understand?"

Yoshida blinked at them a moment longer, taking in their grim expressions and the limp figure of Hugo between them, then carefully set aside the sample tray he was carrying. "And why would I do that?"

"Because I'll cut your throat if you don't."

"Dana," Webb warned. The girl's black eyes burned. Webb braced himself then bent down and hauled Hugo up out of Dana's grip. He carried his friend up the ladder to the hatch, muscles screaming, pushed his way past a protesting Yoshida and laid his burden on the gurney in the surgical bay.

"I can have my guards here in twenty seconds," Yoshida said, scrambling for a communicator on his workbench.

"Look," Webb said, coming forward and putting himself between the flustered medic and Dana who stood in the hatch, bristling. "I think we all know that your Ghost buddies are bit preoccupied right now. So why don't we all just listen to each other?"

"Why should I listen to you? You tried to kill me and he-" he stabbed his finger at Hugo's limp form, "tried to destroy my life's work."

"Well," Webb said, keeping his voice calm with a monumental effort but unable to keep it from gaining volume, "don't you think it will be harder for him to hold up his cloning ban if your work saved his life?"

Yoshida paused, eyes flickering. His hand was on a comm but he stood there in silence. Dana, mercifully, kept silent too. Yoshida's look slid from Webb to Dana and back. He straightened, then folded his arms.

"Ok," he said carefully. "You've got my attention. But you need to give me something more."

"You mean you'll do it?" Dana stepped forward. "You'll give him a new heart?"

"I have one here," Yoshida said. "You're lucky I've just cloned one that's blood-type neutral. Either way, it might not save him, but I will agree to try. On two conditions."

"What conditions?" Webb said.

"One, as you proposed, Commodore and Special Commander Hugo leave me in peace to continue my research legitimately. No more hunting me down. No more restricting my suppliers."

"Yes. What's the second one?"

"Webb," Dana put in but he held up a hand.

"We can persuade him," Webb said to Dana. "If his life depends on it. And if we can't, Harvey can. Yoshida. What's condition number two?"

The medic smiled at him. "You."

"Excuse me?"

Yoshida stepped up close to him. "You, my friend. I will try and save your Serviceman. You can take him home and I'll give you the drugs he'll need to survive the procedure. Providing *you* agree to return to me afterward."

"What for?" Webb asked warily.

"Study," Yoshida said. "More research. Your retention of your predecessor's memories has raised more questions than it's answered. But with time and study, I believe I can get to the bottom of it all."

Dana was shifting about. Her hands were clenched into fists at her sides. She pleaded with him with her eyes but whether she was begging him to say yes or no he couldn't tell.

"Deal," Webb said, stomach clenching. "Now get to work."

"Wait," Yoshida said holding his hand out. "Shake on it. And don't shake and lie. I will know and your friend can die on my gurney for all I care."

The man's other hand still held the comm link. Dana's hand was going to her belt.

"You can't hurt me," Yoshida said smoothly. "Not if you want him to have a chance."

"If Webb's giving himself to you," Dana choked out. "You will save my brother."

"That's not the deal," Yoshida said, eyes calmly sliding back to Webb. "I will try. But either way, you're mine."

"No," Dana said but Webb had reached and gripped the man's hand.

"I said it's a deal," Webb squeezed the medic's hand a little tighter than necessary. "Now get on with it."

A look of satisfaction spread over the small man's face and Webb let his hand go. He nodded and glided through to the surgical bay. He started pulling on scrubs and getting monitors and scanning equipment online. Then he pulled a curtain over the doorway. The last thing Webb saw before the curtain was drawn was Hugo's still and pale face turned their way, eyes fluttering and pain etched into the lines of his brow.

Shaking set into Webb's limbs and he sat heavily on the edge of the hatch, staring out into the darkness of the storage unit.

Dana lowered herself to sit next to him. "What exactly have you agreed to?"

"I don't know."

They sat there in silence. The greyness of exhaustion starting to mist the edges of Webb's vision. He was even too tired to pray.

"We're too late, aren't we?" Dana's voice was small.

Webb shifted to lean on the edge of the hatch. He put his arm around Dana's shoulders and pulled her into him. She settled against him but he didn't answer. He didn't need to.

A faint bleeping startled him just as his thoughts had started to swill away to blank nothing.

"What's that?" Dana murmured sleepily.

Webb patted his pockets and pulled out the gaming panel. A light was blinking in the corner of the screen. "Message," he said.

"From Rami?" Dana said, leaning in.

Webb opened up the reply. His throat tightened. "Her ship is on the way."

Dana turned her face away. Webb put the panel away and deliberately did not think about the fact that they'd be leaving without Ariel… and possibly without Hugo.

Δ

The noise of a door opening tugged at him from somewhere far away. He didn't want to come back. He liked it where he was. It was safe and empty. Something warm was pressed against his side and in the drifting fog all he knew was the comfort of that warmth and blissful absence of thought.

Then there was the sound of feet on metal and Webb blinked his eyes open and pulled in a breath that tasted like bloodgrease, dust and phozone, and everything came crashing back.

He winced and straightened, Dana muttering as she pulled away from under his arm. She blinked sleepily and for an instant looked peaceful and tousled until everything returned to her, too. He watched her face fall.

They both turned, swearing with the stiffness of their muscles. Yoshida was pulling off a surgical mask and his bloodied scrubs. His face was unreadable.

"Well?" Dana demanded, getting shakily to her feet.

"The procedure is done," Yoshida said. "His vitals are good and his body has accepted the implanted heart."

Tears sprang into Dana's eyes and she covered her face in her hands.

"He's ok?" Webb managed.

Yoshida pressed his lips together. "Only time will tell that. But for the moment, everything has gone as it should. Here." He picked up a lock box from the side, went to a locker, keyed in a combination and loaded the box with vials of liquid. He handed the box to Webb. "He will need to be kept on this intravenously for the next four weeks. And this," he continued, pulling a narrow hand-panel from his pocket, "contains all the information needed for his treatment. Give it to his medic."

Dana snatched it from his hand, scrolling through the information. "There's nothing on here about what the drugs are."

Yoshida smiled. "You will just have to trust me."

"Trust you?" Dana said, scowling. "After -"

"Dana," Webb cut her off. "It's not like we have a choice."

"After what?" Yoshida said, eyes narrow and wary.

Webb glanced toward the surgical bay, curtain still drawn. "Can we see him?"

Yoshida stood in silence a moment searching his face, then nodded and stepped aside.

Dana pushed in front and hurried to the surgical bay, shoving back the curtain and stopping in the doorway. Webb came up more slowly behind her.

Hugo lay on the gurney, free of blood and dirt but with a thick layer of dressing taped across his chest, with more bandaging wrapped around his body. The skin around the bandaging was red and angry and the rest of him had an unpleasant yellowish look. His head was angled away, his eyes closed, an oxygen mask over his face. His chest rose and fell steadily, the monitors around him beeped evenly and his face, at last, looked restful.

"You'd almost not believe what a pain in the ass he can be seeing him like this," Webb said, voice steady but only just.

Dana let out a single choked noise then went to him, stepping carefully around the IV stand suspending his blood and drug fluids. She brushed his hair from his face and padded at the skin of his face and neck as if to reassure herself he was still there.

"Let that transfusion finish," Yoshida said from the doorway. "Then you can take him. Ideally, you don't want to move someone so soon after the procedure, but you should get him to wherever he's going for further treatment as soon as possible."

"Yoshida," Webb said, turning on the doctor. He softened his voice. "There's one more thing."

"What?"

Webb chewed the inside of his cheek. "There was...a girl. A girl from Lunar 1."

Yoshida's brow creased.

"The Ghosts had her sister sign over their business in exchange for a procedure. She had the wasting sickness. She needed a new liver."

Yoshida's face slackened. "Yes," he said, after a painful pause. "Yes, I remember. That was an unfortunate case. I told them I hadn't perfected the procedure, that it was too soon to try on live subjects, but they wouldn't listen."

Webb's mouth went dry as he searched the medic's face for signs that he was telling the truth, or a sign that he cared, but the man met his look straight on and couldn't be read.

"I can assure you that that was just an unfortunate occurrence, the result of me being forced to perform a procedure prematurely. Your friend's body has accepted his implant, as I say. Ideally he shouldn't be moved and I won't be held responsible for the ability of his own medical care once he leaves mine. But I have done what I agreed."

"Her sister..." Dana's voice was small. Webb turned to look at her. Her eyes were fixed on Hugo, knuckles white as she gripped the rail of the gurney. "Her sister's after you." She raised her eyes to look at the medic. "She's declared a Black Cross against everyone involved."

Yoshida blinked, looked first at Dana then at Webb.

"Fair warning, Doc," Webb said. "I'd get yourself the hell away from this colony the minute you can."

Yoshida stared at him a second longer, eyes wide then nodded. "Thank you," he said, then went back through to his lab and could be heard jabbering into the communicator.

Webb drifted over to stand by Dana. "How much longer?"

Dana examined the amount of blood left in the bag. "Half an hour, maybe."

"I say we get straight to the *Phoenix* and wait for the cavalry."

Dana nodded.

"Hey," Webb put an arm around her shoulders, though he, too, felt like there was a rock in his stomach. "He's going to be ok."

"If there's no brain damage," Dana whispered. She touched her fingers to Hugo's forehead again. "And if we manage to get him out of here."

Webb gave her a squeeze and let his arm drop, knowing there was nothing to say to that. Neither of them mentioned Ariel.

Δ

"You have your supplies?" Yoshida said. His voice was clipped as he continued to secure lockers and pack away his lab equipment.

"Yes," Webb said, lifting the lock box.

"There's a couple of men coming through with mopeds," Yoshida continued as he worked. "I suggest you do as I'm doing and get yourself away from Haven as fast as you can."

"That's the plan." Webb hesitated then stepped into the medic's way to get his attention. "Thank you. I mean it."

Yoshida frowned. "Just remember our agreement," he said, then pulled something that looked like a gun from one of the drawers in his workbench. "Turn around."

"Whoa," Webb took a step back. "What the hell is that?"

"I'm going to implant a tracking device," Yoshida said, matter-of-factly. "I use them to monitor the progress of my patients.

This way you can't escape our deal, so don't try to."

"Doc," Webb said, raising his hands. "You can trust me."

"Please turn around," Yoshida said, eyes hard.

Webb felt his stomach turn over. That cold look was back in the medic's face. He suppressed a shiver and turned. The metal pressed against the nape of his neck and then there was a sharp pain.

"Ah, you bastard," Webb said, pulling away.

"If you try and remove it," Yoshida said, returning the device to a locked drawer, "I shall know."

"Will you relax?" Webb grumbled. "I've shaken on it, haven't I?"

"The transfusion's finished," Dana said coming through from the surgical bay. She was looking drawn. "Let's get out of here."

Yoshida went back to packing away his lab without another glance at either of them. Webb followed Dana back through to Hugo, neck stinging and mind sliding away from thinking about his agreement. He stood back out of the way as Dana unhooked Hugo's IV lines and mask.

"How much medic training have you actually had?" Webb asked, admiration clear in his voice as she checked his stats before unplugging his monitors.

"Only what's standard at the Academy," she said.

"Never thought I'd be grateful for that place being so thorough," Webb mumbled.

"Me neither," Dana said quietly. "Are his clothes down there?"

Webb searched and found the sweatshirt hooked on the wall behind him. "Jesus," he swore as they struggled to get Hugo upright. "Either he keeps getting heavier or…"

"Or we haven't eaten or slept properly in days," Dana finished. "Come on. He needs to get back on a bloodline as soon as possible."

"Dana?"

They froze.

"Kale?" Dana bent to look in her brother's face. His eyes were open, though his eyelids were heavy. He peered at his sister like he was trying to keep her in focus. "Everything's ok, alright? We're going home. Come on," she said to Webb. "We need to hurry."

"Where am I?" Hugo mumbled.

"Just relax, man," Webb said, keeping his voice light. "Everything's taken care of. This way."

Hugo shivered as his bare feet touched the deck. Webb winced in sympathy. He swayed as he tried to shift his weight on the gurney. They propped him up again. He stared at the deck without seeing it.

"Kale, you still with us?" Dana tried again.

"Let's just get him out of here," Webb said.

Dana nodded, though she still searched her brother's face for any sort of reaction.

They half-supported, half-dragged him out of the bay just as there was the chugging noise of mopeds braking and powering down in the hanger.

"Good luck, Doctor," Dana said as they shuffled past.

Yoshida looked up, surprised. Then he nodded. "You too."

Yoshida's guards gave them wary looks as they dismounted the mopeds but did no more than that. Webb ignored them and mounted one of the mopeds. Dana helped Hugo to climb on behind him.

"Hugo," Webb said. Hugo shifted against his back but didn't reply. "You need to hang on to me. Can you hang on?"

Dana stood by, mouth pinched when he didn't reply but Webb felt an arm come round his waist.

"Just like old times, huh?" Webb said and fired up the engine. "At least we're not on Lunar 1 this time."

"I'm not sure Haven's any improvement on Lunar 1," Dana said, swinging a leg over her own moped.

"Try growing up there," Webb replied, then the men were opening the gates and they were speeding away. They went slow, despite Webb's impatience. Hugo's grip tightened with the movement but he still swayed against Webb's back and he could feel his former captain struggling against unconsciousness.

"Stay with us," Webb said even though he wasn't sure Hugo could hear him. "Almost there, man. Just stay with us."

Dana steered them well clear of the nearest yard but the streets were unnervingly empty, even for mid-shift. After pausing at the second junction and seeing no one outside and no lights in any nearby buildings, Dana took them on the straighter and quicker roads.

"She's berthed in a private dock that's not been used in years," Dana said, sparing a look from the road to look over to Webb and her brother. "We can get to her through Sector 2 and avoid the harbour but…"

Dana cut off and braked. Webb did the same. There was a broad inter-sector avenue ahead. A couple of workers, barely more than children, stood in the centre of the junction, staring at them. They all stayed there in silence for a minute that stretched on and on and then the workers turned and ran away, shouting.

"Shit," Dana punched her palm off the handle bars. "They must have recognised us."

"There's nothing for it," Webb gunned his engine. "Tear it."

Dana didn't hesitate but fired her accelerator and sped out onto the avenue. Webb followed, steering with one hand and keeping Hugo's feeble grip clamped against him with the other. The few people they passed stared after them. Another moped in their path swerved out of their way but Dana was merciless and sped them on, taking a corner at sickening speed onto a street heading back toward Sector 2.

Webb dared to think they were going to make it when the hull was low enough to make out the Sector number, when they turned a corner and had to skid and brake before ploughing into a solid line of people blocking the way.

Webb kept his moped and Hugo upright with an effort, panting heavily and staring around at the dozens of pale, scarred faces. Dana looked about too, fear stiffening her body.

Dana swore. "Those kids must have raised the alarm and told them which direction we were going."

Webb didn't say anything. Hugo shifted against him, mumbling. Webb's hand on the handlebar tightened.

More and more Havenites were joining the crowd, all facing them with dark looks on their faces. Some murmured in groups with heads bent together but the crowd was otherwise silent. Some of the faces were clearly angry. Most were unreadable. Some bore recent injuries. A few had weapons in their hands.

Webb started when he recognised Bryce in the front row, arms folded, glaring death at him. He felt Hugo shift and moan against his back again and tightened his grip on his arm.

"I did not get him this far just to be lynched," Dana said so quietly Webb felt it more said to herself than him.

"Just keep still," was all he could say.

Waiting for something to happen was worse than if the Havenites had all descended on them at once and torn them apart. The scores of eyes pinned them in place and Webb couldn't even think of anything to do or say. Dana didn't look at him but just stared back at the crowd, knuckles white around the handlebars of her moped and face set and frightened.

Webb's blood pounded in his ears and he was just about to gather his breath to yell something, he didn't know what, when the crowd in front of them parted and a small party came forward.

August was amongst them, dark face blank. Simone was behind him along with another Elder, tall for a Havenite with fair hair. Webb didn't recognise him. They were accompanied by four Enforcers, all with long blades or stout sticks ready and each with a secured prisoner in their grip. Three of the prisoners, stumbling along with hands bound, Webb recognised vaguely as Ghosts he'd seen in the recreation rooms in Ariel's stronghold, though now they were dirty, bloodied and so worn out that they weren't even protesting.

The Enforcer in the centre was dragging along Ariel by one elbow of his fine suit. The blade stood tall despite the rough handling, dark eyes looking on all around him with disdain, despite the filth that streaked his face and white hair.

The peculiar party came right up to them and those holding prisoners forced them to their knees. Ariel's black eyes fixed on Webb and burned.

August stepped forward. "Ezekiel Webb, Commodore and Midshipman Hugo," he said, loud enough for everyone to hear. "We are all gathered here to tell you have been spared execution for your crimes on the understanding you leave Haven for good, taking these individuals with you and ensuring all their connections with Haven out in the Orbit are obliterated. Their stronghold is destroyed, their army disbanded. But we can't do anything about the connections and power they have on the Outside. You can."

Webb stared at the older man, brain whirling.

"There are citizens that are owed your heads," the Elder Webb didn't know said, stepping in up next to August. His face was lined and his eyes fierce but he held himself in complete control. People in the crowd shifted and fingered weapons. "But these scum," he glared around the once-finely dressed prisoners, "are the worse kind of traitors. And you are the only way we can make sure no one else can carry on what they've started."

Someone spat. It landed near Ariel's knee. He made no more reaction than to clench his jaw. His eyes were still fixed on Webb's face.

"You will live to regret this, Hadrian," one of the other prisoners said, though she glared at the floor and refused to look at anyone. "It would be better for all of you if you'd hung us."

"There's still time," one of the Enforcers growled.

"No," the Elder, Hadrian, said. "Our judgment is exile. Let

these Outsiders take away all your security and heritage, since you saw fit to disrespect them so violently." Murmuring broke out amongst the crowd again and Hadrian called for silence. "How soon can you be on your way?" he asked Webb.

"We have a ship docked in a private berth near here," Webb said, still keeping very still and trying to ignore Ariel's stare. "There is a Service ship on its way to accompany us back to the Orbit."

"Get them up," August ordered and the Enforcers wrenched the prisoners back to their feet. "We will allow the Service ship to berth in the dock here and will get them on board for you. Then they're your problem."

August wouldn't meet his glance but Simone was looking right at him. Someone muttered something angry in the crowd but was shushed.

"This is our decision," Hadrian's voice boomed around the square. "But you best remember," he turned back to Webb and Dana, heavy face stormy and broad, yard-worker's shoulders bulging. "You are still blacklisted here. If any of you ever dare to enter Haven space again, you will be executed on the spot."

"Message received," Webb said, shifting. Hugo slid against his back and Webb tightened his grip again.

"See that it's done," the Elder said then turned and disappeared into the crowd. Some protests started to erupt and a few people broke off to follow him. Bryce threw a fierce look at Webb then did the same, arguing heatedly but Hadrian shouted right back.

Chatter began to spread amongst the onlookers. Some melted away but a lot of them stayed to stare. More Enforcers came forward, some to help escort the prisoners away. A couple came to take Hugo.

"Be careful," Dana hurried over. "He's hurt."

"Dana," Webb said, standing free of his moped and gently passing a limp Hugo over into the Enforcer's hold. "Go with your brother. Rami will be here any minute. Get him straight to her ship's medical bay. And take these." He fished the lock box Yoshida had given him out of his pocket and the gaming panel that was blinking again. "I'll be right behind you."

"Where are you going?" Dana said, glancing after the Enforcers bearing Hugo away.

"I'll be right there. Go."

She nodded, turned to leave, hesitated, turned back and flung her arms around his neck. "We got him," she whispered in her ear. "We really got him."

Webb hugged her to him. "We sure did. Now if we can just get your brother back alive, we'll chalk this whole thing up as a win, yeah?"

She pulled back and nodded, weak smile warming her face. "Don't be long," she said, then ran after the knot of people heading toward the docks.

Webb left the mopeds in the middle of the street and strode over to August and Simone who were fielding angry questions from the remaining Havenites. As he approached August managed to break away.

"You need to get out of here," he said, taking him by the elbow and leading him away from the gathering. "I'm serious. Lots of people are unhappy with this and the riot's still fresh in their blood. We can't stop them all if they take matters into their own hands."

"I just wanted to thank you, August, whilst I could," he looked over to where he could just about see the white head of Ariel disappear as the Enforcers marched them around a corner. "You've saved our asses."

"What makes you think this was my idea?"

Webb shrugged on shoulder. "Well, yours and Simone's I was guessing."

August shook his shaggy head. He looked very tired. "Hadrian spoke the truth, boy. Stealing, assault, lying about the real reason you brought Hugo aboard? You were closer than I like to think to a public execution. You were lucky we found out about these Ghosts when we did."

"They're done, then?" Webb said.

August nodded gravely. "It took a long time. But we've run out the entire rats' nest of them. With all that gunfire flying about we were bloody lucky we only lost a gatehouse."

"I'm sorry, August," Webb said, making himself look the older man in the eye. "We've really messed things up, I know. But…we had to do this. And we couldn't have told you. You'd've stopped us."

August frowned down the street to where Ariel had gone. "So you were after that blade? Simone reckons so. She remembered something you told her years ago, about your scars. Then when everything kicked off…she reckons you were after him the whole time."

"She was always a smart cookie," Webb said.

"Well I bloody hope it was worth it," August said. "Your friend didn't look too good."

"No, he didn't," Webb said, rubbing his mouth. He took a breath and straightened. "I guess I better get going."

"I would," Simone said as she joined them. "You've caused us quite enough hassle for one lifetime."

"We didn't lie about spying on your yards for the Service, though," Webb said, waggling his finger. "Shame on you, Simone, for thinking so little of me."

"You watch it, lad," Simone said. "There's dozens of people here with fingers itching for your neck and we're the only ones stopping them."

"You wouldn't let anything happen to me," Webb managed a grin. "You like me too much."

"Get your ass out of here, boy," August growled, shoving at his shoulder. "Or I'll kick it myself."

Webb gave a nod, felt his grin melt into something warmer. "Thank you, both of you. I'm glad I got a chance to say goodbye

"Goodbye, Ezekiel," Simone said, patting him on the shoulder. "Now go. Go quick, if you know what's good for you."

Webb threw them a mock salute. "Yes, ma'am. Look after yourselves, ok?"

"And you," August said. "Watch your back, ok?"

Webb smiled for them again and then turned to hurry away. He jogged down the street, aware of all the heavy glances the remaining workers sent his way. He found himself searching the faces for Jazz's, but she was nowhere to be seen.

He told himself that was for the best.

There was an Enforcer waiting for him at the corner and he fell into step next to him without a word. They hurried to the docks. Webb kept his mind reigned in and just thought about getting Hugo to Rami.

He stumbled once when he glanced into the darkness between two buildings and saw a tall figure standing there. The figure was shrouded in darkness but he could feel the eyes on him. There was a suggestion of blood red hair and light glinting off a naked blade. But he blinked and the vision was gone. He told himself he'd imagined her, but the chill the sight had set in his flesh lingered.

"What now?" The Enforcer said as he stopped.

"Nothing," Webb said and allowed himself to be turned down another street. The docks lay ahead, loaders and lifters visible over the buildings and walls. There were yet more people gathered at the gates, but they just stood and watched as Webb was escorted through. The dock workers paused in their work to watch him pass. The gazes here too were a mix of curious, scornful or angry.

Webb sped up his pace.

He could see the wide doorway ahead and the sector's docks beyond. He sped up even more as he caught sight of a Service-class transport navigating through the dock's vacuum shield and into one of the bigger berths. He could see Dana commanding people who were lifting the prone Hugo onto a gurney and the Enforcers and dock workers were rushing about to guide Rami's ship in.

It was only as Webb reached the gate he noticed a figure leaning against a customs shed, cap low on his face and a broad smile almost hidden in a white beard. Webb slowed then stopped.

"I'll be right there," he said to his Enforcer's questioning glance and hurried over to the man. "You shouldn't be here," Webb said as Mac straightened. "We're only alive by the skin of our teeth. If anyone realises -"

"Relax, lad," Mac said clapping him on the shoulder. "I can take care of myself. Heard about everything and thought I'd be able to catch you here. Just wanted the chance to say a proper goodbye."

Webb rubbed the back of his neck and looked at the floor. "This is it then, I guess?"

Mac sighed and lowered his head, face obscured by the peak of his cap. "Well we never say never, do we? But I'm going to have to disappear and disappear good."

Webb nodded, wondering at the feeling of something slumping inside him.

"Maybe I'll try Mars after all," Mac said. "Sounds like that might shape up pretty nice. Reckon I could make myself a life out there. And it's about as far as from the Service Headquarters as you can get."

"I'd say." Webb shifted on his feet, heard Dana calling and looked up and waved to her. "Look, Mac…" he said, turning back to the older man.

"Don't say anything, lad," the older man said. "You don't have to. You owe me nothing and I owe you more than I can ever repay. So let's just part on that and do the best we can, hey?"

"This has helped," Webb said waving towards the motionless Ariel surrounded by Enforcers as the Service ship started lowering ramps.

"You don't have to tell me how important these things can be," Mac said with a sad smile.

Webb felt his chest tighten and nodded. Mac bobbed his head in reply and patted him on the cheek. "You're a good lad. Look after yourself."

"I will if you will," Webb countered.

Mac chuckled. "Deal. See you around, son."

Then he turned and strode back across the dock, head down and coat swirling around him. He disappeared in the crowd at the gate and Webb took a long time to get himself together.

It was Dana calling his name again that brought him back. He turned and ran across the dock as Hugo's gurney was being wheeled aboard the Service ship. Rami stood at the top of the ramp, issuing orders. He felt a catch in his throat at the sight of her. She noticed him, visibly hesitated then smiled and came down the ramp.

"No word for years and then this," she said, looking him and Dana over. "You both look like you've been through hell."

"Is Hugo ok?" Webb asked.

Rami's face fell. "I don't know. What happened to him?"

"It's a long story," Webb said.

"Right, well you can tell me on the way back to Headquarters."

"We can't go with you, Anita," Dana started. "I've got the *Phoenix* here. I promised Marilyn I'd bring her back."

Rami smiled again, warmer than ever and put a hand on Dana's shoulder. "She can come and get it herself, Dana. It may be a few more weeks before they reinstate her pilot's license, but I'm sure she'll be wanting to visit as soon as they do and see what a mess you've made of her colony."

Dana blinked. "Marilyn…is she?"

Rami's smile widened. "She's getting there, at last. Doing much better."

"How?" Dana looked like Webb had never seen her before, hope, relief and exhaustion making her eyes glimmer.

Rami shrugged one shoulder. "When the commodore stopped visiting, she somehow knew why. That thought led on to more.

In her own words, she pulled herself back together so she had the strength to 'tear his head off.'"

Dana pressed her lips together, eyes shining and all she could do was nod. "Good," she managed. "That's…good."

"Come on then," Rami said, nodding towards the ramp. "Let's get you out of here."

"Hugo's going to kill us, isn't he?" Webb murmured to Dana as they both trudged up the ramp.

Dana didn't answer. She'd paused at the top of the ramp to look out over the docking bay. Webb followed her gaze as it swept over the collection of ramshackle ships and work-worn Havenites watching the remaining Servicemen file aboard with suspicious looks.

"I'm glad I'm never coming back," she said, softly, like she was thinking out loud. "But I'm glad I came."

Webb couldn't think of a reply to that but it didn't look like Dana was after one. She gave him a half-smile then drifted onto the ship like someone in a dream. Webb took one moment to type a message to Jazz into his wrist panel:

Thanks for letting me borrow Nod. She's in Sector 4 docking bay with a full tank of gas. Take care of yourself.

He stared at it for a minute, then pressed send and followed Dana in as the ramp started to rise.

Δ

Webb woke from a sleep deeper than any he remembered having for months. The fuzziness in his head from the drugs Rami had insisted on was pleasant and kept pain of her new stitches at bay.

He winced and got up on one elbow, looking across to the other medbay bunk. Hugo was motionless and pale, even against the pristine white sheets. He somehow looked smaller. His closed eyes looked sunken and cheeks hollow. The sight was enough to chase all good feeling from him like smoke in the wind.

He got up and pulled on the clean clothes he found at the end of his bunk, then spent a couple of minutes cracking the code on the drug lock-up and filling a syringe with the first vial he found. Hugo's raspy breathing in his oxygen mask echoed in the confined space. Webb gave his unconscious friend one more glance then padded out the medbay.

Some level of him registered that the *Assurance* was a beautiful vessel. It purred around him as he navigated the passages with top-level displays and walkways shining-new and well-maintained. The few Servicemen he passed gave him wary glances but slid by, otherwise uninterested.

He found the brig without too much trouble. There were three cells. Webb glanced at the cameras over each door and knew he wouldn't have long. He dredged up what he remembered of Rami's favourite code patterns and opened the door of the last cell.

Ariel was sitting bolt upright on the plastic bunk. He was still in his filthy suit but he'd straightened his tie and smoothed his hair - blood, dirt and all - back behind his ears. He looked up as Webb entered, eyes black and empty. Webb pulled the syringe out of his pocket and stood with it in one hand, staring back at the blade with his heart clamouring against his ribs.

Not breaking the eye contact, Ariel reached up, loosened his tie, undid the top button of his shirt and folded back his collar, lifting his chin to expose his neck.

Webb felt his limbs start to tremble. One minute bled into another and still he didn't move. He felt a scalpel lining fire down his ribs and saw a white face smiling above him. Ariel blinked once and it broke the spell and he stepped forward, grabbed the blade by his hair and pulled his head back. He pressed the needle to the skin.

"Don't be tiresome," Ariel sighed when Webb didn't move. "Just get it over with."

Webb tightened his grip in the Havenite's hair and the man winced, then he stepped away, bitterness rising in waves up his throat. The blade put his head on one side and gave him a sardonic look.

"An attack of conscience? Really?"

"No," Webb managed. "I just think this is too good for you." He pocketed the needle again.

"I'm not going to talk," Ariel said smoothly. "Far neater and less troublesome if it all just ended here."

Webb heard booted footsteps somewhere outside the cell.

"You'll talk," Webb said, just as the sound of the lock controls and someone cursing his name came through the door. "You'll talk and they'll destroy you. And I'll be there to watch."

Rami stormed in and hustled him out. He managed to throw one grim smile at the blade before the hatch hissed shut again between them.

XVIII

There was pain, somewhere. A lot of it. And something…not right. He was aware of all this on some level he could ignore, if it weren't for an itch that was forming. Once he was aware of the itch, it was like an anchor stopping him from sliding back into oblivion.

Awareness started to snake back through his mind, spreading like spilled fuel and gaining colour. Under the grey fog of drugs was sucking exhaustion, aching across his shoulders and a fierce ache in his chest. And the itch. The itch was becoming unbearable.

Hugo opened his eyes. They were crusty and the light felt like it was scouring channels through his brain. He tried to curse but his throat was dry and there was something hard in his mouth. He took a deep breath and it rasped and rattled. He took another, more carefully and became aware of the mask over his face, the tube in his throat and the stiff coolness of hospital sheets over his body.

He blinked again and brought a white ceiling into focus. Machines bleeped nearby and the window on his right looked out on a familiar cityscape. He tried to remember why he was here but the effort of thinking exhausted him further and he gave up.

"Kaleb?"

He frowned. It was a nice voice, one that made the uncomfortable throbbing in his chest skip about. There were some shifting noises, rustling fabric and someone scraping chair legs across tiles. The voice came again, closer, saying his name softly.

He turned his head and blinked. He could see yellow hair and a smile that lit fires along his veins.

"Kaleb," she said again, as if she couldn't believe he was there. Brightness pooled in the corners of her green eyes. She reached out cool hands and pressed them against the burning skin of his chest. "Can you hear me? Do you know me?"

He tried to say her name, he wanted to, so badly, but the tube stopped him. He felt wetness on his cheeks.

"It's ok, love," Harvey said, shuffling still closer and pressing those wonderfully cool hands against the skin of his face, neck and shoulders, like she couldn't get enough of touching him. "Don't speak. I'm here, love. I'm here and you're ok."

He managed a nod, unable to stop the tears trickling down his temples into his ears. They tickled. He lifted an arm made of lead. His fingers were stiff and all he managed was to brush the tips through the ends of her curls before it dropped.

Harvey's smile widened, though her eyes were missing something and were set in grey circles. "That's right, love. It's me."

Hugo lifted the arm again and padded at the mask, moaning in his throat.

Harvey glanced behind her, bit her lip then bent over and gently removed the mask. "Rami's going to skin me for this, I hope you know," she said.

Hugo gagged and coughed as the tube slipped from his throat. His mouth, jaw and throat were raw but it felt so much better. He swallowed a couple more times then croaked: "You're ok?"

Harvey laughed. A tear escaped and fell down her face.

"You're a fucking idiot, you know that? Yes, I'm ok. Or I will be, now." She brushed his hair out his face and bent and kissed him on the forehead. "You now need to get better and quick, mister, because I owe you the butt-kicking of a lifetime."

Hugo managed a smile. "It's going to be different now," he croaked. "I promise. I promise I won't leave you again."

Tears shone in her eyes. She put a hand on his face. "I know you won't, my love. I won't let you."

His smile broadened but then grimaced and closed his eyes. Waves of heat were riding through him. He tried to rub at his chest but Harvey's gentle fingers pulled his hands away. "Not yet, love."

"What's happened to me?" he croaked.

"I'll explain everything real soon," she said, patting his hand. He tried to open his eyes again but they didn't seem to want to obey. "Just rest now. Sleep."

"I…"

"Kaleb," Harvey's tone got firmer. "I said later. Just sleep now, ok?"

"Can you…" Hugo coughed and tried again. "My foot. Itches."

He drifted back away to the sound of her chuckling and the feel of her gentle hands rubbing at his feet.

Δ

The next time he drifted awake, everything was clearer. His muscles obeyed him more and he was able to shift about on the sheets, though it made fire dance through his chest. There were voices nearby and he managed to open his eyes and stay awake on the second try and keep Giles and Rami in focus.

"Kale," Giles cut off what he was saying and came forward. "How are you feeling?"

"Shit," Hugo croaked.

Rami pressed her lips together in a way that suggested she wasn't saying what she was thinking, but Giles just let out a low laugh.

"That's not surprising. You don't look all that great either, truth be told. But Anita seems hopeful and that's more hopeful than most things."

"Marilyn?" Hugo croaked, trying to sit up.

"Not so fast, Commodore," Rami came forward to gently push him back down. "There's a long road to go yet. You need to take it easy."

"Where's Marilyn?" Hugo said again, fear building.

"She's ok," Giles said. "She's gone home to rest."

"It wasn't a dream?" Hugo felt his eyes start to prickle again.

"Here," Rami said. She pressed a control to raise the bed and him into a sitting position and pressed a straw between his lips. "Don't gulp, just sip."

All he could do was sip but the water felt better than anything he'd ever tasted and eased his sore throat and mouth.

"No, it wasn't a dream," Rami continued. "You'll both be back to throwing things at each other in the Eclipse control room before you know it."

"Thank you," Hugo said, with a catch in his throat.

"Just doing my job, sir," Rami said.

"I think it's only fair to warn you," Giles said, frowning at his wrist panel. "Mother's on her way."

Hugo felt his heart sink. "Can someone tell me what's happened? Where's Dana? Where's Webb?"

"Never mind about Webb," Dana's said as she came through the door. "Or Mother either. I'm right after Harvey for kicking your ass, Kale. Mother can just get in line."

"Midshipman," Rami warned, stepping round his bed. "He must be allowed to rest."

"Oh drop the act, Anita," Dana grumbled. "The bastard survived, didn't he? Though he might not wish he did when I'm through with him."

"What happened?" Hugo croaked again, rubbing at his chest that burned and ached.

"You got yourself shot is what happened," Dana said, stepping around Rami to loom over him, arms folded. She tried to sound angry but her eyes were large and her voice was thick. "I thought you were a goner for sure, you reckless idiot."

"Shot?" Hugo blinked. His chest heaved and he remembered staring at Paragon's wide eyes and the smell of burning somewhere and Dana calling his name. "I...what...where's Webb?"

"He's getting too agitated," Rami said to the room at large. "I think you should all come back later."

"No," he mumbled, lifting heavy arms to try and push away the mask that Rami was trying to press on his face. "No, tell me."

Dana and Giles exchanged glances as Rami looked at them both.

"Kale, we got Ariel," Dana said, a small smile reaching her face.

Hugo blinked. "We did?"

Dana nodded, smile widening.

"How?"

"Haven turned him over," Dana said. "They spared us on the condition we take down all the Orbit connections him and the Ghosts had with the colony."

"He's in the lowest level of secure lock-up under Headquarters," Giles said. "Along with his friends. They're all falling over each other to try and squeal on the others in exchange for clemency. The Analysts are having a field day. Unofficially, that is, as they were apprehended under, well, less than official circumstances."

Hugo felt something shudder out of him. He closed his eyes and floated on the relief that was so tangible it was like the blood in his veins. It was like a thorn had been removed or an ache suddenly eased. Tightness disappeared from his chest and he breathed more easily than he'd remember doing in a long time.

"We should let him sleep," Giles murmured.

"Wait," Hugo said, looking at his sister. "Dana, tell me where Webb is."

Dana's face fell. Whatever it was that had haunted the back of her eyes now was written all over her face.

"Where is he, Dana?"

She took a breath, glanced at the others in the room for guidance but they looked back at her helplessly. Hugo felt cold build inside him.

"He's ok," Dana said. "As far as I know, anyway."

"What do you mean?"

Dana shut her eyes and let out a breath. "He's with Yoshida."

"What?" Hugo's voice cracked. "Why?"

"They made a deal," Dana said, face hardening.

"What deal?"

Dana's jaw worked. Anger built in her eyes but he didn't think it was at him. Her gaze slid out the window and she started to explain in short sentences and clipped words. Hugo listened. The cold that had settled into him turn to heat. The thumping ache in his chest increased. He tried to swallow but his throat was too tight.

"Ok, enough for now," Rami said firmly after Dana had finished. "I'm putting him back under."

"Mother's nearly here," Giles started but Rami cut him off.

"Well the Special Commander can just wait."

Hugo didn't protest when Rami brought a syringe over to the joint in his IV line. He couldn't move or think. He blinked at the white ceiling and all he could think of was the alien feeling of the cloned organ in his chest. Even when the voices around him faded away and the whiteness melted to black in front of his eyes, he could still feel and hear it beating.

Δ

Time didn't mean anything for Hugo in the days that followed. He found out later that he was in the hospital for weeks whilst Rami took time out from her unit to treat him with Yoshida's drugs, though she never looked happy about it. But whenever he tried to ask her about what had happened to him or about the treatments, she evaded giving her opinion.

"It saved your life, there's no question. But that's all I'll say."

He hurt like he never had before, even with Rami's careful pain management. It was like the very fabric of his body had been ripped to shreds. He passed in and out of consciousness according to Rami's drug regime but it was a long time before he actually began to sleep normally.

His mother came to see him. So did his father. They were grim on the surface, rebuking him for taking matters into his own hands and operating against orders yet again, but they could not hide the pain and relief that flooded their faces in equal measure whenever they looked at him. None of them discussed his return to duty and Hugo found himself relieved knowing that the decision probably wasn't his.

Dana was sent back to the Academy. She sat in his room holding his hand and staring at the wall the day before she left.

"God knows what strings Mother had to pull to get them to take me back," she said. She made a show of being indignant, but Hugo could read her well enough now to tell she was also relieved.

She talked a lot in those seemingly endless days in the white room. All he had to do was sit and listen about what she thought about Rami's treatments, Giles's management decisions for Eclipse or their Mother's dealings with her generals. She never stopped disagreeing, but her voice was soothing and, despite everything, she had an air of contentment over her now that he'd never known in her before.

But they never spoke about Webb and when the conversation steered toward him she went quiet and turned her face away.

By the time Rami finally agreed he could go home to continue his convalescence, it was Harvey that came to get him and that, for a long time, made him forget everything else. She took him back to their home, settled him in their bed and applied for a further leave of absence from Eclipse. She said it was to make sure he didn't do anything else stupid.

Waking up in the night and having her curled against his back was enough to ensure he didn't think about anything else for a long time.

Dana called on the video comm regularly to begin with. She told Harvey about how she'd placed top in Medic Science and Strategy and how she couldn't wait to be sent out in the field and start sorting out the mess that was Service Procedure in the Lunar Strip. She talked to Hugo too, though they found they had less and less to say to each other.

"You're just too alike," Harvey said as she put away the scanning panel Rami had leant them to keep an eye on his vitals. "You always were. You stormed Haven together, but still have nothing to talk about. It's because you think the same. About everything."

As time went on, Dana's calls became less frequent and on some level Hugo knew it was at least partly because every time she called, she was hoping he'd heard from Webb.

But he never had.

It took more time than he cared to consider before he was able to not think about his heartbeat. Rami told him it was psychological and unsurprising, considering. But in quiet moments, laid in bed at night, or when he started to build his strength up again in the Headquarters gym, he was sure it felt different. It felt…wrong.

Harvey told him to stop whining and to consider himself lucky, but when he looked at the scar in the bedroom mirror, he wondered what the cost had been.

Yoshida's shuttle-lab was never found. It wasn't in the official commissioning specs for the *Perseverance* so, as far as the Service was concerned, it never existed. His attempts to engage Analysts fell on deaf ears and Harvey, intercepting some of his messages, scolded him to leave well alone.

"Webb made this deal to save your life," she'd say as patiently as she could. "Whatever you think of it, you're honour-bound to uphold your part."

"I'm not withdrawing my ban," Hugo replied, leaning on his stick to hobble out onto their balcony so he could breathe the fresh air. It usually calmed him. "There will be no more clones. No one will have to live through what he did. Or what I did. Not ever again."

Harvey folded her arms and set her jaw. The breeze off the bay tugged at her curls and for a minute he just watched that, forgetting what he'd been angry about.

"There's good to be done with this science," she said, as she always did. "You'd do far better commissioning it officially and having proper restrictions and monitoring put in place than letting him scurry around in backwaters getting what work and funding he can to carry on."

And that's where the discussion would end. He knew she was right. He also knew that Rami and possibly even his mother thought the same way.

But try as he might, he couldn't set aside the things he'd heard Webb say about himself or the image he had in his mind from Jazz's description of finding him almost dead in an alley because of his inability to cope with what he was. But more often than those things, the image his imagination fed him was one of his friend strapped to a table at Yoshida's mercy, sometimes dead, sometimes not, undergoing studies and testing he couldn't bear to think about, all in the name of this research.

In his bitterest moments, alone in the apartment, staring at the wall, with his alien heart pushing the feelings around his veins, he wondered if it would have been best all round if Paragon had been a better shot, then he wouldn't have to deal with any of this.

Then Harvey would come home and she'd smile at him or tell him off for brooding and the thought would melt away again and he would remember why he did it all.

Epilogue

Hugo's breath was heaving and his muscles were burning by the time he crested the rise. He stood panting and revelled in the feel of the breeze cooling the sweat on his skin and the smell of the water and the trees. The towering shapes of Spacescrapers were grey against the horizon but the sounds of Sydney didn't reach this far. There was only the breeze in the trees and the flurry of birdsong. The water of the secluded reservoir, achingly blue, took his breath away as always. The sky arched overhead in a clear and lighter colour, pure and cool, though the sun beat down fiercely and danced on the water below.

He sat on one of the boulders littering the cliff top and took a long moment just to sit and breathe the air.

"Well, isn't this a turn up for the books?"

Hugo span, reaching for a weapon that wasn't there but then his hand dropped and he gaped. A tall figure clad in a vest and shorts, tattoos on his arms and black hair pulled back into a tail, climbed up to the top of the rise and stood panting from the climb and grinning at him.

"Webb?"

Webb laughed, wiping sweat off his forehead. "Yes it's me, Hugo. Well, you know. Me number two."

Hugo shook his head in disbelief, found himself checking for Ariel's scarring to be sure. "What…how?"

"Harvey said you'd gone out," the clone replied, taking a step up to stand next to him and stare out over the lake. "She said you came here to exercise. I've been trying to catch you up for half an hour," he turned, grin widening and slapped him on the arm. "Guess you're doing good, huh?"

"And you?" Hugo said, taking in his friend's confident stance and the increased muscle along his arms and shoulders. "You look…different. Are you really ok?"

Webb shrugged and looked away. "Yoshida never wanted to hurt me, Hugo," he said, taking in Hugo's look. "He fed me properly, exercised me, monitored me. He just wanted to see if I was, well…" he scratched his head. "Human, I suppose."

"And?"

Webb laughed. "Afraid so. No immortality or super powers for me." His smile, genuine and lacking any kind of edge, told Hugo that something had changed in his friend. "Thanks for my fee, by the way. I had a pretty luxurious trip back."

"You spent it all on space passage?"

His smile widened. "And a new motorbike. Thank your mom for me."

"Mother?"

"I'm assuming she authorised it?"

Hugo gave half a shrug. "Consider it recompense. So…Yoshida? He just…let you go?"

"I wasn't a prisoner," Webb said mildly.

"Then why haven't we heard from you?" Hugo felt heat rush his face. "Not one lousy message, Webb."

Webb raised his eyebrows. "He didn't want me contacting anyone in case you came to find me. I had to stick to his rules, man. I owed him."

Silence fell about them like a curtain. Webb searched his face. Hugo wasn't sure what his friend found there but it clearly didn't please him.

"I knew you'd be pissed about this whole thing," Webb said. "But it's not like I could really ask your opinion at the time, was it?"

Webb was standing with a straight back and folded arms, clearly ready for an argument, but Hugo felt everything evaporate from inside him. He flung his arms round his friend. They stumbled and Webb swore but then hugged him back.

"Steady now, Commodore," he muttered. "I might think you've

gone soft."

"I'm just glad...glad it's over."

"Me too," Webb said, pulling away and grinning. "And we got Ariel, didn't we?"

Hugo looked back over the lake. "We did. But he won't talk. The Analysts say he hasn't said a single word about anything since being taken into custody. We've got information from the others, but Ariel's been reclassified and transferred to a secure hospital."

"I hope the medics have needles," Webb muttered. "Big needles."

"Me too," Hugo said, earning another smile from his friend. "So...are you back? Back for good?"

"Afraid so, Commodore. Yoshida's had all he needs from me."

Hugo sniffed and coughed and looked away. "Have you contacted Dana?"

"I kinda did that first," he said with a lopsided grin. "Hope that's ok."

Hugo took in his bashful expression, trying to figure out just what Webb was asking. "Yes," Hugo aid. "Yes, that's ok."

Webb nodded, looking noticeably relieved. "Good," he said, then rubbed his mouth and took a breath. "There's one other thing. I've come here see...well, to ask..."

"Spit it out."

"I've come to see if you'll give me a job," he said, looking like he was expecting Hugo to laugh.

"A job?"

Webb nodded. "Drifting...well. It's not what it used to be."

Hugo sat on the boulder again and stared out over the lake. He searched inside him for what to say then looked back up at his friend who was now looking a little concerned. "I don't know if I can."

"Why not?"

Hugo leant forward on his elbows and ran his hands through his hair. "Because I don't know if I'm going back myself."

"To the Service?"

Hugo nodded. Webb sighed and perched himself next to him on the boulder. "You once told me the Service wasn't perfect, but it was the only chance the Orbit had. Do you still believe that?"

"I don't know. It was all true, Webb," he said, looking at his hands. "Everything I said to August when we landed on Haven. We've all bled for change that hasn't happened."

"Well it definitely won't happen if you don't go back and make it," Webb said.

"I'm just one man."

"But you've got an advantage this time."

"And what's that?"

Webb grinned again. "Me."

Hugo couldn't fight the smile. "I'm not sure. Your employment record is not exactly the best."

Webb frowned. "I can get you references," he said. "They'll be fake, but I can get them."

Hugo laughed for the first time in as long as he could remember. "It would be good to have someone on my side against the generals."

"Well I don't know about that. I've known you to have some pretty stupid ideas."

"Not as stupid as some of yours."

Webb frowned then smiled. "I take your point," he said, sighed then stood and stepped closer to the edge of the cliff and shaded his hands with his eyes and let out a breath. "You were right, you know. This place is amazing."

"It is, isn't it?" Hugo said stepping up to him. He pointed below to a small, sandy cove between the tree line and the water. "That's where we're getting married."

Webb turned to him. "You?" Hugo nodded. "And Harvey?"

Hugo nodded again and couldn't quite stop the smile from his face. "Two weeks."

"She finally signed the deed then, huh? That's brilliant, Hugo, that's…" Webb heaved a sigh and shook his head. "It's really brilliant."

"You'll have to come."

"Try and stop me," Webb grinned again, then his face fell. "No, wait. There'll be a free bar, right?"

"Yes, why?"

"There's no way I'm attending a social function with your mom without some Dutch courage on standby."

"You'll have to man up. She's the one you're going to have to ask for a job if you really want one," Hugo said, fighting another smile.

Webb visibly blanched. "For real?"

"Webb, you've brought down torturers, terrorists and genocidal revolutionists. You'll be fine."

"If you say so."

"If you get what you want," Hugo mused, looking out over the view again. "She'll be your boss, remember."

Webb mumbled something incomprehensible. "I'll manage if you're there. I think."

"Then anything's possible."

END

About The Author

J.S. Collyer is a UK based author from Lancaster in the north of England. When she isn't writing she likes to look after her cat Marley (though who controls who, is open to speculation...) She likes explosions, lasers, and Sci-Fi.

You can find more of her writings and musings on the Internet: jcollyer.wordpress.com, facebook.com/jscollyer and follow her on Twitter: @jexshinigami

Acknowledgements.

I know everyone always says this, but I really don't know where to begin. So many wonderful people, friends, family, readers, convention attendees, gamers, Tweeters, bloggers, designers and other writers are all instrumental in helping me get this far, to the point where I'm actually seeing the release of my second novel. It's a stone-cut truth that I wouldn't be here without their unending support, encouragement, feedback and unwavering dedication to books, whether that be buying, reading, reviewing, collecting, supporting or designing.

Every last one of you is a legend in your own time and I want to thank you all from the bottom of my spaceship and laser-beam loving heart.

In particular I would like to thank my parents, Ann and Phil, my brother Chris and my Uncle Adam and Aunt Cheryl for their continuing encouragement, support and unflagging belief in me. It is more powerful than any will for success I possess myself and the desire to make them proud is what fires me on my continuing journey.

I have to thank a few people in particular that have gone above and beyond in their support of me and my first tentative ventures into writing and releasing fiction. Those people are Becky Hill, Dom Hayward, Liz Crewe and my partner Andy Bain for all coming to my very first book launch, which was the launch of Zero at Fantasticon 2014. These were the people that stayed by side all day, listened to my reading, cheered me on and made Zero flags and were, in short, the best supporters a debut author could ask for.

I also must thank Amy Wood for being the first person IN THE WORLD to buy and finish reading Zero. She read almost the whole thing on her night shift the day of release and her feedback and encouragement were the most soothing of balms to my release-day jitters.

I have to also thank the wonderfully talented and generous writer M C Dulac, who took on the not-insubstantial job of Beta Reading Haven. The book is worlds better because of her comments and commitment to good fiction and this is something for which my gratitude knows no bounds.

I also have to thank my partner's wonderful family, Stuart, Angela, Jennifer, John and Genna for their both moral and financial support of my writing career. Between them they have assisted in financing crowdfunding campaigns, promotional events and writing retreats, without which the Orbit Series just plainly wouldn't have been possible.

Thanks also to Reg Davey of Dagda Publishing who made all this happen and to Matt Davis of Rock and Hill Studios who put the beautiful face on it.

Last, but by absolutely no means least, I want to thank Paula Disley for not only being a great and supportive friend but also accepting deliveries of boxes and boxes of stock and paperbacks on my behalf. Without her help I would never have anything to show for my efforts and it continues to be very much appreciated.

Peace and love to you all, guys. You all rock beyond measure.

- J.S. Collyer